Also by Meg M. Robinson

Chloe Chadwick Series

Finding Salus

Waking Salus

Remembering Salus

Saving Salus

Megaverse Series

Immortal Love Series

Seeking Eternity

A Fury's Heart

The Last Lemurian

Grim Favors

Dance With Death

The Athenaeum Series

Legacy

Anarchy

Victory

Meg M. Robinson

Chapter 1

THEY WERE GOING TO break into the Sphinx. Sophia couldn't believe it. They were really going to break into the Great Sphinx—if they could manage to find the secret entrance, anyway.

She stood with four others on the side of an empty road, staring at the Sphinx in the predawn light. They'd teleported in only a few minutes ago, and fortunately, it hadn't been sorcery or shadows this time, but divine teleportation. It was much smoother than the other methods, and in any other circumstances, she'd thank Seth for that. Right now he looked furious, and given that he was a Lemurian god—as well as one of the divine patrons of the Athenaeum—she didn't know if she wanted to draw attention to herself. Not that she blamed him for his anger. They were all pissed that the Athenaeum—an ancient repository of texts and relics—had been invaded from within. Which sucked, because this was her first time in Egypt. Rather than the excitement she should be feeling, all she could feel was exhaustion and nausea. And instead of preparing to play tourist, she was planning some major breaking and entering.

College had not prepared her to save the world.

"So the map to the Hall of Records is in there?" she asked of no one in particular, because standing there staring wasn't going to get them into the Sphinx.

"As far as I know," Olivia said from her left. She was a lean woman of average height, with red shoulder-length hair and light blue eyes. And despite being in Egypt, she was completely covered from the neck down in black clothing, including a pair of thin gloves that covered her hands. "I wish I could say there was more to my memories than that, but literally all I know is that the way to the Hall is in there." She shook her head and sighed. "Can't even tell you if it's an actual map, directions, or something else. For all I know, it's got some relic that teleports you there."

"And you said the door is somewhere in the back right leg?" Lucas asked from Sophia's other side.

Olivia nodded. "I did, but again, I don't know where exactly."

It was still a starting part. The Sphinx wasn't exactly tiny, and it wouldn't be easy to search for a hidden entrance without alerting the human authorities. They couldn't exactly save the Athenaeum from her cousin if they were in jail. Sure, they could get out, but that risked alerting humans to the fact that they shared the planet with the Arcane. Then again, better to have humans know magic existed than to have the entire world ruled by Peter and the Miasma. Sophia just wasn't sure how a gargoyle, nightmare, an owl shifter, and a halfling were going to stop something literally as old as the universe.

"I have a house here in the city. We can go there and formulate a plan for how to get in," Erasmus offered.

"And I wish you luck with that," Seth said. "I need to go check in with the other patrons. I may be a new god, and crap with a lot of this stuff, but Isis, Hecate, and the others aren't. They're going to work on getting the wards around the Athenaeum down. Finding out how to stop Peter doesn't do us any fucking good if none of us can get inside."

"No, it doesn't," Sophia said, nodding. "Thank you for getting us this far, Seth. I appreciate it."

"Just find something. I didn't choose to become one of the patron gods just to have to destroy it within a year."

She smiled, but it was bitter. "And I didn't become aspida just to fail it within a month." Not that she'd had a choice. Once the Athenaeum picked her to be the boss of the place, she'd been stuck. No abdicating. She'd checked.

Seth nodded and, as Lucas wrapped his arm around Sophia, vanished with a slight rumble in the ground beneath their feet. She took a moment to lean into Lucas. He was the biggest bright spot in all of this. A gargoyle in charge of the security side of the Athenaeum—the nasaru—he'd become her rock as well as the man she loved. Somehow she'd also become close with Olivia, despite her first conversation with the woman happening just two weeks prior. And her grandfather... That was a much more complicated situation, but she loved him. Family was often complicated, and he wasn't even the most complicated family member she had.

"Let's go," she told them, straightening and looking at Erasmus. He smiled sadly at her, then turned and began walking through the streets of Cairo with a confidence that came from familiarity. Sophia, Lucas, and Olivia followed him, saying nothing as he led them to an older house. He walked right up to the front door and turned the knob, which made her wonder why he hadn't locked it. Cairo wasn't a war zone, but surely it was still smarter to lock up.

Once they were inside, he shut the door behind them and motioned for them to stay close. "Touch the door, please."

Sophia exchanged a confused look with Lucas, but they crowded in around Erasmus and each of them laid a hand on the door. He spoke a few syllables then nodded. "Keys are easy to lose, so I locked the door with magic decades ago," he explained. "Now the three of you can come and go as you need."

That was cool, and if they made it out of this alive, she was going to ask him to teach her that spell. That spell and probably a hundred others. For now, she looked around, surprised to see it looked like a normal house. Sure, the decor was heavy on Egyptian art and artifacts, but it could be a house in America—if it belonged to an Egyptologist. It was also clean, and she had to wonder if this had been her grandfather's home base since his 'death.' Regardless, there was a couch, so she walked over to it and dropped onto it with a soft huff. She hadn't really been on her feet that long, but it felt like she'd walked miles.

Desperate to get this whole situation dealt with, she dove in, though her head was starting to ache. "Okay. Olivia, how certain are you that the Hall has the answer about to how to free everyone in the Athenaeum from the Miasma?"

"As certain as I can be without ever having stepped foot in there," Olivia said as she took a seat in a chair across from Sophia. "The records my ancestor found made them certain it held information that was old back when the Sphinx was first built. Since it's technically the oldest library in the world—even older than the Athenaeum—it has to have stuff we haven't seen before."

If it still existed—or ever did—but Sophia kept those doubts to herself. If the Hall didn't exist, they had literally nothing to go on. She needed hope, even if it was thin and fragile.

"I have to agree with her," Erasmus said, taking a seat on the other side of the couch, leaving a little space between them. She appreciated it. She might be thrilled he wasn't actually dead, but she was still mad about the deception. "Before I left, I knew something was wrong. I had no idea it could be the Miasma, but I knew it was powerful and old. I had never come across anything similar in the Athenaeum—not even in the Vault—so I was trying to find the Hall as well. I don't have Olivia's memories, but I've come across enough references to it over the years to believe it to be everything Olivia says it is."

Something pricked at Sophia's memories, and she chased it while the others talked. Lucas sat on the arm of the couch next to her, resting a hand on her shoulder. She appreciated the support, even if it didn't help much at the moment.

"Do you know more about this Miasma?" he asked. "I'd never heard of it before Olivia mentioned it a little bit ago. Sophia said something about violent change?"

Erasmus nodded and explained. "When the creators were done making the universe, there was an excess of five substances. Five essential substances, to be specific. When concentrated, they were dangerous, but since they were necessary to life, they couldn't be destroyed. Instead, they were hidden away. Miasma is one of them. Every reference I've found to it has labeled it similarly. Essence of violence, the violence of change and emotion...Which does make sense that it's what is infecting the Athenaeum."

"And that people were attacking Sophia," Olivia said, nodding. "Even if they weren't being controlled by Peter, Sophia represents a pretty big change. If they were primed to be violent, who else would they be violent toward?"

"It does make sense, unfortunately," Erasmus agreed.

"You said there were five of these substances, though?" Lucas pressed.

"I did. There are essences of peace, violence, chaos, matter, and something I have only seen referred to as the Wellspring. I'm afraid I do not know what it could be."

"Grandpa?" Sophia asked as she realized what had been bugging her.

"Yes?"

"You said you've seen several references to the Hall, but Olivia said a human not too long ago gave it that name. So what else is it called?"

"I can't tell you its true name, but it's been referred to by several names, depending on where it's mentioned. Hall of Wisdom, the Great Library, and other things of that nature. Once it was even called Sozu, but I don't know why. No other reference I found for that name led to anything resembling the Hall."

Sophia made a noncommittal sound and mulled that over. "Olivia said it was ancient when the Sphinx was built, so could it be a language lost even to the Arcane? I know we're long-lived, but other than people like Olivia, things still get lost from one generation to another."

"It could," Olivia answered with a frown. "Because I know a lot of languages, even some dead ones, and that sounds like a word in a couple of them, but it doesn't really work. Closest I could say would be Japanese. Sosen means ancestor, which kind of works, but it's not an old enough language if that's anywhere close to the original name for the Hall."

Sophia nodded. "Maybe we'll find out its original name when we get there. For now, any ideas on how to find the entrance into the Sphinx? I don't imagine it would be easy to find, or someone would have already gotten into it."

"Someone may have gotten into it," Lucas said. "Just because no one advertised finding it doesn't mean it didn't happen. Plenty of people from the Athenaeum have gotten in lost places, but only others from the Athenaeum know about it. Not everyone wants to share their discoveries with the world."

She inclined her head to him, because it was a good point. Unfortunately, it didn't answer her question. "Can sorcery locate something like this?"

"It might," Erasmus said slowly. "Between the four of us, we know a great deal of sorcery, and three of us have gone on several retrieval jobs. Olivia and Lucas might not have ever been venatores, but I was for a time. When your job is to go find and retrieve items for the Athenaeum, you quickly learn sorcery to help you find hidden rooms and doorways."

"You don't sound too sure of that."

"Because I'm not," he admitted with a faint smile. "I am confident we can avoid the cameras and guards—invisibility is one of the first spells any guard or venator learns—but not all spells to lock and hide doors are the same. We don't even know who hid it."

"He's right," Olivia added. "For all we know, a god did the hiding, which means sorcery might not be able to get through their wards to find the door, much less open it."

"You know, until last week, I was always happy being what I was," Sophia said, letting her head fall against the back of the couch. "I could shift into an owl and heal bumps and bruises, which were the worst injuries I ever had to deal with. But right now I really wish I was a witch."

Lucas gave her shoulder a squeeze. "Never wish you were something you aren't. It's pointless and can't help anything."

"Agreed, but she does have a point. A witch might be useful," Erasmus mused. "Especially someone skilled and used to...less than ideals situations."

"What about Blanche?" Sophia asked. She'd only met the woman once, but she was a witch—a necromancer—as well as Death's wife. Necromancers might have a bad reputation among the Arcane, but Sophia liked her. Plus, there might be ghosts hanging around the Sphinx, and a necromancer might help. On the other hand, it would also potentially be putting Death's *wife* in danger, and that didn't sound great for anyone's life expectancy.

"You know Blanche?" Erasmus asked, the surprise obvious on his face.

"Mmhmm," was Sophia's answer, and though she was glad she'd met Blanche, she was aware the sound wasn't a happy one.

"Death, too," Lucas added dryly. "They both showed up a couple of weeks ago."

For a moment, Erasmus was distracted from the current problem. "You met Death?" He straightened and leaned forward. "What was that like? Did he feel as powerful as I expect he would? Did—" He broke off and frowned. "Why did you meet Death?"

"Do you remember giving Suni a summoning spell?" Sophia asked.

"I do... Blanche used it."

"Yeah, well, apparently Death really hates being summoned. He came looking for you, wanting the spell destroyed."

"Oh my," he breathed. "I am so sorry, Sophia. I had no idea—"

She waved a hand and shook her head as she cut him off. "It's fine. I ended up finding the spell a couple of days later. Didn't destroy it, but I did leave an impossible to miss note on it so no one else would use it. Blanche said she'd make sure he'd be okay with that."

Erasmus nodded slowly, but he looked troubled now. "It sounds like Seth hasn't filled me in on everything."

Lucas asked, "Does that mean you know about the rest?"

"If by the rest you mean Agatha and Dion, then yes." He shook his head, sorrow etched in every line of his face. "I can't believe my nephew was involved in this. He was always hungry for knowledge, but I never would have dreamed he would end up hungry for power."

"He wasn't," Sophia said gently. "When I met Death, I asked him if I could talk to Dion. Dion was innocent. Peter..." No, she couldn't talk about that right now. "Dion was actually killed because he was a good man."

Relief and grief battled for dominance in Erasmus, and in the end, grief won. It lingered for a few moments before he lifted his chin. "Blanche is a strong witch, yes, but her talents are with the dead."

"And I don't know that Death would be too thrilled with us dragging his wife into this shit show," Lucas added.

"No, I don't think he would," Erasmus agreed. "But I do know of another witch who might be useful. From what I understand, his powers are more varied, and he has experience with...treasure hunts, shall we say?"

"You want us to call in a treasure hunter?" Sophia asked, a little stunned.

Erasmus chuckled. "Seth was a treasure hunter before he became a Lemurian god," he pointed out. "The fact that he hunted the treasures either for the Athenaeum or human museums doesn't change that fact. But no, this witch is actually someone who would make a good venator, if he was so inclined. I met him when Seth took me to Lemuria, so it's someone even our patron trusts."

Olivia and Lucas both looked at her, and while she was happy they were trusting her enough to make the decision, she was starting to get sick of so much resting on her shoulders. She wasn't sure how she felt about bringing in a stranger on Athenaeum business, but they were cut off from most of the people they'd call on, so their choices were limited."Hell, if Seth trusts the guy, I'd be stupid not to. Who is he, and can you get him here in time?"

"I think we'd be better off going at night, when there are fewer people around, so it gives us a little more time to get the guy here," Lucas offered.

"I agree, and I do think he'll be willing. Julian has a thirst for knowledge that rivals even mine. Perhaps surpasses it."

"Then I say call him. See if he can be here by... What do you think? Eight?" Sophia asked, glancing up at Lucas, who nodded his agreement.

Erasmus nodded and drew out his phone. To her surprise, he put it on speaker.

"Hello?" The man had an English accent and sounded curious. She wondered about that, since Erasmus had said he knew the man.

"Hello, Julian."

There was a lengthy pause from the other end of the phone. "Erasmus?" Julian asked, voice tinged with surprise and suspicion.

"Yes, it's me, Julian," Erasmus confirmed.

The suspicion grew. "How? Suni said she spoke to Blanche, and she'd been told you'd died."

Erasmus sighed. "That bit of trickery is going to follow me for a while, I think," he murmured, more to himself than to Julian. "It was a ruse. I assure you, I'm quite alive."

"I'm afraid I can't simply take your word on that. When the woman who is apparently now married to Death says someone is dead, I would be a fool not to believe her."

"Would an imposter know that I am—or was—head of the Athenaeum and that when we met on Lemuria, you pressed myself and every god present with questions until several of us were certain one of those divine beings was going to send you to the afterlife to escape those very questions?"

Sophia was a little intrigued, but also uncertain about having this man help. Then again, in the same situation, she might have done the same.

"No, I suppose they wouldn't." The surprise remained in Julian's voice, but it sounded like he accepted Erasmus was who he claimed to be. "Am I correct in assuming you want your status among the living to remain quiet for now?"

"You are, though I trust both Suni and Blanche." His eyes met Sophia's for a moment. "I don't want to cause them any more grief than is necessary." She was still hurt, but she believed that. "But I'm afraid this isn't a social call."

It was Julian's turn to sigh. "Unfortunately, it never is. Does this have something to do with the reason you apparently faked your own death?"

"It does. And I can get into that later, but for now, I have need of a witch, and one who's experienced in...adventures, we'll say."

"It has been a few months since I did more than give the Hunters information on demons," Julian said thoughtfully. "What is this adventure you need help with?"

Erasmus arched a brow at Sophia. It took her only a moment to realize he was giving her one last chance to back out of accepting outside help. She appreciated it, especially since he was far more experienced than she was. But she could admit to herself that part of her considered him the true aspida, now that she knew he was alive. But since he was asking, she nodded. "How do you feel about helping a few of us from the Athenaeum locate the Hall of Records?"

There was more silence from Julian. "It isn't a human myth?" Though his words should indicate doubt, even a stranger like herself could hear the excitement in his tone.

"I have no concrete evidence, but I do have strong reason to believe it exists."

The excitement grew more noticeable. "What do you need from me? And when?"

"Tonight, around eight Cairo time. We will most likely need help to find and open a magically sealed and hidden doorway."

Sophia noted that he refrained from mentioning that the door was in the Sphinx, and wondered why.

"And where am I meeting you? Where you are now?"

"That's preferable, yes."

"I will absolutely be there."

"Thank you, Julian," Erasmus said before hanging up.

"Just how well do you know this guy?" Olivia asked.

"I've only met him in person once," he admitted. "But Suni and Blanche know him well, and even Seth trusts him." He smiled. "I know he seems eager, but he's just interested in learning something new."

"As long as he's useful and not dead weight I don't care. But for now, we should get something to eat and grab some sleep while we can," Lucas said. "I have a feeling we're not going to get enough sleep over the next two weeks, and dawn isn't that far away."

Olivia groaned and rested a hand on her belly. "I'm all for the food."

Sophia wasn't sure how much she could eat, but knew she needed to. "That works."

Erasmus looked uncertain when he asked, "Could the two of you get the food? I'd like to speak to my granddaughter...if that's all right with you."

Sophia wasn't all that sure she was up for such a conversation, but it might be better to get it out before they really got into finding the Hall and a cure for the Athenaeum. She had no idea what they'd be facing, and distractions could potentially be dangerous. "Yeah," she decided, "that's fine."

Lucas studied her face for a minute before he accepted her answer. "Anything in particular you want?"

"No, just something light."

He nodded and bent to kiss the top of her head. "We'll be back in a bit," he told her, getting to his feet.

"We probably shouldn't use our credit cards," Olivia pointed out as she stood.

Erasmus drew out his wallet and selected a card, offering it to Lucas. "Use this one. No one in the Athenaeum has any reason to track it."

Lucas accepted the card, gave Sophia one last look, then he and Olivia left the house, leaving Sophia alone with her no longer dead grandfather.

Chapter 2

Neither of them spoke for several minutes after Olivia and Lucas left. It was more than a little awkward. Sophia had discovered Erasmus existed, gotten just a couple of days with him, then saw him horrifically 'die.' Even if she had barely known him, it had still been a traumatizing experience for her. The fact that she could count the number of living family members on one hand didn't help.

Erasmus was the one to break the silence, though his voice was quiet and uncertain. Sincere, though, she had to give him that. "I know you're angry with me, Sophia, and you have every right to be. But I do want to say again that I am truly, truly sorry that you had to witness that. It was never my intention to hurt you."

She pursed her lips together as she studied his face, a face that was both familiar to her and not. He looked his age—which Lucas had told her was somewhere around nine hundred—with white hair and a lengthy beard. Honestly, he looked like the human's version of a wizard, which was accurate enough, considering how much sorcery he no doubt knew. His eyes were kind, and the same shade and shape as her own green ones. And now that he was no longer feigning illness, he looked surprisingly fit for a man in his tenth century. No doubt at least part of that was due to having a demigod healer looking after him

15

for quite some time. But what really drew her attention was the true regret written on every one of his features, held within the set of his shoulders.

Part of her wanted to tell him she forgave him, that she loved him and understood. To an extent, it was true, but emotions didn't care about logic."I know you are, but I really don't understand why you had Carla and Nick bring me to the Athenaeum to meet you when you knew you were disappearing in a few days. Didn't you realize it would hurt?"

Shame crept onto his face. "I'll confess, while I hoped you would come to care for me, I perhaps did not think it through as thoroughly as I should. All I could think of was that I'd never met my granddaughter, and I wanted to at least once. Since I had no guarantee that I would survive rooting out the poison in the Athenaeum, I knew it might be my only chance. But I know it was...selfish of me."

Maybe, but could Sophia really blame him for that? Not really. She'd been pissed at her mom when she'd discovered she had family, and had been prepared to go against Heather's wishes to meet Erasmus, so she might have done the same thing. Except... "If the illness was faked, why did you have to die when I was there? It was hardly a peaceful death."

"As I mentioned before, the timing was off. To avoid arousing suspicion, the effects of the poison were real—magical and non-lethal, but real—even if the mithridate removed all traces of it from my system. I should have had another few hours, and I had planned to tell you I was tired so you would leave before having to witness my death. But it was, to an extent, automated, for lack of a better word."

"I take one or more of the patrons helped you?" She couldn't think of another way he could have fooled Sergei. The son of Apollo wasn't likely to have missed a fake illness any other way.

Erasmus nodded. "Hecate and Isis, yes."

Sophia nodded and rubbed her hands on her denim-covered thighs, trying to move past her emotions. "Did you know? That I'd be the next aspida, I mean?" If so, it was going to be way harder to forgive him. The job had its perks, but overall? It sucked sideways.

He smiled with genuine pride and shook his head. "I didn't, no, but I wasn't at all surprised when Seth told me. It's why I left you a note, just in case." His smile wavered a little. "Did you find the note?"

Her eyes narrowed as she remembered finding that letter. "I did. Why in the hell do so many things in that place just pop open without warning? It scared the crap out of me."

He chuckled, finally starting to relax. "It only happens to aspides. I take it you learned how to operate that bit of magic?"

"Yeah. That and that aspida room."

Brightening, he said, "You found that, too? And in such a short period of time! It took me three months to find it after I became aspida."

"By accident," she admitted. "Remember, I found that spell to summon Death, and that's where it was."

"Oh yes, you're right. What do you mean you found it by accident? Not that I'm surprised, but I'm curious what accident led you to it."

"Everything was pretty much shit after you died, and I was kind of just wandering, trying to take my mind off things and hating that I was named aspida, then the door opened and it also scared the crap out of me."

"It scared me, too," he admitted with a nod. "Fascinating room, though, wasn't it?"

"It was, but it also scared me. That grimoire?" She both loved and hated that book. It definitely terrified her a little.

Understanding, he gave another nod. "They spells are in there for a reason. They may be dangerous and scary, but they'd be more terrifying if anyone else was able to get their hands on them."

"Not all of them sounded that bad, but enough of them were scary enough to make me really hope Peter isn't able to get in there."

Erasmus thought for a moment, then shook his head. "I can't guarantee it, but I don't believe he could. The magic of that room is such that it will only open if the aspida is there. I'm not even certain it would open for the aspida if they weren't alone."

"Yeah, but he shouldn't have been able to keep Seth from teleporting into the Athenaeum."

"Mmm. Yes, that is a good point." And it troubled him, much as it did her. "Even so, I don't think it would be an easy matter for him. Especially since it isn't likely that he even knows of the room's existence."

Sophia frowned and made an uncertain sound. "He might."

"How so?"

"Since Dion's death, I'd been going down there a couple times a week. Trying to find a solution or something, you know?" When he nodded his understanding, she went on. "A few nights ago, I was headed down there but never made it. Someone—probably Peter, unless he made someone else do it—pushed me down the stairs and threatened me. Lucas checked the cameras, and they'd been turned off around when I left my room. I can't swear he hadn't been stalking the cameras and noticed me going down there."

"He might have realized you were going to that particular hallway, but magic protects that room, remember? Not just hiding the door and opening it for the aspida, but ensuring it's difficult to discover. When we first installed the cameras, I was concerned about that very thing, and when I checked, all I saw was myself standing in the hallway, looking at urns and reading the steles."

That was something, at least, and Sophia felt some of that tension ease out of her shoulders. "But he can get in the Vault."

Erasmus sighed and inclined his head to her. "Probably, yes. He can certainly get past the technological locks, given he was the one who installed them. There's magic surrounding that room, but given all he's done so far, I would not be surprised if he could bypass that as well."

"Which means we can probably look forward to a whole lot of trouble when we go back there," she said grimly, remembering the things she'd seen in the Vault. Hell, just that Tablet of Destiny Olivia had found would be a disaster. Causing floods and channeling a god's power? Yeah, they really didn't need Peter to get his hands on that particular item.

"Most likely, yes," he agreed. "But don't discount us. I may not be as physically formidable as Lucas, but I know quite a bit of sorcery. Olivia likely rivals me in that regard, and she's also quite a skilled guard."

"Yeah, then there's me." Sophia couldn't keep the bitterness out of her voice. She really should never had been chosen as aspida. She wasn't experienced enough, and she could count the number of spells she knew on both hands.

He cocked his head, one brow arching. "You make it sound like you're useless, but that couldn't be further from the truth."

"Right, I'm the only one who can use the failsafe." A spell she'd begrudgingly memorized, that would essentially vaporize the Athenaeum and everything in it.

"Sophia," he began, voice sharp, "while it's true you have not learned as much as others, that doesn't make you useless. You have your owl, which makes you an excellent spy and lookout. You know your Greek gods and lore—which is more applicable in Egypt than most people realize. You're also adaptable, smart, and determined, which are three traits I would wager on over experience when it comes to something like this. Because what you don't seem to understand is that *none* of us are experienced in a situation like this. I've never had my family try to kill me and kill others I cared about. I've never had my home invaded from within. I've certainly never had a deadline to neutralize one of the building blocks of the universe in order to save the world."

When he put it that way, she felt like a bratty child for complaining about her lack of experience. "I'll do what I can," she promised.

"That's all any of us can do," he said, his tone gentle now. "These are not good odds that we're faced with, but I genuinely believe that we have a chance of succeeding. Just have faith. In yourself, and in us."

"I'll try." And if she thought about it, ignoring how she felt about being aspida, she wasn't actually doing that bad a job. She had gotten Lucas and Olivia out alive, and Olivia had memories stretching back thousands of years. Maybe she hadn't been able to get Sergei out, but no one was perfect and this whole thing had begun before she ever learned any of it existed. And she realized she wasn't quite as angry with Erasmus as she had been. It wasn't a perfect situation, and it sounded like he'd done the best he could. And she really couldn't blame him for wanting to meet her before he potentially went off to a true death.

The door opened and they both looked over. Lucas peeked inside and arched a brow questioningly at her. "It's fine," she told him, and he and Olivia entered, carrying pizza boxes and a bag.

"Everything okay?" he asked as he sat beside Sophia and put the pizzas on the table. Olivia took sodas out of her bag and set them beside the pizzas before she reclaimed her earlier spot.

Sophia wasn't sure why she was surprised they'd found pizza, but a little familiarity couldn't hurt. "Yeah, okay's a good word considering the situation," she said as Erasmus rose and left the room. She frowned a little until Lucas nudged her.

"Seriously, are you okay?" he murmured.

"I'm freaking out, but I'm not as mad as I was," she admitted.

Understanding, he nodded and kissed her cheek. "We'll get through this," he said as Erasmus came back with plates and napkins.

Silently, everyone grabbed some food and began eating. Normally, Sophia enjoyed conversation with her meals—especially pizza—but just didn't feel like it today. Besides, if they were like her, they were contemplating what was to come. Like how in the hell they were going to pull off breaking into the Sphinx—and what they'd find there.

Though Sophia hadn't been sure she could eat, she was surprised when she realized she'd eaten three slices. But now that they were relatively safe and her belly was full, she felt exhaustion pulling on her. She hadn't pulled an all-nighter in months, and never under these circumstances, so that wasn't surprising.

Lucas noticed, taking the plate from her and setting it on the table. "You need sleep," he said in a tone that allowed no argument. Not that she was planning on it.

"There are a couple of bedrooms. Down the hall, either door on the left," Erasmus told her.

She nodded and got to her feet, her movements slow as her body was way ahead of her in the going to bed department. Lucas rose and rested a hand on her back, starting to walk with her back to the bedroom. Before they could reach the hallway, Erasmus spoke up.

"Lucas? Could I speak with you before you go to bed?"

Lucas paused and glanced back at his former boss. "Yeah, just let me get her settled first."

"Of course."

They continued down the hall to the first door on the left. The bedroom was beautiful and the bed looked comfortable, but Sophia had a feeling she'd be able to sleep on a stone slab or broken glass right now. She was so tired she was surprised she was able to move.

After collapsing on the bed, she felt Lucas removing her shoes and smiled a little. He was normally a grumpy man, but he took such good care of her. She would have gotten to her shoes in a minute, but he just got it done, then shifted her to pull the covers out from beneath her so he could tuck them around her.

"Sleep well, love," he whispered, kissing her lightly.

"Don't stay away too long."

"I won't," he promised before leaving the room, closing the door quietly behind him. Not that it mattered. By the time he reached it, she was already out.

Chapter 3

WHEN LUCAS GOT BACK to the others, Olivia was hyperfocused on her pizza, and Erasmus was standing by the door. When Lucas's eyes landed on the older man, he inclined his head to the door. Lucas had no problem with stepping outside for this conversation, so nodded and followed Erasmus out.

They didn't go far, and it was still just shy of dawn, so there weren't any others around. It was probably as private as they'd get for a while. That was good, because Lucas was furious with Erasmus and had a few things he wanted to say. "What did you want to talk about?" he asked, knowing his voice was pissy, but he didn't care. He also realized he had automatically switched to Greek, as it was the language he normally used when speaking with his former aspida.

"I wanted to apologize to you," Erasmus began in the same language. "I know you're angry with me, and you have every right to be, as does Sophia. But with you, it's almost harder. I had an instant connection with her, given that she's my granddaughter, but you have been my friend for many years. My true friend."

"Then why in the hell did you not trust me enough to let me know what was going on?" Lucas snapped. "Not just because I was your friend, but because I'm the head of the nasaru. It's literally my job to protect you and the Athenaeum. Or was, now it's my job to protect your granddaughter—a job I would have been a hell of a lot better prepared for if you'd just told me what the fuck was going on!"

"I understand how you—"

Lucas cut him off, not wanting apology or understanding from Erasmus. Not yet, in any case. "What? Understand how I feel? So you've had someone you've been friends with for years decide to ignore your job and those years of friendship and work with the gods and a demigod to fake his own death? And do you understand how you left the Athenaeum open to more deaths, all because you couldn't tell me you'd been poisoned?" He shook his head, his hands curled into fists. Worse, he was dangerously close to turning to stone, which wouldn't be good, even though the area seemed empty of humans. In this decade there were cameras everywhere, and it was hard to know exactly where you'd been seen by one. "No, I don't think you know how I feel."

"No," Erasmus agreed calmly, "I don't know exactly how you feel, but I do know how it feels to have a member of my family, one I trusted completely, turn on me and kill people. Try to kill me. If Suni hadn't rediscovered the mithridate, I likely would be as dead as Thomas, Agatha, and Dion. But," he continued when Lucas started to speak, "I do understand you feel like I didn't trust you. I truly do, Lucas. And I know it's worse because I told Sergei, but in all honesty, if I hadn't needed his healing abilities in the beginning, before I realized what was going on, I likely would not have told him, either."

Lucas closed his eyes and rubbed at them. "Erasmus?" He dropped his hand. "You know I respect you. You're an intelligent man who has learned more than anyone I know—except maybe Olivia, but she cheated. You were a fair and knowledgeable aspida, and one who truly cared about the Athenaeum. Keep all that in mind when I tell you that you're stupid."

Erasmus blinked like the owl he was and cocked his head. "Pardon?" he asked, surprised more than offended.

"You're stupid," Lucas repeated. "I get not wanting to tell everyone in the Athenaeum. I really do. That was smart. Back then, you didn't know who was involved. But while you're experienced and probably know more sorcery than anyone else on the planet, with the possible exception of Olivia and Hecate, you're just one man. It's a hell of a lot harder for one person to solve something like this than two or four. Four of us have been working on it for the last month, and it took all of us to figure out it was Peter and the Miasma. Beyond that? If you didn't trust me as head of security, then I shouldn't have been head of security."

The older man actually looked his age as he thought of what Lucas had said, and after a minute, he nodded. "You're right. Not that I'm stupid, but I will admit to a certain amount of hubris. I did contact the patrons, obviously, but I didn't want to involve anyone from the Athenaeum. I thought I could deal with it myself." He shook his head and sighed. "I knew whatever the ultimate goal was, it wasn't good, but I never would have imagined it would be something like this. Something so...heinous and with such global implications."

"You should have," Lucas said, not yet over his anger. "If you knew they were blocking six *gods* from seeing what was going on, when those gods were looking hard, that should have given you a fucking clue."

"Yes, you're right," Erasmus agreed in a low murmur. "All I can say is I'm sorry. Truly sorry. I couldn't believe it was you, but part of me...I felt I had to play it safe. But can we really afford to remain angry with each other, given what we know?"

"Oh, I can be pissed and still stop Peter. I can be furious and still listen to you when you're not being an idiot. But all that's also in the past and can't be changed, so you're just going to have to accept that I'm going to stay pissed for a while. Sophia grieved, but I did, too. I thought my best friend was dead."

"Again, I am deeply sorry for that." His eyes narrowed. "Speaking of my granddaughter, though...Are you sleeping with her?"

Some men would have frozen or sputtered when asked that question. Others would have hedged or flat out lied. Lucas did none of those things. He arched a brow and said bluntly, "Yes." He intended to leave it at that, but despite his anger, he really did respect Erasmus, and saw him as a second father. "I love her, so if you have a problem with it, you're just going to have to deal with it. I don't—"

"A problem with it?" Erasmus asked, brows lifted, his voice pitched higher in surprise. "No, no. I have no problems whatsoever. Long before all this came to light, I always harbored the hope that Sophia would come to the Athenaeum and you two would gravitate toward one another."

Now Lucas was surprised. "You did?"

"Of course! You know I followed Sophia's progress as much as I could, despite Heather's insistence to remain distanced from the Athenaeum, and you are someone I respect as well as like. My granddaughter could certainly do far worse than you, and not much better."

Lucas had to replay that twice in his mind before it really sank in. "Oh. Well, good. Because I don't want Sophia suffering for our relationship. She's suffered far too much in the past month already.

I want to give her peace, not put her in the middle of two men she loves."

That made Erasmus beam, and he patted Lucas's shoulder. "Good. She deserves someone who puts her first—at least when she lets them."

Lucas chuckled, knowing how true that last part was. "We should get some sleep before your friend gets here. If we're lucky, Olivia will even make sure we don't have any nightmares."

"I am surprised to find her with you," Erasmus admitted. "Not that I mind by any stretch of the imagination, it's just that Olivia always tended to try to keep to herself."

"That's Sophia's doing. Seems she liked Olivia right off the bat, then when she was trying to find a replacement for Dion, she dragged Olivia in. My guess is Olivia's bloodline had something to do with it, but I doubt it was the whole reason."

"It does make her uniquely qualified to be in charge of the entire library, if for no other reason than the languages she speaks. Did you know she's fluent in more languages than I am?"

"Yeah, but like I said earlier, she cheated. Still, it's handy for a curator. More handy for a head curator."

"Indeed. Now, let's try to sleep."

They went inside and discovered Olivia had already withdrawn to one of the bedrooms. After dealing with the remains of dinner, Lucas quietly let himself into Sophia's room. To his relief, she was already asleep. Given how the past few hours had gone, he was sure she was going to have trouble falling asleep, but supposed exhaustion trumped trauma in this case.

He took a moment to just look at her in the fading moonlight. When sleeping she looked small, though she was about five four. Her lean form was more toned than it had been when she'd first arrived in the Athenaeum, and he found her newfound strength sexy. He brushed a strand of brown hair out of her face, then traced the tip of his finger down her cheek. She had delicate features, and he'd taken enough time to just look at her that he knew every inch of her face as well as his own. But while she looked young, fresh, and sweet, he knew there was a core of steel within her. There had to be, to deal with everything that had been thrust on her shoulders.

Taking off his shoes and shirt, he slipped beneath the covers and wrapped his arms around Sophia. It no longer surprised him when she turned to him in her sleep and cuddled up, but it was always a nice feeling. A comforting one. He hoped he'd fall asleep as easily as she had, but the sun had long broken the horizon before he was able to sink into sleep.

The sun had started to set before Sophia woke. Lucas had his arm wrapped around her and had pulled her partially on top of him at some point during the day. Thoughts of what had happened at the Athenaeum remain buried beneath the fog of sleep and she smiled, shifting higher so she could press her lips to his. He made a soft sound, and when she repeated the caress, he began to return it as he fought his way to consciousness. She could tell the moment he managed it, because he took control of the kiss. Not that she minded. It was thrilling, though she'd always hated when men had tried to take control in the bedroom. Maybe there was something to those sappy lines, and everything was different with the right person.

Just as she was really starting to get into it, as Lucas's hand was sliding up her ribs toward her breast, there was a knock on the door before Olivia called through the wood. "Wake up, you two. Food's here."

Groaning, Sophia rested her forehead against his neck and sighed. Couldn't they have given her a little longer before reminding her of what they were facing? Especially since this could very well be the last time for the next few weeks that she'd have a room with a door.

"I agree completely," Lucas said, kissing her brow. "Don't worry, I'll make sure we get some time alone. Even if I have to send the others off on a wild goose chase for an hour or drag you away."

She lifted her head and smiled. "I'm holding you to that."

They climbed out of bed and got ready. Lucas headed out to the living room while Sophia veered into the bathroom. After dealing with necessities, she took a couple of minutes to pat a cold washcloth over her face and prepare to face what was coming. If she looked at it through the eyes of an optimist, it wasn't all bad. They might be the ones to rediscover the Hall of Records. Not only would that definitely make a mark on her tenure as aspida, it would be a fantastic find. Especially if it was remotely close to how Olivia had explained. Given that Erasmus had been searching for it over the past month, it was obvious he believed it was.

Of course, if they didn't manage to stop Peter and figure out a way to keep the Miasma from infecting the whole world, it wouldn't matter what she did.

Sighing, Sophia dried her face and went out to face the others, hoping they'd be able to help keep the intrusive thoughts out of her head.

She stopped at the end of the hallway, because there was a stranger sitting across from Erasmus. He looked like he was near Lucas's six foot three height, and that wasn't where the similarities ended. Both had brown hair cut short, though Lucas's was a little more military than the stranger's, and a darker shade as well. And where Lucas had green eyes, the new man had brown. Lucas tended to wear clothes like what he wore today—cargo pants and a tee-shirt—but the stranger wore more business casual. He also held himself more stiffly than Lucas did.

He noticed Sophia before the others and offered a polite smile. "Hello. You must be Sophia." The English accent told her she was probably Julian.

"I am, yes. Julian?"

"I am," he echoed.

"And a man who would be quite at home in the Athenaeum," Erasmus said, motioning for Sophia to join them.

"If you ever offer me an invitation to come see it," Julian said, playful pouting in his tone. Sophia had a feeling his words were more true than he wanted to let on.

"Are you an academic?" Sophia asked as she took a seat next to Lucas. They'd gone for burgers tonight, which surprised her. Pizza last night, she could understand. It was easy and familiar. But burgers?

They were in Cairo. Why not local dishes? Still, she grabbed one and some of the fries before she noticed the bottles of Coke. Since she desperately needed caffeine, she grabbed one and took a deep drink before letting her focus shift to the food.

"After a fashion," Julian agreed with a nod. "Most call me a demonologist, though."

The burger halted inches from Sophia's mouth and she blinked at him. "Demons are real?" They were talked about by the Arcane, of course, but in the same way humans talked about Nessie or Santa—as interesting myths. When Julian had mentioned them on the phone earlier, she'd thought...well, she wasn't sure what she thought. A metaphor, maybe? Or just research?

"As real as any of us," he confirmed. "There's actually an organization similar to yours that's devoted to tracking them down and ensuring they don't harm people here on Earth. It's a great deal less secret, though. I'm a little surprised you haven't heard of it before."

She finally took the first bite of her food and considered before she shrugged. "I guess it never came up before I moved to the Athenaeum, and after, I had too many other things to focus on."

He inclined his head to her. "Understandable."

"Erasmus said you had some experience in stuff like finding the Hall?"

"Mmm. I haven't ever searched for something precisely like the Hall, but yes. A year ago, my wife, a friend, and I found pieces of a relic that had been broken and hidden all across the globe."

Sophia's brows lifted. "Seriously? That sounds awesome." And definitely put him in the same category as the venatores.

He smiled, but it was tight. "The end result certainly was, but it was far from safe. We came across jaguars in the Amazon rainforest, starving elementals in an Antarctic cave, and territorial mers in Lake Baikal in Russia. Not to mention several hundred snakes right here in Egypt."

"No, I don't guess any of that was fun." But it did sound like something right out of some of the movies she loved. She could do without the danger, but going on an adventure like that without the world-affecting risks would be nice.

"It wasn't. But I imagine you have all sorts of relics in the Athenaeum?"

She might still be waking up, but she could recognize fishing when she heard it. "We have all sorts of everything in the Athenaeum."

Erasmus chuckled. "Don't think my granddaughter is going to crack any easier than I did," he chided Julian, but it was clear he didn't mind. It almost sounded like Julian fishing and Erasmus blocking had become routine between them.

"I had to try," Julian said without shame. "But if you aren't going to tell me more about the Athenaeum, then would any of you care to fill in some of the details? Finding the Hall of Records is quite the incentive, but I would appreciate a bit more information."

Not for the first time, three sets of eyes turned toward her, then Julian's did as well. One of these days, she might get used to being the boss, but today wasn't that day.

Her stomach suddenly a little queasy, she set her burger down and wiped her fingers on a napkin. This wasn't an easy question, and she wasn't sure if she should tell him about the Miasma. Not because he wasn't part of the Athenaeum, either. She hadn't told most of the

Nasaru either, nor would she have, even if they'd been in their right minds. Still, if he was going to help them find the Hall, he might help them find whatever could counter the Miasma, which meant he needed to know.

"Have you ever heard of Miasma?" she asked.

Julian frowned. "The sentient disease?"

It was Sophia's turn to frown, but Olivia spoke before she could. "What do you mean, sentient disease?"

"In Greek lore, it was a disease, usually said to have been sent by the gods to punish someone of wrongdoing. Unlike most diseases, it had sentience, and would continue to infect and spread until the wrongdoing was atoned for. Is that not what you're meaning?"

Sophia shrugged. "I don't know about sentient, and the gods don't seem to have anything to do with it, but the rest sounds right." He looked curious, and she continued before he could press. "This is to be kept to yourself, but long story short? Everyone in the Athenaeum—except for the four of us—has been infected by some substance that is at least partly magical and, they are being controlled somehow by one person. Olivia said it sounded like Miasma, except the only reference I found for Miasma didn't describe it like you did."

"I have questions—several of them—but can we begin with what description you did find?"

"It was one of five elements or substances that were left over when the universe was created. They were hidden away because, while necessary, in concentrated form they were dangerous. Miasma was the violence of change and emotion."

"One of five? What were the other four?"

"Focus, Julian," Lucas said mildly. "The other four haven't taken over the Athenaeum. Which means they're not in danger of ruining the world."

"Oh. Yes, right. You said one person was controlling the infected. Was that person infected as well?"

"I don't know," Sophia admitted. "Our healer never told me he was, so I'm not sure if he was checked or not."

Julian nodded slowly. "What happens if we can't find the Hall?"

"Worst case scenario? He tries to infect as many people outside the Athenaeum as he can until we hit the two week deadline the gods who protect the Athenaeum have given us. When that happens, the Athenaeum and everyone inside it will be destroyed. Problem is, it might not actually solve the problem. We have people who go all over the world. Some of those who have already left might be infected. Or he might be sending more people out right now for the specific purpose of infecting people. And right now, the best we have is a way to temporarily break someone free."

"Temporarily?" Julian asked at the same time Erasmus said, "You broke someone free?"

"Yes and yes," she answered. "Using demigod healing and Isis's tyet, we were able to heal one of our people. Or so we thought. But not long after, when we went to try to end all this, he was right back under the Miasma's control."

Julian nodded. "Do you know how they were being infected?"

Thinking of that made her think of Sergei, still back in the Athenaeum and at Peter's mercy. Lucas must have noticed something off, because he rubbed her knee and said, "The water. Some of the Miasma was put into our water supply, so every time we came into contact with it, we were getting dosed. Our healer said it didn't metabolize and leave the body like other substances, so it just kept building up until it changed people's behavior."

"It was a gradual thing?"

"Except for Lachlan," Olivia said bitterly.

"What happened to him?"

"He went crazy and started attacking people," Sophia explained. "Didn't seem to matter who they were. If he saw them, he was attacking them. He was also the one we thought we'd cured."

"Poor Lachlan," Erasmus murmured. "We'll get him back," he told Sophia. "Him and everyone else in the Athenaeum."

"I know we will." They had to. "So our plan is to find the Hall, because it's supposed to have stuff in it that was old when the Athenaeum was founded. If anywhere has information about Miasma, it's there, because even the gods don't know."

"Or some of them do and aren't sharing for their own personal reasons," Julian said. Something told her he'd not had the best experience with the gods, but didn't pry. They didn't have time for it right now.

"It's a possibility," she agreed.

"Do you have a starting place for where to look for the Hall?"

Since it was Olivia's memory, Sophia glanced at her and the nightmare answered. "Nothing definite, but I have good reason to believe we'll find the way to the Hall beneath the Sphinx. Not sure if it's directions or a map, but I'm sure something's there."

"I hope you have something more specific than just beneath the Sphinx."

Olivia nodded. "The door's supposed to be hidden in the back right leg. But none of us are witches, and while we're all skilled in sorcery to one degree or another, we can't guarantee it'll be enough to find and open a door sealed magically."

Julian smiled for a second and shook his head. "Well, it won't be the first hidden door I've found in Egypt."

"It's not?" Sophia asked.

He shook his head. "It isn't. I was helping a friend do much the same thing the last time I was here. So the plan is to go to the Sphinx and just search until we find the door?"

"Basically. We're going to go at night, with an invisibility spell over all of us," Sophia confirmed.

"When do you want to go?"

Sophia glanced at Lucas with that question, since strategy was more his forte than hers. "A little after midnight," he answered.

Julian nodded. "Then shall we spend the time between now and then trying to consider alternatives in case the Hall doesn't have the answer?"

Sophia hated the thought that it might not, but he was right. So for the next few hours, they discussed how they might cure the Miasma infection while her anxiety grew.

Chapter 4

The hours they were forced to wait in Erasmus's home wore on Sophia. Lucas wasn't sure the others could see it, but he did. She sounded calm and put on a good face, but there was a tightness to her eyes and shoulders that wasn't normally there. Still, she didn't back down from discussing plans and theories and didn't let herself succumb to despair. This might be all new territory for her, but she kept up, and better than a lot of people would. She really was an amazing woman, and he hoped they could finish this soon so she could start to actually enjoy the Athenaeum. The joys of ancient texts. The thrill of learning something new. And the hope that came from being part of a family that all had the same goal in common. And despite his anger with Erasmus, he wanted Sophia to get to know her grandfather. Neither the Athenaeum nor her grandfather had been particularly pleasant experiences for her so far, and they should have been. He remembered his first month in the Athenaeum, and he'd spent it in a dazed kind of glee. And those with more academic backgrounds tended to go far beyond anything as simple as glee.

The time finally came for them to stop talking and head out. Lucas ensured Sophia still had the knife he'd given her before they'd confronted Peter. The Hall might be abandoned, but it could also be guarded and he wanted her to have every protection he could give her. He just wished he'd had time to show her how to properly use it—or any weapon.

They gathered in the middle of the living room, most of them empty-handed, but Julian slid a backpack onto his shoulders. Then, when they started casting protective spells, Julian's eyes widened and his right hand twitched as he studied them in fascination. "You said none of you are witches? I apologize for the rudeness, but might I ask what you are?" he asked, his words polite, even if there was eagerness in his voice. It wasn't taboo to ask such a question, but some Arcane did find it rude. Julian was fortunate that no one protested for now.

"I'm half elf, half owl shifter," Sophia began with a shrug. "Grandpa is full shifter, Olivia's a nightmare, and Lucas is a gargoyle."

"Fascinating," Julian murmured. "I have never really spent time focusing on sorcery—I've never truly needed to—but I might need to start. None of you should be able to create shields, but I can sense them. Strong ones, too."

Erasmus chuckled. "If you think that's impressive, then brace yourself."

Julian gave him a curious look, but said nothing as Erasmus spoke sounds that were familiar to Lucas, but gibberish to anyone not familiar with the spell. Nothing obvious happened, and Julian's brow furrowed. "What am I bracing myself for? I can feel you did something, but not what."

"We're invisible," Olivia answered with a grin. "To anyone who isn't the five of us, anyway."

His brows lowered further as he gave them each a long, hard look. No doubt using his magic to sense the spell. Or try to. "With a few syllables? You're able to do that?"

"Sorcery can do anything, so long as you know the right spell and have the will to make it happen," Sophia answered. "But trust me, it takes work to have it do what you really want it to," she said, grinning at Lucas. "Remember the grapes?"

Lucas would forever remember the sight of her face after he'd pelted her in the chest with the small fruits. He laughed and nodded. "I do. But we should go, because the spell won't last forever."

"Right. Everyone ready?" Olivia asked, turning the lights off then motioning them into a tighter group. When everyone had agreed, she shifted them through the shadows to the rear of the Sphinx. Lucas and Sophia were prepared for the unsettling feeling that accompanied such travel—like their soul was snapping back into their bodies—but Erasmus and Julian looked a little ill. Lucas understood, as he felt the same way, he just wasn't caught off guard like they were. He probably should have warned them, but honestly hadn't thought about it until it was too late.

"I really don't like that form of teleportation," Julian said, a hand resting on his stomach.

"Sorry. I always forget that those who aren't nightmares find it unpleasant, but it is effective," Olivia said with a shrug.

Sophia gave them only a minute—during which she looked around nervously—before she spoke, voice quiet. "All right. Let's get started. I don't want to risk being caught. We've got enough problems without adding humans into the mix."

It wasn't going to be easy. It only took a few syllables from the sorcerers and a quick check from Julian to realize there was magic permeating this entire area, which they'd expected. Narrowing it down to just the doorway would take a great deal more expertise than he had. Which was why he was watching for humans. Olivia had opted to help, since she could further hide them in shadows if needed. And he'd seen the interest and desperate hope in Sophia's eyes when they were discussing the details of their plan. She wanted to help, even if she didn't have the skills to do so now. Watching Erasmus and Julian work might give her some of the experience she lacked.

Though he took his role as lookout seriously, he couldn't help but glance back to the three working. Julian was a few feet from Sophia and Erasmus, with the latter murmuring to his granddaughter. Explaining what she could do to help them locate the door, he assumed.

Curious, he took a moment to feel the magics around him, unsurprised when there were flashes of it coming from the witch and sorcerers. Then it began to build, and he hoped they'd located the door and were trying to force it to open.

"Guards," Olivia hissed. Both she and Lucas moved closer to the others and the Sphinx, pressing their backs against the stone. Though Sophia, Erasmus, and Julian were already against the monument, Sophia all but plastered herself against it. Lucas got it. They'd warned her that the invisibility spell didn't prevent the guards from hearing them or running into them, only hid them from sight. Since this was far from her comfort zone, she was clearly being overly cautious. Honestly, he applauded it. It took everyone a little while to adjust to doing this kind of thing. For some, it only took a couple of retrievals. For others, he'd seen it take years.

The guards were taking their sweet time. They were only a dozen or so feet from them, but didn't seem to be in a hurry to continue their rounds. Worse, one of the two wandered entirely too close to Olivia. He saw her inhale, then hold her breath, all while glaring at the man. Then he noticed something that was even scarier than a human getting too close to an invisible Olivia. Sophia looked like she was trying very hard not to sneeze—probably due to her face being pressed against the sandy side of the monument—and both guards had stopped and were chatting about one of the men's girlfriend.

Lucas waved until he caught Erasmus's attention, then pointed to Sophia. The older man shook his head in confusion and Lucas mouthed 'sneeze.' Erasmus grimaced and glanced at the guards, then his lips moved in a nearly silent whisper. Lucas wasn't sure what spell he'd just cast, but the guards started moving again, at a brisk pace now. In under a minute, they were far enough away that the group could speak quietly and not worry that someone would hear them breathing and moving.

"You okay?" Lucas whispered to Sophia when it looked like her need to sneeze had passed.

She nodded, but also looked a little paler than usual. "Yeah, but maybe I don't want to be a venator if it's always like this," she half-joked.

He grinned at her and went back to watching for other guards. Erasmus might have been able to send the first two on their way, but there was no guarantee they'd stay gone. And there was no telling how long it would take them to get the door open.

Sophia really wasn't cut out for this sort of thing, but she couldn't deny how interesting it was to watch Julian and her grandfather search for the way into the Sphinx. Though she'd focused on Greece in her own studies, even she knew there were several known openings in the Sphinx. But none of those—as far as she knew—actually led to anything even remotely like Olivia had mentioned. In fact, she was pretty sure most weren't big or deep, and some were dead ends.

Julian and her grandfather were using a mixture of methods in their search, including running their fingers along the stone. Julian spoke little other than to confer with Erasmus, but witches didn't need to speak to weave their magic. Erasmus, on the other hand, was almost constantly murmuring spell after spell. Normally she couldn't feel magic unless it was exceptionally strong—like when Death had visited the Athenaeum—but Erasmus had taught her a variation of the spell to sense magic that let her do more than get a snapshot of what had been cast in the past. She paid close attention as they worked, surrounded by magic from every direction.

The two men were separated by about ten feet, and Sophia stayed between them so she could alternate her attention as they worked down the stones that made up the hind leg of the Sphinx. Then, as Julian took a step to the left, she frowned and moved to his other side, resting a hand on the tail of the Sphinx as she stared at the stone. "Olivia," she whispered, glancing at the nightmare.

"Yeah?"

"You sure it's actually in the leg?"

Olivia didn't answer right away, but seemed to think as she watched for more approaching humans. "Can't say for certain," she admitted. "Why?"

"Not sure," Sophia answered vaguely before she shifted closer to Julian. "You checking just the leg itself, or have you checked the tail?"

Julian paused and took a step back, his head cocking as his gaze moved over the stone tail. "I was focusing on the leg," he said with a nod. "Not ignoring the rest, just not focusing on it."

"Try?" she asked. The new magic she was using had a learning curve, but there was something about a section of the tail that bugged her. It was probably nothing, especially if Julian and Erasmus had bypassed it, but none of them really understood the Sphinx. Even with Arcane living so much longer than humans, they'd still lost a lot of their ancient past. That was part of why the Athenaeum existed. So important things didn't get lost to time.

He nodded again and ran his hands carefully along the top of the tail, his brow furrowed, eyes narrowed in concentration. As seconds ticked past and the humans made their way further along their route back toward them, he repeated his action not once, but twice, before making a thoughtful sound. "Erasmus? Come over here?" Gone was the eager, excited tone he'd had earlier. He was all business now, and Sophia appreciated it.

Erasmus joined them, and it only took a nod to the tail before he was checking as well. "I think you're onto something, *louloudi mou*," he said with a distracted smile. She was briefly distracted herself at the endearment—my flower—but forced herself back to the moment.

Once again, they resumed their staring and muttering, and Sophia felt the magic build. It felt different from the few types of magic she'd felt before, so she closed her eyes in order to better focus. Given her particular brand of magic, sometimes it was difficult for her to remember that sight often interfered with her other senses. Now that she was blocking out that part of the world, she could feel the magic more clearly and in a way she didn't expect. The new spell was damn impressive—as was the magic her grandfather and Julian were doing.

"Hurry up. You've got maybe five minutes before the guards are back," Lucas warned quietly.

Neither man answered him, but she felt a sudden push of magic—from Julian, she thought, since Erasmus didn't speak a syllable.

"Two minutes," came the next warning, more urgency in Lucas's tone.

The magic built further, and she heard her grandfather speak just as there was another burst from Julian. Then she heard a soft grinding sound. Eyes opening, she saw that it wasn't a doorway that had opened in the Sphinx's leg, but one revealed by the tail shifting up.

"Quickly," Julian said as he started forward, having to hunch over to dip beneath the tail. "They most likely heard that."

No one hesitated, and the moment all five of them were inside some sort of corridor, Julian released another burst of magic and touched the side of the door. Opening the door might have been difficult, but closing it was much easier, as the tail slid smoothly down, covering the hidden entrance once again. Leaving them in complete darkness.

Chapter 5

Sophia really wished the battery was in her phone, because this level of darkness was more than a little eerie, even for someone who was part owl. She might be able to see well in the dark, and better when she was in owl form, but even she couldn't see if there was an absolute absence of light. And the smell didn't help. She'd become used to the scent of old books, tablets, and the like, but this was different. Not musty, and nothing she could place. It wasn't even bad, just extremely odd to her senses. It made her wonder if it was unique to the interior of the Sphinx, or if all structures from ancient Egypt smelled this way.

"Did any of us geniuses remember to grab a flashlight?" Lucas asked dryly.

There was a chuckle before a light turned on and blinded them all for a moment. When she could see again, she saw Julian grinning with a headlamp shining from his forehead. "I had a feeling this might become an issue," he admitted, digging into his backpack before he offered each of them a light. "This isn't the first time I've dealt with this kind of situation. Though I am relieved to see there aren't stairs."

Sophia got her light turned on and settled on her forehead before she really looked at the area around them. Corridor was a good name for where they were, and like Julian had said, there were no stairs.

Instead, the floor sloped downward and after what looked like about fifty feet, it made a ninety degree turn. It likely did a second turn around the corner and continued further beneath the Sphinx.

The walls looked like those in other temples—or at least looked like photos she'd seen of them—in that they were covered in pictures and hieroglyphics. They were beautifully done, but they didn't look quite right. It reminded her of a chart she'd seen once showing the evolution of Greek letters. The symbols had been similar to ones she was familiar with, but most of them were altered in some way.

She turned to find Olivia and saw the nightmare was studying the walls as well. Maybe she was thrown by the differences, too? "These look weird to you? Like an older version of the hieroglyphics we know?"

"No, they aren't weird, but they are an older version," Olivia confirmed with a nod. "And not one the human archaeologists have come across."

"What do you mean?" Lucas asked, moving to stand beside her.

"These are the hieroglyphics the Arcane used back then."

"Wait. We had our own version of hieroglyphics?" Sophia asked, momentarily forgetting about why they were inside the Sphinx.

"Of course. Magic was more commonplace and accepted back then, even by humans, but we didn't want them having all our secrets," Olivia said with a smile. "I'll tell you more after we kick Peter's ass."

"I'm holding you to that."

They turned toward the way deeper into the Sphinx, and to no one's surprise, Lucas moved to the front. Unwilling to be cast to the back of the group, Sophia hurried to walk right behind him. She wasn't dumb enough to be in the front, not when she was squishy and he could turn to stone in an instant, but she didn't want to be coddled like a helpless child, either. If Erasmus and Lucas had their way, she knew she would be.

The corridor did switch back on itself, leading deeper, but it also did more than that. As soon as Lucas's foot hit the first landing, torches in the next section lit with a soft whoosh. Sophia blinked against the increase in light, and though she shut her headlamp off, she didn't remove it. Knowing their luck, they'd reach a section where there weren't any torches and be blind again. The others apparently had the same idea, because they did the same thing.

Continuing down, they had to switch directions four times. Sophia wasn't sure how far beneath the Sphinx they were at that point, but guessed it was at least a couple hundred feet. Fortunately, living in the Athenaeum for a month had gotten her over any apprehension she might have had about being so far underground. Especially in an ancient structure. Besides, it had held up this long, so it would hold up for a few hours more. Or so she hoped.

But this felt too easy, and if she'd learned anything from the movies she loved, it was that if something felt too easy, everything was about to go to hell.

After going back and forth a couple more times, the sloped path ended at a doorway. "Everyone ready?" Lucas asked.

Sophia cast her shield spell again, just to make sure, and she heard Erasmus casting one, too. When everyone had answered Lucas, he nodded and eased into the room beyond the doorway.

It was a tall chamber, roughly thirty feet square with a ceiling about ten feet high, and at first glance, there was only one way in or out. It was also completely full of all kinds of treasure and one unexpected item.

There was an Egyptian sarcophagus in the middle of the room, with a good five feet of empty space surrounding it. It was made of a pale tan stone and intricately carved with symbols. From what she knew of ancient burial rituals, there was likely a coffin inside, similar to the one King Tut had been found in. Not that she intended to open it and find out. The dead were meant to be left in peace, and she'd do her best to see that this tomb's inhabitant wasn't disturbed.

Disturbing them was how horror movies began. Especially in an Egyptian tomb.

Though impressive, the stone box was greatly overshadowed by the rest of what lay in this long forgotten chamber. There were tables, shelves, and open chests simply brimming with gold and gem-encrusted objects. Goblets, statues, jewelry, headdresses, weapons, and things she couldn't even identify. Hell, some of the stones set into the various items were ones she couldn't recognize. They might just be rare gemstones she'd never encountered, but she wouldn't be surprised if some of them were magical. But they all shared one trait; they were exquisitely crafted. Modern technology couldn't have made these items any more perfectly.

"There has to be millions of dollars worth of gold in here," Sophia breathed, though she honestly had no idea of the value of any of this. Her own jewelry was mostly costume jewelry, with a few silver pieces mixed in. Not that she regularly wore any of it. This? It looked like the highest quality, both in craftsmanship and historical value. She loved it.

"At least," Erasmus agreed with a nod. "Especially when you add in historical value. But I wouldn't recommend touching any of it."

"Why not?" The Athenaeum might not be hurting for money—assuming Peter hadn't changed that in the last day—but even a fraction of this treasure might allow them to purchase more items that would make their jobs easier. And safer. Gods, they could use some safer.

Julian smiled at her. "You haven't been in many tombs, have you?"

"This is my first," she admitted, since she wasn't sure the crypts in the Athenaeum really counted in this instance. They were more like a local cemetery, they just happened to be underground.

"Quite a few ancient tombs—especially those associated with the Arcane—have traps or curses. And the curses tend to be centered on the treasure that was meant to go with a deceased individual to the afterlife. I couldn't tell you for certain without thoroughly studying it, but this treasure could be cursed."

"And we don't have time to deal with curses," Lucas said absently as he made his way to the sarcophagus.

No, they didn't, but while Lucas was focused on the sarcophagus, she decided to check out the rest of the room. It wasn't that she didn't think the sarcophagus could hold some clue, she just didn't relish getting too close to a dead body. Ashes were one thing, mummies were another beast completely. Besides, he wasn't the only one looking it over, as Julian had joined him. Since they didn't have much time, divide and conquer was probably their best bet, so she wandered past Lucas and Julian, searching for signs of other things hidden amongst the treasure. The problem was, there was a hell of a lot of treasure.

It was easy to try to dismiss the golden artifacts, but for all she knew, one of the statues or rings could be the map. Or one of those chests encrusted in jewels might have maps inside. Hell, one of the statues could have it inside for all she knew. That was the problem with ancient Arcane—they had been tricky as hell. And that wasn't even considering that one of these items might take them directly to the Hall when touched. It was worse than the needle in a haystack. At least then you knew exactly what you were looking for.

But there was more to this room than a dead body and treasure. One of the walls was split into sections roughly seven feet wide, and each section was written in one of what looked like four languages. The hieroglyphics she recognized, as she did the Sumerian cuneiform, even if she couldn't read it. Of the other two, one was vaguely familiar, but she couldn't place it, and the other was completely alien. No, maybe not completely. There was something about it that felt like she should know it, but she would put money on never having seen it before in her life.

"Olivia? Have you looked at the walls?"

"I glanced at them, yeah. They're stories, from what I can tell."

"What languages are those? I recognize the hieroglyphics and cuneiform, but I'm not sure what the other two are."

Olivia walked over and stood beside Sophia as she stared at one of the panels covered in the last language. "I can't actually read all of this one," she admitted. "It's one of the few languages I'm not completely fluent in, because none of my ancestors were able to study it completely enough."

"What is it? I guarantee I've never seen it before, but it...I feel like I *should* know it."

"Really?" Olivia took a longer look at the panel, frowning at it before she shrugged. "No idea why. It's Lemurian, so unless there was something hidden in the Vault, there's no reason why you would have come into contact with it."

Sophia stared at the symbols which were comprised of swirls and straight lines. It was kind of pretty, but she hadn't been expecting it to be Lemurian. "You're sure?"

Olivia smiled faintly. "Pretty sure. If you want confirmation, though, we can call Seth."

Sophia shook her head. No, Seth needed to be working to get the Athenaeum's wards down. Verifying the language wasn't as high a priority. "No, I believe you. I'm just not sure why Lemurian writing is in a chamber a hundred feet beneath the Egyptian Sphinx."

"Now that I've got no clue on. Just because one of our patrons is a Lemurian god doesn't mean we're experts in the place. I don't even know if most of the Athenaeum knows he's Lemurian, and Erasmus is the only one of us who's been there."

Since Sophia had nothing either, she just nodded to the other unknown language. This one was closer to the hieroglyphics than the Lemurian, as it was made of symbols—some that resembled pictures, and some that didn't. "What's that language?"

"Minoan, though you probably know it as Linear A."

Holy shit, was all Sophia could think as her mouth went slack. Of course she'd heard of Linear A. She wanted to geek out, but forced herself to stay calm. When they'd stopped Peter, she could come back and study it to her heart's content—after she'd picked Olivia's brain for everything she knew about this language. The humans couldn't decipher this language, and even the Arcane thought it was undecipherable. It had been lost millennia ago, and there weren't enough writings left to allow anyone to figure it out. Other than those like Olivia. "Please tell me you're a hundred percent on that and fluent in it."

Olivia laughed and bumped her shoulder against Sophia's. "Of course. And yes, I'll add it to the list of languages to teach you when this is over."

"Thank you," Sophia said, tempted to hug the other woman.

"Does anyone recognize the map on the ceiling?" Lucas asked.

Map? She hadn't noticed any map, but then, she hadn't looked up. There was so much on the walls and surrounding her that she'd been overwhelmed. Lifting her gaze, she saw he was right. The entire ceiling was covered with an intricately detailed color map of what looked like an island. It was a long land mass, with what looked like forests and mountains, and even something she thought was a volcano. But to answer Lucas's question, it wasn't even remotely familiar. No, she wasn't an expert on geography, but most of the places around today should strike at least a hint of a chord within her. "I don't. Looks like an island, though." Wait, lost islands. Could it be Atlantis? Sure, the humans thought it was a myth, but they also thought shapeshifters and witches were myths. Then again, even the Arcane believed Atlantis to be just a story.

"I do," Erasmus answered, but his tone was thoughtful rather than excited. "To a point, in any case. It isn't exact, but it looks like a map Seth showed me of Lemuria. Ancient Lemuria."

"Lemuria?" Sophia frowned at her grandfather. "Why in the hell is there a map of Lemuria and Lemurian writing in a chamber beneath the Egyptian Sphinx? Greek stuff would make sense, because the Greeks and Egyptians interacted, but the Lemurian stuff?"

Erasmus shook his head and dropped his gaze from the map to the sarcophagus. "I don't know. Even having been there, I don't know as much about the place as I'd like. Seth would tell me, I'm sure—though they're very protective of their home—but there hasn't been time. But this," he stepped closer to the sarcophagus and touched a corner delicately. "This might provide some answers."

Julian was still studying the sarcophagus as well, though Lucas was staring up at the map. Half turning, she saw Olivia was looking at the symbols on the walls. Sophia nearly smiled when she realized they were surrounded by millions of dollars worth of gold and jewels, and not one of them was paying it any attention. The urge disappeared quickly because they still had to figure out what in this mess of treasure and carved walls would lead them to the Hall. And as much as she'd like to let her grandfather take the lead as the one with the most experience, he was looking at her as though waiting for her to make a decision. Dammit, they were taking the fact that she was the aspida seriously.

She blew out a breath. "Lucas?"

"Yeah?"

"You said you knew about the Sumerians. Did you mean the language, too?"

"I did," he agreed.

Sophia nodded. "Then can you and Olivia work on seeing if there's anything but stories on the walls? Grandpa, Julian, you two check the sarcophagus."

"Can do," Lucas said, walking toward one of the Sumerian panels. Olivia nodded absently, the motion mirrored by Julian.

Erasmus smiled and nodded. "What do you plan on doing?"

"I'm going to try to get a hold of Seth and see if he has any insight as to why Lemuria is popping up in here, of all places." The language was one thing, but with the addition of the map, it might be important enough to draw him away from brainstorming with the other patrons. Getting into the Athenaeum did no good if they didn't have a way of fixing the problem.

Again he nodded, before he reached into his pocket and pulled out a phone. "I know you three disabled your phones, so you can use mine if you want."

That made sense. If Seth was dealing with the other patron gods, he might not be able to pop over to see her, but he should be able to answer a call or text. "Thank you," she told him, taking the phone. Once she had, he immediately started studying the sarcophagus again. She woke the phone and went to the contacts. Seth's name was one of the few on the list, which was good because, like most people in the last few decades, she programmed numbers rather than remembering them.

Walking to the far side of the room so she wouldn't disturb the others, she called pressed the button to call a god.

"Hey Erasmus," Seth said when he answered. His voice was strained, but she couldn't blame him. "Tell me you found something."

"It's Sophia. And...sort of."

"What do you mean, sort of?"

Deciding to go with the old saying about a picture being worth a thousand words, she quickly snapped a shot of the ceiling map and texted it to him. "We're in a chamber beneath the Sphinx and found that. And there's what Olivia assures me is Lemurian writing on the walls. A few other languages, too, but Lemurian's there."

Seth was quiet for a moment, and when he spoke again, he sounded baffled more than stressed. "I'm guessing Erasmus figured out that was Lemuria before it sank?"

"Maybe? He just said it looked like a map of Lemuria that you showed him."

"Shit. Okay. I've only been a Lemurian for a year and my focus is pretty well split between trying to stop Peter and making sure my pregnant wife is okay. I'm going to see if Vazi can help out."

"Vazi?"

"The only other Lemurian god currently around. He's an old one, too, so he knows more about it and the Lemurians than I do."

"If he's willing to help, I'm more than happy to accept it."

"Let me talk to him and I'll text you."

He hung up without saying goodbye and Sophia lowered the phone, suddenly nervous. She'd gotten used to Seth, but it hadn't hurt that he'd been a normal Arcane for most of his life. It meant he acted like a normal person. Meeting an elder god was kind of terrifying, but if he could help them get to the Hall, she'd suck it up and deal with it.

The phone buzzed in her hand and she turned it to look at the screen.

Seth: He'll be there.

She'd barely finished reading the text when she felt a brief breeze accompanied by a soft burst of power. Glancing up, she saw a tall man—taller than Lucas by several inches—with an athletic build, blonde hair that just brushed his jaw, and pretty blue eyes. He was handsome, but also had an aggravated look on his face.

"Which one of you is Sophia?" he demanded.

Chapter 6

The god's words drew the gazes of the others. Erasmus, she noted, smiled slightly and nodded to the man, but Lucas immediately looked at Sophia, his skin taking on a gray cast. She really loved how protective he was over the people he cared about. Especially her, though she was sure he'd protect Olivia and Erasmus as well.

Though nervous, she didn't hesitate to lift a hand. "I am," she answered as she moved back toward the others. "Vazi, I assume?"

"Unless you asked for another god. And what the hell is on your head?"

Of course, Seth had sent her a snarky god. Couldn't he have warned her? Normally, she would go for respectful since this was a god and thus a person capable of crushing her with his pinky. She was tired of giving into bullies, though, no matter how little say she'd had previously. And while Vazi might not be a bully per se, she still wasn't going to let herself be steamrolled. "Actually, I didn't ask for you. I asked for Seth. He just thought you'd be more help. And it's a headlamp, since none of us can see in total darkness."

Vazi smirked and shook his head. "I think I might like you. So why am I here? Seth told me it had to do with Lemuria and the trouble in the Athenaeum, but gave me no details."

Sophia thought about going into a long explanation, but remembered how useful the explanation she'd given to Seth had been, so kept it short. "We're trying to find the Hall of Records for something that can counter Miasma and we found that," she pointed to the writing Olivia was standing in front of, "and that," she finished, now pointing straight up.

Expression curious, Vazi looked at the writing first, which caused his brow to furrow. Silently, his gaze shifted to the map, and the frown deepened. "And we're in Egypt? Beneath some monument that had to have been built after Lemuria sank?"

"Um...I don't know when Lemuria sank, but the Sphinx was built something like four thousand years ago, if that helps?"

"To be a little more precise, Isis said the Sphinx was built roughly five thousand years ago," Erasmus offered.

"So yes, it was built after Lemuria sank," Vazi said with a single, sharp nod. "Is there anything else Lemurian in here?"

"I don't know," Sophia admitted when no one else immediately spoke up. "We've avoided the treasure because it might be cursed and we only have two weeks to stop Peter. The sarcophagus is an Egyptian style, but I haven't really looked at the carvings. Erasmus thinks it might help explain the Lemurian writing and map, though."

"Why?" Vazi asked Erasmus.

"It would be logical," Erasmus answered with a shrug. "There are two main anomalies in here; the sarcophagus and the Lemurian. It's also the only one here, and the Sphinx isn't known to be a tomb, despite being surrounded by monumental tombs like the pyramids."

Vazi nodded and strode toward the sarcophagus. "Have you been able to read any of the inscriptions?" he asked.

"I have. They're in Egyptian rather than Lemurian. However, being able to understand the words doesn't mean I understand the intent behind them."

"What do you mean?" Sophia asked as she followed Vazi toward the sarcophagus.

Her grandfather turned back to the top of the sarcophagus and, in the same way Sophia did, let his fingers trace the air above the writing as he read aloud. She also noted there was no hesitation with the language as there was when she read the language, proving his fluency.

"My heart will be lifted if these words are ever read again. I do not write these words in the language of my homeland, as I am the last of my kind. It is a great sorrow to me, and I know my soul will be joining my brothers and sisters before much longer. My kind have been hunted almost to extinction, until only I remain. I have taken measures to return my body here when my pursuers run me down, so whatever magic of mine remains after I pass into the beyond will ensure what I have left behind for you will not be abused.

"Knowledge is the greatest ambition, the highest pursuit after one's family. Here, in what I hope has become my resting place, I have left the path to what I have spent the last years of my life protecting. Only one worthy of it will find the true treasure that surrounds me."

Erasmus paused for a second, then looking up, his eyes lingering on Vazi for only a second before shifting to Sophia as he read the last line. "I am Akila, the last survivor of Lemuria."

No one spoke for several minutes. For Sophia, though Erasmus's voice had been even, the words he spoke had given her chills. This woman had known she would die—would be murdered—which couldn't have been easy. And while she'd read stuff written by people who had died centuries ago before, something about these words struck her more deeply. It felt like they'd been written with her in mind, though the chances of that were beyond slim. Still, if she pushed past the emotions that the inscription created within her—which wasn't easy, as she wanted to cry for this Akila—she realized it sounded like this Lemurian had left them clues to the Hall of Records. At least she hoped it was the Hall.

Sophia wasn't the only one moved. Frowning hard, Vazi stepped up to the sarcophagus and laid his hand on it, his index finger tracing over one of the symbols. "She was one of mine," he said, voice quiet and rough. "I even knew her. Not well, but we spent more time among our people than most of the other gods did. They were our children—both figuratively and literally, in some cases. I knew only some of them survived Lemuria's destruction. I even knew only one survived to this time. But this?" He shook his head and his hand stilled as he took another minute to settle.

Vazi let his hand drop to his side and turned to Sophia. "I was going to help because Seth asked me to and I know how dangerous it could be if the Athenaeum isn't retaken, but now I'm going to help because one of my people was hunted down and killed because she was one of mine. Because her last thoughts were of this place, of protecting it."

Sophia could only nod for a moment, because he sounded like he was genuinely mourning a woman who had been dead for what was probably a few thousand years. From what she'd heard of the gods, they didn't normally care about mortals like that. It gave her a new respect for the Lemurians and for him. "I'm sorry your people suffered like Akila and others. And I'm really sorry I had to bring it all back like this."

He shook his head. "You weren't responsible. And finding this Hall might help me reclaim a part of my people I thought was lost."

"What do you mean?"

"Akila was like you and Erasmus." Sorrow was replaced by amused resignation when he glanced to Julian. "And him." Turning back to Sophia, he continued. "She mentioned knowledge being the greatest ambition, and it was definitely hers. I met her through one of my brothers. Our god of wisdom. If she is connected to this Hall, it might have writings from my people. So, as of this moment, I'm as invested in finding it as you are."

Sophia was torn. If he reverted back to his earlier aggravated self, what promised to be a stressful two weeks might get even worse. But having a god on their side, especially one who was apparently ancient, definitely couldn't hurt. Even if they found some way to free the Athenaeum from Peter and the Miasma, it might not be an easy thing for them to actually accomplish. Having a cure didn't mean you could distribute it. "Then do you have any idea how to use what's here to find the Hall? Olivia found something that said the map to the Hall was here, but..." She shrugged and made a gesture to indicate the rest of the room. "We've got a few stories on the walls, a map of Lemuria on the ceiling, a sarcophagus, and a shitload of possibly cursed treasure."

Vazi chuckled. "Not yet, but let's see what we've got. Do you need help with the writings?" he asked, jerking his thumb toward a panel in Lemurian.

"Nah, I got that," Olivia answered. "Might miss a few nuances, but I can read it."

He arched a brow but nodded. "Then I'll start on the map, since I know that better than any of you—even if you've come across a map of it before."

"That works. Thank you," Sophia said. He went right into the task, studying the map intently. The others went back to their tasks as well, which meant Sophia now needed to figure out where she could help. The sarcophagus was well taken care of by Erasmus and Julian, so she decided to join Lucas and Olivia. She knew at least a little of those languages.

Lucas noticed the moment Sophia stepped beside him, and he looked away from the Sumerian writing to check on her. "You doing okay?" he murmured, sliding an arm around her waist and pulling her in closer. He had a feeling Vazi's offer to help had both added to her stress and given her hope.

"Kind of. It's just a lot, and this woman didn't give us much to go on."

He nodded. "True, but we're all smart. We can piece together what she did leave and find the Hall."

"Anything jumping out at you so far?" she asked, leaning her head against his shoulder.

"Maybe?" He didn't want to give her false hope, but there was something bugging him. He didn't know the other three languages, so he'd been focusing on the Sumerian. He wasn't a linguist like so many in the Athenaeum, but it was one of the languages he was fluent in. Despite that, there was something off about this. Most of it he could figure out—like adjusting for slight dialect shifts or being able to read typos—but there were a few parts that were confusing him.

She knew him well, though, and gave him a reassuring squeeze. "Talk me through it?" she suggested. "Sometimes talking something out with someone else helps you figure stuff out."

It wasn't a bad idea, so he nodded. "I've read through it a couple of times now. For the most part, it's what Olivia was saying. A story about a little girl finding a magical world. There are some parts where the writing isn't quite right, but I can make it out. Like if someone was telling you about a cat but spelled it K-A-T, you'd still understand, you know?" She nodded, but stayed quiet. "That stuff is fine. It's no worse than reading the old texts. But there are some symbols that don't fit."

"What do you mean?"

"You'll be following along with a sentence, then there's a stray word or sound that just doesn't match."

"Like reading a text with bad autocorrect?"

"Sort of." Deciding an example would be better than an explanation, he said, "More like if I was talking to you about how much I liked flying with you, how much I umbrella want to do it again."

Sophia blinked up at him, her head cocked. "Is it really that far out? Not like they messed up when they were writing a word?"

He shook his head. "No, it's totally separate from other things around it."

"Hmm." She stepped away from him to look at the hieroglyphics. For several minutes, she studied them in silence, her brow furrowing the longer she did. "Olivia?"

"Yeah?" came the distracted reply.

"You gotten a chance to read through both the Minoan and Lemurian sections?"

"Yeah." This time, Olivia looked away from the wall and to Sophia. "You found something?"

She shook her head and jerked her thumb in his direction. "Lucas did. There are random sounds and words interspersed in with the story on the Sumerian panel. From what I can tell, it's the same for the hieroglyphics."

Olivia nodded and frowned at the wall again. "Same here. I was trying to figure out if I was mistranslating it, but the odds of this many errors are slim. For a normal person it might be fine, but if this woman was connected to a god of wisdom, she was probably smarter than that. And if it's in multiple languages, you have to wonder why. And Lemurian? It was likely her native tongue."

"That's what I was thinking. It seems intentional."

"I think that's what was tripping me up," Lucas admitted as he turned back to the Sumerian. He wasn't a dumb man, but when he'd been on retrievals, he'd been focused on the safety of the venatores, not on getting through security measures—which included ancient riddles now and again. Which meant he hadn't been thinking like a venator. He needed to start if they were going to stop Peter. While still keeping Sophia safe.

"Me too," Olivia agreed. "But if it is intentional, why?"

"Julian?" Lucas called, looking back at the scholar who was still studying the sarcophagus.

"Yes? Did you find something?"

"We think so, but we're not sure. I know you brought some things with you. Any chance there's paper and a pen in it?"

"Actually, yes." Julian took off his backpack, retrieving a leather-bound journal with a pen held against the spine. "Should I ask?" he questioned as he walked over to offer the items to Lucas.

"Not yet. Thanks."

Opening the journal, Lucas started writing the out-of-place words from the Sumerian section of the wall, including both the Sumerian and the translation. When he had it down he studied it, but it seemed like nonsense. "Sophia, you want to write the extra Egyptian symbols?"

She hesitated, then shook her head, motioning toward Olivia. "I'm not fluent, so it might not be completely accurate, but it's a good idea. Be smarter to let her do it. Could be we'll find a pattern."

He nodded and gave the journal to Olivia, and while she focused on getting down the words for the other three sections, he went back to the Sumerian. Despite trying to put the random words and sounds together in different orders, they didn't seem to fit together. Taking a step back, he tried to see if there was a pattern to how they were placed on the wall.

"Sophia, how many did you find in the hieroglyphics?"

"Five. Why?"

"I found six in the Sumerian. Trying to figure out a pattern."

"Anything promising?"

"Not yet, but let's see what Olivia finds. Easier to find a pattern in four things than two."

She nodded, and fortunately Olivia finished only a few minutes later and walked over to them. "I followed your example and wrote the original and the translation."

"How many did you find in each language?" Lucas asked.

"Six per."

Sophia blew out a breath, and he had a feeling it was from missing the sixth on the Egyptian panel. "Definitely not a coincidence, then," she said, nodding.

Lucas looked over the pages. "Were any of them placed in the same position on the wall as another language?"

"No, they were in seemingly random spots," Olivia answered.

"Could it be sorcery?" Sophia wondered aloud.

"Anything's possible, but if it is, it might not work unless we know what it's supposed to do. We'd be missing the intent. And I'd be happy to give it a go, but it's twenty-four syllables and we don't know what order they should go in, so we could be trying thousands of possibilities. And that's if we need to use all twenty-four."

"Could be there's more on the sarcophagus," Sophia suggested. "An instruction manual or key or something."

"If this is a spell, it would make sense," Olivia agreed. "A few words wouldn't be too difficult to figure out, but with this many, there has to be more for us to find."

Lucas agreed, so they made their way over to the three by the sarcophagus. "Did you find anything?"

"Possibly," Erasmus said as he straightened. "The lid is what I read before, telling us who is inside. The sides are different. Each one is in a different language, and the content isn't the same."

"Let me guess," Sophia said with a sigh. "Hieroglyphics, Sumerian, Minoan, and Lemurian?"

"Precisely," he confirmed with a nod. "One of you said they were stories? On the walls, I mean?"

"For the most part," Olivia told him. "We found six out-of-place words or syllables in each section, though. We're thinking it's part of a spell."

"That makes sense," Julian said as he frowned at the top side of the sarcophagus. "There are out of place words here, as well. Not syllables, but full words."

"Did they make sense?" Sophia asked. "Because ours didn't."

Julian hesitated and Erasmus took over. "If we have the order correct, it says 'speak to find knowledge not found on a map.'"

Sophia blinked at him. "That's...not helpful. Even if it means speak the words and sounds from the walls, which ones? What order?"

Erasmus shifted a shoulder in a shrug. "I don't know. But in addition to those words, we also found eight numbers. Akila clearly meant them to be more difficult to find, because they were literally hidden in the words."

Olivia asked, "Were they grouped in any way?"

Julian nodded. "Four groups of two."

"What are they?"

"One and three, seven and two, seven and four, and nine and five."

Lucas stepped closer to Olivia and looked at their notes on the walls. "That fits."

Olivia nodded, glancing from the notes to the walls and back. "It does."

"What fits?" Sophia asked, crowding in to look as well.

"One and three. That syllable on the Sumerian panel? It's the third word on the first row. And this one? That's the second syllable on the seventh row of the Lemurian," he explained.

Since none of the others were dumb, they immediately caught on to what he'd noticed.

"That narrows it down to four syllables. In order, even. We just need to figure out which one is first," Sophia said, sounding excited again. Good. She could worry about Peter after they found what they were looking for.

"And figure out what she meant by finding knowledge not on a map," Erasmus reminded her.

"If this really is the way to the Hall, then it's definitely not some-place on a map," Olivia said, though she didn't sound completely certain.

"Beyond that, there is something on a map," Vazi said, smiling a little as his gaze slid upward once more.

"There is? What?" Lucas asked, as everyone else looked back to the ceiling.

The breeze was back, and this time it lifted Vazi smoothly off his feet and up to the map. "I don't think Akila meant for anyone but someone familiar with Lemuria to find this Hall, at least not without great difficulty. You see how there are multiple things marked on the map? Mountains, rivers, forests?"

Olivia nodded and handed Julian the now closed journal and pen. "Yeah?"

He pointed to a symbol Sophia didn't recognize. "There are also several of these marked. Not normal marks for a map, then or now." His magic moved him to a different part of the map, where he showed them another identical symbol. "They aren't letters, but seem to be more like..." He slowly lowered back to the floor as he thought and scowled. "I believe Seth says X marks the spot?"

Erasmus smiled. "It's a common misconception that treasure or an end point on a map is always marked with an X, but yes. Essentially, it's just a symbol to say 'this thing is here,'" he explained.

"It's the same for this map. And if you're familiar with Lemuria as it was, and I mean very familiar, then you'll notice that there is one thing all these symbols have in common." Vazi smiled smugly and crossed his arms over his chest. "They're all hot springs." The smile dimmed. "Though they're all destroyed now."

"Would it really need to be one on Lemuria? If she marked several of them, maybe it's just meant to say you have to say the spell at a hot spring?" Sophia wondered aloud.

"From what I know of Akila, she would be purposefully vague," Vazi began as he looked at the top of the sarcophagus. "If she did know how to get to this Hall, and it is as Seth described to me, then she would want to ensure only intelligent people managed to find it. But that said, she wouldn't want to make it impossible. What good would a place full of knowledge be if no one could learn from it?"

"So you think if it was a specific spring, she'd have clues leading to it?"

Vazi nodded. "I do. And I don't think she'd have marked all those springs if only one would do."

"Okay. We have the words, we have a general location. Now we just need a hot spring. Anyone know of one?"

"I do, actually," Julian said with a smile. "I can take us there if you like."

Of course the man wanted to come with them. Lucas wasn't against it. Hell, he wouldn't mind if Vazi wanted to join. Having another god on their side couldn't hurt. Especially since they were dealing with some insidious primordial substance.

"First, just in case this doesn't work, can you get us back in here if we need to come back to see if there's something else we're missing?" Sophia asked.

Julian hesitated, his eyes going unfocused. Before he could speak, Vazi said, "I can. And I'm going with you." He didn't ask, but Lucas wasn't surprised. Gods didn't tend to ask anything of mortals.

Rather than simply conceding, Sophia cocked her head and studied the god. "All right," she agreed after a moment. "We don't know what we're going to find at the Hall, or where we'll need to go after. And we're definitely going to need help when we go back to the Athenaeum. I don't want to kill anyone if we don't have to. The infected are innocent in all this."

"I agree," Erasmus said quietly. "I'd even prefer if we didn't have to kill Peter, but I've resigned myself to the fact that it may be necessary."

Sophia glanced down, her face closing down, her shoulders hunching. "I know." Drawing in a slow breath, she looked up at each person's face. "We ready to go?" When everyone had nodded, she focused on Julian. "Whenever you're ready."

Julian nodded and motioned for everyone to gather closer. "We'll drop by my house first. We need supplies." The words were just out of his mouth when the world melted away.

Chapter 7

Julian's home was, from what Sophia could tell after only one glance, an estate. Old and big, but comfortable rather than stuffy or overly modern. She liked it, but she wasn't exactly sure what he meant by supplies, so she asked as their group began to follow him through the house.

Julian smiled and smoothly shrugged one shoulder. "Do you know how long we'll be in the Hall? An hour? A day? Do you know where we'll need to go to after that? Because it could be that we find a spell there that can counter the Miasma, but chances are it will lead us someplace else that has what we need. Which means more time spent traveling. At the very least we need a little food and water."

Sophia felt like an idiot, because he was absolutely right. She really wasn't cut out to be a venator. No, she told herself, she needed to stop that. She wasn't thinking like a venator because she'd never had to act like one before. This was the first time she'd done anything like this, so she needed to cut herself some slack. Everyone had to learn when confronted with something new.

As they walked, Sophia caught a scent in the air and sniffed. Despite everything, her mood was lifted when she recognized the smell of fresh cookies. When they walked into the kitchen, there was a woman with brilliant red hair pulled up in a messy bun, wearing jeans, a tank top, and an apron, mixing something in a bowl, despite the fact that it was probably very early in the morning. She was slender and pretty, with a smear of flour on her jaw. When she spotted Julian, everything about her brightened. Almost immediately she noticed the group of people behind him, and her brow knit with worry. Then her eyes landed on Erasmus and she smiled again. "Erasmus. It's good to see you again," she said, her voice a soft murmur, the English accent only making it smoother.

"Good to see you as well, Paige," Erasmus said, smiling back at her. "I'm sorry to intrude."

"No need. I don't mind company." She set her bowl down and wiped her hands on her apron as she focused on Julian. "Is everything all right?"

Julian didn't pause as he strode toward her. After using his thumb to wipe the flour off her face, he bent his head to kiss her lightly. "It isn't, but it will be. And don't worry," he said, gently resting his thumb against her mouth before she could express her concerns. "I'm not in any danger at the moment. Besides, you remember Vazi, don't you? How much trouble could I find with a god backing us up?"

Paige didn't look convinced and muttered something that sounded like "Judging on past experience? A lot." But after a soft sigh, she nodded. "You can't stay, then?"

He shook his head. "Just here to get some supplies. I may be gone for a few days. You might want to invite your father. I know you don't like staying home when it's just you."

"It's too big a house for just me," she said absently. "But I can help with supplies. Unless you think you might need me?"

Sophia didn't know what skills Paige had, but Julian didn't hesitate before shaking his head. "Not this time."

Paige arched a brow. "Is that true, or do you just want to keep me out of harm's way?"

Uncaring about their audience or the flour on Paige's apron, he pulled her into his arms and smiled unapologetically. "You're eight weeks pregnant. I'm absolutely wanting to keep you out of harm's way."

"You're pregnant?" Erasmus asked, sounding delighted.

"Congratulations," Vazi said, not quite as enthusiastically, but he still sounded happy for the couple.

Paige peeked around Julian and smiled. "Thank you, and I am. Just found out two weeks ago."

"How wonderful! But I agree with Julian," Erasmus told her. "The first few months are too important, as are both you and that child. I promise I will do everything I can to return your husband to you in the same condition he leaves in. Even if it means sending him home."

"I appreciate that. And because I do, I'll help you with the supplies." She drew away from Julian and the two started getting what they needed. It seemed she'd done this before, because she didn't question what he was wanting to take. Several insulated bottles got filled with water and they grabbed food that wouldn't spoil even if they were gone for several days; jerky, protein bars, and what looked like dried fruit. The fact that they had all three on hand made Sophia wonder how often they did things like this.

When a timer dinged, Julian left the kitchen while Paige pulled a sheet of cookies out of the oven. "If any of you want a biscuit, you're welcome to them," she offered.

Since Sophia was hungry and they smelled really good, she happily accepted the offer, thrilled when she realized they were chocolate chip. To her surprise, Vazi and Olivia also accepted. Julian returned just as she was finishing her cookie, holding several backpacks. They all looked partially filled, but he proceeded to divvy up the food and water bottles between them before offering each person one. "I also grabbed some rope, a couple extra headlamps, a compass, a GPS, and a few other things, just in case," he told them as Sophia and the others slid the backpacks on. Even Vazi accepted his without complaint, though she was sure he didn't need anything the backpack held. Couldn't he just snap his fingers and manifest a feast or something? Then again, she didn't really know anything about god powers. Maybe his were limited to what he was the god of? Now that she was thinking about it she was curious, but she wasn't sure she was curious enough to ask the grumpy god.

"We'll give you a few minutes to say goodbye to Paige," Sophia told Julian before smiling at the woman. "It was nice to meet you. Thank you for the cookie, and congrats on the baby," she offered, then ushered the rest of her group out of the kitchen.

"Do you really think we'll need all this?" Olivia asked while they waited for Julian.

"We might," Lucas said, shrugging. "It's not like we have a lot of information on the Hall, and like Julian said, we don't know where we'll be going after. I'd rather have the food and other supplies and not need them, than end up stuck somewhere without them."

"True," she conceded then turned to Vazi. "So I'm fuzzy on the Lemurian gods since there's almost no information on them and I haven't gotten to sit down with Seth. What are you the god of?" she asked bluntly. Okay, so she was more curious than she'd realized.

"We kind of like it that way," Vazi admitted. "There's not many of us, and not all the other gods are thrilled we exist, so right now we're pretending like we don't." The words themselves were innocent enough, but there was a threat in them. Clearly if any of them decided to go talking about the Lemurians, they could expect an unpleasant visit from Vazi. "But I'm the god of the sky."

"Like Zeus?" Sophia asked, then recoiled at the look of pure hatred he turned on her.

"I am *nothing* like that pompous, treacherous child of a god," he snarled at her.

Sophia couldn't prevent herself from taking a step back. She'd never encountered a pissed off god before, and found she didn't like it at all. Especially when she was the one who had pissed him off. "I'm sorry," she quickly said, even as Lucas stepped partially in front of her. "I just meant the general sky part. Lightning, storms, all that."

"No," he said, voice clipped. "He's a pale imitation and doesn't have nearly the same powers I do."

"And she didn't know that you clearly have a hate on for the guy, so why don't you tone it down?" Lucas suggested.

For several long seconds, Vazi glared at Lucas, then he took a step back and took several slow breaths. "You're right. But for future reference, no one associated with Lemuria has any fond thoughts of that god."

"Understood," Sophia assured him. She didn't understand the hatred for Zeus, but had to admit he didn't exactly come off in the best of light in the stories she'd heard of him. If even half of them were true, he was a bastard, to put it mildly. This time she knew she wasn't curious enough to ask what Zeus had done to piss the Lemurians off so badly. She wanted to live to see the Athenaeum free of Peter's control.

Julian returned, which helped cut through the tension. "Everyone ready?" he asked, a little smile playing over his lips. Clearly he'd had a pleasant goodbye with Paige.

"Yes," she answered quickly, wanting to get them further from her misstep.

Again he used his magic to draw them to another place, and she had to admit it was one of the smoothest teleportations she'd experienced. Certainly easier on the body than either her sorcery or Olivia's shadow travel. Okay, so Seth's had been the easiest, but Julian was definitely practiced at it.

It was still night where he'd taken them, and darker due to the fact that it was pouring down rain. They were in a forest, but the trees didn't do much to shield them from the storm. As they pressed against the trees in a bid to keep dry, several of them turned their headlamps on. Unfortunately, it was dark enough, and it was raining hard enough, that it didn't really do much good. It certainly didn't help with the rain itself.

Rather than trying to shelter himself next to a tree like most of the others—Vazi chose to use his powers to divert the rain from landing on him—Julian frowned up at the sky. "It shouldn't be raining," he said, sounding baffled.

"What do you mean?" Sophia asked while she considered Vazi. Deciding to give something a try, she envisioned her shield, but above her rather than surrounding her, then spoke the spell. It wasn't perfect, but it did seem to help lessen the amount of rain that landed on her.

She'd practice, if she thought she'd be in this sort of situation ever again.

"I checked the weather just a few minutes ago, and it said it was cloudy but dry," he answered as he pulled out his phone.

"So? When are any weather people a hundred percent accurate?" Olivia countered.

Julian frowned harder at his phone. "Something is very wrong."

"What?" Lucas asked, again moving in front of Sophia. One of these days she was going to talk with him about being overly protective, but she'd wait until she'd gotten a bit more experience under her belt.

"In addition to a completely unexpected, sudden storm here, there's been quite a few other major incidents."

"Such as?" Erasmus asked, drawing out his own phone.

"A massive earthquake in Italy, another in California. A large tornado in Georgia—the state, not the country." He continued reading, then added, "And reports just showed up about other freak storms like this one in places where it was sunny or cloud-free only minutes before."

"Earthquakes in California aren't really uncommon," Sophia weakly protested. Then she had to ask, "Where in Georgia did the tornado touch down?"

"Ah..." A bit of tapping and scrolling, before he answered, "Athens?"

She could almost feel herself go pale. "I lived in Athens," she whispered. But as much as that thought terrified her, another was worse. "Um...Grandpa?"

"Yes?" Erasmus asked, leaving the shelter of his tree to join her.

"You're really familiar with the stuff in the Athenaeum, right? Especially the stuff on the lower levels?"

"I am. I'm also probably thinking the same thing you are. These aren't natural occurrences."

"You think Peter's doing this?" Olivia asked.

"I kind of do," Sophia admitted. "I'm just not sure why."

"If it is Peter, he knows where you used to live," Lucas pointed out. "The tornado could have very well been sent in case you'd gone home—which you did."

"And the Ekklesia has their headquarters in Italy," Erasmus added. The so-called ruling body of the Arcane didn't so much rule as they ensured the Arcane weren't exposed to humanity. In extreme circumstances, they acted as judge and jury for heinous crimes.

"Why would he go after them? You don't think he wants to let the humans know we exist, do you?" Sophia asked, horrified at the idea. The Arcane might have magic, but the humans had sheer numbers—and their weapons weren't exactly ineffective. A nuclear bomb could kill an Arcane as easily as it could a human.

"I don't know, but if this weather isn't natural, then we should get a move on," Vazi pointed out. "Where's the hot spring?"

Julian shook his head and put his phone away. "This way," he told them and started down a narrow path. It only took a couple of minutes before they stopped in front of a small spring. It was only about ten feet across, and eight long, but there was steam wisping up from the surface, proving it was definitely warm.

"We should get in, just to be sure," Olivia suggested.

Since none of them could get any wetter—aside from Vazi—they all got in the spring, though none of them got deeper than their knees. "I don't know how this works, but maybe we should hold hands, to make sure we all end up in the same place," Sophia told them. Once they had she looked at Olivia. "You probably know the sounds better than the rest of us. You want the honors?" They only had four possibilities for the order of the words, so it shouldn't take too long to get it right—assuming they hadn't missed anything in the Sphinx chamber.

"Sure." Olivia spoke the syllables in a clear, firm voice, then paused.

"Nothing," Vazi told her with a shake of his head. "Try again."

Since he would know if the words had caused magic to build, Olivia nodded and tried the second.

"That's doing something. Keep going," he encouraged.

She repeated the spell and this time Sophia felt magic beginning to tingle over her skin. After the third time, she felt like something was pulling at her navel, a second before that something yanked and she was pulled through space and into darkness.

Chapter 8

It didn't really surprise Lucas when they ended up surrounded by darkness. Fortunately, the headlamps prevented them from being totally blind. From what he could see, they were on a circular stone platform that stood just a foot above the surrounding floor. They were all—including Vazi—dripping water onto it, but no one paid much attention to that. The room they were in was large and circular as well, with a set of stairs curving up along one wall, leading up to the next floor. There was one doorway to his left, but that was the only other exit he saw. When he turned, he found a vertical ring behind them, a faint shimmer in the air within it hinting that it was a portal. It didn't hurt that it glowed with a pale silvery light. Hopefully that meant when they were ready to leave, they could just step through it, but he wasn't sure if it would deposit them back at the spring, or someplace else entirely. Didn't most portals only go to one place? Though he supposed it could be possible that they could have multiple destinations.

There were four statues placed equidistant from each other around the platform. He couldn't tell who they were, though all four were facing inward. Two were women, two men, and all four had wings. After looking for a moment longer, he could see there was a snake worked somewhere into each statue. One of the women had a serpent coiled loosely around her throat, while the other wore one like a belt. One of the men had a snake wound around each arm, while the other man held one in his extended hand.

"Anyone recognize those statues?" he asked. He heard answers in the negative, but he'd expected that. Whoever these statues were made to resemble, they'd probably died long ago.

"More importantly, can anyone do something about my clothes?" Olivia asked. "Wet clothes aren't exactly comfortable. The last thing any of us need is to get sick right before we head back to the Athenaeum."

"I can," Julian promised. A minute later, their clothes were perfectly dry. A little stiffer than they had been, maybe, but dry. Lucas wasn't about to bitch.

"This place is Lemurian," Vazi said, emotion thickening his words.

"We're on Lemuria?" Sophia asked, twin threads of surprise and delight in her voice.

He shook his head slowly as he looked around the darkened room. "No, we're not. We aren't even on Earth any longer. But this place is Lemurian. It was built with Lemurian magic. Most likely by Grovek. The god of wisdom. He wasn't a builder, but his sole purpose in life seemed to be learning anything and everything he could. That could have included magical construction techniques."

This was a first for Lucas, and he wasn't sure he liked it. They were in some other realm or dimension? Sure, the ring behind them looked like a portal, but despite his earlier thoughts, there was no guarantee it would work—and if it did, they really could emerge anywhere. He was happy for Vazi to find this connection to his people, he honestly was, but there was something about this place that scared the hell out of him. It didn't have the same feel the Athenaeum did. Both were ancient repositories of knowledge, but the Athenaeum felt like home while this felt more like a tomb. He couldn't explain why he felt that way. There was no dust, no cobwebs, no signs of dead bodies or coffins. Even the air tasted fresh and clean. But he couldn't shake the feeling. He wanted them to find what they were looking for and get the hell out of this place.

Sophia stepped off the platform before Lucas could urge her to be careful, and the moment her foot touched the floor, torches he hadn't noticed flickered to life, bathing the room in soft light. That was fine. It had happened in the Sphinx, too, but then a figure appeared just a few feet in front of Sophia, close enough to touch, which was not fine.

It was a woman, perhaps only five feet tall, with long, perfectly straight black hair, dusky skin, and kohl around her eyes. She wore a garment that reminded him of Egypt, but it wasn't exactly right. But the most notable thing was that she wasn't quite solid. He could see through her with very little effort and had to wonder if she was a ghost. Whatever she was, he didn't like how close she was to Sophia, and took two steps forward until he was beside Sophia. Before he could ask who she was, she spoke.

"I am Akila," she said, her voice holding a trace of an accent he couldn't place. His initial thought was Lemurian, but Vazi didn't sound like she did, so he wasn't sure. That wasn't the biggest question, though. If the sarcophagus in Giza had really held Akila's body, then was really this her ghost? Or was it something else entirely? And if it was Akila's ghost, how was it speaking English? It hadn't existed thousands of years ago. Then again, they didn't know when she'd died or when the chamber they'd found had even been created. She might have left that message long before she'd actually been killed.

There were too many unknowns for his taste, and Akila wasn't done speaking.

"The fact that you are here in Sozu demonstrates that you possess a measure of wisdom, which makes you welcome. However, I must warn you against misusing this holy library. This is a sanctuary for knowledge, not personal gain. If you seek to use what can be found here for power or to harm others, then leave now before you suffer the consequences. In addition, nothing here may be taken outside of Sozu. If you can abide by these rules, then you are welcome to explore. If you need help, call for me."

She disappeared before anyone could respond. No one spoke for a minute longer, then Olivia broke the silence as she switched off her headlamp. "That was kind of creepy and ominous."

"Definitely ominous. But uh...isn't she the one whose tomb we were just in?" Sophia asked as she turned her light off, too.

"That wasn't actually Akila," Julian said, a tone of wonder in his voice. "From what I can tell, it was some sort of...magical hologram."

"You're partially correct," Vazi said, stepping down from the platform and staring at the spot Akila's image had just occupied. "It wasn't her physical form, no, but it was a piece of her. I would wager that if we do call for her, she'll respond as she would have when she was alive."

"That is some astonishing magic," Erasmus said. "I don't think we need to worry about her warnings, though. I'll admit it would be tempting to take some texts back to the Athenaeum, but we certainly aren't here for personal gain. What we find here quite literally will determine the fate of the world. That is the least selfish reason we could have for coming here."

"Agreed," Vazi says, turning and looking at the four statues. They made him frown, but Lucas wasn't sure they had time to get into why they seemed to displease him.

"Right. Let's split up. We have a better chance of finding what we need more quickly if we break into groups," Sophia said after Lucas gave her a gentle nudge. She was still getting used to being in charge, and it couldn't be easy taking that control when a god was in the room.

"Makes sense," Olivia said with a nod. "I know Seth gave us two weeks, but if Peter's already breaking out forbidden magic, the sooner the better."

"Exactly," Sophia agreed. "Okay. Julian, Grandpa, and Olivia, you want to start upstairs? Lucas, Vazi, and I will see what's down here."

No one had a problem with that, so the other three started up the stairs that circled upward around the room while the rest of them headed for the single doorway. Though Lucas was sure Vazi could handle himself, he still ensured he was first through the doorway.

He stopped just outside, finding himself in a hallway. It curved back on both sides, proving that it at least partially surrounded the room they'd just left. It wasn't empty, though. Other than torches—which lit magically like the others—there were more statues and simple pedestals with a variety of objects on them. Directly across from him was a heavy wooden door, the only exit he could see from their current vantage point.

"Down the hall or check the door first?" Lucas asked.

"Door," Vazi said, stepping past Lucas and opening it. He needed only a second before he sighed. "Grovek is all over this room."

There was sorrow in his voice and Sophia felt for the guy. She glanced at Lucas, then stepped forward, glancing into the room. It reminded her a little of the hidden room in the Athenaeum she'd visited so many times, searching for answers. There was a round wooden table in the middle of the room with several clay tablets and what looked like papyrus sheets spread over its surface. There were also a few other stone shelves and shorter tables that had things she couldn't identify. But the only things with writing she could see were those on the center table. "Do you want to go through those, or do you want us to help?" she asked Vazi quietly.

"I'd like to do it."

She nodded and considered if she should try to help him. They didn't have a lot of time, but Vazi was a person—a divine one—who deserved ten minutes. Beyond that, he'd be more effective if he wasn't upset. Returning to Lucas as Vazi started to look over the tablets, she whispered, "Can you see what else is down the hallway? I want to talk to him, but I'm not sure he'll open up if there's someone else here." More specifically, another man, but she wasn't going to say that aloud. Men were so weird about opening up sometimes.

Lucas smiled, though it was a little tight, and gave her a light kiss. "Sure. I'm wondering if there are other doors, anyway. Yell if you need me."

He backed out and continued down the hall. When he was out of sight, she turned back to Vazi. "Are you doing okay?" He might not want to talk to someone he'd only just met, but she had never been the sort to ignore someone else's pain.

"I miss my people. Both the mortals and the other gods," he admitted without looking up from the tablet. "Seth is a Lemurian god, with all the powers of one of the originals, but he never saw Lemuria as it used to be. I don't have the history with him I had with so many of my pantheon. Nor do we think the same way, since he spent most of his life mortal and ignorant of Lemuria. Which means this is the closest I've been to any of the original Lemurian gods since our home was destroyed. Having his wife on Lemuria helps, too, because she was alive then, before it sank, and she was a friend, but I can't put everything on her, especially not with her pregnant." He glanced at her briefly. "Her child will be the first Lemurian born in more centuries than I care to count." He lifted his head and looked around the room, a tiny smile trying to form on his lips. "Grovek's magic is in every inch of this place. The structure, the furniture, these tablets. I don't know how, but he used himself to create it."

She was curious as to how long he'd been without those Lemurians, but it didn't feel right to ask. She knew it was more than five thousand years, which was far too long. "What was he like?"

"Grovek? He...was a lot like Julian, actually. Always needed to learn something new. Other people needed food and water to survive, but he lived on knowledge. The smartest man I've ever met, and he absorbed new information like a sponge, but that made sense, given that he was the god of wisdom."

"Did he just hole up in here?"

Vazi shook his head. "No. I didn't know this place existed, but he spent plenty of time on Earth. There was always something new to learn. And he loved teaching, too. He would never hoard what he knew, but wanted to share it with people. And not in a way that made you want to hit him with a lightning bolt, either. There was no pushiness in him, just a sincere desire to help others learn. He helped the other gods when they needed it, and he always had apprentices. Akila was, I believe, the last one."

"If he didn't hoard what he knew, then what was this place for?" Sophia wondered.

"I can only guess, but I would imagine a safe, distraction-free place to write down what he'd learned and to teach his apprentices," Vazi said with a shrug. "And that's assuming there's more here than this," he added, waving a hand at the tablets.

"Based on what I found, I'm hoping your assumption is right," Lucas said as he returned.

"What did you find?"

"The hallway goes in a circle all the way around that room we arrived in, and there are four doors. This one and three bedrooms," Lucas answered. "Unless this guy was secretly the god of partying as well as wisdom, I doubt he wasted the space upstairs with just having a bunch more bedrooms."

"Then, unless you found something here, should we join the others?" Sophia suggested.

Vazi glanced down to the tablets and shook his head. "Nothing pertinent to the Miasma, no. One is about a new plant he found, and the others are about a group of people he'd found in a desert region between two rivers. He thought they were developing toward becoming something like the Lemurians were. Unlike the other mortals, they were settling down and starting to farm."

Lucas frowned. "That sounds like the Sumerians, but you're right, that isn't relevant right now."

"Then upstairs we go. I'm sure we'll find something," Sophia said, though she hoped her voice sounded more optimistic than she felt.

They weren't exactly off to a good start, and so far, the Hall of Records wasn't shaping up to be all that impressive.

Chapter 9

THE SECOND FLOOR HAD another large circular room, and the stairs continued up to a third. Like the first floor, there was one doorway leading out of the room. Unlike the first floor, this room didn't have a platform and portal ring, but instead had several tables and chairs. There was no sign of the others, and no writings for them to check out, so they left through the doorway. Again, there was a hallway with statues and a door across from them. This time, the door was open, showing full shelves, as well as the rest of their group. The shelves had plenty of materials on them, but Sophia noticed there were no books and nothing that looked like paper. It was all tablets, papyrus sheets, and scrolls of some material she couldn't identify. It made sense, though. Books weren't really a thing in ancient times. Honestly, she was a little surprised to see the scrolls.

All three people inside were busy looking at different things as Sophia entered the room.

"Find anything promising?" she asked as she walked over to one of the tablets. It wasn't in a language she knew, but while disappointing, it wasn't a surprise. It looked like it was probably Lemurian, since it had those interesting swirls.

"No, though it isn't exactly easy to tell for sure, since I'm the only one who reads Lemurian, and these are almost all in Lemurian," Olivia answered, setting her papyrus back down.

"All?" Sophia asked, disheartened.

"Almost," Olivia corrected. "There are a couple in a language that none of us recognize."

"Let me see?" Vazi asked, striding toward her. Olivia picked up another sheet and offered it to him. His brows knit and he shook his head. "I can't read this either. Which shouldn't be possible. I can read every language, even if I haven't encountered it before."

"You did say Grovek was the god of wisdom, and that he built this place," Erasmus mused aloud. "Could it be that it's a language or code of his own creation, intentionally made to not be read by anyone else? Including other gods?"

Vazi set the sheet down and nodded. "That is entirely possible."

Julian walked over to them, looking as pessimistic as Sophia felt. "We glanced around the rest of this floor. There are four rooms, including this one. They all seem to be basically the same."

"So we need to figure out how the rooms are organized so we can figure out where information on the Miasma could be," Sophia said as she frowned at one of the shelves.

"What about Akila?" Lucas suggested.

"It can't hurt," Erasmus said, nodding. "If she was his apprentice, surely she would know how he organized his materials."

"Akila?" Sophia called out, feeling a little silly for doing so. "We need some help."

It took only a breath before the ghostly woman appeared. "How may I be of assistance?"

"Is there anything in here about Miasma?" she asked, getting right to the point.

"There are several texts about Miasma, yes. They're all on the fifth floor, in the north room."

"North?" Julian asked. "Which way is north?"

"This room is the east room on the second floor. Does that help?"

"It does, actually. Thank you," he said politely.

"You're welcome," Akila said before disappearing again.

"So go to the fifth floor and turn left?" Sophia said before she left the room to head that way.

"Sounds that way," Lucas agreed.

The only reason her legs weren't screaming by the time they reached the fifth floor was all the stairs she'd had to climb back in the Athenaeum. She still wasn't happy, but doubted she would be again until they had reclaimed the Athenaeum.

The fifth floor—at least the first room of it—looked basically the same as the three below it did. Tables and chairs spaced around the room, torches on the walls. Unlike the other rooms, the stairs stopped here, proving this was the highest level of the building. And it occurred to her that she hadn't seen any windows or doors that led out of this structure. It made her wonder what the hell was outside. Or if there was anything outside.

They crossed to the doorway then turned left to go to the next door, hoping they were right and it was the north room. It was odd to think of cardinal directions in a place that wasn't even Earth. Did the magnetic field work the same in every realm? It didn't really matter, but it did serve to distract her for a few seconds.

They found the room almost a mirror image of the one they'd been looking through on the second floor, right down to the types of writings. Sophia appreciated ancient things, she really did, but found herself wishing for an ordinary book. Or at least something she could read.

Vazi, Olivia, and Erasmus took the lead on diving into the materials, but rather than settling in to read and dismiss, Erasmus frowned after only a minute. "Vazi, I don't mean to probe at raw wounds, but when was it that Lemuria..."

"When was it destroyed?" Vazi asked in a chilly voice.

"I'm sorry, but yes," Erasmus answered, sounding like he genuinely hated having to ask, but it meant it was probably something important.

"According to Seth's calculations, it was in 4349 BC. Why?"

Erasmus nodded. "I expected it was somewhere around there. And I ask because no other language is supposed to go back that far. Sumerian—as far as we can tell—didn't come into use for a thousand years after that. Neither did the Egyptian hieroglyphics. Yet this tablet," he lifted his hand to indicate the tablet in it, "is in Sumerian. And that one?" He pointed to one on the shelf next to him. "That's Egyptian. Even if we accept that Akila lived for a thousand years after Lemuria sank, would she have taken the time to copy all these into a new language?"

The anger drained from Vazi's face as Erasmus's words penetrated, and he looked at some of the writings around him. "It doesn't sound likely, no. If she was intending to take them back to Earth, possibly, but then why didn't she do that? And if that was her plan, we would likely find the Lemurian originals here."

"Do you know what Akila was?" Julian asked. "Was it possible she had a vision of the future and knew these would be needed in languages other than Lemurian?"

Vazi frowned harder before he shook his head, but he didn't look certain. "I think she was a shifter. Maybe a siren? Either way, not a race given to prophecy. But then, I don't know what magics Grovek was toying with, or what he taught his students. It's as likely a guess as anything else."

"Not to sound dismissive," Olivia began, still going through tablets and pages. "But does it really matter? As long as what we're looking for is here, we're good. And having Sumerian and whatever just means that more people can search."

"She's not wrong," Sophia said, smiling at her friend's bluntness. It also pushed her into action. She had planned to just stay out of the way of those who could read and translate, but now she started to look for pieces she could read, relieved when she found one fairly quickly. She was even happier when it was in Greek. While she could muddle through hieroglyphics, this was one of the languages she'd really focused on and could read almost as easily as she could English.

Even with the six of them all searching, it took time before anyone discovered something relevant.

"Found something," Olivia called. She was sitting in a chair, her legs crossed, feet resting on the table in front of her. It was a relaxed pose, despite the tension on her face.

"About Miasma?" Lucas asked. He'd stuck close to Sophia, but hadn't slacked in sifting through the hundreds of items in the room. The two of them were currently sitting on the floor, backs to the wall, a pile of materials around them to check.

"Sort of. It talks about the creation of the universe and how five substances called Amzirana were crucial. I don't know if it's just what Grovek called them, or if that's the name the creators—he calls them the Anunnaki—gave them, but it's the Miasma and four other substances."

"The Anunnaki?" Sophia asked, confused. "The scroll I found in the Vault called the creators the Ethereals."

"They have many names," Erasmus told her. "The Anunnaki, Celestials, Ethereals, the Hidden Ones...It seems like each culture gave them a different name, but if Grovek called them the Anunnaki..." He trailed off and looked to Vazi.

Vazi sighed and nodded. "Yes, the Anunnaki are their true names. I know Seth told me they're now associated with the Sumerians, but they created the Sumerian pantheon, as well as my own."

"Is Amzirana the real name for the Miasma, Quintessence, and other substances, then?" Sophia asked.

"I don't know," he admitted. "It wasn't something I ever concerned myself with."

"And again, it doesn't really matter," Olivia cut in. "It does talk about how all five of these substances were hidden beneath the Earth, so the Miasma isn't the only thing that was literally buried."

She was right, so Sophia got back on topic. "Since you haven't said anything, I'm guessing it doesn't have any hints for how to cure the Athenaeum of it?"

Olivia shook her head. "No, but it does prove there's information about it here."

She was right about that, too, so Sophia got back to work, feeling a spark of hope.

It took more time—she wasn't sure how much—before anyone else spoke. Erasmus glanced up from the papyrus he was reading. "You were right, Vazi. Grovek did create this place. He named it Sozu—wisdom in Lemurian, for those who don't speak it—because he wanted it to be a sort of treasury for just that. Someplace he could store things that didn't necessarily need to be learned by everyone."

"Like the Miasma," Vazi said, nodding. "Smart. He was absolutely a man who would want to document anything important, even if he intended it to be only for himself."

It sounded to Sophia like this place was Grovek's personal Athenaeum. It made the place seem a little more welcoming, but still didn't solve their problems.

"Hey guys, I think I found it. Well, possibly," Lucas said, pushing to his feet. "It talks about those Amzirana. What they are, mostly. Quintessence, Miasma, Chaos, Oskila, and the Wellspring. Seems like he found where three of them were hidden."

He glanced away from the tablet he was holding to look down at Sophia. "He was in the Miasma chamber, before the Athenaeum was created above it."

"Does he say how you can fight it?" Sophia asked.

"Actually," he said, lips curving into a smile, "he does have a theory."

"Don't keep it to yourself, man. Out with it," Julian said, exasperation in his voice.

"He says he thought that Oskila and Miasma were in direct opposition to one another and could be used to counter one another. He does warn that the two should never come in direct physical contact, but apparently proximity is enough to affect people in most cases."

"Great. So all we need to do is find a place that was hidden by the freaking creators of the universe," Olivia said dryly.

"No need. He found it already. He gives descriptions of the route he took, and there's a map. There's no way it's going to be a hundred percent accurate, not after several thousands of years, but it could get us in the general vicinity."

"That's all well and good, but what is Oskila?" Julian asked.

Erasmus looked at Sophia and simultaneously arched a brow and smiled at her. It was nice, having him trust that she knew the answer, but it still wasn't enough to make up for having watching him die. "You know how Miasma is the violence of change and emotion? Oskila is basically the opposite. It's peace in physical form."

"An extremely soft, light purple mineral, apparently," Lucas said, his eyes back on the tablet.

"It makes sense, then. Peace countering violence—or even other strong emotions," Julian said, nodding. "Let's see this map, see if we can sort out where we need to go."

Lucas moved to the table in the middle of the room and laid not one, but two tablets on the surface. One had cuneiform on it, while the other had a map. It wasn't as neat or detailed as she was used to seeing on maps, but it was also the first one she'd ever seen on a clay tablet. She couldn't quite call it crude, but it was fairly basic. However, there was a very clear circle with an X through it to indicate where the Oskila was.

It seemed X sometimes really did mark the spot.

"These are mountains," Vazi said, tracing his finger along a chain of inverted V's. They were almost in a straight line, with just a slight rise on the right. "This means water. Something large, like an ocean or sea," he continued, indicating an area that had shallow diagonal lines covering it. That took up the top of the map. "This is probably a river," he said a minute later. It wiggled across the map from right to left. There probably weren't too many places on Earth that looked like that, but it wasn't anyplace Sophia recognized. Then she realized something.

"If that is an ocean, we need to account for a changed coastline. A lot of this," Sophia said, waving her finger around the area where land met water, "could be underwater now."

"Underwater?" Erasmus frowned and leaned in closer until the table was only a foot from his nose. "I think I know where this might be. Not the chamber specifically, but the map in general."

"Where?" Lucas asked.

"Alaska. If I'm right, this is the Bering Land Bridge, this is the Brooks range, and this is the Yukon River."

"I think you're right," Olivia said after studying it for a minute longer. "It's a little different, but geography can change in a few decades, much less a few thousand years. If you cut the land off here," she said as she rested the side of her hand on the tablet, "it works. Problem is, Alaska is a big damn place. Even with the chamber being marked, it's still a couple hundred square miles to search. At least."

"You said he described his route?" Julian asked Lucas.

"Mmhmm," Lucas agreed, referring back to the tablet. "He followed a small river into the tall, ice-covered mountains, then found a tributary and followed that. It led to a frozen waterfall, he felt the Oskila beyond it, and found a passage behind it. The deeper he got into the cave, the more he started feeling the effects of the Oskila. Sounds like it's pretty deep, which makes sense. If the Miasma is beneath the

Athenaeum, it has to be pretty damn deep, too. Can't really be hidden if it's on the surface and easy to find. Or affecting everyone who walks by."

"That still doesn't really narrow it down though, does it?" Sophia asked.

They spent the next half hour throwing out ideas for how they might pinpoint the entrance to this cave with so little to go on. Eventually, they decided to check out some of the smaller and harder to reach tributaries in the mountain range, each of them paying close attention to their senses. If that didn't work, they'd call in Seth. Since he was the god of mountains, he should be able to sense any caves and help them find the right one.

Then they had to figure out how they could avoid the effects of the Oskila. If even Grovek had been affected, then most of their group would likely be even more susceptible. Lucas jokingly suggested they all drink large amounts of caffeine, but Vazi had said it couldn't hurt. It wasn't something they'd known about when Lemuria had been destroyed, and he'd seen firsthand how it could ramp a person up.

Coffee could save the world. Who knew?

Joking aside, Olivia had asked for Akila's help, who said Grovek had never found a surefire method, but had theorized that layers of protection would be the most effective. She added that he had noted the Oskila affected him more when he had stopped moving. With that information, they'd decided to go with caffeine, constant movement, and a spell to shield from outside influences. None of them were particularly confident, which is why they'd also agreed that everyone would stick with someone who could teleport. At the first sign that someone was succumbing, they'd be teleported out of range. It wasn't perfect, but it was the best they could come up with.

That done, Julian looked at his watch and sighed. "Before we go hiking through the mountains, we should probably rest. We left for the Sphinx after midnight, and it's now almost eight in the evening. None of us—barring possibly Vazi—could handle hiking in Alaska without rest. It might be summer, but that doesn't mean it will be easy."

"Yeah, Alaska isn't exactly known for being super accessible," Sophia agreed. Now that he'd said something, she realized she wasn't just tired, she was starving.

"I found three bedrooms down on the first floor," Lucas informed the others. "Might have to double up, but it's doable."

"I don't need much rest," Vazi said, shaking his head. "I think my time would be better served seeing what Seth and the other gods have learned, especially with the extreme weather. Hecate or Isis might have some ideas for defending from the Oskila, too. But you should be able to go back through the portal when you wake up and return to the hot spring we left from, then teleport where you wish from there."

"I do need rest," Julian said with a faint smile, "but rather than double up with one of you—as lovely as you all are—I think I'd rather one last night with my wife before I brave the American wilderness."

"Understandable," Sophia said, nodding. "Meet us back in Egypt at my grandpa's house in eight or so hours?" It might be prudent to try to skimp on sleep time and get going, but she wasn't sure they could get to the cave if they didn't get a full night's rest.

"I can do that. I'll see what other equipment I have, as well. This might not be as simple as walking through the woods. In fact, I'd be shocked if it was."

"Seth used to do things like this all the time. I'll ask him for equipment. But keep in mind that you won't need the same equipment the mortals do," Vazi said, smirking. "I don't normally like doing...parlor tricks, as Seth calls them...but for something like this, I'll help the five of you cheat."

"And we really appreciate it," Sophia said sincerely. They would need all the help they could get.

Chapter 10

As it turned out, even Vazi wasn't able to teleport out of Sozu, so both he and Julian joined them as they made their way back down the stairs to the first level. Vazi and Julian walked through the portal back to Earth while the rest of them each claimed one of the bedrooms.

Lucas closed the door to the room Sophia had chosen—the south room, according to Akila—and watched her take in the ancient bedroom. In all honesty, it didn't look that out of the ordinary. Yes, the walls, floor, and ceiling were stone, but she was used to that by now. Even the torches weren't that out of the ordinary for them. The bed was heavier and of an older style than either of them were accustomed to, but the bedding smelled fresh and looked clean. There wasn't, of course, a modern bathroom, but there were facilities, and a large, smooth stone tub. He wasn't sure where the water for it would come from, but didn't dwell on it too long. They were in a tower-like structure built in another dimension with no doors or windows offering access to the outside—accepting the improbable was kind of a requirement.

Sophia dropped onto the bed and pulled off her backpack. They'd been sipping from their water bottles off and on while researching, but none of them had really thought about food. Which meant she now grabbed out one of the protein bars, downing it in fewer bites than he would have thought possible. Since he was hungry, too, he sat beside her and did the same thing while studying her face.

As soon as the door had closed behind them, shielding her from everyone else, she'd dropped all attempts at hiding her expression. He'd seen her grow more and more stressed as the weeks had passed after she'd been named aspida, but it paled compared to the tension on her face now. Added to that, her shoulders were high and hunched, which meant they'd probably feel like stone. She'd forgotten that was his job, not hers.

"Talk to me," he said after she'd devoured her second protein bar and washed it down with several gulps of water.

"I thought that if we could actually find the Hall of Records—a place I didn't think actually existed—that all our problems would be solved," she said quietly. "Wasn't this place supposed to be like the Athenaeum on steroids? Full of ancient secrets and forbidden knowledge?" she asked, her voice firming, but it also allowed him to hear her frustration.

"What makes you think it isn't just that? We looked in exactly two rooms and were basically ignoring anything that didn't involve Miasma," he pointed out, setting his bag aside and rising. As he spoke, he walked over to the tub and started trying to figure out how to get it to work. There was a stone spout that came out of the wall, but he didn't see a nozzle or any way to get water to flow out of it. "And we did find what we were looking for. From the sounds of it, even the Athenaeum didn't have that much information on it. And no, we didn't find anything as simple as casting a spell and curing everyone, but we have a lead. We have the writings of someone who researched these substances extensively, and who actually found a possible cure. We even have a plan. We gear up, go to Alaska, get some of this Oskila stuff, and use it to break everyone there free of Peter's control. Then we kick Peter's ass and get your Athenaeum back." He knew it wasn't going to be that simple, but he refused to let her hear any of his doubts.

He paused and frowned at the tub, his eyes narrowed in consideration. "Water, hot," he said, doubting it would work, but a second later, water began pouring out of the spout and filling the tub, little tendrils of steam rolling off it. Glancing over his shoulder, he told Sophia, "Strip. You're getting a bath."

"I don't need a bath. I need to find a better way of finding that Oskila," she protested stubbornly.

"No," he said as he tested the temperature of the water. It was just shy of too hot. Perfect. "What you need is to relax, get a good night's sleep, then kick some ass."

She looked like she was going to continue to argue, then huffed and started pulling her clothes off more roughly than normal. He understood what she was going through. Honestly, he wasn't much better. Head of security might not be aspida, but a lot of this fell on him just as much as it did her. Not only that, but he'd known all those people for years. He'd trusted them—even Peter. He hadn't seen what was going on right beneath his nose, and he really should have. And he might not be dumb, but he knew he couldn't keep up with minds like Erasmus's or Julian's. Since there wasn't anything to physically fight right now, it meant he wasn't exactly feeling useful. Yeah, he'd found Grovek's account of the Oskila chamber, but that was just luck. Almost everyone else in the room could have read it, too.

Lucas always enjoyed seeing Sophia nude, but right now he just wanted to take care of her, and held her hand as she stepped into the deep tub and eased herself down in the water. She let out a soft hiss, but it quickly turned into a low moan of pleasure.

"Okay, this wasn't a horrible idea," she admitted as she got settled and tilted her head back. She was quiet for several long minutes, and he said nothing, hoping her mind was relaxing as much as her body was. When she spoke, he knew it wasn't.

"And you've got a point, but it's Alaska, Lucas. You know how fucking big that place is. And our big clue is a river in the mountains? I don't know how many rivers are in those mountains, but I have no doubt it's a lot."

"It is a lot," he admitted, moving to the bed. He set their bags aside and pulled back the quilt, nodding when he saw the sheets were as clean as he'd hoped. "But you can't be pessimistic. Does the situation suck? Abso-fucking-lutely. Is it going to be easy? Hell no. But look at who we've got on our side. We've got a god who may be the most ancient person on the planet, a man who has spent nine hundred years learning everything he can—including sorcery—a woman who has the memories of at least a few dozen people, and a man who, from what I hear, spends pretty much all his time learning. Not to mention the two of us. And if we need to, we can call in Seth, who is working with five powerful and intelligent gods. If I were a betting man, I'd put money on us over your little weasel of a cousin."

"Except my cousin is backed by a substance as old as the universe," Sophia pointed out, but he noted her voice wasn't quite as tense. It still wasn't happy, but baby steps were still steps.

"So what?" Lucas asked bluntly. "We're going to be backed by one, too. And you've got something he doesn't."

"What's that?"

"You've got a connection to the Athenaeum he doesn't and never will."

"Except I'm not in the Athenaeum."

He shrugged and walked back to the tub, gesturing for her to stand up and take his hands. She did with a sigh and he grabbed one of the towels he'd spotted—which was not terrycloth like he was used to, but just a rectangle of some kind of thick cloth. He used it to dry her off, then led her to the bed. His reassurances and the warm water weren't doing much to help, so he decided to go another route.

"On your stomach," he instructed. She gave him an odd look, but complied, making a small happy sound as she settled on the bed. He would have thought a bed this old would suck compared to modern beds, but either he was wrong, or she was too exhausted to care if she slept on a rock.

Now, Lucas's focus was on trying to put her mind at ease, even if only for a little while, but he wasn't dead. The sight of her lying on the bed, completely nude, gave him ideas. Depending on how she reacted to what he had in store, he might even be able to act on some of those ideas.

Stripping off his shirt and shoes, he climbed on the bed and straddled her hips. And while he didn't intentionally press against her, he also didn't care if she happened to realize he was semi-hard. It wouldn't be the first time. But for now, all he did was lay his hands on her shoulders and press his thumbs into the knots he found all too easily. He was immediately rewarded by a low groan. Not surprising.

He wouldn't be this tense even if he was in his gargoyle form. Resolved to keep massaging until her body was loose and she'd forgotten to stress, his hands slowly moved over her back and shoulders. Not that he could ignore that the way she was moving sinuously beneath him and moaning in pleasure had him hardening fully in his pants. But he wasn't a teenager. He could restrain himself...at least for a little while longer.

He eased himself a little lower, so he could get the last of the knots out of her back, the ones just above her perfectly shaped ass.

"Lucas?" she murmured, turning her head a little farther so she could see him out of the corner of her eye.

"Yes, love?" he asked, dragging his gaze from her butt to her face.

"Don't get me wrong, I needed the massage, and I love that you're taking care of me, but I need a different kind of attention."

He smiled and let his thumbs sweep downward, brushing over the top of her butt. "Oh yeah? What kind of attention?"

She groaned and arched into the gentle caress. "You know perfectly well what kind of attention."

Lucas bent and pressed a kiss against her spine. She sighed and relaxed beneath him, so he began to slide down, letting his lips trail over her skin in soft caresses and teasing kisses. By the time he reached the small of her back, she was making small, encouraging noises, and his pants were entirely too tight. He reached down and unbuttoned them, eyes closing for a second in relief.

"I do know," he murmured before lightly nipping at her right cheek. "And I'll give you that attention, but you're going to have to just lay there and take it."

"Happily."

He chuckled and gave the other cheek a quick bite as well. "Oh no. I mean, you'll have to take it until I decide I'm done with you." Today he wouldn't be content with just letting her come once then joining her. Not even close. He was going to love her until she'd forgotten about Peter and the Miasma. Until she was so well pleasured and exhausted that she'd slip right into sleep.

Rather than taking his words as a warning, she shivered and moaned softly. "Happily," she repeated, looking over her shoulder at him. "I'll take everything you have to give me."

The words were simple, but they turned him on more than he would have expected. And though she likely meant it sexually, it felt more profound than that. It didn't matter that they'd known each other for such a short time. He loved her, and if he had his way, he was going to spend the next few centuries loving her and watching her grow as aspida. Which meant he was going to find the way to kick Peter's ass. Tomorrow. Right now, he was going to turn her to mush, even if it killed him in the process.

Shifting off her, he rolled her onto her back, then nudged her legs open so he could kneel between them. She was so beautiful, especially like this. Her cheeks were flushed, her eyes half-lidded. As his gaze roamed down, he saw she was breathing more rapidly and her nipples were already tight with arousal. He trailed a finger between her breasts, keeping his eyes on her face. She kept alternating between watching the progress of his finger and looking into his eyes, and he just smiled. Moving further down, he skimmed across her navel, and when he neared her core, her breathing sped up a little more. Though teasing her was always enjoyable, he thought she'd already suffered enough. His suffering was just beginning.

Sinking a finger slowly into her already wet sex, he pressed against her clit with his thumb, the combination making her gasp softly and press against his hand. He rocked it back and forth for a minute, just long enough to get her moving and starting to grip the pillow. Without stopping, he braced his other hand beside her head and leaned down to kiss her. Immediately, she let go of the pillow and wrapped her arms around him, pulling him flush against her. His only complaint was that he was still wearing his pants and boots, but the feel of her warm, smooth skin against his chest had him groaning and kissing her harder. It was so damn difficult to remember his plan, much less to follow through with it, but he wanted to see a satisfied smile on her face rather than the line between her brows.

Sophia's arms loosened, and she slid her hands down his chest. When he felt her fingers brush over his crotch, he hissed in a breath and pressed his thumb more firmly against her clit. She moaned into the kiss, but didn't allow herself to be distracted, though her fingers trembled lightly as she undid his pants. One of those hands started to ease into his pants, but he jerked his hips back, knowing that if she touched him, he'd be inside her and his plans would disappear in a rush of lust. She made a sound of complaint and reached for him again. He grabbed her wrist and lifted it above her head, pinning it to the bed. That made her shiver and he lifted his head, taking in the eager, nearly frantic look in her eyes.

"If you want me to fuck you, then come. I'm not giving in until you do," he warned, hoping he could follow through on his threat.

"Lucas," she protested, but he just added another finger to the first, causing whatever else she was going to say to be lost in a gasp.

He quickened the movement of his fingers and shifted to capture her nipple between his lips. Her free hand cupped the back of his head as teased the stiff peak, alternating between sucking and stroking the tip of his tongue against it. As she rocked and writhed beneath him, he prayed that she'd find her release soon, because this was killing him. He never would have thought he'd be so damn turned on in the middle of a major catastrophe, but he hadn't been this desperate to be inside someone since he'd first started having sex.

Then he felt the most glorious sensation in the world, coupled with the most wonderful sound; she started to tighten around his fingers then moaned as the first wave of pleasure peaked. It had barely registered in his mind before she was saying, in a sultry, passion-filled voice, "Give in."

He couldn't have resisted her, even if it meant saving the world. Releasing her wrist and withdrawing his hand, he shoved his pants down, then in the next motion was thrusting into her. They groaned in unison, even though Lucas had to hold still for a minute, as she was fluttering around him as the orgasm ebbed. If he'd moved, even a little, it would have all been over.

"Lucas." The word was still breathless, but it wasn't a plea. It was a demand, and one he was more than happy to obey.

Drawing back, his eyes locked on hers, he waited until she was about to make another demand, withdrew, then slammed into her, pulling a beautiful cry from her kiss-swollen lips. He slid an arm beneath her, making her back arch so her breasts pressed against his chest. He ground against her, not willing to let the pleasure or passion fade, and nipped at her jaw before nuzzling her neck. "Hold on," he told her. Once her arms were around him, he started to move again, pulling her against him at the same time his hips pressed forward, so he pounded hard into her.

Sophia's hands clenched and he groaned as her nails pressed against his back. He loved it. Knowing she was lost to the sensations made the earlier denial of his own pleasure worth it. So now he pushed through his body's demands and kept moving with her, into her, drawing more noises from her throat, while he kept his face buried against her shoulder. But when she started to clench around him again, and those noises became more desperate and frequent, he could only clench his jaw and hope he could hold out a little longer.

Then she moaned his name and wrapped her legs around him, letting him sink just a little deeper. Groaning with something entirely too close to desperation, he thrust twice more, then, buried inside her, he lost it, emptying himself into her.

Though his goal had been to exhaust and relax her, he found himself unable to do anything more than crush her for several minutes. When he could move, it was just to roll over and land beside her, staring up at the stone ceiling. Her hand brushed his and he glanced down to see her lacing her fingers with his. Glancing up at her face, he managed a smile when he saw her eyes were closed. It was the last thing she'd been able to do before falling asleep.

Leaning over, he kissed her cheek, then dragged the blanket over them and let himself follow her, hoping they could both keep this memory in mind over the coming weeks.

Chapter 11

Sophia woke with a smile and a languid stretch. The night before had been unexpected, but also exactly what she'd needed. Lucas somehow always knew, and had since before they'd gotten involved with one another. When she'd freaked out over being named aspida, he hadn't gone with the soothing words and gentle manner like her mother had, but had given her a brusk talking to that had snapped her out of it. And last night, when she'd been sinking deeper into despondency, he'd taken her mind off it and reminded her why they needed to stop Peter. It was a knack she definitely appreciated.

"Sleep well?"

She opened her eyes and saw him in the tub, briskly washing away the last two days. "Better than I have in a while," she admitted. "And given that we've been sleeping together for a while, that's saying something."

He chuckled before rinsing suds off his skin and climbing out of the tub. Though her body was well satisfied, she still took a minute to enjoy looking over his hard, muscular body, from the short, dark brown hair, past his rugged features and green eyes, over his perfectly sculpted torso, to his powerful legs. She hadn't been looking for a guy when she first arrived in Greece, but she'd sure as hell lucked out in finding one.

"I love you," she said, unable to hold the words back. She knew he wasn't perfect. He was overprotective, hovered at times, and wasn't always the most sensitive of people, but he was perfect for her, which was all she needed. Hell, it was all she wanted.

He paused in drying himself and walked over to the bed, bending to give her a lingering kiss. "I love you, too," he murmured before straightening. "But as much as I'd like to let you lounge about in bed—especially with me—you should probably get up."

"I could use a bath myself," she admitted. And since there was no coffee pot here, it was needed to help wake her up.

"You could," he agreed, only to grin when she gave him an offended look.

"Are you saying I stink?" she asked, gaping at him.

He held up a hand, two fingers held a quarter inch apart. "Maybe a little," he said teasingly.

Gasping in feigned shock, she tossed a pillow at him, but he only chuckled, picked it up, and threw it back on the bed. Still, she did refill the tub and wash, though she was quick about it. She didn't want the others to have to wait on her. When they were dressed, they left the bedroom and headed back to the central room. Erasmus and Olivia were already there, sitting on the edge of the platform, talking.

"I want to go take a few pictures of that tablet before we go, just in case we need it," Lucas told them, heading for the stairs.

"Already done," Erasmus said as he stood. "We thought much the same thing."

"I suggested he take pictures of all the tablets, not just the Oskila one," Olivia added.

"Smart," Sophia said, smiling. "I get why nothing can be taken, but I'll admit it is tempting."

"It is," her grandfather said, "but we know how to get back here later. We can always make copies for the Athenaeum."

"Just for the Vault?" Lucas asked.

"Probably. Most people have no need to know about Miasma or the other..." He glanced at Olivia. "What did the tablet call them again?"

"Amzirana," she answered.

Erasmus nodded. "Yes. As Peter has proven, some things should not be out in the world."

"On the other hand, if it was a little easier to find information about it, we might have recognized him using Miasma sooner," Sophia argued. "Things might not have gotten to this point if we'd known what we were facing."

"True," Erasmus agreed. "Perhaps we should have summaries for instances like this, and put them in the most accessible place for future aspides?"

"That's not a bad idea. Not just the Amzirana, but other potentially world ending things."

"You two can figure that out after we stop this world ending thing," Lucas prompted, resting a hand on Sophia's back and encouraging her toward the platform.

"True," Sophia said, smiling up at him.

Not knowing how long had truly passed on Earth, they put on their headlamps and switched them on before stepping through the portal. They returned to the spring—in the spring, actually—and it was raining just as hard as it had been when they left. The sun was setting but still visible, so at least it wasn't total darkness like it had been the last time. That didn't make it any less miserable.

She really wished they could have teleported to the Hall from the Sphinx. At least there they'd be dry. Sighing and making no effort to hide from the downpour, she looked at Olivia. "Can you get us back to Grandpa's house from here?"

"Probably not," Olivia admitted. "I'm not exactly sure what country we're in, but it's definitely not anywhere close to Egypt. If it was full night, it might be possible, but I wouldn't wager on it."

"You got us from Greece to Georgia," Lucas told Sophia. "Could you get us to his house now? It's one more person, but you're not being swarmed by a Miasma infected mob this time."

Erasmus's brows lifted and shock tinged his voice. "You did what? How?"

Sophia shrugged and refused to feel bad for what she'd done. "A spell I shouldn't have used, but it was that or be killed, so we didn't have a choice."

"From the grimoire?" She nodded and he sighed. "I'm sorry you had to learn any spell from that book, but under the circumstances, I'm glad you did. And while Lucas is technically correct that your life isn't in any eminent danger, I do think these circumstances warrant using that spell again."

Sophia was afraid that was going to be his answer, so nodded. "All right. Everyone get close and grab an arm or shoulder or something." When they had, she blew out a breath and closed her eyes, bringing the spell back to mind, then picturing Erasmus's living room. When she had it clear, she said the spell and felt them pulled through space.

To her relief, they reappeared right where she'd wanted to go. Even better? The world didn't go dark this time. Maybe because she'd had time to prepare? Or had actually pictured a destination in her mind? Probably the latter, but it didn't matter much at the moment.

Erasmus pulled out his phone, now that they had a signal again. "It's a little after four. Julian and Vazi will probably be joining us soon. We should eat while we can."

No one argued, so they immediately descended on the kitchen to get breakfast. The protein bars had assuaged the worst of her hunger the night before, but she'd burned off a lot of those calories, and hiking through Alaska was going to be tough on her. Erasmus, too, she imagined. As guards, Olivia and Lucas were both in good shape, and even Julian looked like he didn't just hole up in a study, which meant she was a little worried she'd hold them back.

"Anything here we can add to our packs?" Lucas asked after they'd finished eating—and had coffee, thank the gods.

There was a soft sound, like the displacement of air, and she turned to see Julian and Vazi in the living room. They had ditched the little backpacks they'd used before, replacing them with bigger hiking packs.

"Good, you're already here," Vazi said, nodding. "How long do you need?"

"Depends on what's in those packs," Lucas answered, nodding to them.

"Everything we should need for a week trekking through Alaska," Julian answered. "Sleeping bags, two-person tents, food, canteens, rope. I even have a GPS unit and another notebook. And, of course, coffee and caffeine pills."

"I can refill the canteens so you don't have to worry about fresh water," Vazi answered. "And I'll outfit the five of you in appropriate clothing when we arrive. Julian tells me this place we're going to tends to be cold, even this time of year."

"Yeah, but it shouldn't drop below zero, which it does a lot during the winter," Sophia agreed. "Did Seth and the other gods have any news?"

Vazi scowled at the question and shook his head. "They haven't made any progress getting into the Athenaeum. These wards are strong, and they aren't even sure how he's managing it."

"What about other weather anomalies?" Erasmus asked.

This time, Vazi nodded. "Quite a few. Flooding, earthquakes, tornadoes…Even some formerly dormant volcanoes are showing activity, and they're near populated areas. If this man is going for chaos, he's succeeding. The humans are panicking and the Arcane aren't much better. There are even multiple pantheons looking into it. So far, they haven't been able to pinpoint the source. I don't know if it's a result of whatever is being used to cause these disasters, or the wards on the Athenaeum."

"Do you have any good news?" Olivia asked dryly.

"Actually," he said in a similar tone, "I do. I told the Athenaeum patrons the plan. Isis and Hecate were able to give me a spell that should help with the Oskila trying to put us all on our asses. They can't guarantee how much it will block the effects, but it's better than nothing. And they gave me a jar that should do much the same, so we can safely collect some of the Oskila to take to the Athenaeum."

"And I have news as well," Julian admitted, but he sounded a little uncertain.

"Is it bad news?" Sophia asked, not sure she wanted to hear it.

"No...But I may have overstepped."

"Just tell them," Vazi prompted, rolling his eyes.

"You've said the people in the Athenaeum are innocent other than Peter, correct?"

Sophia cocked her head. "They are..."

"Then I assume when we try to take it back from him, you will want to avoid killing if at all possible. That might be easier with more people—especially well-trained people."

"So you invited friends to play?" Olivia asked, arching a brow.

Julian nodded. "I didn't give them too many specifics, but if we need them, they'll come. Seth knows most of them. Erasmus even knows some of them."

"Who are you thinking of?" Erasmus asked.

"Suni and Evane, Wade and Samara, Aaron, and Kara."

Erasmus looked pleased as he nodded, but Sophia was confused. She knew Suni was a healer who had worked with the Athenaeum before, and the one who had given them the formula for a potent antidote, but the others were strangers. "These are good people, then?" she asked.

Erasmus answered. "Wade is a bounty hunter for the Arcane, and his wife, Samara, is an assassin. Her brother, Evane, is just as skilled, and he is married to Suni, who is one of the best healers in the world."

"Aaron used to be Seth's competition and is a tiger," Vazi added. "Kara is a stone witch. Both are skilled."

While it relieved her to know these people were known by Erasmus and Seth, Sophia wasn't sure how she felt about inviting strangers into the Athenaeum. On the other hand, if it was a choice between exposing it to a few people or Peter destroying the world as they knew it, was it really a question? Lucas bent his head to whisper to her. "I've met Evane and Suni, too. Having an uninfected healer would be a major asset, since we don't want anyone to die."

That was also a good point. She could technically heal, but not to the level that would be needed in a fight. Or a battle, which was probably going to be more accurate. "If you can vouch for them and they're willing to not only help but also keep the Athenaeum a secret, I'm more than happy to have them."

"I can and they all know the meaning of discretion," Julian assured her.

"Two of them live on Lemuria, so I can second that," Vazi said with a nod.

"Fantastic. But we can't go back to the Athenaeum until we find the Oskila, so...everyone ready?" Sophia asked, looking from face to face. Everyone nodded and she looked at Vazi. "Are you our transport?"

"I am. Everyone grab a pack, then we'll go." After everyone had slid the packs over their shoulders, he took them out of Erasmus's comfortable Egyptian house, and right into a cold kind of hell. As soon as they appeared in Alaska, they were assaulted from above. Sophia ducked her head and covered it with her arms as she was hit with what felt like hundreds of jagged rocks.

"Did anyone think to check the weather?" Lucas asked as he covered her with his body. Since he'd transformed into his stone skin, he likely wasn't bothered. And the reprieve allowed Sophia to look around. They were in a forest, and judging by the near freezing temperature, it was definitely in Alaska. Just to their left was a small river, still flowing freely. It might all have been pretty, except everything was wet and it was currently hailing. There were chunks of ice scattered around that ranged from the size of a pea to the size of a golf ball. No wonder it felt like she had dozens of bruises on her back and shoulders.

Olivia and Erasmus had taken shelter against a tree, while Julian had a hand held up above him, palm toward the sky, apparently holding a magical shield, because the hail was bouncing off thin air and avoiding him. Vazi, however, had his hands on his hips and was scowling at the sky, his eyes narrowed. The hail began to come less frequently, then after a minute, it finally stopped. "I do not like this," he said darkly. "Whatever is being used to cause this weather is not something that should be in the hands of anyone."

"Which is why it was hidden away in the Athenaeum," Erasmus pointed out, carefully stepping away from the tree.

"Then, if you want to keep it, you should ensure this will never happen again," Vazi warned.

Sophia was offended for the Athenaeum and its people, especially since she'd read the gods had guided the first aspida to the cave that had become the Athenaeum. Likely as an added layer of protection for the Miasma chamber, but it still put the location for it firmly in their hands. Which meant they bore some of the responsibility for their current predicament.

That was why her voice was a little short when she spoke, despite speaking to a god. "Can we just get proper clothes and get started? The sooner we get back to the Athenaeum and stop Peter, the sooner the weird weather will stop."

Vazi arched a brow and stared at her, but she wasn't going to back down or look away. He wasn't going to smite her down or anything, at least not now, and she was tired of always being the one to give way.

She was smart and capable, and she was aspida. She might not be Vazi's boss, but she was a boss. It was time she acted like it. This, not looking away first from a god, was the first step.

After an extremely long minute, he smiled slightly. "Very well." He waved a hand, and her sodden jeans and tee-shirt turned into a fleece-lined pair of cargo pants, long-sleeved shirt, and fur-lined, hooded coat. He'd even changed her tennis shoes to hiking boots, and given her gloves. A quick look around proved that everyone was dressed in nearly identical clothes. The fits and sizes were different, of course, but otherwise they looked the same. The important thing was she was no longer cold.

Julian pulled a small electronic device out of his pack. It was about the size of a phone, but thicker. The GPS, maybe? He pushed a few buttons then slid it into his coat pocket. "Does anyone feel anything out of the ordinary?" he asked.

Everyone, Vazi included, went still, several of them closing their eyes. Eventually, they all responded in the negative.

"I would recommend we head along the river for a while, paying close attention to any signs of magic or the Oskila," Erasmus said.

Sophia nodded. "It's a good idea. Say, for an hour? Then we hit a different river? I'm not super familiar with Alaska's geography, but there are a bunch of rivers and tributaries, I think."

Julian said. "I pulled up a map last night. There aren't that many actual rivers, but certainly plenty of tributaries and streams."

"Then I think that's our plan. Though for people not familiar with Alaska, keep an eye open. There might not be that many people outside of the cities, but there are a lot of animals, and not all of them are going to be afraid of people."

"Some of them will flat out attack," Lucas confirmed. "Bears, moose, wolves...It shouldn't be a problem, but if we're surprised, someone could get hurt."

With everyone aware of the dangers, they started moving upstream. This was a wild part of the state, which meant the only paths—when they found them—were game trails. Sophia wasn't used to traversing the outdoors, and Erasmus wasn't always too steady on his feet either, so there was a bit of slipping and extremely careful stepping. Though Sophia felt a little stupid, none of the others did anything but help and support her whenever her foot landed wrong or she stepped on a slick rock.

After a little while, they did find a more level part of the forest and things got easier for a bit. It didn't take long before Sophia noticed the others pulling ahead of her, all except for Olivia. Even Lucas quickened his pace after giving her a quick kiss on the cheek. When Olivia started walking alongside her, Sophia asked, "So, should I be worried that you got everyone away so you could apparently talk to me alone?"

Olivia grinned and shook her head as she stepped over a small fallen branch. "No. I just figured you might want to talk, especially to someone who wasn't full of testosterone. You've been through a hell of a lot the last few days. Everything at the Athenaeum, having to retreat, breaking into the Sphinx, visiting another realm, and now this. And since it's all because of a cousin I know you liked, I know it's hard. And while Lucas is a good guy, he's still a guy."

"He is, but he's also been doing what he can to take care of me," Sophia admitted. "I don't think I would have been able to sleep last night if it wasn't for him." She watched Lucas as he walked beside Julian, the two chatting much like she and Olivia were. Though she'd never thought of him as the outdoorsy type, he seemed at home here. Despite everything they were facing, he even looked more relaxed out here, which was nice. "I love him."

Olivia laughed softly and nodded. "Yeah, I know. I think we all do. It's not exactly hard to see. You guys have that lovey-dovey look anytime you look at each other."

"It's really that obvious?"

"Pretty much," she answered cheerfully. "But I'm glad he's helping. That doesn't mean I'm not here to listen if you want to vent."

Sophia considered if she wanted to. She'd done it some the night before to Lucas, but she had to admit it might be nice to talk about it to Olivia. "I just can't believe Peter is doing all this. Any one thing would be bad enough, but he's attacking the fucking world, Olivia. Not just me, not just the Athenaeum, the *world*, and I can't figure out why."

"I'd love to give you an answer," Olivia said after a long pause, "but I don't have one. It could be he was just born a psychopath. Or maybe he was influenced by someone."

"Or something," Sophia muttered.

"Or something," Olivia agreed. "But right now, the reason doesn't matter. He is doing it, and we need to stop him. Which is why we're in Alaska, of all the godsforsaken places, trying to find a cave no mortal or god was ever supposed to find."

Sophia sighed and gave a small nod. "True. I really hope this Oskila stuff can fix everyone in the Athenaeum."

"It may, but we probably shouldn't count on that. We may need to incapacitate people if it doesn't, until we find some way of knocking Peter's influence out of them."

"Probably, but I honestly hadn't thought about that too much," she admitted. "At least not the infection part. I'm more worried about the fight I'm sure will happen when we go back. You know I'm not great at that stuff. I've only had a few weeks of training, and almost none of it was magical."

"First, don't discount that shield spell I heard you're good with. Didn't it save you guys from getting killed when you went to Delphi?"

The day Peter had hired someone to kill her. Sophia hated to think of that day. "Three of us still got shot, but yeah, it could have been worse. A lot worse. But you can't win a fight hiding behind a shield."

"Not this kind of fight, no," Olivia agreed, "but you know some sorcery. No reason you can't learn more, and we've got a couple hours walking through freaking Alaska."

"You know some spells that could help?" Olivia just arched a brow and smirked, reminding Sophia about her unique memory. "Right. Dumb question. You probably know at least as much sorcery as my grandfather."

"Probably," Olivia agreed. "And I've got a couple in mind that could help."

Over the next hour, she taught Sophia two different spells. The first allowed her to summon an object from anywhere. It had to be a real object, and she had to either see it or know it well enough to visualize it. So she could summon her laptop since she knew every inch of it, but she couldn't get Excalibur, as she'd never seen it. They practiced a bit until Sophia got the hang of it, but she was limited—so far—to things she could see or those she knew as well as her own face. But it meant she could grab objects to attack or defend with, or retrieve a weapon if she lost it in a fight. True, her only weapon was the little knife Lucas had given her, but she didn't really want to be defenseless.

The second spell was one Sophia was a little more hesitant to use, both in the moment or on the people of the Athenaeum. It was one to create and control fire. Definitely an offensive spell, and she could envision too many ways using it could go horribly wrong. After the others learned what they were doing, though, each and every one of them insisted she practice. Fortunately, they all promised they could prevent her from burning down the entire forest, so she gave in. She was extremely hesitant at first, but Vazi did something that prevented the fire from getting out of control, and Lucas—in partial gargoyle form—stomped out any stray flames. After a little while, she grew more comfortable with it and actually started to have fun. It was also surprising how easy it was to create fire. Probably because everyone was familiar with fire. It wasn't hard to envision a flame or how it moved. How quickly a dry leaf would curl and turn black.

She was still practicing when they reached the end of the first hour, and she immediately felt guilty. She hadn't been focusing on feeling any stray magic. Fortunately, Erasmus, Vazi, and Lucas had been, and none had felt so much of a twinge. Which meant they were onto the next stop in their wild goose chase.

Chapter 12

LUCAS WAS RELIEVED WHEN Olivia had started teaching Sophia offensive spells. Even after they dealt with Peter, it wouldn't be a bad thing for her to be able to kick some ass if she needed to. She was actually doing pretty good with the fire when they stopped to change locations. It might not be enough to counter a fire elemental, but she was safer than she had been.

Part of him wished she didn't have to go with them when they tried to take the Athenaeum back from Peter. Even Erasmus knew how to handle himself in a fight better than she did, which meant she'd be at risk. But not only would she refuse to let herself be left behind, she was the only one who could perform the failsafe. She had to go.

The second spot Vazi took them to looked remarkably similar to the first, but he wasn't surprised. They couldn't really be that far from where they had been, and it was all northern Alaska. It wasn't like they were going to go from river and forest to desert or plains. At least they shouldn't.

They took a few minutes to check, and again they felt nothing. At least nothing magical, though a scant ten minutes after they started walking, it began hailing again.

"This is starting to piss me off," Vazi said in a low, angry tone as he glared up at the sky. He was able to make it stop, but it seemed like it took more effort from him than it did the last time. That worried Lucas. A lot. If the oldest sky god on the planet was having trouble with the weather, then Peter had really gotten into some dark and dangerous magic. Magic Lucas wouldn't have thought existed, even inside the Athenaeum.

Before Lucas could go back and talk to Sophia, Erasmus decided to beat him to it. Then he made Lucas smile when the former aspida also got on the sorcery instructor bandwagon. He wasn't sure what spell was being taught at first, not until he glanced back and saw *two* Sophias walking beside Erasmus. He tripped, but caught himself before he faceplanted. That didn't mean the love of his life didn't see it, though, which she verified by laughing before he'd fully straightened.

Erasmus was grinning. "Just teaching her a nice spell to cause a distraction. I think you proved very well how effective it is."

"What the hell spell is that?" Lucas asked as he studied the doppelganger.

"He called it a twin spell," Sophia said, smiling, too. "She's not real, though," she explained, waving a hand through the solid-looking figure.

"It's actually a very difficult spell to learn," Erasmus told him proudly, and Sophia flushed with pleasure.

"Oh shit," Olivia said from ahead of them.

Lucas went on alert, facing forward again. It only took him a second to spot what had caught her attention. A brown bear. Not good. Worse, it had just spotted them. It let out a roar and started to charge toward them, making him wonder if it had cubs nearby. He might not be the type to enjoy tromping through the woods, but even he knew you didn't fuck with a mama bear and her cubs. He transformed into stone and prepared to face the beast, but Vazi sent a blast of air toward it. The bear slowed for a second, but didn't stop. Then Sophia appeared directly in front of the bear, making his heart stop. The bear lunged at her, but went right through her, making him realize what had just happened. And as Erasmus had said, it made a hell of a distraction. The bear looked supremely confused, and another gust from Vazi had it deciding they weren't worth the trouble. Turning, it ambled off the way it had come.

"Nice one, Soph," Olivia said when the bear was out of sight.

"Thanks," Sophia said, a little breathless. Which he got. A bear charging toward you was never fun.

They started walking again, and just five minutes after the bear, fat, white flakes started to fall from the sky, resulting in Vazi letting out a string of what had to be Lemurian curses. "Stop!" he shouted at the sky, which had the desired effect of causing it to cease abruptly as the flakes melted once they hit the ground.

"Grandpa, you know what's in the Athenaeum better than anyone," Sophia began. "What could he be using to do that?"

"It could be a couple of things. If he got into the Vault, there are several spells and relics which could be used to control the weather. I can't think of anything powerful enough to annoy Vazi, though," he admitted. "But even I haven't been able to go through everything in the Athenaeum. That's why we have multiple people cataloging it."

The fact that none of them knew exactly what Peter was doing kept them all quiet for the rest of the hour, though Sophia continued to practice her new spells. They popped to a third location, and he really hoped the third time would be the charm.

After about thirty minutes, the snow began again. But rather than soft, lazy flakes, it began coming down hard, the snow swirling around violently while freezing wind slapped their faces. It went from gray skies to a blizzard in less than a minute, the temperature dropping drastically. While Vazi was pissed by yet another weather anomaly, he went to work on clearing it up. When it took longer for him to dispel the snowstorm, everyone else started huddling together for protection and warmth. They watched the sky, but the sheer amount of power pouring off Vazi was noticeable to all of them, especially when the air around him began crackling and smelling like ozone. Lucas doubted the effort he was having to use was completely to blame for the phenomenon. It was likely just as much his emotions causing the effect. Peter had better hope anyone other than Vazi found him. The god might kill him for this alone, even if the others found a way to save him.

Gradually, the snow began to lessen, then stop altogether, though a full inch had accumulated on the ground while Vazi had been at work.

"Peter has much to answer for," Vazi said darkly as he stalked off, not waiting for the rest of them to join him.

The mood was more subdued over the next half hour until Vazi stopped. "Where's the next tributary?" he asked Julian.

The witch didn't answer right away, but had paused, head cocked and brow furrowed.

"Julian?" Olivia asked, walking to his side. "What is it?"

"I believe...I feel something. It's faint, and I can't tell where it's coming from, but I swear there is...something," he answered absently as he turned in a slow circle, his eyes closed.

"I'll be back," Vazi said before he disappeared.

Lucas tried to see if he could sense whatever Julian had felt, but it felt just like it had the last two dozen times he'd focused beyond the forest. Unsurprising, since witches were more in tune with things like that than most of the other Arcane races. None of the others admitted to feeling anything, either.

"While Vazi's gone, we should probably take a break," Sophia said, finding a rock to sit on. "We haven't eaten anything since we got out here."

Everyone agreed and found a place to sit, digging in their packs to pull out jerky or protein bars. They'd need something more substantial soon, but if they were close to the cave Grovek had written about, they'd probably wait until they reached it. Besides, being in a cave would offer them more protection, especially if the weather continued to fight against Vazi.

He watched Sophia's face as he took a bite of his bar. She looked stressed, but not as much as she had twelve hours ago. There was tiredness on her features, too, but they had been trekking through Alaska for the past several hours while she practiced sorcery, both of which were quite a work out. It was possible the learning had been enough of a distraction, at least for a little while.

It was about twenty minutes later when Vazi returned. He didn't look annoyed any longer, but was smiling. Not that it was really a pleasant looking expression. A pissed off but pleased god? Not ever a sight he wanted to see, even if the god was on his side.

"You found something," Erasmus said, pushing up from the log he'd been sitting on.

"I found something," Vazi confirmed. "Flew around to try to find what Julian was feeling, and I think I found it."

"Where?" Olivia asked as she stood beside Erasmus.

"Found another river, smaller than this one. Followed it upstream, and I started to feel something, too. The urge to just sit down and rest, to let my eyes close and allow peace to wash over me. It was far from overwhelming, but I felt it."

"Tell me you found the waterfall," Sophia said, slowly getting to her feet.

Vazi grinned. "I found a waterfall. Frozen around the edges, even. The feeling was the strongest there. I didn't see a cave, but I didn't look for long. You five ready for me to take you there?"

Everyone scrambled to get their packs on before nodding. "Let's go," Sophia told him with a faint smile of her own.

The forest disappeared, and when they reappeared, it was on the bank of a river. It was only five feet wide, though it did open up into a small pool right beneath the waterfall. That was only twenty feet high, and normally he might consider it pretty, especially with the bits of ice reflecting the sunlight. Now, though, his focus was on the sensation that even he could feel. It took a moment, because it wasn't something obvious, like an electrical charge in the air. It was more a feeling of peace, but not a natural peace. The urge to curl up where he was crept into his mind, and he knew it could become overwhelming if he got any closer to the source. Out here, it would probably just result in the world's most relaxing nap.

He glanced at the faces of the others, and saw signs they were feeling it, too.

"We should find that cave quick, then start chugging the coffee," Sophia suggested.

"And cast that spell on all of us," Vazi agreed. "I would do it now, but Isis and Hecate weren't sure how long it would last, and I'd rather wait until we're closer and the effects are stronger."

"Wise, especially if the cave is as deep as Grovek insinuated," Erasmus said, nodding.

"Speaking of," Olivia said, frowning. "We aren't all gods, and even with the coffee and caffeine pills, we're going to need to rest at some point. If we need to keep moving down there, maybe we should rest before we get into the cave, so we don't have to stop."

"So, find the cave, rest, then load up on spells and caffeine and get down there?" Lucas asked.

"Probably the smartest plan," Sophia said. "I don't think we can spare eight hours, but a couple hours now could mean the difference between making it and dying somewhere in that cave."

"Agreed," Vazi said, nodding. "I'll even rest this time, though I'll set a ward to make sure no more wildlife tries to interrupt us."

"Appreciated," she said, meaning it. They got to work, then, converging on the waterfall and the stones surrounding it. Remembering how she'd missed the opening that led to the Athenaeum, Sophia didn't go straight for the area behind the waterfall. It was obvious, which meant at least one of the others would be searching there. Beyond that, the rocks she would have been stepping on looked slick, and while she wasn't a complete klutz, she didn't think she was light enough on her feet to avoid slipping and falling into the icy water. The last thing any of them needed was hypothermia.

As they began searching, the weather started to shift again. At the first sign of snow, she sighed and glanced toward Vazi. He glared up at the sky and muttered something, but this time it only took a few moments before the flakes eased, then stopped. Again. She wasn't sure what purpose her cousin could have in messing with the weather in Alaska, but she was getting almost as sick of it as Vazi was. The tornado near her house made sense, in a sad way, but she wasn't sure about any of the rest. Was he just trying to cause as much destruction as possible, or was there an actual reason behind it? Did he have enemies in all the locations? People he was afraid could stop him? It made as much sense as him trying to kill Erasmus.

And what was the purpose of all of it? Ruling the world? If so, that was a supremely stupid reason. There were plenty of movies and books about people who wanted to rule a world, but it never made sense to her. Who wanted the headache? Running the Athenaeum was bad enough, but the world? Especially if it was taken over forcibly, like he was trying to do? He'd always be dealing with rebellions. How was that enjoyable? She shook her head and continued to run her fingers and eyes over the rock, inch by inch. Glancing at the others, she saw they were employing much the same methods. Well, except for Vazi, who had his eyes closed and one hand extended. She wasn't sure what he was doing, but she wasn't going to question the methods of a god.

"I think I found it," Julian called after half an hour of looking, pointing to a depression in the stone.

"How sure are you?" Lucas asked.

Julian wiggled his head from side to side and shrugged. "As sure as I can be without climbing inside. And I do mean climbing. It isn't a tall enough hole for any of us to get inside without being on all fours."

"I'll check," Vazi said before he disappeared. In only a few seconds, he reappeared right where he had been. "It's definitely a cave, and without delving too deeply, I would be fairly confident in saying it's the one we're looking for. I haven't sensed any other openings." He paused, then added reluctantly, "Though to be truthful, I didn't sense this one until it was pointed out."

"That makes sense, though," Olivia pointed out. "If the Eternals or Anunnaki or whatever they call themselves wanted to keep these places hidden, doesn't it stand to reason that they would have done something to make it hard to spot?"

"Well, we found it. Let's get the tents set up, get some hot food, and some rest," Sophia said, relieved she could stop scraping her fingers on the stone—though she wasn't thrilled that she was going to have to brave those slippery rocks in four hours.

There were three tents, so doubling up was going to be a necessity. Sophia and Lucas sharing was a given. Olivia and Erasmus decided to bunk together, and Julian and Vazi would take the third tent. Not that the witch looked particularly happy about that. She didn't blame him. She wouldn't want to share a tent with a grumpy god, either. Of course, Vazi didn't thrilled either, but that amused her. A little.

Sophia had never been camping in her life, so she was happy Lucas knew how to set their tent up. She helped where she could, then unrolled the sleeping bags inside, pleased when she realized they'd zip together so they didn't have to sleep in separate bags.

When all three tents were set up, they broke out the freeze-dried food. Vazi was kind enough to help them boil the water without needing to build a fire, so they all had a hot meal. Sophia was extremely skeptical about it, but was surprised to find it wasn't half bad. It wasn't something she'd seek out to eat, but she wouldn't balk if they ever decided to go camping for fun and took that with them.

After eating and spending a few minutes in the woods away from the others, Sophia climbed into the tent. After removing her shoes, she reluctantly took off her coat and gloves, then got into the sleeping bag as quickly as she could. It would warm up, she knew that, but the first few seconds were an unpleasant shock.

Lucas saw her reaction, and chuckled as he removed his shoes and coat as well. "Little chilly?" he teased.

"Shut up and get your ass in here with me," she said, yanking the thick covering up over half her face. She didn't remember ever being this cold. Yes, in Georgia winters the temperatures got this low, but she had always done the sane thing and stayed indoors. When she did have to venture out, she'd never taken off her coat.

He did as she asked, but it was then she realized he wasn't as warm as she was hoping he'd be. Then it hit her; he was stone. Okay, so he didn't look it right now, but it was an integral part of his being. Of course, he'd run a little cooler than others. It was no different from how she and a large chunk of other shifters ran a little hotter. It didn't stop her from curling herself around him.

He wrapped his arms around her in return, his chin resting lightly on top of her head. "So does that mean you don't want to take off a few more pieces of clothing and see how quiet you can be?" he asked.

The tone was playful, but she had a feeling he would be more than willing to do just that if she agreed.

"I love you, but I'm not taking anything else off until we're at least twenty degrees further south. Thirty would be better."

He rubbed his hand over her back and smiled. "That's okay. You don't really need to. Roll over," he instructed, gently helping her to do just that.

When she was on her side facing away from him, she scooted back against him. "Okay, why did I do that?"

"Because if you're not taking any clothes off, then I have to get creative," he said, slipping the button of her pants free then easing down the zipper.

"Creative? That just feels like you're about to take my pants off," she said blandly, but she was fighting a smile.

"Nope, they're staying on," he said as he nuzzled the back of her neck. "Doesn't mean I can't open them up enough to do this," he said as he slid his hand into her pants and beneath her panties.

Five minutes ago she would have said her libido was colder than the weather outside, but when his fingers grazed over her clit, then her opening, she decided that she liked his idea of creative. And if he got too much more creative, it might end up being warm enough for her to get rid of her pants.

Maybe.

"I'm okay with this," she murmured as he stroked her lazily.

"Good, because I don't want to stop." He scraped his teeth over her neck. "Just remember, you have to be quiet."

Quiet? Only if he went easy on her, and she wasn't sure he knew how to be easy on her. Then she stopped worrying when he slid a finger into her. She started to moan, but caught herself and swallowed the sound.

No, he wasn't going to go easy on her. He used the heel of his hand to press against her clit while his finger slid in and out of her. And his mouth? It didn't stay idle either, kissing and nipping along her neck and beneath her ear. Then he pressed his hips forward and she could feel the hard ridge against her ass that proved he was enjoying toying with her as much as she was enjoying being toyed with.

He slid another finger into her and her breath caught. She closed her eyes to try to focus on not crying out, but it just helped her pay more attention to every sensation. This time she couldn't prevent her moan, but pressed the sleeping bag against her face to muffle it.

He tsked against her ear, and the feel of his warm breath made her shiver and press back against him. "You're supposed to be quiet," he whispered, as he quickened his fingers, no doubt knowing it would make it harder for her to avoid making noise.

"Shut up," she breathed, rubbing against his cock, hoping to get his control to loosen like hers. He released a sharp breath, which made her smile and grind more insistently against him.

He nipped at her neck again, a little harder than before, so she could feel a sting of pain mixed in with the pleasure. "Stop that or your pants are coming off."

Sophia reached a hand up and back, sinking in into his short hair to hold his mouth against her. "No. I've got other plans for you."

Lucas gave a low growl she felt more than heard, then slid his free arm beneath her and ensured every inch of her was plastered to him. She didn't mind, though she did wish their clothes were gone. One of her favorite things was lying beside him, skin to skin.

He didn't stop, but he did whisper against her ear, "Tell me about these plans." It was hard for her to focus on the demand, because she'd never come so close to orgasm when fully clothed before. Especially not when in a tent in freaking Alaska. Not that she was going to argue, not when she felt the pressure building within her with every stroke of his fingers.

Then it crested and she had to turn her face into the sleeping bag, though the only sound that escaped was a breathy gasp. He heard it though, felt her come, and smiled against her skin as he ground his cock against her.

His fingers gentled as the orgasm ebbed, and he pressed soft kisses over her throat as she started to relax.

"So about these plans," he murmured as he slowly drew his fingers out of her.

She found herself able to laugh as she turned around to face him. "What if I said it was kissing you brainless, then going to sleep?"

"Then I'd have to call you a dirty liar," he answered without hesitation.

"You'd be right." But she did kiss him, if only because she would never get tired of doing that. It didn't matter whether it was soft and loving, or hard and passionate, like it was now. She loved that he got so hot and worked up teasing her, but then again, it also went the other way.

Ignoring how her pants hung open, she slid down in the sleeping bag. She knew it would prevent her from seeing him, but that was okay. She'd be able to feel him, hear him, and that would be enough.

Sophia opened his pants by feel alone, and carefully slid the zipper down. A sudden hint of light made her look up, and she grinned as she saw him peering down at her, the bag lifted. She said nothing as she pulled his shaft out of his pants, and kept her gaze on his as her hand wrapped around him and stroked slowly up, then back down, making his eyes darken to gray. It wasn't enough, so she lowered her head and took him into her mouth. His jaw clenched as her mouth slid down, taking him inch by inch until the angle prevented her from taking anymore.

Sophia would love to take an hour playing with him, pleasuring him, but knew they really did need sleep before they went underground. Besides, it was fun to push him hard and fast, to see him break and lose control. It made her feel strong, powerful, and sexy.

She sucked and moved her mouth over him, never giving him time to relax or settle. No, she wanted him off balance and consumed by pleasure. She might not have the mobility she was used to, trapped in the sleeping bag as she was, but it didn't seem to matter, not with how taut his body was or how hot his eyes were. He whispered her name, and it was as tense as the rest of him, so she drew him in as deep as she could, sucked until her cheeks hollowed. It seemed to be enough.

His head fell back, his eyes squeezing shut as he went over the edge. Ridiculously pleased to have brought such a strong man to his knees—metaphorically, anyway—she swallowed him down and moved her mouth gently over him until he relaxed beneath her. She drew her lips off him and smiled, wiggling her way back up in the bag.

"I like your plans," he told her in a husky voice as he wrapped his arms around her.

"Me too. And I'm not cold anymore."

He smiled lazily, his eyes still closed. "Good. You really should sleep now. I've been in a handful of caves, and they generally aren't anything to scoff at."

"What could we run into?" she asked. While part of her was afraid to know, she felt she needed to know what she might be in for.

"There's no way to know for sure," he admitted. "Every cave is different. Could be narrow passages that we have to crawl through, or huge caverns full of stalagmites. There's one I heard of in Mexico that's full of huge crystals. They call it the Cave of Swords, if that gives you an idea what it's like."

"Sounds kind of pretty."

"Maybe, but it probably wouldn't be the easiest to navigate. All I know is it's going to be dirty and rough, but we'll get to the bottom. We'll find the Oskila."

She said nothing for a long moment, then she gave voice to one of her greatest fears. "What if the Oskila doesn't cure everyone in the Athenaeum?"

"Then we'll find another way. Olivia's still got the Tyet, we've got Grovek's theories, and once we stop Peter, we'll have more time to focus on them," he answered without hesitation.

She didn't know how confident he really was, but he sounded pretty sure, if tired, so she nodded and closed her eyes, though she wasn't sure how easily sleep would come to her. Probably easier than it would have without their mutual plans.

He kissed her temple and tugged the sleeping bag up a little higher around her. "Sleep. Worrying won't change anything. It'll just stress you out again. And if you're going to succeed in step three of saving the world, you need the rest."

"Step three?"

"Finding the secret chamber in the Sphinx was step one. Step two was finding the mythical Hall of Records."

"Sozu," she murmured.

"What?"

"It was actually called Sozu."

He chuckled and nodded. "Sleep," was all he said. With the Oskila chamber somewhere beneath them, she couldn't help but do just that.

Chapter 13

Just over four hours later, they were all awake and miserable. While they'd slept, the blizzard had begun again, leaving a full foot of snow on the ground, with more swirling around, propelled by a wind strong enough to be painful. Despite that, the tents and sleeping bags got packed up. After some quick discussion, they decided to leave both behind. It was extra weight, and while the Oskila shouldn't necessarily make them drowsy, it would encourage them to opt for the lazier route. Or that was how they'd interpreted the various writings about it. Anything they could do to avoid fatigue and inactivity could be the difference between making it out alive or dying down below.

After they had gathered around the narrow opening, Lucas stopped Vazi before he could be the first inside. "Before we go in there, I think we need to talk about what happens if one of us starts to be affected—severely—by the Oskila. Because if this is like caves I've been in, carrying a person won't be a feasible option for long."

"We've got a couple of people who can teleport," Olivia said, inclining her head to Julian, Sophia, and Vazi. "How about if one of us starts to nod off or whatever, they teleport if they're able, or someone else takes them if they're not? It's kind of what we talked about before.

We could shoot for Erasmus's house, maybe, since it's someplace we've all been?"

"It's a good idea," Julian agreed. "It wouldn't be wise to leave anyone behind. We don't know what prolonged exposure to Oskila would do."

"I agree," Sophia said as well.

"And I'm perfectly happy using my house as our...what's the word, Lucas? Rendezvous point?"

"That's it," Lucas confirmed.

"Great. We've got a plan. Can we get moving now?" Vazi grumbled.

"After you," Sophia said, waving a hand toward the opening.

Though Vazi didn't bother with the headlamp, the rest of them put theirs in place and turned them on while they waited for the god to get inside. Except he cheated. The rest of them would have to crawl on their hands and knees, while he just disappeared, presumably reappearing inside where he could stand.

Lucas sent Olivia next. It wasn't that he didn't trust Vazi—surprisingly, he did—but he wanted someone with a better attention span and longer fuse on the other side before Sophia went through. After Olivia and Sophia, he urged Julian, then Erasmus through, before he followed them all inside.

It wasn't unexpected when he had to crawl for a while before the passage finally opened up. His knees would have preferred if a while hadn't been close to five minutes, but if that was the price he had to pay to save everyone from Peter, so be it. Though as soon as he was able to stand up, he asked, "Vazi? Any chance of you adding knee pads to the rest of this gear?"

"Oh, yes, I suppose that would make it more comfortable, wouldn't it?" the god said, as though it had only just occurred to him. But he did as asked, and soon the five mortals all had knee pads on.

With that concern out of the way, Lucas looked around. The passage may have opened up, but he wouldn't call the area they were clustered in a chamber. It was only an inch or so higher than he was tall, and narrow enough that he could reach both sides at the same time. There was moisture coating almost every inch of the stone, which worried him. Slick, smooth rock made for uncertain footing. Then again, the ground seemed surprisingly uneven. It might provide enough traction to keep everyone upright. Unless some of that texture was gravel, which could easily slide.

Then there were organic dangers. Bats tended to love caves, though he wasn't sure if they lived this far north. There also tended to be insects and various reptiles and amphibians, but he wasn't sure how dangerous any cave-dwelling types were. And those were just the potential threats he knew about. "Everyone, be very careful about where you step. Smooth stone and water don't mix. And if we're the first people down here since Grovek, then we don't know how stable anything is. I doubt we'll find any sinkholes or have any cave ins, but I'd rather us be prepared just in case."

After everyone had acknowledged his warnings, they started further into the cave, walking in the same order they'd entered the cave. It only took a few minutes for them to realize this was not going to be a leisurely descent to the Oskila chamber. First, the passage opened up into a small chamber, no bigger than the average living room. Then it split into five passages. The first one they'd chosen had been the biggest, but it had ended in a rock slide just ten minutes later. One that was impassable without a large expenditure of energy, so they'd opted not to try, at least not right away. After backtracking, they tried the next passage over—and the second largest. This one didn't end, but it did rise sharply at one point in a pile of boulders and rocks, causing them to climb. Once, Olivia accidentally loosened a rock which had smacked into Sophia's arm, but it only left a scrape and blossoming bruise, which Julian had quickly healed.

The multiple passages and pile of rocks weren't the only issues they ran into, either. This was definitely not a journey for the weak. It didn't help that they couldn't stop and rest, and he knew they would all benefit from a few minutes here and there. The best he could allow was walking more slowly as they drank water and—after the first hour—down more caffeine pills.

Through all of it, Lucas didn't see a single sign of life. More signs of water, absolutely, but no insects, no animals, not even a trace of moss. He hoped that wasn't an omen.

The passage had finally widened enough for them to walk with two people side-by-side instead of single file. He took the opportunity to move up beside Sophia. "You doing okay?" She was struggling, though not as much as he might have expected. The training over the past month had done her good, even if it wasn't being used in a fight. At least not the traditional sort. The sex hadn't hurt either, he thought with an internal grin.

"Not really. I'd love to stop, but..." She trailed off and shrugged, lifting her canteen for another drink of water. "I'm suddenly glad the Athenaeum had all those fucking stairs, though, otherwise I'd be crying for someone to teleport me out of here."

He grinned because he understood. He'd been in good shape when he'd first gone to the Athenaeum, and he'd had issues with them at first.. "If we're lucky, we'll find this place soon. And we can slow down if we need to, just not stop. I know it isn't perfect, but it helps."

"Not when it's like that," she said dryly, nodding to the way ahead. He followed her gaze and saw that it dipped down sharply, then climbed at an even steeper angle. Stalagmites and rocks littered the way, too, so they would have to zigzag across to the other side and occasionally climb over rocks. Even he wasn't looking forward to it. Not just because of the physical exertion, but because the Oskila was starting to be more noticeable the deeper into the cave they got. It wasn't horrible now, but he wasn't sure if it was because they weren't close enough yet, or because of the precautions they'd taken. Or it could be like the Miasma; a cumulative effect over time.

Other than Vazi, they were all dragging by the time they reached the topside of the next rise, and when they reached that point, each and every one of them stopped. The view ahead of them called for a minute of gaping, though. Gaping and many, many pictures, Lucas thought, and Erasmus agreed, since he pulled out his phone to do just that.

The passage opened up into a cavern that had to be at least as big as a football field. Not only was it long and wide, it was tall. Sixty feet, if he had to guess, but it was hard to tell by the light of headlamps. That wasn't what had caused all of them to stare in awe. It was the forest that filled the cavern.

Oh, it wasn't a forest like the one they'd left outside; there was no green anywhere, and it was as silent as a grave, but in front of them were the unmistakable shapes of hundreds of trees. They were all gray with hints of red and orange, each with branches stretching out and up. There wasn't a single leaf on any of them, but it didn't matter. Finding a forest this far below ground wasn't something any of them had expected to find.

"How is there a forest in a cave?" Sophia asked.

"I...don't know," Vazi admitted, sounding as baffled as Lucas felt. "But they don't look right."

"No, they don't. I think I know why, though," Olivia said as she started forward. It took a minute before anyone followed after her, and her pace was quicker, so she was soon standing at the base of one of the trees. It dwarfed her. They obviously weren't as tall as the redwoods in California, but the trunks were a good ten feet across, so they weren't small.

"They're petrified," she called, laying a hand on the tree, a reverence in her voice he'd never heard before.

"I still don't understand," Julian said as he joined her, studying the tree. "The petrification, that makes sense. Water, minerals, it could happen. There's a cave in England that petrifies anything left there, in fact. What I don't understand, though, is how there was ever a forest beneath the earth. Trees need sunlight, nutrients. We could argue the nutrients were carried here by water that's no longer here, but I don't see any possible way they could have gotten sunlight, much less enough to have grown to this size. Underground, even if they had survived without sunlight, they should be...stunted, small."

Vazi rested both hands flush against the tree, his head tilted back so he could stare up into the bare branches. When he spoke, his voice was quiet and almost awed. It was an odd tone for a god to have. "You forget. We are standing in a chamber created by the ones who created everything. The Anunnaki were the ones who were responsible for the Oskila, the Miasma, and everything else in the universe. If they had the power to create that, why is it so difficult for you to accept that they could create a forest where no forest should be?" He looked over at Julian. "The only reason forests are on the surface, drinking of the sun, is because that is how they designed them." His gaze slid back to the barren branches. "Perhaps this is how forests were in the beginning, until the Anunnaki chose a new way. It wouldn't be the first time they'd done such a thing."

"What do you mean?" Sophia asked.

"The Lemurian gods were feared when we were all active. Not because we were the oldest, though we were. It was because we were different. The gods who came after us were created differently than we were." He didn't explain how, and Lucas wasn't going to press. Vazi might be working with them, and might even trust them to an extent, but he was fully aware they weren't in his inner circle. When this was all over, he'd go back to Lemuria and they'd go back to their homes. Hell, they might never see the god again.

"We should keep moving," Erasmus suggested. Since his voice was a little slurred, it wasn't hard to guess why he had spoken up. Honestly, they never should have stopped, but for a sight like this, none of them had even thought about resisting the urge to take it in.

"We should," Sophia agreed. As she started moving, she also fished out another caffeine pill, washing it down with a large gulp of coffee.

Lucas didn't blame her. It was odd, but it was like his brain was trying to shut off before his body. He didn't feel tired, not really, just...like he wanted to stop. Stopping would be a very good thing, really. No more stress, no more fighting. All he would need to do was stop moving and stop thinking. He'd drift off to sleep and be able to dream for eternity. How wonderful would that be? And if Sophia stopped, too, she might dream with him, which would be just about perfect.

Olivia stumbled into a tree, but rather than straighten herself, she leaned against it and let her body begin to slide down. It felt like that should be significant, something he should worry about, but he just wasn't. In fact, he was seriously starting to consider sitting down next to her. It would be a nice place to rest, in an ancient, underground forest. There weren't many better views.

Then Sophia tripped and fell to her hands and knees, and he was jolted out of the haze that had started enveloping him. "Sophia!" He ran to her and helped her to her feet. "Are you okay?"

Her expression was a little dazed, but she nodded. "I think so. Might have a bruise or two, but I'm okay. Just...wasn't watching where I was going, I guess."

He shook his head. "No, it's not just you. Look at Olivia."

She did and even in the light of the headlamp he could see she paled. "Oh gods," she whispered. "Vazi?"

"Mmm?" was the god's response.

"Vazi!" she said, raising her voice. She didn't get much of a response the second time. Before Lucas could take a shot at getting Vazi's attention, she flung out a hand and hissed out a few syllables.

Vazi rocked like he'd been hit, but it got a reaction. A strong breeze poured off him as he turned back toward them, glaring at Sophia. "Careful, mortal," he warned.

"We're slipping, Vazi. The Oskila is getting stronger. It's time to use that spell," she explained, and Lucas smiled at her response. No apology, just telling him what he needed to do. She'd grown so much since he'd first met her. Hell, she'd grown since they'd left the Athenaeum. Their situation had forced her to accept her position.

Vazi frowned at her for a second before slowly nodding. "Yes. Good idea. Sorry." He closed his eyes and tilted his chin, speaking in a low voice, in a language Lucas didn't recognize. The effects were immediate. The veil of disinterest began to lift, allowing him to think more clearly. It wasn't gone, but the spell did help.

Julian pulled Olivia to her feet while Erasmus shook his head. "That's dangerous. I didn't even notice how strong it was getting until it eased."

"Neither did I," Sophia admitted.

"Until Sophia fell, I was seriously thinking about just sitting down and going to sleep. Forever," Lucas added. "We should hurry."

"Agreed," Olivia said.

They quickened their pace as much as they were able as they passed through the forest. Before, it had seemed beautiful in a way, but now it was just eerie. Dead. Normally Lucas liked old things, but this ancient forest was now one of the creepiest places he'd ever been. The light of their headlamps reflected off crystal spots in the trees, reminding him of animal eyes in the darkness. And if they weren't careful, they might end up as still and lifeless as those trees.

It felt like hours before they reached the other side of the forest. The fact that the chamber narrowed to another single passage was a little worrying, but they didn't have any other options. They hadn't seen another way without backtracking almost to the beginning of the cave system.

"I don't like this," Olivia said, though she didn't hesitate to follow Vazi into the almost claustrophobic passage.

"Unfortunately, we just gotta suck it up," Lucas said, turning sideways to get past an exceptionally narrow part of the passage. But honestly, he didn't like it either.

Fifteen minutes later, the path widened just enough to allow them some breathing room, but it also sloped downward at a steep angle. Worse, it had loose gravel and sand, making it more dangerous. Vazi didn't seem to have any trouble, but Lucas didn't expect anything less. Olivia was almost as good as the god, but then Julian's foot hit wrong and he went down hard. The incline and gravel meant that once his ass hit the ground, he started sliding down, and fast. He knocked into Erasmus, who fell partially on top of him, then they kept going. The pair knocked into the back of Sophia's legs, and she landed on top of them both. She must have hit more than soft flesh, because she let out a quick cry of pain as continued sliding.

Lucas began moving quicker, hoping to get to them and grab them before they could hit one of the stalagmites and really hurt themselves. Olivia tried to catch them, but while she was strong, she didn't have a good way of bracing herself where she was at, and had to choose between trying to hold on to them or going down with them. Vazi didn't have that problem. He shoved a hand out and the three stopped, their hair lifting and swirling, telling Lucas the god was using wind to hold them in place. It allowed them to steady then untangle themselves with Olivia and Lucas's help.

Julian and Erasmus both had some scrapes. Sophia had lucked out of that particular injury, but once she was on her feet, Lucas saw her cradling her arm and he frowned, looking her over. "What's wrong?"

"Hit my elbow on a rock when I fell," she admitted.

"Julian," he demanded.

"Of course," Julian agreed easily, resting his hand on Sophia's arm. The tension around her eyes eased as the pain did.

"Thank you," she told him with a faint smile.

Though he knew they needed to get moving again, Lucas drew her into his arms and held her for a moment. "Don't scare me like that again," he whispered against her hair.

"I'll try not to," she promised, tilting her head back so she could kiss him lightly. Only then did he let her go.

The ground leveled out a few minutes later, and a few minutes after that, the walls spread out. Not that it was much easier for them to pass, since there were formations and rocks everywhere. They had to wind their way across the chamber, while picking their steps carefully. They might not slide downhill here, but they could still fall on a stalagmite and hurt themselves.

"This feels too easy," Sophia said, turning her head to shine the light from her headlamp around. "Further back it was all multiple passages and stuff, but now it's just one way? No hunting needed?"

"Could be that nothing else was needed, since the Oskila is so much stronger here," Julian suggested.

"True. If you didn't know what was down—"

That was as far as she got before a crack sounded from above their heads. Lucas glanced up in time to see a stalactite separate from the cave ceiling and come crashing down. There wasn't any time for him to react, though it was heading right for Olivia. She jumped back, barely avoiding being impaled. As it was, the centuries-old formation scraped her arm before it hit the ground and broke, sending natural shrapnel flying.

"Fuck!" Olivia said as she scowled at the remains of the stalactite, then looked down at her legs. There were small tears in her sleeve and the fabric of her pants, but she said, "Didn't break skin. Just be careful," she called, looking up and glaring at the other missiles waiting to fall on them.

Thankfully, while another one did fall, it was further away from them. But the cave floor began sloping down again, and the effects of the Oskila grew stronger. Lucas realized his thoughts were drifting back to those of peace and dreams, and transformed to his gargoyle form, careful to keep his wings tucked in close. It might not do anything, but at this point, he had to try.

After a few minutes, he realized there were only four people in front of him, not five. Frowning, he turned and looked around, spotting Julian about fifty feet behind them, leaning against the cave wall, his eyes closed. "Hold up," he called to the others. "Julian's out."

They walked back to him, finding that his words were more true than they knew. The man was actually dozing off on his feet. "Julian," Lucas said, shaking his shoulder. "You need to wake up." There was no response, and Lucas felt a little ball of fear form in his belly. "Julian," he repeated, louder this time.

"Oh, let me," Vazi said, his voice nearly a purr. "I owe him for the first time we met," he said, touching Julian's face. Electricity sparked against the witch's skin, which literally jolted him awake.

"Ow!" Julian rubbed at his cheek, frowning at Vazi. "What did you do that for?"

"You were asleep."

"And what was it payback for?" Olivia wondered.

"For pestering me incessantly with questions."

"Ah. Fair enough," she said, nodding in understanding.

"I was sleeping?" Julian asked, sounding like he was still half in that state.

"You were," Sophia confirmed. "Which means it's time for you to leave. Go back to Erasmus's house."

He frowned, like her words weren't quite registering. "Leave? No...I can't leave. I..." He shook his head and rubbed at his temple. "I'm supposed to be doing something, aren't I?"

"You're supposed to be heading to Erasmus's house in Egypt," Sophia said, her tone sharp rather than soothing. The last thing any of them needed was more soothing.

"Oh. Right." He nodded. "I'll do that, then." He disappeared, and Lucas hoped he actually made it to Egypt and not just somewhere else in the cave.

When they resumed their journey, Sophia walked beside him rather than behind Olivia. Though the cave made their voices echo, she kept hers low enough that Vazi was probably the only one who could hear her.

"I don't think my grandfather is going to last much longer."

Lucas focused on the man and saw his steps were slower, his feet dragging a little along the ground. He might be old, but the man had never acted like it other than when he'd been feigning illness. But he also knew the man well enough to know he wouldn't give in until he had to. Not without a good reason.

"I'm not sure any of us will unless the chamber is close by," Lucas admitted. "The spell is helping, and so is being in gargoyle form, but I don't know if it's enough if we have to deal with hours more of this."

"How long have we been down here?"

"Probably close to five hours," Lucas estimated. It felt like longer, much longer, but realistically, he was probably pretty close.

Sophia groaned and leaned into him for a moment, not caring that he was made of rock at the moment. "This stuff had better work."

He agreed, so didn't say anything, just rubbed a hand over her back.

Further conversation was halted when Olivia stumbled, then went down. She didn't get back up, but wasn't out like Julian had been, because she murmured, "Well fuck." Being more aware didn't mean she made any effort to rise, though, which worried Lucas.

"Time for you to go, too," Vazi said, pulling her to her feet before Lucas and Sophia could reach her.

"You too, Grandpa," Sophia added.

"No, I'm fine," Erasmus argued.

"You're not," she said firmly, then she went for the kill. "And you owe me. You made me watch you die, so you're going to let Olivia teleport both of you to your house where I know you'll be safe."

Erasmus's face fell, but he nodded and looked at Olivia. "Can you move us both right now?"

"I...Yes, I think so. Shadow travel is as natural as breathing," Olivia said, nodding as she reached out to him and hooked her arm in his. "Your house?"

"Yes, his house," Lucas answered when Erasmus only frowned in apparent confusion. Lucas felt the same way. There was something he felt like he should be remembering, but he couldn't bring it to mind.

Olivia nodded, held Erasmus's arm tighter, then they faded into the shadows. It was the first time he'd seen it happen to someone else and had to admit it was kind of a creepy—but cool—method of teleportation.

"We should get going, before we have to leave, too," Sophia said, moving past Vazi and continuing deeper into the cave.

Chapter 14

This was not how this was supposed to go. Half their people were gone, and Sophia's mind was constantly foggy with thoughts of resting, of stopping until she fell into dreams and oblivion. Lucas seemed to be okay, especially after he'd transformed, but she saw signs that he was more affected than he was letting on. A faraway look on his face, a scrape of his foot along the floor, reaching a hand out to the wall to steady himself. Even Vazi wasn't as confident as he'd been when they first entered the cave.

They pressed on, though, because they had no other choice. This was the only thing they knew of that would give them a chance to stop the Miasma, and she felt responsible. Peter was her cousin, the Athenaeum was supposed to have been under her protection. The others might choose to quit, but she couldn't.

Sophia was so deep in thought, she nearly walked right over the edge of a pit. She caught herself just in time, but her arms pinwheeled for a moment as she caught her balance, then took three quick steps back. Lucas was there in an instant, grabbing her shoulder to further steady her.

Frowning, she looked around and saw the hole was large. Maybe thirty feet across and ten wide. Too far to jump, except there wasn't anywhere to jump to. Other than the section where she stood, it was surrounded by vertical walls. At first she thought it was a dead end, but then she realized the feeling of the Oskila was stronger here than it had been anywhere else.

"You feel that?" she asked Lucas.

"You mean the nearly overwhelming urge to sit down and just stay there for the rest of eternity?" Lucas asked dryly.

"Yeah. Like maybe the Oskila is..." She crept forward until her toes were at the edge, then carefully leaned over and looked down, letting her light shine into the pit. "Down there," she finished.

"I think you're right," Vazi said as he stepped between them and peered down as well. He held a hand out over the pit and cocked his head. "I know Julian said he packed rope, but I don't think it's long enough to get the two of you down there."

"But if the Oskila is down there, we have to get down there," Sophia argued.

"Yes, we do," he agreed, an instant before he shoved both of them forward and over the edge.

Heights didn't normally bother Sophia. Neither did falling. She was part shapeshifter and had been turning into an owl and flying for all her life. It was a completely different situation when an ally shoved her into the unknown. She cut off her scream, but not before it echoed around her. "Asshole!" she yelled instead, before she started to shift. Just before she could complete the transformation, she felt air envelop her and wanted to roll her eyes. At least he had planned on a way to get them to the bottom safely. Still, he was going to pay for that stunt. On the other hand, it did serve to jolt her a little further out of the effects of the Oskila.

Glancing over, she saw Lucas had his wings spread and shook her head, but felt a hint of amusement. Not that she'd let Vazi know that.

When they reached the bottom, Vazi was already there, standing in a small, round area with a single opening.

"We can both fly," Lucas told the god in a dry tone.

Vazi shrugged without a hint of remorse. "This was quicker. And more fun." He nodded to the opening and pointed. "The Oskila's in there."

"You got the jar?" Sophia asked, staring at the sliver of the next chamber she could see from her current position. It wasn't much, but she saw a pale, powdery looking substance covering the walls and floor.

He lifted his hand and a jar appeared in it. "Right here." She glanced over, then did a double take. It resembled an Egyptian canopic jar, but there was one thing off about it. "Is that...an owl? I thought those things only had images of like Anubis or..." She couldn't actually remember what other animal heads she'd seen on them, but owls definitely weren't it.

"It is. Isis insisted on the deviation," he answered with a shrug. "Shall we?"

"Caffeine pills first," Lucas insisted, digging some of them out and offering one each to Sophia and Vazi. They took them without complaint before they stepped cautiously into the room.

Sophia was a little concerned about walking on the Oskila if it really was this pale powder, but her first step didn't knock her out. Not that it eased her mind in the least. She did relax, though, but it was definitely against her will.

"Hurry," Lucas said, his voice sluggish.

Vazi nodded, but for once didn't have any snarky remarks. He removed the lid and handed it to Sophia, then knelt beside a spot where the powder looked thicker. He swayed and nearly fell over, which would have put his hand directly in the Oskila. She doubted even he could withstand that, so grabbed his arm, preventing that fall. It took some effort, since he was far from a small man and she wasn't at her best.

Lucas pulled out a pocket knife, opened it, and bent in front of Vazi. "Hold the jar, I'll scrape it in." Vazi gave another nod and held the jar down next to the floor, while Sophia worked on steadying them both. She hadn't anticipated that it would take three people to do the actual collecting, but as long as it got done safely, she didn't care.

No one was moving exceptionally quick now that they were literally standing on the Oskila, so it took more minutes than any of them would have liked to fill the jar. When it was, Sophia placed the lid on top, and Vazi made sure it was airtight.

Both men rose, then Sophia led the way back to the outer chamber. "We should..." She frowned when she lost her train of thought. It took another minute for her to catch it again. "We should try to get the stuff off our shoes, so we don't carry it back to Egypt."

Vazi gave a quick flick of his fingers, which had all three of them levitating a foot in the air. A breeze brushed over their lower bodies and feet, cleaning the Oskila from them and sending it back into the next chamber.

With them still in the air, Vazi asked, "Everyone ready?" He didn't wait for an answer before he teleported them all back to Erasmus's house. Immediately, she felt better. She could feel the effects of the

Oskila Vazi carried, but it was much easier to ignore—and to resist. The change was abrupt, but entirely welcome.

Julian was sitting on the couch, his head in one hand, elbow braced on his knee, while the other held a cup of what smelled like fresh coffee.

"Where are Erasmus and Olivia?" Lucas asked as he shifted back to his human form.

Julian lifted his head and frowned. "They aren't with you?"

Sophia and Lucas exchanged a look. "They left not long after you did," she explained.

"She said she travels via shadows?" Vazi asked.

"Yeah. She's a nightmare," Lucas answered.

"It was daylight. She might not have had enough shadows to get far." After a second, he sighed and set the jar on the table. "Give me a minute to ensure I'm no longer being overly affected by that," he said, waving a hand at said jar, "then I'll go get them."

Julian straightened, his eyes fixed on the jar. "You got it? That's the Oskila?"

Sophia nodded. "It is. Basically full, too."

"Good. I'm glad you were able to collect it." Shame crossed his features. "I'm sorry I wasn't able to continue helping you."

"No," she said quickly. "It wasn't your fault. Erasmus and Olivia didn't make it to the chamber either. And yeah, Lucas, Vazi, and I made it, but that didn't mean it wasn't close. Damn close."

Julian didn't look convinced, but nodded.

"I'll be back in a minute," Vazi, apparently recovered, told them before he disappeared. She prayed Olivia and Erasmus weren't too deep in the cave, because none of them could handle too much more.

This was why Vazi rarely dealt with mortals. Aside from those from and currently on Lemuria, anyway. Lemurians were different. The rest were always complaining and sticking their noses where they didn't belong. And wasn't that proven by the fact that all of this was a result of a single mortal interfering with something even the gods didn't dare touch?

To be fair, he couldn't blame Olivia and Erasmus for their current situation. He would never admit it, but he'd come closer than he'd like to succumbing to the effects of the Oskila, so he could hardly berate mortals for being more susceptible.

Sending himself back to Alaska, he started at the opening of the cave. The supplies they'd abandoned were still there, buried in the snow, and he sent them back to Julian's house. It wasn't likely anyone else would be this way anytime soon, but he couldn't see leaving them in the forest.

Transforming to air so he could move quickly and easily, he flew into the cave and went in search of their missing people. It took less than a minute before he found them, not too far from the mouth of the cave. They were passed out and lying in a heap against one of the walls. Returning to his physical form, he waved a hand and brought all three of them back to Erasmus's house. Though he wasn't known as a kind god—even if he liked to think the Lemurians had always seen him as fair—he put them on the couch rather than on the floor.

Ignoring the others, who had stood and were clearly concerned, he laid a hand on both their chests and sent a light jolt through them, which cleared the worst of the peaceful effects from the cave, waking them both.

Olivia gasped, hand covering the point where he'd sent a minuscule bolt of lightning into them. "What happened?"

"You didn't make it back here," Lucas answered.

"I found you not too far from the opening of the cave," Vazi explained, selecting a chair and sinking down into it. It might not be a throne, but he had to admit it was comfortable enough. It wasn't a terrible sacrifice to make in order to protect the world from this megalomaniac of a mortal they were fighting against.

"Thank you for coming back for us," Erasmus said, also rubbing his chest. Maybe he should have chosen a different method of waking them, but it was the most expedient. Besides, Julian had shown he had some healing abilities. And if he hadn't been up to the task, Vazi knew where to find Suni. She owed him a favor. Not that he'd like to waste it on saving one mortal, but he knew Seth was fond of this one. To be honest, he was growing fond of him as well. Okay, the others as well, not that he would allow them to get even an inkling of that fondness. Mortals tended to abuse such things, and he had enough to worry about without being badgered for minor favors.

"Is there somewhere we can keep that until we're ready to use it?" Sophia asked, pointing to the container holding the Oskila. "The jar seems to be doing its job, but I can still feel it poking at my mind."

"I could send it someplace only Seth and I can access," Vazi offered.

"That sounds perfect," she said, nodding.

He waved a hand and it disappeared. Even he could notice a difference, and was sorry he hadn't thought of doing that sooner.

"Thank you," she told him, relief clear on her face and in her voice. "I think it'll be easier to plan how to use it without it nearby."

"Agreed," Julian said, nodding. "But I do have a question. Are you wanting to do the planning before or after we get everyone else here?"

Sophia stilled and Vazi cocked his head as he watched the emotions moving over her face. From what Seth had told him, she was young—in every way—and had only been head of the Athenaeum for a month. Odds were she knew nothing about battle strategy, which did not fill him with confidence. Unfortunately, she and the other mortals knew more about what they were up against than he did.

"I'd recommend waiting until you meet the others. They might have powers or skills we can use," Lucas murmured to her.

She nodded. "That's a good point. But I don't know if we can fit that many people in here comfortably. Especially since I don't want us to rush that planning. We've still got ten days until Seth's deadline, though I'd prefer not to use it all since Peter's messing with the weather. Every day's delay could mean deaths."

Olivia nodded. "Same here. But if we go in half-cocked, with a half-assed plan, it's not going to matter how many days we have left. Losing tomorrow or losing in a week still means losing."

"If I might suggest something?" Erasmus said, looking at Sophia. When she nodded, he went on. "We find someplace able to accommodate so many people, then we take two days to recover and plan. That gives us time to figure out who can do what, and the best way to use the Oskila. It might also be enough time to let the patrons figure out a way through the wards Peter has placed on the Athenaeum. It does mean there will likely be increasingly bad weather for two days, but I would rather some natural disasters than the world changing irrevocably—and not for the better."

"I might be able to help with the weather," Vazi said before he could think better of it.

"You can?" Sophia asked, and his eyes narrowed at the surprise in her voice.

"I am the god of the sky. That includes weather, as you saw in Alaska. If I don't have to worry about Oskila or anything else, I can monitor these freak storms and at least lessen their impact. It all depends on how strong they are, and how many I'm having to deal with at once." He could feel a breeze coming from his skin, along with small arcs of electricity as his anger built. When he discovered what had been used to achieve this weather, he was going to destroy it, regardless of what it was or if Seth and the others in the Athenaeum protested. Anything that could make him work this hard to fix the weather was not something that needed to exist.

"Thank you. That would give us a little more breathing room."

Vazi inclined his head in acknowledgment but said nothing.

"We can regroup at my home," Julian offered. "It's big enough for everyone."

"Works as good as anywhere I can think of," Sophia said, nodding.

"Then I recommend we go now. The sooner we plan, the sooner we can stop all this," Lucas said.

Vazi asked, "Is everyone ready now?" When they'd agreed, he brought them all to the room he'd found Julian in before. The entrance of his home, he imagined.

"Paige!" Julian called.

A minute later, the red-haired woman came down the stairs, smiling brightly when she saw her husband. She rushed to him and threw her arms around him, not hesitating to kiss him.

Vazi rolled his eyes to the ceiling until someone cleared their throat, breaking the couple apart.

"Sorry," Paige said, still holding Julian. "I'm glad everyone is all right."

"It's not over yet," Julian warned her. "And we're going to have more company."

Paige's brow furrowed. "Who?"

"Shouldn't be anyone you haven't met yet. Wade and Samara, Evane and Suni, and some people from Lemuria."

She nodded slowly. "Now?"

Julian glanced at Sophia, who hesitated before shaking her head. "Not all, no. I don't know about the others, but I still feel like I'm dragging. I think we'll all plan better after some rest and recover."

Olivia shook her head. "We might not recover. Or more specifically, Vazi, Sophia, and Lucas might not."

Vazi narrowed his eyes at her. "What do you mean?"

"Oh," Sophia breathed. "I'd forgotten about that."

"Forgotten about what?" Vazi asked, starting to lose his patience.

"Sergei and I were getting infected by the Miasma—it was in the aquifer," Olivia explained. "One of our other people was severely infected. Sergei realized it wasn't metabolizing and didn't leave the body by natural means. We ended up having to use a relic and Sergei's healing to get it out of us."

"Except it didn't last with Lachlan," Lucas pointed out.

"Not necessarily," she argued. "He was out of contact with us for a while. He could have been reinfected. It wouldn't have taken much."

"True."

"Well, that's fantastic," Julian muttered. "What kind of relic? I can heal—to an extent—but I don't have any relics that might do that."

"I actually still have it," Olivia said with a smile, pulling a golden tyet out of one of the pockets on the side of her thigh.

"Vazi, can you sense the Oskila we might have inhaled?" Sophia asked.

Vazi closed his eyes and searched his own body, displeased when he did find something foreign. To be thorough, he checked the others as well. There was something akin to a residue on Julian, Olivia, and Erasmus, but nothing inside them like he found within Lucas and Sophia. "I can. And Olivia was correct. Those of us who were in the chamber have something inside us. The others are basically clear."

"Let's see if your healing and the tyet can fix them, too," Olivia told Julian.

Julian nodded, and Sophia walked over to them, offering her hands to them after she'd removed her gloves. Vazi cocked his head and watched as they worked their magic. Surprisingly, when they drew back, Sophia was clean. She had the same residue as the others, but it was more like a lingering scent than anything. He wasn't sure it would have worked if they'd inhaled anymore of the Oskila. For that matter, he wasn't sure how any relic had worked.

"It works," he assured them, and they were quick to repeat the process with Lucas and himself.

"I don't know what's going on, and I'm not sure I want to, so I'm going to go put on some tea and order some food," Paige said, smiling uncertainly at them before she retreated further into the house.

"If I'm going to keep a handle on the weather while you five recover, I'll need to focus elsewhere. I know you said you don't want everyone here yet, but I'll bring the Lemurians now. I do want to be here while you plan, but I can catch up if I need to," Vazi told them. "Just call out to me when you're ready to start planning, and I'll be back as soon as I can."

"We will," Sophia told him. "And thank you."

Not wanting her thanks—not now anyway—he popped back to Lemuria. To his surprise, everyone he was meant to collect was in Tempest's home. Everyone plus two additions. Aelia and a vampire named Logan who had only come to Lemuria a month before. He didn't seem to be a bad guy, but Vazi hadn't spent much time with him. Aelia, on the other hand, was an impressive woman. Technically human, she was almost as old as Tempest, and arguably just as powerful. She was also the reason why any Lemurians were currently both alive and awake. If it weren't for her, Tempest likely would have been killed, Seth would still be mortal, and Vazi would still be slumbering.

"If you aren't going to help Seth and the others, speak up now or you're going regardless," Vazi ordered, but his voice softened when he looked at Tempest. "Except you, of course. You just rest and take care of that baby." The child she carried would be the first new Lemurian in thousands of years. Everyone was more than a little protective of them both.

"I'm too big to do anything else at this point," Tempest complained. "Especially if it involves trying to get out of this chair or a bed without someone to pull me to my feet."

Vazi chuckled and walked over to her, kissing the top of her head. "Liar. You can use your power to get up."

"Yeah, but my power can't rub my feet," she said, pouting.

"Seth will, as soon as he comes back."

"Any idea when that's going to happen?"

"Two days, I hope." Unless everything went extremely wrong.

"We're all going," Kara told Vazi when he turned back to them. "Logan offered, and he could be a help."

"You do know the goal is as few casualties as possible, right?" Vazi asked the vampire.

Logan nodded. "I do. That's not a problem."

Vazi studied his face for a second, then nodded. "Be safe while we're gone, Tempest," he said before he took them all to Julian's house. As soon as they were all present, he retreated to Thelaria, the home of the Lemurian gods. Which, since Seth insisted on living on Lemuria with his wife, meant he was its sole occupant. A fact he would never cease resenting.

Chapter 15

Everyone was still in the entry of Julian's house when Vazi returned, dropping off four people Lucas had never met. Despite Julian's assurances, it made him a little itchy. It didn't help that Vazi disappeared before making any introductions. It made no sense that he actually liked the guy, but put that aside to study the strangers who had come to help the Athenaeum.

There were two men and two women. One of the men was about Lucas's height, with shaggy black hair, blue eyes, and a muscular build. Hopefully, they weren't muscles earned solely for aesthetics. They needed people who would actually be useful in a fight. The other man was an inch or two shorter, with blonde hair cut shorter on the sides. This one had a lean build, more like a swimmer than a fighter, but Lucas knew looks could be deceiving. And he noticed the guy stayed well away from the windows, making him wonder if they'd brought a vampire.

The first woman was of average height, with brown hair pulled into a ponytail. Her skin was tanned, and she had unusual eyes he could best describe as hazel, but that wasn't quite right. He just didn't have the right word to name the color. It was the other woman who made him stop and narrow his eyes. He knew that face, but he would wager an extremely large sum of money he'd met her before. It only took a minute before he realized how he knew her, and it worried him.

"I saw a statue of you in the Hall of Records," he said, taking a step closer to Sophia. If this woman had been around that long ago, she wasn't a normal woman, which meant she was probably dangerous.

The woman cocked her head and frowned. "The Hall of Records?" she asked. Her confusion sounded genuine, but he wasn't sure he trusted it. Though he had to admit there were cases where genetics resulted in near twins across generations, he doubted that was the case now. Besides, it would have been a lot of generations if that was what was happening here.

"What statue? I didn't see one that looked like her," Olivia said, stepping to Sophia's other side.

"Neither did I," Sophia said, but she had her gaze fixed on the woman's face. He wasn't surprised she hadn't noticed the statue, though, not with the mood she'd been in.

"On the first floor. It was outside of the bedroom we stayed in. Far side from the door to the central room," Lucas answered without looking away from the woman.

The woman went still and her face went completely blank. "Describe this Hall of Records."

"Perhaps I should make introductions," Erasmus said quickly as he inserted himself between the group from Lemuria and the group from the Athenaeum. Looking at the Lemurians, he started gesturing to people as he named them. "This is Sophia, my granddaughter, Lucas, her boyfriend and the head of the Athenaeum's security, and Olivia, also from the Athenaeum." He turned to do the same in reverse. "Sophia, this is Aelia. I've known her for many years, though I sadly only met her in person a few months ago. The other woman is Kara, who is Seth's best friend. He," he pointed to the black-haired man, "is Aaron, who was Seth's longtime professional rival until they settled on Lemuria." He paused, then added, "I'm afraid I haven't met their companion."

"Logan," the leaner of the two men answered. "And I've only been on Lemuria for a month, so you wouldn't have met me."

"Erasmus, what Hall are they talking about?" Aelia asked, sounding like she was fighting back some strong emotion.

"One we recently found that at the very least rivals the Athenaeum, and could potentially surpass it when it comes to texts. Apparently, its original name was Sozu."

"Sozu," Aelia said at the same time he did.

"How did you know that?" Sophia asked, glancing at her grandfather, then back to Aelia.

Aelia blew out a breath, looking uncomfortable. Aaron stepped closer, partially moving in front of her. It was, Lucas realized, the same move he often made with Sophia. Aaron whispered something to her, but she shook her head. "No, it's okay. They have a right to ask. I just...I didn't know anyone else alive had ever been there."

"You've been there?" Olivia asked.

Aelia nodded, her face full of sorrow. "I have, yes. Many times. Though I've only returned twice since Lemuria sank."

"What do you mean? Wasn't Lemuria lost thousands of years ago? How could you have been to the Hall before Lemuria sank?" Sophia asked. Lucas had to admit he had mixed feelings about her sounding so suspicious. Not trusting everyone was a good trait to have, but it also made him a little sad that she was losing so much of her innocence. He could punch Peter for that alone, and found the desire to do so almost overwhelming.

Aelia glanced at Aaron and Kara. It was Aaron who shrugged and said, "You don't know most of these people. You don't owe them anything." Kara just rubbed Aelia's shoulder comfortingly.

"I owe them a little, if this problem involved going to Sozu for a solution," she corrected before turning to Erasmus. "I was apprenticed to the one who built the Hall, as you call it. Not for long, since the war happened only about a year later. But something happened—no, I will not tell you what—that led to me having...an increased lifespan."

"Seriously? We didn't need to go under the Sphinx to get to that place?" Olivia muttered.

Lucas nearly missed the tiny smile on Aelia's lips. "I'm sorry," she added directly after, and sounded sincere. "If I had known you had an issue that severe, especially with Erasmus involved, I would have offered to help. But what is it that we're dealing with? From what I've heard of the Athenaeum, it should have at least a little about everything you could possibly want to know."

Sophia didn't answer right away, and Lucas touched her lower back gently, which made her sigh and speak. "I won't get into all the details until everyone is here, but...If you were in the Hall multiple times, did you come across anything about Miasma?"

That caused the first unguarded expression on Aelia's face; shock. "Miasma?" She sighed and shook her head. "I...I know it's one of the oldest things in the universe and that it acts like a sentient infection. There were rumors that it could be controlled, but only with extreme difficulty."

"Did you ever read of any way that the infection could be cured?" Erasmus asked.

Aelia shook her head slowly. "No, but everything there was written by the one who taught me, and those he taught. We could only document what we learned, and there wasn't exactly a lot of experimentation on Miasma. And I have to say, while I'm still willing to help, I'm more than a little terrified that this situation involves Miasma."

"Trust me, you're not alone in that," Sophia muttered.

"Anyone want to explain what this Miasma bullshit is?" Kara asked.

"One of the five elements that help make up all of creation. It's basically violence contained within a pool," Aelia explained.

"We'll explain more tomorrow. Vazi brought you all early so he can focus on making sure the world isn't destroyed with earthquakes and hurricanes before we can stop it," Lucas added. "We just got back from getting another one of those five elements and are wiped. Without some downtime, we'll be next to useless."

"First, you'll have tea and something to eat," Paige said as she came out of the kitchen. "Food should be here in a few minutes, and if you don't relax a little before you sleep, you won't rest as well."

Lucas wanted to argue, as he could still feel the weight of the Oskila, but Sophia nodded, and he knew how much all this was bothering her. A few minutes spent with food and distraction wouldn't be a bad thing.

They followed Paige into the dining room, where she had an honest to god tea service, along with enough cups for everyone. She glanced at Julian, nothing more, and he turned around and went back the way they'd come while she started serving tea. It took only one sniff to recognize it as some sort of chamomile blend. Not that they really needed any further relaxation, but it might soothe the mind as well as the body. And while he wasn't much of a tea drinker, he wasn't going to turn down Paige's hospitality, especially not with them taking her husband away on a very dangerous trip.

Lucas scented the pizza Julian brought back before he ever saw the man and the five boxes he was carrying. That was all he needed to realize he was starving. The protein bars and freeze-dried meals provided calories, but they'd burned quite a few trekking through the Alaskan cave. Pizza, on the other hand, was the food of the gods.

Once everyone had access to the pizza, the Nasaru—and Julian—all dug in like starving wolves, just with better manners. The Lemurians grabbed a few slices, but were more civilized about it.

"How long have you guys lived on Lemuria?" Sophia asked when she was done with her first slice and transferring a second from the box.

"About seven months for most of us," Aaron said with a shrug. "A month for Logan."

"What's it like, living on a mythical continent?"

"What's it like living in a mythical library?"

Sophia inclined her head to him, though Lucas was sure she was dying to ask to visit. Not that he thought she had anything to worry about. If—when—they pulled this off, Seth would likely give her most anything within his power. And he had taken Erasmus already, so it wasn't like outsiders were forbidden.

"I know you said you don't want to go into details until others arrive, but how serious is this situation?" Aelia asked.

"It's very serious," Sophia said, setting the slice down with only one bite taken out of it. Instead, she sipped at the tea. "There are seven gods working on this with us, including Vazi and Seth. Let's just say that you really, really want to help us come up with a good plan."

"I had a feeling that was the case," Aelia said, nodding. "Who else is coming?"

"After we get some rest, I'm going to get the twins, Wade, and Suni," Julian answered. "We'll have Seth and Vazi, of course. If we're lucky, Evane and Samara can get their mother on board as well."

"The twins?" Lucas asked.

"Ah, yes. It is probably better you three know now, so you can adjust," Erasmus said, shifting uncomfortably in his chair.

Lucas narrowed his eyes as he glanced between Erasmus and Julian. "Adjust to what?"

"The fact that they're demons," Julian said bluntly.

"Demons?" Olivia asked, sounding as pleased as Lucas felt.

"What he doesn't say is that they are the twin children of a goddess who was forced to become a demon, and that they're nothing like demons you've read about," Kara said, rolling her eyes. "I've met them. They're a little archaic, and can absolutely be lethal in a fight, but they're not evil, monstrous people."

"Have you met them?" Sophia asked Erasmus.

"I have, and I agree with Kara," he answered. "And before you ask, because I know you will," he said, smiling, "their mother is Echidna."

"The mother of monsters? And you say they're not monstrous?" she asked, doubt in every syllable.

"Don't believe all the propaganda Zeus puts out there about people," Aaron said darkly.

Sophia frowned in obvious confusion, but said nothing. Lucas knew her well enough to know she was processing that and trying to read between the lines. He didn't blame her. Even he had heard of Echidna. More than that, he also knew the reputation of demons. The Arcane had a group whose sole purpose was to eliminate any demons who came to Earth, and for good reason. They tended to make Peter's particular brand of crazy look normal. Which made him wonder if the Hunters knew about these twins.

None of that mattered when he saw Sophia try to hide a yawn. He finished the last of his pizza, and was even polite enough to drink the rest of his tea before he pushed his chair back. "I think it's time we started on the resting portion of the afternoon. Could one of you point us to where we'll be sleeping?"

"Absolutely," Paige said, rising immediately. "Erasmus, Olivia, what about the two of you?"

"I would honestly love that," Erasmus admitted, while Olivia only nodded.

Paige led the way up the stairs, showing Erasmus and Olivia to rooms across from one another. Lucas expected to get the next room, but Paige led them to the far end of the hallway, putting a good six rooms between them. "I thought you might like some privacy," she said, smiling as she opened the door and gestured inside. "There's a bathroom, too. I can probably find some clothes for you, Sophia, and I'll see if Julian has some that will fit you, Lucas. If I do, I'll leave them outside the door."

"Thank you. I definitely need a shower," Sophia said, nodding.

"Absolutely. Sleep well," Paige said, shutting the door after they were both inside.

Sleep wasn't going to be the problem, Lucas knew, especially for Sophia. The nightmares were.

Chapter 16

As soon as the door was closed, Sophia started for the bathroom, ignoring the fabulous bedroom full of antique furniture. The coat was stripped off and dropped, followed quickly by her shirt, then her bra. Normally she wasn't so sloppy, but she wanted to shower off Alaska almost as much as she wanted to reclaim the Athenaeum. She paused at the door to bend down and unlace her boots, shoving them off while she undid her pants.

"You feel that dirty?" Lucas asked, following her at a more sedate pace, though she heard his clothes coming off, too.

"I haven't showered since we realized the aquifer was tainted," she explained as she shimmied out of her pants and underwear. "Yeah, I bathed in the Hall, but it's not the same as a shower. Besides, after that we went hiking through Alaska and spelunking in a mystical cave. And sure, Vazi cleaned the Oskila off of us, but it's like I can still feel it on me. So yeah, I feel that dirty," she told him over her shoulder before she turned the water on. Later she might be charmed by the large claw-foot tub that had been turned into a shower, but right now all she cared about was the hot water and soap it held.

"So you won't be doing much venator work when we get the Athenaeum back, huh?" he teased as she tested the water, waiting for it to heat up.

"Oh no, you're not tricking me that easily. I know half the venatores stay in cities. Auctions, private sales, and things like that." But she was pretty sure she'd been turned off of real field world for the foreseeable future.

She stepped into the shower and sighed as the hot water slid over her skin. And though she'd love to just stay like that for an hour, she wasn't sure how much longer her body had before she was forced to sleep. After wetting her hair, she grabbed the shampoo and stepped back so Lucas could get under the water. The shampoo was more floral than she normally went for, but it wasn't bad, and as long as it got her hair clean, she wouldn't complain.

"True," he admitted as he stepped in. "But honestly, no one would blame you if you didn't go on retrievals. Most aspides don't, or at least not often. I think Erasmus has only been on retrievals three or four times since I joined the Athenaeum."

She only nodded, and the rest of the shower was spent in silence as they alternated who was under the water and who was washing. It was one of the few times where they'd kept their hands off each other, and Sophia had to wonder if it was exhaustion, stress, or something else. Lucas might be a gargoyle, but he was definitely not cold-blooded.

Sophia got out and dried off, but when she checked, she realized Paige hadn't yet brought any clothes, and she couldn't bring herself to put her dirty clothes back on, so she wrapped a towel around her and sat on the beautiful four-poster bed as she started to dry her hair. She dimly realized Lucas had done much the same, though his towel was wrapped around his hips. While she should be taking in the sight of his damp skin and hard muscles, she found herself frowning at the floor as she wondered if they could do this.

Aelia had been around since the time of Lemuria and actually studied in the Hall of Records, but she didn't know of a cure. Grovek had only theorized about the Oskila helping, so they might be walking into the metaphorical gunfight with a knife. And what if the Oskila did worse than not help, and just put them in that overly relaxed state while the infected were hyped up on the Miasma? It could be a massacre. One in which she'd lose everyone she cared about, on top of those she was responsible for.

Lucas sat beside her and pulled her onto his lap, into his arms. "Stop."

"Stop what?" she asked, letting herself lean into him.

"Doubting. You're doing a great job in a shitty situation, so snap out of it."

"Easier said than done," she muttered. "You do realize how bad a situation we're in, right?"

"I do, but stressing isn't going to help. Hell, it could make matters worse. You keep worrying about the worst-case scenario, then when we get back to the Athenaeum, you'll be distracted. Distractions during a fight—and this will be a fight—can get you killed. I'm going to be royally pissed if you get killed."

He wasn't wrong. She might not have been in the military and sure as hell wasn't a guard, but even she knew he was right. "Do you really think the Oskila is the answer?"

"I don't know," he admitted with a shrug. "Maybe it is, but we're dealing with stuff no mortal should even think of fucking with. I don't even think the gods should be dealing with this stuff. If the creators—whatever you want to call them—had been smart, they would have destroyed this stuff or sealed it away. Caves can, obviously, be gotten into. I won't be upset when I can go back to normal guarding and security. I'm not cut out for this end of the world crap."

"Neither am I."

He shrugged and tightened his arms around her. "I don't know about that. I don't think you've been doing a bad job. Besides, you really should be more optimistic. And that's not a suggestion, by the way," he said firmly.

She leaned back and narrowed her eyes at him. "It's not? Aren't I supposed to be the one giving you orders? I assume I am still aspida, anyway."

He gave her a grin that promised many things, and all of them wicked. "You are, but if we don't stop Peter and save the world, then things won't calm down enough so I can propose."

Sophia laughed and shook her head. "Yeah, right. Save the world so you can propose?" This was a new tactic for him. Sometimes he went with supportive, but most of the time, his pep talks were sharp, meant to snap her out of a funk. Humor wasn't so much his thing, though he could be funny at times. Then again, this could kind of be another way of snapping her to reality. Shocking enough to be effective.

Except he wasn't laughing. The grin had even left his face, leaving him looking as serious as she'd ever seen him. Her laughter died, and she cocked her head as she studied his face, looked into his eyes. His expression now caused flutters of nerves and something more pleasant in her belly. "You're serious."

Lucas nodded and rubbed a hand slowly up and down her back. "I am. I love you, Sophia, you know that. And no, we haven't been together long, but I'm not an indecisive man. I'm also not the sort of man to ignore something just because it might not be manly to admit it. I love you, and whether you're aspida or I'm head of your security, I don't plan on going anywhere. I want to marry you. I want to wake up every morning with you beside me, and go to sleep every night with you in my arms. One day I want us to talk about family. I want to take you to some of the places you've always wanted to see, for pleasure, rather than to save the world. I want to take care of you and love you. Is any of that really so hard to believe?"

Sophia couldn't speak for a moment. She'd heard of people getting choked up, but had never really experienced it before. It took her two tries before she shook her head and said, "I do know you love me. And no, it isn't so hard to believe." And she realized this might be the last night they would have before more people invaded Julian's house and they lost the privacy they had. As much as she fought for optimism, it might be the last night they'd ever have together, and she didn't want to waste it. She sure as hell didn't want to waste the emotions quickening her pulse.

Twisting in his arms, she straddled him, letting the towel slide down to her waist, baring her breasts, and she didn't care when the bottom of it rode up to her hips. It wasn't like she intended to be covered for long. She wrapped her arms around him and crushed her mouth to his. She tried to convey everything she was feeling in that kiss; her hope, her fear, the nervous anticipation, her appreciation for everything he'd done to help her get to where she was now. And, of course, the ever-growing love she felt for him.

His response was immediate. Groaning against her mouth, his hands cupped her towel-covered butt and pulled her hips in tight against his, so she could feel how quickly he hardened beneath her. Almost immediately, he lifted her so she was up on her knees, tearing his own towel off and letting hers fall to the floor. When he pulled her down again, it was to feel flesh against flesh, and she shivered with excitement as the kiss broke. It didn't matter whether they made love or fucked, whether there was foreplay or not. He never failed to leave her feeling both satisfied and cherished. Still, she had a feeling tonight was going to be different, but in an amazing way.

Lucas stood, taking her with him, and she wrapped her legs around his waist, moaning as his cock pressed fully against her. Even better, when he walked, he rubbed against her, bumping her clit with each step. She had no idea where he was going, and she didn't care. They hadn't really done anything yet, but she couldn't recall ever being this turned on in her life.

He stopped and set her on the edge of the dresser, then urged her legs wider. A hand dipped between them and he sank two fingers into her without warning, making her gasp and cling to his shoulders. She tried to pull him closer, and he resisted...for two seconds. The kiss he gave her demanded, it took, and when she gave everything, it was returned just as intensely.

Sliding his fingers out of her, he dragged the head of his shaft against her folds, then pressed into her. She expected hard and fast, but instead felt a slow, sensual joining of his body with hers. He didn't stop until he was buried inside her, then he went wild, giving her the fast, hard, and deep she'd been expecting. It shot her from extremely aroused to feeling the sharp press of an orgasm starting to bear down on her.

It was more intense than anything else she'd experienced, and all she could do was hold on to him and ride it out.

With her seated on the dresser, it rocked the piece of furniture, heavy though it was. A fact she didn't notice until the mirror started to bang against the wall each time he slammed into her. She might not have even noticed then, except it seemed to annoy him, as he glared at the mirror. After urging one leg to wrap around him, he lifted her off the dresser. Her other leg fell without the dresser to support them, but he didn't go far, simply turning, taking three steps, and pressing her back firmly against the wall. She was at just the right height to touch the floor with her foot, though she was on her toes. It might cause some discomfort later, but she right now she didn't give a damn.

His hips pinned hers, and he dropped a hand to her raised thigh to balance and support her. His other hand to pulled her arms from around his neck, grabbed both her wrists, and pressed them against the wall above her head. For all intents and purposes, she was trapped, yet she didn't feel that way. No, she felt protected and desired in a way she never had before. He'd been demanding in bed before, he'd even gone a little wild when she'd driven him crazy, but this was somehow different.

With no other way to encourage him, she leaned her head forward for a kiss. He allowed it for a moment before drawing back and pressing his hips forward to grind against her. She gasped and threw her head back against the wall, her eyes closing before he growled. Her eyes flew open and he shook his head once, a clear demand that she not do that again. When she kept her gaze on his, he finally started to move again.

She moaned as he slid into her over and over again, holding back only enough to avoid hurting her. Unable to touch him, to kiss him, she could only rock her hips forward to meet his thrusts, but soon she found herself trembling with the force of the sensations building inside her.

As if he knew just how close she was, he captured her lips for another kiss just before she came, muffling her cry of pleasure and responding with a low groan of his own. And he didn't stop. He pounded into her through her orgasm, kissing her just as fiercely, so it felt like the climax went on forever. He'd given her amazing orgasms before, but something about this one felt more intense, more important. Knowing he wanted to marry her probably had a lot to do with it. That was her last thought before her brain shut off, so she acted purely on instinct, returning his kiss as she rocked against him, desperate to prolong the pleasure for even one more second.

It left her legs weak, and even pinned, it wasn't easy for her to help support herself. She tried, not wanting this to end, not just yet, but again it was almost like he could read her mind, because he released her wrists and pulled her away from the wall. It meant he had to draw out of her, but he wasn't done with her yet, thank the gods. He half carried her to the bed and fell onto it with her. Almost immediately, he was back inside her, hooking a hand behind one of her knees to draw it up against his side.

This time, he didn't stop her from touching him. Though she loved running her hands over his warm flesh and hard muscles, she had to hold on to him instead of teasing or caressing. After the orgasm he'd given her, she didn't have the energy to do anything else. One hand grabbed his bicep while the other found his shoulder. But holding on to him didn't stop him, it didn't even slow him down. He thrust into her over and over until she came again, this time crying out to the ceiling as her body trembled and she clung to him.

She was still dealing with the aftershocks when his arm slid beneath her and he lifted, just as he sat back on his heels. The position drove him deeper, and she moaned, wrapping herself around him. It was more intimate, and she stared into his eyes as he lifted her, then used his strength and gravity to slam her down onto him again.

Nothing had been said since she first kissed him. There hadn't been any need for it, not when their bodies spoke more fluently than words ever could. She felt the urge now, though with her brain so foggy, she could only form the simplest of statements.

"I love you."

The groan vibrated from his chest into hers as he quickened his pace, and one hand lifted from her back to tangle in her hair. He tilted her head back, then pressed his lips against the side of her throat as she felt him drive into her once more before finally giving in to his own climax.

Sighing as she stroked her hands over his back, she let her eyes close as his mouth gentled on her skin, his lips trailing up to her jaw, then over to her lips. In direct contrast to the way he'd loved her, his kiss was tender and lazy. He held her carefully as he leaned them to the side, giving her time to move her legs, until they lay tangled with each other on the bed.

He stroked his hand over her cheek. "Just remember," he murmured, "I was being serious."

It took her a minute to remember what they had been talking about when she'd instigated their lovemaking, and by the time she had, his eyes were closed and his breathing had slowed and deepened.

Smiling, she cuddled a little closer and let her own eyes close. "So was I," she whispered.

Chapter 17

By the time they woke, Paige had left clothes for them. The tee-shirt fit Sophia perfectly, though the jeans were a little snug. Not that Lucas seemed to mind. When she'd put them on, he'd eyed her butt like he was considering whether they had enough time for another go in the sheets. Unfortunately, priorities meant they didn't, but she'd have to remember how much he liked her in tight jeans.

They found everyone in the kitchen, with Paige and Julian making breakfast. After everyone had eaten—and gotten at least one cup of coffee—Julian left to collect the rest of his volunteers. Sophia could admit she was a little nervous. Even with the people who had already agreed to help, it was a lot of strangers she was supposed to lead. At least with the current situation no one expected her to come up with all the plans by herself. It would absolutely be a team effort, especially considering the experience some of these people had. She was grateful for that.

When Julian returned, four people in tow, he quickly introduced everyone. The muscular blonde man with arms covered in tattoos was Wade, the bounty hunter and wolf shifter. The woman he had his arm around, Samara, was a few inches taller than Sophia, with long black hair and black eyes. Her brother, Evane, was a much taller, more muscled version of her, though his hair only reached his shoulders. Sophia had to admit the twin's black eyes were a little off-putting. Or it could be that they were demons, and she'd never met one before. Heard of them, absolutely. Everyone in the Arcane had heard the stories, but other than the Hunters, she wasn't sure many had ever actually met one.

The last member of the group was a woman who could only be described as petite, with short, spiky black hair and the most intense blue eyes Sophia had ever seen. Where the demons had a dangerous aura, Suni gave off one of comfort and warmth. Since Sophia had heard many stories about Suni's healing, she expected that was the cause. Most healers had a soothing aura. It was part of their magic. Those like Julian, who only had some healing magic, didn't have that extra, though Sophia wasn't sure where the line was between someone who could heal and someone who was a healer.

"Suni!" Erasmus said warmly, rising and moving to take the healer's hands. "I know I've said it before, but I must thank you again for the mithridate."

"Ah...Is that how you're alive when I'd heard more than one rumor that you'd died?" Suni asked, accepting Erasmus's hands, though she looked thrown, her eyes wide, her voice distracted.

"Oh, yes. I apologize for that," he said, glancing at Sophia before he returned his focus to the tiny witch. "It is, yes, and I'm truly sorry for the deception. It was necessary."

"She cried," Evane said darkly.

"Again, I apologize," Erasmus said contritely.

While he'd been greeting Suni, Wade and Samara had been saying hi to Paige, with the wolf giving her a tight hug that lifted her off her feet as he let out a whoop. It seemed she'd told him about her pregnancy.

Once everyone had calmed down, they moved into the parlor where there was more space, and they sat down to plan. Unfortunately, in this case, it was up to her to begin.

"First, I want to thank all of you for coming to help," she said, looking at each person as she did. "Second, while I know you're all trustworthy, I do have to ask that you not reveal any of what I'm about to say to anyone who doesn't go with us." They all promised without hesitation, and Sophia took a deep breath to explain what was going on, before she realized Seth should probably be in on the planning. And Vazi had asked to be informed as well. "One moment," she told them, closing her eyes and mentally calling out to Seth.

It took only the space of three breaths before he appeared, with another god in tow. Not Vazi this time, but one she recognized from the statues in the entrance hall of the Athenaeum. Athena. Fitting that he'd bring her, since she was the goddess of wisdom and warcraft. Who better to help plan what was essentially going to be a battle?

There were more greetings to Seth, though they were more subdued. Perhaps they'd realized the severity of the situation, or maybe it was the presence of a goddess none of them truly knew personally. Aside from Erasmus, because he seemed quite familiar with the patron.

Sophia took another moment to call out to Vazi, but he didn't respond. He had said he might be late, so she didn't worry too much. Maybe her mind went to horrible thoughts of all the weather he was trying to prevent, but she didn't let herself dwell on it.

Again she took a deep breath, but this time there was nothing that would allow her to stall any longer. "I don't know how much any of you know about any of this, so I'm going to act like none of you know anything, just so I don't miss any details," she began. "Some of us," she motioned to Lucas, Olivia, and Erasmus, "live and work in the Athenaeum, which is an ancient library and collection of relics. Some time ago—we don't know long—one of our own started using a substance called Miasma to infect the rest of the people in the Athenaeum." She went on to explain what the Miasma was, what they'd learned about it, and about the Oskila. That was when Seth jumped in.

"Peter—the one infecting people—has closed the Athenaeum off so even Athena and I can't get inside," he explained. "Problem is, the Miasma is going to want to keep infecting people, and could easily take over the world, especially with Peter having access to everything inside the Athenaeum. And just to point out how serious it is, the extreme weather that's been seen around the world? We're almost positive it's his fault, though we aren't sure how he's doing it."

Erasmus nodded. "The Athenaeum has relics more powerful than can normally be found out in the world, and magic that hasn't been seen in hundreds, if not thousands of years. So it could be a number of things, or several things being used in conjunction with one another."

"When you say take over the world, what exactly do you mean?" Wade asked. His pose was casual—leaned back, arm around Sam, one foot propped on the opposite knee—but Sophia could see his body wasn't as relaxed as his tone might suggest.

Sophia smiled sadly. "To give you just one example, in about a week, this infection turned my mom against me. And when I said turned her against me, I mean she was part of a mob that tried to kill me, Lucas, and Olivia. And there wasn't a hint of hesitation in her. She wasn't the only one, either. Everyone in the Athenaeum—which is a few dozen people—was infected, other than the four of us. And if he infected another water source, he could infect hundreds or thousands more in a very short period of time."

His jaw tightened and he nodded. "So why exactly are we here? From what you've said, we can't do shit about the Miasma. You want us to go in and kill this guy who's infecting everyone?"

"No!" The word burst out of Sophia before she could temper her reaction. It caused a few raised brows, and she inhaled slowly before shaking her head. "No, not if we don't have to. That guy is my cousin. I'd prefer we imprison him if at all possible. And the others? They're infected, so none of what's going on is their fault. I want them knocked out and restrained until we can cure them of the Miasma infection."

"That's why you wanted so many of us?" Kara asked. "Having greater numbers gives you more options for getting through all those people and to your cousin?"

"That's part of it," Sophia agreed. "The Oskila we collected should help calm them, and might even help with the infection, but we're not positive about that. It may do nothing."

Lucas rubbed her arm lightly and added on to what she'd said. "The main goals are to reclaim the Athenaeum and stop Peter before he can either cause more destruction with the weather magic or infect more with the Miasma. If we can't do that, then the alternative is completely destroying the Athenaeum and *hoping*," he emphasized the word, "that it'll also stop the Miasma from spreading any further than it already has."

"What are we looking at as far as defenses go?" Evane asked. "You said an impenetrable ward—and I hope you've got an idea of how to get through that—but what kind of structure is it, how many people are we looking at dealing with, and how are they armed?"

Sophia glanced at Lucas and he answered. "No idea on the ward. That's not the sort of magic I deal with. But the structure itself can be both blessing and curse. It's basically a small underground city. There's a cave opening, a labyrinth, then several levels of carved out hallways and rooms, with stairs leading between them. Weaponry? There's enough there to arm several hundred people if necessary, and most of them don't really need it. We've got talented witches, shifters, elementals... Most Arcane races are represented there, actually. And there isn't a one of them that doesn't know at least some sorcery."

Logan frowned. "How many should we expect to find?"

"If it's just the people we left there, we're looking at about thirty people, so we're outnumbered," Lucas admitted.

"Yeah, but you'll have me, Vazi, and Athena going in with you," Seth told him. "And while we're in there, Thoth, Mimir, Hecate, and Isis are going to be on the outside, containing anything that comes out, while doing their best to keep the weather fairly normal."

"How narrow are the hallways?" Sam asked. "Are we going to be fighting in close quarters? Because if we're outnumbered and trying to keep the deaths to a minimum, that's going to make it more difficult."

"Not as wide as you're hoping," Erasmus answered. "Eight feet in most places, but the first two levels do have large open rooms. Including one just after the labyrinth and entrance."

They continued to ask questions and point out problems, with Olivia, Erasmus, and Lucas giving answers or counters. In all honesty, it was overwhelming. Sophia had never been part of a war council, and that's basically what this was. She didn't have the knowledge or experience to deal with tactics, and listening to the others talk about them made it all the more real. And pointed out where she was severely lacking.

She could sense the panic she'd felt upon being named aspida rising, so she whispered, "Be right back," to Lucas, borrowed her grandfather's phone, and went looking for a door outside. She needed some fresh air.

It took her a few minutes to find it, but ended up in a garden. The weather was actually nice for the moment, so she sat on a bench, closed her eyes, and just breathed until the worst of the building panic calmed. But it was a temporary solution. What she needed was advice from someone who wasn't a battle-hardened warrior, which everyone inside seemed to be.

Searching through the meager contact list on her grandfather's burner phone, she found the name she'd seen last time she'd borrowed his phone. Blanche. She really wished she had her own phone, but hit the call button and tried to relax. It only took Blanche a moment to answer.

"Hello?"

"Blanche? It's Sophia."

"Oh. Hi, I didn't recognize the number."

"It's not my phone," she explained. "I borrowed my grandfather's phone." As soon as the words were out, she realized Blanche wasn't in the know about that. "Oh, right. You know how you said he wasn't in the Underworld?"

"I do…"

"That's because he faked his death with the help of at least one god," Sophia said, unable to keep the bitterness out of her voice.

"Uh…huh. Yeah, that does explain a few things. But why don't you sound happy about that?"

Sophia grimaced and shook her head, even if Blanche couldn't see it. "I am happy. I get to actually get to know him now, and spend time with him, but I'm also pissed that he faked his death—very realistically and in front of me—and besides that, I'm in a hell of a lot of trouble."

"Wow. Didn't see any of that coming." There was a slight rustling, like she was getting settled. "Okay, what's going on?"

For the next ten minutes, Sophia found herself detailing basically everything that had happened since the last time she'd spoken to Blanche. The woman had been to the Athenaeum and was married to Death, so there was no real point in trying to hide things from her. Besides, she considered the woman a friend, despite having only met her face to face once and spoken to her a few times afterward.

She wrapped up her explanation and rant with, "And I just don't know how we're going to do this. There are at least thirty people in there, armed with sorcery, their natural magic, and a few thousand years worth of relics, and we've got about fifteen. We also don't have any guaranteed way of dealing with the Miasma. People are going to die, Blanche, and I just don't want that. I don't even want Peter dead, but there's no guarantee the Oskila will be any help at all. And worse, because I've never been in anything like this, I don't have anyone else I can call in who can be trusted not to abuse the Athenaeum when this is all over. Basically everyone who's helping was called by someone else. Seth has some of his Lemurians, and Julian brought in some of his friends."

"That's a lot," Blanche admitted. "First thing, I want you to breathe. Second, who all is there to help?" Sophia rattled off the names, leaving Paige out since she would likely be staying home. If Julian didn't want her going to Egypt or Alaska, he sure as hell wasn't going to be okay with his pregnant wife risking Miasma infection. Sophia wouldn't be okay with her going, either. "Okay, I know most of them—or at least of them—and they're good people to have at your back. I'd offer to help, but I'm not much of a fighter, and almost all my powers revolve around death. Since you don't want people to die, I should stay out of it. Same goes for Death. He could drop everyone there in an instant, and honestly, he probably would if I told him what was going on."

That thought chilled her, and she prayed that Blanche wouldn't tell her husband. Not yet, anyway. "If we can't stop Peter, and destroying the Athenaeum doesn't kill him, then that might be what we need," Sophia said quietly, hating that she had to say that.

"You're not there yet, but if you let me know before you head in, and I don't hear from you within, I don't know, a day after that, I'll check it out. If the worst has happened, I'll ask Death to take care of Peter."

Sophia wasn't sure Death could kill someone in control of the Miasma, but she appreciated having a backup plan, even if it was a horrible one. "Thank you."

"You're welcome. But just because Death and I can't come doesn't mean I don't know anyone who could help. It's a couple trustworthy enough that Death had them hold on to his scythe for a while, and Julian's actually met them. I can call and see if they can help out, and give them this number if they are."

"They're good in a fight?"

"Again, they had Death's scythe for a while. That thing can do more damage than all the relics in the Athenaeum," Blanche explained, and she sounded like she meant it. Sophia could believe it. "Anyone who's protecting something like that isn't going to be helpless."

"Good point. Yes, please ask them."

"I will. Remember, let me know when you head back to the Athenaeum, or I'm going to assume the worst. And good luck."

"Thank you."

Sophia hung up and tried to decide if she felt better or not. The thought of two more people was good, but part of her resented that she'd just resigned Peter to death if she couldn't stop him. On the other hand, Miasma or not, one of the gods going in with them could probably kill him, too. And while it was a decision she hated having to make, if it was a choice between Peter or the billions of other people on the planet, she had to choose the billions.

Being in charge really, really sucked.

"Sophia?"

Turning, she saw Paige standing a few feet away, a concerned look furrowing her brow. "Paige, hi. Sorry, I just needed to get away for a few minutes."

Paige smiled faintly and nodded, walking over to her. "I know. Empath," she explained, sitting on the other side of the bench. "Not that it takes an empath to know you're in quite the difficult situation.

Anyone would be upset, especially if they felt responsible because they were the boss."

"It's not just that. Them?" Sophia gestured toward the house. "They've all been in situations like this. Maybe not on this scale, but they just dove into tactics and defenses and stuff. A month ago I was a grad student studying history and language. This is so far out of my comfort zone, it isn't funny."

Paige nodded understandingly. "I was in a similar situation not that long ago. Not world ending, but dealing with traps set by the gods, and fending off assassins sent by them as well."

"Oh shit. I'm sorry. You must hate having gods in your house, then." She hadn't even asked if Paige minded the invasion, with or without the gods.

But Paige shook her head. "I don't hate the gods. Not all of them, anyway. There's one I'm quite fond of, in fact, and I've never had any issues with Seth or Vazi. But I think you need to have more faith in yourself, Sophia. I can't go—my talents are all mental, and it wouldn't be smart to go there with the baby—but I have a feeling that the world will still be here in a week. And mostly intact."

"Don't suppose one of those mental powers is prophecy, is it?" Sophia asked, smiling weakly, though she had to hope Paige had seen something.

"No, not prophecy," Paige answered, dashing that hope, "but that doesn't mean that feelings can't be accurate at times."

Sophia nodded, but after a moment, found herself admitting, "I'm scared, Paige. More scared than I've ever been in my life. And that includes when my cousin pushed me down a flight of stairs and strangled me."

Paige patted her knee. "Any sane person would be. But you're not running away from the problem, you're trying to solve it. Which is all anyone—sane or not—can do. And don't discount those people inside the house. They are fantastic people with some amazing talents and hearts bigger than you would expect. I think you'll all do better than you expect."

"How can you be so calm, knowing what's going on?"

Paige laughed and shrugged. "Because I have had a lot of practice processing emotions, since I'm all too often consumed by the emotions of others."

"Yeah, that'll do it." She turned the phone over when it rang and saw a number she didn't recognize. Blanche's friend? "Sorry, I need to take this."

"Of course. I'll be inside if you need me," Paige said, rising and heading back the way she came.

"Hello?"

"Is this Sophia?" a woman asked.

"It is."

"I'm Brigit, a friend of Blanche's. She said you're in a bind and could use another two swords. So to speak, anyway."

"I am and I absolutely could," Sophia said without hesitation. She might not know this woman, but everyone else who was helping was a stranger being vouched for by a friend, so why not two more? "Did she tell you the situation?"

"She did."

"And you're still willing to help?"

"I am."

Sophia closed her eyes and let herself smile a little. Something might be going right. "How soon can you get here? We're in England right now."

There was a bit of delay before she heard a man's voice, and not through the phone. "Now."

Her eyes flew open and she looked up at a man and woman. The man was about Lucas's height, but broader and even more muscled. His eyes were green, and his light-brown hair fell to his shoulder in soft waves. His mustache and beard were full, and the overall effect was one that said viking to Sophia. The woman was only a few inches shorter, and where he was muscular, she was curvy. Her skin was pale, which actually made her blue eyes look paler than Sophia thought they were. Her blonde hair was the longest she'd ever seen on anyone in person, reaching down to her butt—and that was with the dozen or so braids that were visible.

"Uh...Brigit?" Sophia asked, lowering the phone.

The woman smiled and nodded. "I am. And this is Rune."

Sophia slipped the phone into her pocket and rose. "Thank you both for coming, especially knowing what we're up against."

"Isn't that the best reason to come, though?" Brigit asked. "If you lose this fight, we all suffer, not just you. It only makes sense to help."

"I'm happy you feel that way. You ready to go inside and meet the others?"

"We'd love to."

Wondering what the group was going to think about these two last minute additions, she led the way.

Chapter 18

Lucas was starting to get worried. Sophia had been gone for a good half hour, but when he'd started to go after her a few minutes ago, Paige had intervened and asked him to let her go. He'd reluctantly agreed, but she had come back in a few minutes ago and Sophia hadn't. Paige didn't look concerned, but it didn't ease his mind.

Just before he got to his feet, she walked in, followed by a tall, curvaceous woman, and a powerfully-built man he'd never seen before. Eyes narrowing, he rose. "Sophia?" was all he said, keeping his gaze on the strangers.

She smiled tightly and looked around. "Everyone, this is Brigit and Rune. They're also going to help." Her eyes focused on him again. "Blanche vouched for them."

"As will I," Julian said, though he didn't sound as certain as Sophia did. "We met them a couple of months ago. Powerful, from what I could gather."

"Very powerful," Suni agreed in a murmur. "It's nice to see you both again."

"It's nice to see you as well. Everything worked out, I see," Brigit said, smiling as she sat on the arm of a chair, while Rune sat in the chair itself, his arm loosely looping around her waist.

"Yes, I suppose it did," Suni said, glancing at her husband.

Lucas wasn't sure what to think about these two, but with several trusted people accepting them, he didn't voice any protest.

"Have you figured anything out?" Sophia asked as she took the spot beside Lucas, leaning lightly into him.

"We were actually just discussing how best to use the Oskila," Lucas informed her. "That's really going to be the first step, so everyone inside will—hopefully—be less combative."

"Vazi can use his power to circulate the powder through the entire Athenaeum, so it should hit everyone inside," Seth said.

Athena shook her head. "I'm not sure he'll be able to, not with the wards. It wouldn't let us even see inside. Our powers basically stop at the edge of the ward, even ones that aren't physical. It might be different for him, but since we created the original wards, we also would have thought we could get through them easily."

"I have an idea about that," Aelia said, lips pursing. "The wards, I mean. I don't think you're going to like it, Lucas."

Lucas huffed softly. "I'm thinking you're probably right, but what is it?"

"Based on what everyone has said about the aspida and relationship to the Athenaeum, it's possible that Sophia may be able to breech the wards—"

The idea of Sophia being the only one of them inside the wards had Lucas's skin turning gray and a low growl slipping out, which caused Aelia to break off what she was saying. Except Sophia elbowed him not so gently. "Let's hear her out."

"I told you that you wouldn't like it," Aelia said with a shrug and sympathetic look. "Anyway. I know a spell that can dispel wards from the inside. It was meant to get rid of powerful ones that seemed impenetrable otherwise, which is exactly what we're dealing with here."

He hated to admit it, but it was probably the best plan they had. Even if Vazi could use his powers to circulate the Oskila, it didn't do them a damn bit of good if none of them could step foot inside.

Sophia leaned more fully against him and rested her hand on his thigh, no doubt realizing how hard it was for him to stay quiet. "How difficult is this spell?" she asked.

"It's not complicated, but that doesn't mean it's easy," Aelia confessed. "It needs a great deal of focus or it will backlash and you definitely won't be having a good time. And it needs a few things I don't currently have easy access to. Unless we have time for me to make a trip to Sozu."

Frowning, Seth asked, "Sozu?"

"Original name for the Hall of Records," Olivia supplied.

"It's real?" Athena asked, leaning forward in excitement, before she shook her head and reined herself in. "What does it need?"

Aelia hesitated a moment, blew out a breath, then answered. "Powdered dragon scale, and ash of a rowan tree."

"How many scales?" Athena asked while Lucas was thinking of the scales he'd seen when he visited the Athenaeum Vault just days before.

"Just one will do," Aelia told her.

"Dragons are real?" Sophia asked, and the shock was mirrored on the faces of several others.

"They are—or at least, they were," Aelia said, nodding. "They were Lemurian and hunted just as eagerly as the Lemurian people were."

"Very true, but I do happen to have a scale. I'll bring it when we're ready to go in. And the rowan tree ash won't be a problem either,"

Athena assured Aelia. "If all that does get us inside, I will be able to lead everyone through the labyrinth. Even if Peter has altered the magic, it's still my creation—or partly." Lucas wasn't as sure as that, as the entire Athenaeum was partly her creation, but he said nothing. They needed to hope, and if she couldn't get them safely through, they'd just have to deal with it when they got there. They didn't have any other options.

"I think we should split up after that," Olivia said, tapping on her knee thoughtfully.

"Why?" Sophia wanted to know.

The tapping continued. "We'll need some people neutralizing—without killing—the other Nasaru, and of course someone needs to find Peter, but I think we should also have a group go to the Vault, see if we can find out how to stop the Miasma. Or how to counter whatever he's been doing with the weather."

"I think that might be our wisest option," Erasmus agreed. "Though I think each group should have someone familiar with the Athenaeum. The layout isn't complicated, but it isn't a small facility."

"I agree with that," Sophia said, still leaning against Lucas. "But I'll be in the group looking for Peter. I know some of you think we should just kill him, but I have to try to at least subdue him, even if he doesn't feel guilty for what he's done."

Erasmus exchanged a look with Lucas, as neither of them wanted her anywhere close to Peter, but they didn't argue with her. "Then I should go to the Vault. Peter thought I was dead, so he might not have revoked my access."

"He might have kept it to use it," Lucas agreed with a thoughtful nod.

"It's a possibility."

Wade leaned forward and arched a brow, but there was a faint grin on his lips. "So we're the muscle to knock out or tie up all your people while you go get the glory?"

"No," Sophia told him with a decisive shake of her head. "You're the ones keeping our people alive. A small group against a large group, there would be deaths no matter how you look at it. Having more people means we're less likely to get overwhelmed and have to resort to fatal measures."

He just chuckled and leaned back, his arm going around Samara's shoulders again. "I'm fine either way. I'm a bounty hunter. This is kind of what I do."

"So what are the groups going to be, then?" Logan asked.

Lucas glanced down at Sophia, who was frowning as she thought. After a moment, she glanced up at him. "I'm guessing you're going with me no matter what I say?"

"Damn straight."

"There's only four of us, though, and if we need to be guides…"

"I can guide a group," Athena offered, then she smiled. "I did help create it, so I daresay I know it better than anyone else here."

"Oh," Sophia said sheepishly. "I hadn't thought of that, but yes. So Lucas and I in the first group, Erasmus in the second, Athena in the third, and Olivia the fourth. I don't know what everyone's specialties are, so I don't think I should assign anything beyond that."

"I'm in your group," Seth said without a hint of flexibility in his tone. "When we find Peter, I want to be there."

Lucas got it. Everyone felt betrayed by Peter's actions. And while the Athenaeum had six divine patrons, Seth had been the most in-volved—at least in the last few months since he'd become a god. Probably because he'd been what had amounted to a freelance venator for years prior to that.

"That's fine," Sophia accepted with a nod.

Brigit trailed her nails lightly along Rune's bicep as she spoke. "I'd like to be in your group as well."

The request coming from a woman he'd just met had Lucas studying her more intently. It didn't really make sense. Suni had welcomed the woman, as had Julian. And getting the approval of Death's wife couldn't be easy either. She was just as much a stranger to him as the Lemurians and Julian's friends, but there was something about her that bugged him. Rune too, but to a lesser extent, and that could be explained away because the man was the bulkiest guy Lucas had ever seen. He wasn't the tallest one here—Evane won that prize—he just had the biggest muscles. Of course, the physical strength could be compensating for weak powers, but Lucas didn't think that was it.

Sophia took longer to respond to Brigit than she had to Seth, and though he wanted to warn her away from accepting the offer, he remained silent. This had to be her decision. "Can I ask why?"

Brigit smiled, and it was a warm, sympathetic smile, but it didn't make his misgivings go away. "Blanche spoke rather highly of you, and when she asked if we'd be willing to help, she seemed most concerned about you. I'd hardly be doing my job as her friend if I didn't try to keep you safe. I promise, I'm not just arm candy."

"Pardon me for being rude," Erasmus broke in, "but might I ask what you are? You and your...husband?"

"Mate," Rune corrected in a terse, gruff voice.

"Mate, then," Erasmus said, inclining his head to the man.

"You're the grandfather, right?" Brigit asked, still smiling.

"I am, yes."

"Then you're not being rude, you're protecting your granddaughter. Wanting to make sure she's protected as much as possible. Any parent would understand that. Rune is a witch, and I'm a halfling. Banshee and snake shifter."

"Banshee?" he asked, gaze flicking to Brigit's hair.

That made her grin brightly. "What? You've never heard of a bleach? All banshees might have natural red hair, but even humans can dye their hair."

"And we're getting off topic," Sophia broke in. "Yes, you can come with us to find Peter. Anyone else know which team they want to be on?"

"I'd like to go with Erasmus's team," Aelia said at the same time Julian asked, "Can I be on the team going to the Vault?"

Erasmus chuckled while Seth muttered, "Called that."

"Can you be trusted in the Vault?" Lucas asked Julian, fighting his own grin.

"Yeah, not sure we want to let Julian near that many relics and ancient texts," Olivia added, smiling impishly. "We might never get him out."

"No, we'd get him out," Sophia argued, her own lips twitching. "It might be in a few months when Paige has the baby, but we'd get him out."

Julian rolled his eyes. "I'm not that bad," he protested, only to be met by a chorus of "Yes, you are."

"Up to you," Sophia told Erasmus. "From what I've seen, he'd be an asset. And Aelia? She might be the best person to help who hasn't been in the Athenaeum before."

"I agree," Erasmus said, nodding. "On both counts, actually."

"If Aelia's going with you, then I'm going, too," Aaron said stubbornly. "I know Julian can throw a fireball, but if the three of you all have your noses in a book, you're going to need someone watching your back."

"That would be fine, and is a very good point."

After a bit more discussion, they decided Vazi would also go with the Vault team, since he would be able to read everything in there. Wade and Sam insisted on staying together, and Kara, Logan, and Athena would join them. Evane, Suni, Olivia, and Rune would make up the last group. It left the more fight-heavy people subduing the Nasaru, but had someone familiar with the Athenaeum in each group. It wasn't perfect, but Lucas thought it was the best they were probably going to get on short notice.

"You're going to come across people with a wide variety of powers," Lucas warned the others. "And the guards are all extremely well trained, in weapons, hand to hand, and magic. There are several magic users in the guard, and the rest have learned a variety of offensive and defensive spells. It's one of the things I insist on. Never thought it would come back to bite me in the ass."

"That's not just your doing," Olivia said with a shake of her head. "Guards have always trained in sorcery."

"True," he allowed. "Even what you would consider our librarians know at least some spells. Just keep in mind that everyone there is a scholar, even the guards, so don't underestimate their intelligence."

"What kind of weaponry will they have?" Wade asked.

"Heavy on old school weapons—swords, knives, even spears—but we keep a stock of guns, too."

The wolf made a face at the last bit, but nodded. "I don't know that any of us carry guns, but I know some of us like edged weapons."

"Which you can't use unless it's life or death," Sophia broke in.

Evane smirked. "We've got magic, too. I can drop large groups of people with pain. It's unpleasant, but generally not lethal. And if anyone reacts badly…" He trailed off and looked down at his wife, his expression softening. "Suni can heal just about anything." His gaze hardened again as he looked at Olivia and Rune—the other members of his team. "So make damn sure you protect her. Short of that god Apollo, she's probably the best healer on the planet."

"Sergei might argue that," Sophia whispered to him, and Lucas chuckled.

"He's worked with her, and was actually really impressed by her skills, so he might not," he explained. But Evane's comments brought something to mind. "Athena, Seth, can either of you get a hold of any magic-nulling cuffs? There are a couple of pairs in the Athenaeum, but I don't know if we'll be able to get a hold of them. It might help in neutralizing some of the Nasaru without killing them."

Athena's lips thinned. "There aren't many outside of the Athenaeum. When Zeus outlawed the creation of powerful relics, those were on his list, so most were destroyed. I'm sure there are a few…contraband, we'll say…cuffs out there, but I know of a couple pairs I can get my hands on. I'll bring them."

"I think we've got the basic plan down," Sophia began, shifting and drawing her legs beneath her, "but I've got one very important question before we start fine tuning things."

"What's that?" Olivia asked.

"Where the hell is the Miasma chamber? I know I didn't get a chance to read through everything, but I never saw anything pointing that out, and I've got a feeling Peter's going to be in or near that chamber."

Olivia looked blank and shifted her focus to the two gods. Even Erasmus cocked his head and focused on them, which meant Sophia probably hadn't missed anything.

"There's a hidden door on the same level as the Vault door," Athena answered. "I'll draw you a map and go over how to get inside."

"Good. Thank you," Sophia said, smiling.

For the next few hours, they went over more of the details. Maps were drawn and various places were pointed out as likely spots where the Nasaru might gather—or where they could set up an ambush. Fortunately, Lucas had gone over various invasion scenarios with the guards, so he knew where they might go to regroup or set traps.

Occasionally, Paige—sometimes with help—would bring in food or drink, or people would wander off for a break or to stretch, but they remained mostly focused on the task at hand.

Then, when the two groups that were going to be dealing with the masses were discussing their strategies, Lucas got to his feet and reached for Sophia's hand. She gave him a curious look, but rose and moved to follow him. And if he happened to notice Erasmus arching a brow at him, he ignored it. Lucas wasn't going to hide how much he loved his woman, nor was he going to just sit by while she got more and more stressed as the fight that would decide the fate of the world drew closer.

Erasmus listened with half an ear as he watched Lucas draw Sophia out of the room, and hid a little smile. He hadn't been lying when he'd told Lucas he had hoped the two of them would meet one day. It hadn't mattered that he'd never met his only granddaughter in person, though he'd paid attention to her life. He'd known when she graduated high school, when she'd started her undergrad studies. She was bright and curious and lovely—and looked so much like her father. Erasmus truly missed his son, but he saw pieces of Gregory in Sophia, which comforted him a great deal. And he'd always known she'd be a lot like her father, so when he'd come to know Lucas, a man who had become one of his best friends, how could he not hope for the two of them to meet?

That was why, when he'd first seen how the two of them acted together just days ago, he couldn't help but be happy despite the circumstances. The two of them truly deserved each other. They were both strong and smart, driven and kind, and best of all, they clearly loved one another. It gave him a sliver of light in this disturbing time.

He only wished he hadn't hurt both of them so badly. That was something he would regret for the rest of his life. At the time, he had honestly thought he was doing the right thing, warning no one of his plans, but he understood why Lucas was not only hurt, but insulted.

The problem had been that he hadn't known who he could trust. It had been inconceivable that any of the Nasaru had been responsible for Thomas's death, and trying to choose one person who seemed less trustworthy than the others had been a monumental task.

Erasmus never would have even suspected it would have been his own family. Though in a part of his mind he didn't want to acknowledge, had to admit he would have suspected Peter over Lucas, and that hurt him deeply. Family was extremely important to him, perhaps in part because he had so few members of it left.

Glancing at the doorway they'd disappeared through, he almost smiled again, because it looked like his family was going to be growing by one. And if he was very, very lucky, perhaps even by more than that. He loved babies, and thought Lucas and Sophia would make beautiful, brilliant babies.

Turning back to the rest of the group when he heard his name, he shook his head. "I do apologize. I missed what you said."

Julian arched a brow. "Are you all right?"

"I am, yes. I just got distracted for a moment. What was the question?"

"Who are the people we should most be wary of?"

"Peter, of course," he began. "It will be impossible to miss him, as he is the only person in the Athenaeum with a blue mohawk. The guards will all be formidable, but Ray and Carla would be the two I'd least want to fight. They're both extremely skilled."

"I saw Carla practicing once, and she was a badass," Seth agreed with a nod.

"She is. But the honest fact is that every person inside the Athenaeum could be deadly," Erasmus admitted. "There are certain spells everyone is expected to know, but we don't discourage people from learning on their own, either. Sometimes that leans toward history, science, or language, but since we don't see sorcery as taboo, it's extremely common for our members to learn more than the basics."

Athena nodded. "And they have always been encouraged to hone their own innate abilities as well. They should be a joy to have as well as a way of protecting themselves, but it does mean they are more skilled than the average witch or shifter."

The discussion shifted to the types of people in the Athenaeum, and Erasmus found his mind wandering back to his granddaughter again.

He hoped they did manage to get through their assault of the Athenaeum without any casualties, because he'd very much like to start making things up to Sophia and Lucas.

Chapter 19

"Where are we going?" Sophia asked as he led her through the house. Lucas had seen the gardens through the window earlier, and was fairly certain she'd never gotten to fully enjoy such a place. Certainly not in the way he intended her to.

Lucas grinned and gave her hand a squeeze. "Taking a break. We both need one." Her more than him, but it was to be expected. This wasn't entirely familiar to him, but it wasn't unfamiliar, either. The scale was, sure, but not the actual act of forming a plan.

She must have heard something in his voice, because she made an uncertain noise and glanced back to the house. "We really should be helping with the planning. I'm all for sex, but don't we have bigger things to worry about?"

Now he laughed. "Love, have you not noticed how anytime two people take a break at the same time, that it's a couple? Evane and Suni, Wade and Samara? I guarantee they're not just stretching out their backs and having a nice chat. And you, more than anyone else, deserve to take half an hour to relieve some stress."

"Oh gods…You really think…oh gods!" She pressed her face against his arm and groaned. "It hadn't occurred to me, but now I can't get those images out of my head. And while I like them—as much as I can without knowing them—I do *not* want that image of them in my head."

"I can help with that," he promised, drawing her outside. It was a little overcast, but warm enough for what he had in mind. Maybe a little warmer than he might like, but not bad. Just to be on the safe side, he took her around the side and behind a hedge framed by some shorter, flowering trees. It would provide both privacy and shade, and maybe even a hint of romance. It certainly smelled nice, with the blossoms releasing their fragrance into the air. He couldn't have said what types of trees they were, but they were pretty and smelled good. "Besides, I have a feeling that you, my beautiful nerd, have never been crazy enough to have sex outside."

She wrinkled her nose at him before she laughed softly and shook her head. "I'd like to bitch at you for making assumptions, but you're right."

He stopped and drew her into his arms. "There's a first time for everything. So shut that brain of yours off for a little bit. You can go back to worrying when we get inside," he told her, bending his head to kiss her. She responded immediately, but he could feel her inner struggle with responsibility. A short-lived struggle, as after a few seconds, she gave in and set that aside, letting herself be in the moment. Be with him.

Lucas kissed her until he could feel her heart pounding in her chest and her fingers were gripping his shirt. His arms wrapped around her, he began to sink down to his knees, drawing her with him. That was when she surprised him. Her hands slid from his back to his chest, then she pressed her palms flat against him and pushed. Since he wasn't expecting it, he fell back in the grass, propped up on his elbows and blinking in surprise at her.

She was grinning wickedly as she crawled forward on all fours until her face was above his. "You wanted crazy, didn't you?" she teased.

"I guess I asked for that," he agreed, laughing. Sophia wasn't a prude or overly reserved, but he hadn't been kidding earlier about her not being crazy earlier. When in public, she was more sedate about these sorts of things. That meant the spontaneity was strangely arousing, and he felt himself hardening, and immediately wishing his pants were a little looser. Though he hoped he wouldn't be wearing them for much longer.

"Well, in for a penny and all that," she teased before resuming their earlier kiss. It was only a moment before he felt one of her hands on his pants, and he stroked his hands lightly over her chest as she pulled down the zipper. Sitting back, she tugged his pants open and down enough to free his cock. She looked satisfied when her gaze moved over him, and she trailed the tip of one finger up his shaft and over the sensitive head, making him hiss in a soft breath. "It amazes me how someone made of stone can be so soft," she murmured, shifting back so her knees were on either side of his. "And feel so good."

She bent, and he held his breath when her tongue followed the same path her finger had just taken, then exhaled on a groan when she teased the tip. He gently pushed her hair back from her face so he could see her beautiful eyes as she let her tongue slide over him. Except that teasing was all she seemed inclined to do and it was driving him mad.

Clenching his jaw, he was only able to withstand another thirty seconds of that torment before his free hand dug into the grass. With the last vestiges of responsibility—and to save his sanity—he growled, "Stop toying with me."

Sophia gave him a wicked smile, followed by a long, slow lick. "But I like toying with you."

The hand that had been holding her hair back fisted, tugged just a little, and her lids grew heavy, a small sound escaping her lips. It was his turn to smile, as he kept the tension on her hair. "Play with me, and I'll play right back," he warned, sitting up and urging her back as he did.

"I like that, too," she breathed when he got up on his knees, back in the same position they'd started in.

"Good." He turned her around, then dropped his hand to her jeans, undoing them and shoving them down to her thighs. Fingers stroked between her legs, and she whimpered as he smiled, unsurprised to find her damp. This woman really was amazing. Brilliant, beautiful, stubborn...and the most amazing lover he'd ever had. And an absolutely perfect match for him in every way.

His free hand wrapped around his cock and he positioned himself against her, while the hand in her hair drew her head back so he could kiss her. "Be quiet, or everyone inside will hear," he whispered, before thrusting his hips forward and burying himself inside her.

She arched and her mouth opened, but she managed to hold in the cry. One of his arms wound around her stomach, holding her to him as he drew his hips back, then slid into her again. This time she gasped, but he wanted more. He wanted to make her struggle not to lose control—then make her lose it anyway.

Tugging her head back a little more, he pressed a gentle kiss to the curve where her shoulder met her neck, then bit, careful to tantalize rather than hurt. The second he did, she clenched around him and moaned, which caused his next stroke to be harder, go deeper. He never would have guessed she'd like a little pain with her pleasure, but he wasn't against giving it to her. This woman kept surprising him, and he couldn't wait to see what else she'd surprise him with over the next year—or century.

"More," she begged, rocking her hips as much as her position allowed, while tilting her head a little further. He couldn't resist her, especially not like this. He bit harder, thrust harder, and tugged on her hair just a little harder. She covered the forearm over her stomach with one hand, and reached the other up to cup his head, to hold him against her.

It started to rain as they moved together in the garden. He spared one glance to the sky, but even a freak storm wouldn't make him stop, not unless it would endanger Sophia. It started to come down harder, but she seemed to be of the same mind as him, as she demanded, "Don't stop. Don't fucking stop."

"Never," he breathed against her ear before his teeth found her throat again. She couldn't hold in her cry this time, though it was masked by a boom of thunder. It was fitting, really. This felt primal, and she had finally let down all her guards, so she was as uninhibited as he'd ever experienced. Despite being outside, in a place where they could be caught, she didn't seem to care. She'd stopped worrying, stopped stressing, and was simply in the moment. It was exactly what he'd wanted. What she'd needed.

His hand slipped down from her stomach until his fingers found her clit. Immediately, her nails pressed against his scalp and her hips bucked, like she couldn't decide if she wanted to press against his hand or his cock. He closed his eyes and savored her reaction, but began stroking her clit as their clothes grew sodden and rain dripped down his face.

She whispered his name and he let go of her hair, instead wrapped his arm around her, needing to hold her to him when she came, and she was close. "Sophia," he groaned as she started to flutter around him and his arm tightened, his finger pressing more firmly.

Her head hit his shoulder as she clenched around him and cried out his name. While normally he could hold on for a little while when he felt that, this time he was helpless to do anything but fall with her. Fall even harder for her.

Lucas groaned and gentled his grip on her while they ground together, trying to make the moment last as long as possible. Her hair stuck to his neck and her face, and their clothes clung to them, but neither really noticed or cared.

When he could breathe again normally, he drew out of her and sat back, not trusting his balance right then. He cradled her in his lap and kissed her before resting his brow against hers. For a minute they remained like that, content to do nothing else, but then she started to giggle. He blinked and drew back enough to look at her face. "What's so funny?"

The giggles transformed into laughter. While he was happy to hear it, he was still baffled as to the source. "Lucas, we're soaked, probably muddy, and there's no way we can pretend that didn't just happen when we go back inside. Not to mention my ass is still hanging out."

"So's my dick," he retorted, but he grinned, seeing the humor in their situation. "But you're right on not being able to pretend. But if we ask nicely, I'm sure one of those dozen people can dry and clean these clothes since we don't exactly have anything else to put on."

"Okay, but you're doing the asking. I don't know—oh gods." She changed what she was saying mid-sentence, and pressed her face into his chest. "My grandfather is in there!"

Lucas bit his lip to keep from laughing. "I'm pretty sure Erasmus knows we're sleeping together." Especially since he'd asked point blank, and Lucas hadn't lied to the man. She still looked distressed, so he kissed her forehead. "I'll ask Seth to come out and take care of our clothes before we join the others," he promised.

"Still embarrassing, but at least he's not my grandfather."

"Then come on, let's get inside before this storm gets any worse," he said, urging her up.

"Not sure how much worse it can get," she said, pulling her pants up with a faint grimace.

"We haven't been struck by lightning," he pointed out as he fixed his own clothes.

"Good point."

They didn't bother hurrying back inside the house—it wasn't like they could get any wetter. Instead of going in to get Seth, which he knew would further embarrass her, he mentally called out to the god. It was the first time he'd done such a thing, but this was also the closest he'd ever been to a deity. Fortunately, it worked.

As soon as Seth saw them, he grinned and shook his head. "I had a feeling that's what you two were doing, but what did you do? Stick a rain magnet in your pocket?"

"Seth?" Sophia said, calmer than he was sure she felt.

"Yeah, Soph?"

"I like you, but if you finish ruining what's left of my afterglow, I'm going to seriously debate the wisdom of smacking a god upside the head."

Lucas knew she wasn't serious, and judging by his laugh, Seth did as well.

"Fair enough. But why did you call me out here?" Seth asked.

Lucas grimaced. "We didn't exactly pack before leaving the Athenaeum, and even these clothes are borrowed."

"So you don't have anything dry and clean to change into," Seth finished with a nod. "I get it." He flicked his fingers toward them and they were suddenly dry from head to toe. "Better?"

"Much," Sophia said, nodding. "Thank you."

"No problem. Ready to get back in there? We could use a distraction."

Lucas frowned. "Why? What's going on?"

"Nothing like what I'm sure you're thinking," Seth quickly assured him. "Mostly Wade and Evane are arguing about the best ways to take people down without killing them."

"Samara is Wade's wife and Evane's sister, right? Why isn't she stepping in?" Sophia wondered.

Seth snorted and shook his head. "She was an assassin for two millennia and a soldier as well. She's offering ways of bettering their suggestions, not stopping it."

"Oh. Then yeah, we should probably get back in there. Though I'm glad they're talking about non-lethal measures," Sophia said, starting back toward the others at a brisk walk.

Seth grabbed Lucas's arm before he could follow. "Something wrong?"

"Just everything," Seth answered. "No, I just wanted to say...I'm happy for you."

That was the last thing he was expecting and just said, "What?"

Seth inclined his head in the direction Sophia had gone. "Her. Didn't know you well before I became a Lemurian, but I knew you well enough to know you were a guy like I used to be. Devoted to my job, not a lot else going for me. Had more acquaintances than friends."

Lucas couldn't exactly argue with that, so just nodded.

"Then I met Tempest, my wife. Had Zeus's assassins after us, found a place everyone thought was a myth, went up against a god who killed her, Aaron, and Kara—and yes, I mean literally—but everything changed. She changed me. I have friends, a family. A purpose beyond my job. A real reason to get up and be happy every day. Which, okay, is why Peter's pissing me off so much, but the rest of it? Just makes me happy. And it seems like Sophia's doing that for you."

"She is." It was as simple as that.

"Just be good to her. I've come to like her since she became aspida. Hell, I was primed to like her before that, just from listening to Erasmus."

"Seth, I love her. Hurting her is the last thing I want to do. And you know me well enough to know what I'll do to the one who tries to fuck with her." And those who already had. Which was why it was going to be so hard to keep from killing Peter when they found him.

"Good. C'mon. Not sure even Sophia can break up Evane and Wade when they get going. Those two act more like brothers than brothers-in-law sometimes."

That could be entertaining, but if he wanted this over and done with, they needed to get back to work.

Chapter 20

Vazi finally showed up when they broke for dinner, looking annoyed and exhausted, but after eating, he jumped right in with the strategy. They planned and refined those plans until around eleven that night, when everyone went to their respective beds, with the warning that they'd be leaving before dawn. Not just so Logan wouldn't have to be exposed to the sun, but so hopefully they'd catch everyone in the Athenaeum off guard.

It was an hour before sunrise when they gathered in the entrance hall of Julian's home, including all three gods. The rest of the patrons were, Athena assured them, already in place to help and ensure no infected individuals escaped. They did a last check to make sure everyone knew where they were going and what they were doing, and had whatever they needed to do their respective jobs. Sophia made sure she had the knife Lucas had given her a week ago, now attached to her hip, and cast her shield spell. She started to include her threat sensing spell, but realized that every corner of the Athenaeum would be a threat to her right now. Most likely, it would distract her rather than help her. Besides, having just the shield spell up would allow her to focus on strengthening it instead of splitting her focus. A much better use of her time.

They'd also, in anticipation of the plan to circulate Oskila through-out the Athenaeum, all drank the strongest energy drinks they could find. Honestly, after this, Sophia might be off coffee and all other caffeinated beverages for a while.

Remembering Blanche's request, she borrowed Erasmus's phone and shot her a text, letting her know they were heading to the Athenaeum. Blanche responded within a minute.

Blanche: Good luck. Stay safe. I don't want to see any of you here for a long time.

When they were ready, Seth took the whole group to the estate just down the mountain from the Athenaeum's entrance. It was used for storing the dozens of cars the Athenaeum and Nasaru owned, pro-viding cover for the influx of people coming and going, and allowed them to own the land the entrance was on, so it wasn't accidentally discovered by anyone else. Not only that, but some people stayed there rather than in the Athenaeum. Like Carla and Nick, who had two young twin girls. Since they didn't want the girls to grow up completely underground, they spent half their nights at the estate. It was a good system, though the trail wasn't exactly fun.

Sophia had wanted to teleport to the cave entrance, but Seth and Athena had been adamant that the wards wouldn't allow it. So as the minutes ticked by to dawn, the eighteen of them trekked up the mountain. There was one bright spot in it all. When Sophia had first come to the Athenaeum a month before, this hike had killed her legs, but now it barely strained them. All the training, walking up all the steps, and the adventure in Alaska had definitely strengthened her muscles and increased her stamina. Having regular, occasionally athletic sex probably hadn't hurt either. She still didn't really like the trail.

When they'd reached the edge of the ward, Sophia could see where the opening into the mountain was. It looked like it had those weeks ago, but in the darkness it seemed ominous. Though it was probably all in her head, she thought she could feel the Miasma beneath their feet, waiting, plotting. Creeping even deeper into the minds of all the Nasaru trapped inside. A shiver ran through her and she rubbed her arms, but it did nothing to combat the sudden chill fear caused.

"The ward is as strong as ever," Athena confirmed after holding her hands up against it for a minute.

"Then let us see if it prevents my power from entering," Vazi said, bending and scooping up a handful of dirt. He broke it up so it was fine particles rather than clumps, then blew gently on it. Sophia watched as the wind he created picked up the dirt, lifted it, and swirled it through the air...only to stop and collect on the invisible wall of the ward. After a second, it fell to the ground, on the wrong side of the ward.

Vazi muttered some rather uncomplimentary words she didn't understand, but she caught the intent behind them. In a fit of temper, he flung a hand out toward the ward. Though wind swirled around all of them, whipping at their hair and clothes, nothing got past the magic protecting the Athenaeum, and after a minute, he dropped his hand and the wind faded. It was far from reassuring that the oldest known god in existence was unable to get through magic caused by a mer in his twenties. Whatever he had used to create such a thing would no doubt be destroyed by that very god when this was all over.

Though Sophia really didn't want to do it, she turned to Athena. "Did you get the dragon scale and ashes?"

The goddess nodded as she looked away from the ward. "I did." She held a hand out, palm up, and a small leather pouch tied with a cord appeared.

Before Sophia could take it, Erasmus laid a hand on Sophia's shoulder and took the pouch from Athena. "Let me try first."

She shook her head. "If Aelia's theory is right, it'll be me who can get through."

"You are aspida, yes," he conceded, "but I have a connection as well. It wasn't long ago that I was aspida, and I was connected to the Athenaeum for decades."

"Yeah, but you were replaced," she said bluntly, not wanting to risk his safety.

"Magic is rarely that black and white, and a situation like this has never before occurred," he argued, giving her shoulder a squeeze. "I know you're still angry with me, but I need to do this."

"Will one of you just try already so we can get on with it?" Vazi snapped. "We don't have time for stalling."

Sophia wasn't sure it was really stalling, but the anger from the god and the stubbornness on her grandfather's face had her sighing and motioning toward the ward. "Just be careful." She didn't want to lose anyone today, and especially not before they'd even gotten inside. Worse, she knew this was going to be the easiest part of taking back control of the Athenaeum.

Erasmus approached Athena, who still stood beside the ward. Tentatively, he lifted his hands and let them hover just before the ward. After taking a slow, deep breath, he pushed his hands forward.

No one had to wonder where exactly the ward was, because the instant Erasmus touched it, a low thrumming sound hit their eardrums. In the same instant, he was thrown back with a burst of light. Before he could hit the ground, Lucas caught him, then lowered him carefully to the ground.

"Suni!"

The petite woman was already moving, as was Rune. They knelt beside the unconscious man, with Rune nudging Lucas out of the way with perhaps a little more force than was necessary. Lucas narrowed his eyes at the witch but said nothing as both Rune and Suni laid their hands on Erasmus and began working their magic. With the two working in tandem, it only took a moment for Erasmus to open his eyes and try to sit up.

"Take it easy for a minute more," Suni told him soothingly, while Rune just planted one big hand in the middle of Erasmus's chest to keep him from moving. Rune's method was the more effective of the two.

"Sophia?" Erasmus called, sounding winded.

"Yes, Grandpa?" she answered, kneeling beside him, Rune moving to make room for her.

"You were right."

She smiled faintly and patted his hand. "Yes, I was. Keep that in mind next time you try to be stubborn. I'm glad you're all right, though." She glanced up to Suni, then Rune. "Thank you both."

"It's my job," Suni said with a warm smile as she rose and moved back to Evane's side.

"While he recovers, why don't you try the ward?" Evane asked, though he was staring at the opening instead of her.

"It would be good to know now," Seth admitted. "If you can't, then we'll need all the time we can get for plan B. And to help you, too."

Sophia nodded and took the pouch from where it had fallen out of Erasmus's hand, then turned toward the entrance to the Athenaeum.

"I don't like it," Lucas said, moving to stand between Sophia and the ward. "His logic was sound and look at what happened to him."

"I don't like it either," she said quietly, taking one of his hands with her free one and squeezing, "but what other choice do we have? The gods can't get through the ward, and I'm the best chance we have of getting inside. We *need* to get inside or we won't be able to stop Peter." She'd already been worried about trying to use her position as aspida to bypass the ward, but after seeing what had happened to Erasmus, she was terrified. True, he was okay now, but it could have gone so much worse. And what if the ward somehow could sense attempts made on it and would grow more powerful each time someone tried to get through it? Or if Peter could sense those attempts and would send people out to attack from that side?

And what ifs didn't do any damn good.

She almost wanted to laugh when she realized at least she had a friend in the afterlife if things went too wrong. And she'd probably finally be able to meet her dad. Blanche could probably arrange that.

Lucas looked more worried than she'd ever seen him, and she tried to smile for him. "I'll be okay. Trust me."

"It's not you I don't trust," he whispered before kissing her. He kept it brief, but it still left her a little unsteady. It also pushed some of the fear back, enough to allow her to approach the wards.

Without giving herself too much time to think, she stepped forward. If she did anything else, she might chicken out, and they couldn't afford that. To her relief, it didn't zap her like it had Erasmus, but she could feel the wards. They pushed back at her, making it feel like she was trying to walk through thick mud. Each step took a great deal of effort, and moving through the ward was like being bitten by hundreds of bugs on every inch of her skin. It was bearable—for now—but extremely unpleasant, and if it lasted too much longer, she wasn't going to be able to contain a scream. This was like an itch that couldn't scratch; something mild that turned maddening.

It took every bit of willpower she had to keep moving forward, to just put one foot in front of the other, but she did it. And after several long minutes, the prickling disappeared and her foot was able to move unhindered. She nearly fell to all fours, even wanted to, but was able to make do with putting her hands on her knees and bending over, relearning how to breathe.

When her heart had stopped pounding in her ears, she heard her name and forced herself to straighten and turn. Lucas stood at the edge of the ward, being held back by Seth and Wade, and despite their strength, they were struggling to hold him.

"I'm okay," she said, but it was barely a whisper. Though only a few feet separated them, she doubted he could hear her. She tried again, able to get some volume this time. "I'm okay. It just...fought me."

He nodded curtly, and the two men holding him seemed to relax, suggesting he wasn't fighting them as hard.

"Aelia...what's the spell?" Sophia asked, standing up straight and loosening the tie on the pouch. "What do I need to do?"

"A couple of things first. Not just for you," Aelia said, stepping up beside Seth. "As soon as you bring the ward down, the one who put it up will probably feel it. So everyone will need to be on alert. As soon as the ward is down, at least one of us needs to get to Sophia, because this is going to take a lot of focus and energy." When everyone had acknowledged her words, her eyes settled on Sophia. "I mean it about the focus. Block out everything else."

The words were simple enough, even for a warning, but coupled with the tone and the look in the ancient woman's eyes, Sophia paid close attention. When Aelia just kept watching her, Sophia slowly nodded. "I will," she promised.

Aelia slowly spoke the syllables, repeating them several times until Sophia had them. "Say that, then take a handful of the scales and ash and blow them at the ward. The entire time, picture the wards disappearing, starting where the mixture touches, then spreading from there. Dissolving. Sort of like water on cotton candy."

Sophia went over the chant again in her head, then grabbed a handful of the powdered scales and tree ash, preparing it for the next step. Closing her eyes to block out the image of Lucas's worried face, she tried to imagine the wards going down, just like Aelia had told her. She carefully spoke the chant, enunciating clearly. As each syllable of the spell was spoken, she felt the magic begin to build. Once the last syllable left her lips, she opened her eyes, lifted her hand, and blew the powder at the ward.

The tiny particles hit the magical barrier and Sophia felt a jolt deep in her chest, one that dropped her to a knee. The small, rational part of her brain realized it was a result of the ward snapping, but all she could focus on was how much it hurt. But she wasn't alone. No sooner than the sting of her knee hitting the ground had registered, Lucas's arms were around her, and the faces of Olivia and Erasmus were in her field of vision, further proving she'd done it.

"I've got you," Lucas murmured, before there was a deep sound—more a vibration—from beneath their feet.

"Earthquake?" she heard Kara ask while she leaned into Lucas, waiting for the pain to ebb.

"No," she whispered, shaking her head. "I think that was Peter."

"I think so, too," Erasmus said, cupping her face. "We'll stop him soon enough, *louloudi mou*," he promised softly. "Suni or Rune, could one of you help her?"

"Yes," came the gruff voice of Rune. He really wasn't a man of many words, but he knelt beside her grandfather and took her hand. Gentle warmth flowed through her, radiating out from where his skin touched hers. It was like a magical hug, though she felt a little silly just thinking that. But whatever it felt like, when it faded, it took the pain with it and she could finally take a deep breath.

"Thank you," she told him, smiling and getting to her feet. Lucas helped and pulled her into a real hug—though a brief one—the moment she was up.

"We should move quickly," Athena said. "Vazi?"

The Lemurian nodded and moved past Sophia to the opening in the mountain. He summoned the Oskila jar to him and removed the lid. Immediately, Sophia could feel the effects gently pressing against her, but Vazi didn't stop there. Hand above the opening, he made a grasping gesture that had the powder swirling up from the ceramic vessel, then pushed his hand, palm first, toward the opening. The Oskila followed his direction, rapidly flying into the crevice and disappearing. When it had all flown into the mountain, the effects eased.

Vazi closed his eyes and kept his arm outstretched. Guiding it throughout the Athenaeum, she assumed, but whatever he was doing, no one moved much or said a thing for several minutes, not until he opened his eyes and lowered his arm. "I can't guarantee it's reached everyone, but the Oskila is there."

"That's going to be a bitch to clean when we're done," Sophia murmured, knowing it was just a momentary distraction from what came next.

"We will help," Athena assured her. "But now, it is time to enter and reclaim the Athenaeum. Is everyone ready?"

After she'd received confirmation, the goddess touched Sophia's shoulder lightly, then stepped past, disappearing into the mountain.

Taking her last Oskila-free breath, Sophia followed, Lucas at her side.

Chapter 21

THE CAVE THAT SERVED as the first room of the Athenaeum looked no different than the last time Lucas had seen it, but when they stepped into the labyrinth that was the Athenaeum's first line of defense, he frowned. He'd been through this maze hundreds of times and had always been able to clearly see the path that led the way through it. It was a magic inherent to the Athenaeum, and every member could see it as easily as if someone had painted a line in neon paint. But now there was nothing. It was just stone, dirt, and cave formations.

"It's gone. The path's gone," he said, unsure if he felt anger or grief over that fact.

"Not gone," Sophia disagreed, with a slow shake of her head, "it's just extremely faint."

Lucas tried, but couldn't make it out, no matter how hard he tried. He could only guess that she was more closely connected to the Athenaeum as aspida, and thus was harder to magically push out. How else could she have gotten through the ward even if Erasmus couldn't?

"Just follow me," Athena said once everyone was inside. Despite her apparent confidence, she didn't move with the quick, sure movements he was used to seeing from people navigating the labyrinth. There was more hesitation, slower steps, and at least one moment of indecision as she led them through. Not a single person said a word, not even Wade, and Lucas had quickly learned the wolf was normally a sarcastic bastard. A trait he honestly appreciated, but he was grateful Wade kept quiet for now. No one needed any added stress. And tempers were hot as it was, so the wrong comment might cause someone to snap. No one needed that. Especially not if it was a god snapping. Vazi was certainly on the edge.

The rumble they had felt earlier might have been Peter, but now the ground shook in a way that really did feel like an earthquake. Not that it was that surprising. If he had been causing earthquakes around the world, why wouldn't he try to take out the invaders now that he knew they were here? It worried him. Normal earthquakes were bad enough when only the ground beneath his feet was shaking, but now they had stone above their heads as well. If Peter hit the ground in just the right place, he could take all of them out.

"Can you do anything about the quakes?" he asked Seth.

Seth scowled and shook his head. "I've been trying. It's like with the weather and Vazi. I can lessen it, even stop it temporarily, but I can't flat out stop it. And I haven't had the centuries of practice like Vazi has."

His ability to lessen it failed just a few minutes later, when a stalactite detached from the ceiling and scraped Kara's shoulder and arm as it fell. A few inches more to the right, and it would have killed her, just like what had happened in Alaska with Olivia. He wondered if that was meant to be a sign. But dealing with the now, it took barely more than a touch from Suni to fix her up, but after that, they were all careful to look up when they were walking, not just down.

Normally it took about five minutes to get through the labyrinth, but it took them close to half an hour until they stepped into the entrance hall. Where the labyrinth had looked natural, this room was clearly manmade. Two rows of pillars lined the room, each one carved in a different language and stating the purpose of the Nasaru. Six statues watched over the room, one for each of the patrons. It was honestly a beautiful room, especially lit by the soft glow of magic. Except it wasn't empty this morning, as it almost always was.

Athena was first, followed by Sophia and himself, and then the first attack came. A fireball hit Athena square in the chest, while a second person fired a gun at Sophia. They were lucky, in that Athena was unbothered by the magic, and Sophia's shield was still intact or had been renewed, stopping the bullet before it could reach her. One downside was that the sound of the gun echoed around the stone chamber.

"Remember, subdue only," Sophia called as the rest of their group rushed into the entrance hall to help.

Lucas understood where she was coming from, but he wasn't willing to risk her. Transforming into his stone form, he stepped in front of her and flicked magic at the first person he saw peek out from behind a pillar. Since a gun fell from the man's hand as he dropped, he knew it had been the person who had shot at Sophia.

Logan shot past them, utilizing what Lucas realized was vampiric speed as he raced toward the spell-slinger and tackled him.

A third person ducked out to try to attack, but Julian reached out with his magic, lifting the woman and knocking her against one of the pillars. It had the same effect Logan's tackle did, knocking the woman out.

They cleared the rest of the room and Lucas was surprised to find those three were the only ones. The man he'd hit was quickly put to sleep with a touch from Suni, but Lucas's concern was elsewhere.

"I don't recognize any of these people," Sophia said, studying the face of the one Logan had tackled.

"Nor do I," Erasmus agreed.

"Can one of you check and see if they're infected?" Lucas asked.

"I can," Athena said, kneeling beside the first man. After only a moment, she moved onto the second, then the third. "They all hold the Miasma inside them."

"Shit." Olivia's simple statement mirrored his own feelings. "So Peter's been recruiting, which means we don't know how many people we're going to be up against when we step through that door."

"No, we don't," Seth agreed, "but that doesn't change the basic plan. It does mean you nine are going to have a harder time subduing everyone," he said, glancing at those who weren't going after Peter or the Vault.

"Just means more of a challenge," Wade said, shrugging. "We can handle it. You guys just stop this."

Sophia touched the writing on one of the pillars, her face looking like her heart had broken. "He's abused everything we stand for," she murmured.

"And we're going to stop him," Erasmus told her, rubbing her arm. "We can mourn for the boy he used to be later, when everyone is safe."

She sighed, nodded, and let her hand drop. "I know. Let's go."

Sophia didn't wait for anyone else to agree, just started for the doors at the other end of the hall. Within only a few steps, she had Lucas on one side, Seth on the other, and everyone else quickly followed.

"Remember," Lucas said as they reached the large doors, "this is the area the guards have trained to hold. If there were three people in here, then there will be at least five times that on the other side."

"We know," Samara said with a nod. "We've got this, Lucas," she assured him with a faint smile. Her black eyes still unnerved him, but after hearing about her skills, he was happy to have her with them. As long as she remembered this wasn't an assassination. But he had to be optimistic, given the talents of the people who had agreed to help them. The fact that they had a couple of gods helping should mean it would be relatively easy...right?

"I'll get the doors," Rune said, in the longest sentence Lucas had heard him utter yet. He nodded, and they all readied themselves for what they'd find on the other side. With a sweep of one hand, Rune flung the doors open and they rushed through, finding chaos on the other side.

It took only a glance to see the gathered defensive force was a mix of Nasaru and people like the ones in the last room—outside people Peter had recruited or lured, then infected. That made it harder. The Nasaru were his family, just as much as his siblings were. More, in some ways, since he lived with these people, ate with them, fought beside them. To be fighting against them now hurt in a way he couldn't describe. He wasn't sure if it was better or worse that it wasn't their doing. True betrayal would hurt more, wouldn't it? But as it stood, some of these people were going to be hurt, possibly killed, for something that was in no way their fault.

No, betrayal would definitely be better than this.

Sophia couldn't believe how things had progressed between her and the Nasaru. Friends, to dirty looks, and now there was Jericho, flinging what looked like icicles at them. The first one shattered on Lucas's stone chest, but the second sliced across Aaron's shoulder. When he threw a third, she shot out a hand and hissed one of the spells she'd learned just days before. The icicle disappeared and reappeared in her hand, then she threw it back at him. Her aim wasn't as great as his had been, and she didn't have his strength, but it still hit his stomach. Ice elemental or not, it temporarily stopped him from throwing more frozen missiles at them. Not willing to let him recover, she used the first spell Lucas had ever taught her, throwing magic in a punch toward the man who had been so nasty to her. This time, her aim was better, and he flew back, hitting the stone floor. When his head smacked hard on the floor, it fortunately knocked him unconscious.

There was a brief hint of satisfaction in taking down the man who had spoken out time and time again about how useless she'd be as aspida, but it dissipated quickly. Jericho might be an ass, but he was one of her people. And he wasn't the only face she recognized. Samara was fighting Valerie—the woman who handled all the Athenaeum's finances—while Brigit was facing off against Catherine, another one of the curators. Julian and Penny were exchanging magical blows, while the rest of the group who had come with her was spread out across the room, doing their best to avoid killing anyone. It wasn't easy, she knew that. When someone was trying to kill you—especially with magic—the quickest and most efficient way of stopping them was to fight back hard, which could result in a fatal blow.

Lucas stuck close to her, absorbing both physical and magical attacks as they slowly began downing the people who had become the enemy. It was the first true fight she'd ever been in—more a battle, really—and she decided that she hated it. Sure, part of it could be because of who they were fighting, but most of it was just that she hated this kind of fighting. Any kind of fighting, to be honest. She didn't let herself shy away from it, though. She used what magic she knew, and when someone got too close for her to get a spell off in time, she used her fists or her feet.

The weeks of training may not have made Sophia a warrior, but her hits were more effective than she'd expected them to be. No, she didn't knock anyone out in one punch, but she was able to do enough damage that they ended up that way—or close to it.

When everyone was on the ground, Lucas, Olivia, and Erasmus went around, putting the magic-dampening cuffs on the wrists of those they deemed the most magically dangerous. Jericho was on that list.

Not all of the knockouts had been bloodless, and the normally clean, pale stone that made up the wall and floors was splattered with crimson. Nor were the injuries restricted to the infected. In addition to Aaron's icicle-induced wound, Aelia had a bloody nose and was holding her left wrist at an odd angle, Brigit had one eye partially closed from a hit to the face, and someone had used a blade of some sort to slice deeply across Wade's stomach. It all made her feel a little nauseous, but Suni, Rune, and Julian were making the rounds and healing everyone—infected and non. They also ensured the infected would remain unconscious while they cleared the rest of the Athenaeum and hunted for Peter.

There weren't as many injuries as she'd feared, but counting faces she recognized, she realized the majority of the Nasaru hadn't been here. That meant there were at least twenty more skilled people hiding somewhere down here, waiting to attack. Fantastic.

When everyone was healed and they were sure the infected wouldn't be rejoining the fight, they gathered in the middle of the room. "Everyone know where they're going?" Sophia asked.

"We're going that way," Wade said, jerking his thumb to the hallway to the left.

"And we'll go that way," Olivia said, nodding to the right. "Go, find Peter. Stop all this bullshit," she said, starting toward her chosen hallway.

Rune stared at Sophia for a long moment before he turned to join Olivia, Evane, and Suni. The man was an enigma. He spoke very little, and despite his obvious strength, he had a surprisingly gentle nature. Or maybe she only thought that because he was a skilled healer. And he made her a little nervous. It wasn't that she thought he'd hurt her—she honestly believed he wouldn't—but there was just...something. Something she couldn't put a name to, so she forced herself to shove it aside until later.

"You can do this," Athena said solemnly before she went to her hallway, along with the rest of her team.

Sophia looked at those remaining. While most of them were going to the Vault, they all needed to get to the same level. Considering that there could be people scattered all throughout the Athenaeum, it wasn't the worst idea for them to stay grouped until they reached the Vault level. And though most of her would love to procrastinate, she knew she couldn't.

"Time to find Peter," she said, starting for the stairs. Surprising no one, Lucas—still in stone form—was quickly at her side and half a step ahead. Given what Peter had already done, and the fact that they had only come across one guard, she wasn't going to argue.

Chapter 22

THIS HAD BEEN ENTIRELY too easy so far, and Lucas didn't like it. Peter's first line of defense had been random people he'd brought in, one guard, and a handful of people more at home in a library than a battlefield? Yes, he'd warned the others that everyone here could be dangerous—and they were—but the fact remained that some had combat training and others didn't. Jericho was the only one they'd come across who had. Which meant Peter would likely have the bulk of the guards around him. Him and the Miasma chamber, if he wasn't there himself. On a good note, it meant those on the first level would probably have an easy time clearing it. Of course, that meant his group was probably going to get hammered.

While he cared about everyone in the Athenaeum, he wasn't going to hesitate to do what was needed to protect Sophia and prevent Peter's evil from extending out into the world. Even if that meant striking a fatal blow on someone he had considered family only a week ago. Maybe it wouldn't come to that. Gods, he hoped it wouldn't come to that. He'd do it, but he wouldn't be happy about it.

They made it past the residential level without seeing a single person, then past the level which held the crypts and the room where aspides were chosen.

They were on the second level of the library when they came across the first group of infected. Joshua, Alicia, Farid, and Theo stood there, along with Nicolas, Jeremiah, and seven people he didn't recognize. Not good. The first four were very skilled guards. Nicolas wasn't a guard, but he was married to one, and Lucas knew Carla made him train, just in case he went on a retrieval. Jeremiah was a venator, but he trained almost as hard as the guards, because accidents did happen when they were trying to bring something back to the Athenaeum.

Before Lucas could even begin to warn the others, Jeremiah opened his mouth and let out a sound that was like nails on a chalkboard, but infinitely worse. Nails on a chalkboard annoyed. This felt like someone was hammering spikes into his ears.

Every member of his group cringed and covered their ears. Even Lucas, who was currently stone, wasn't immune, and found himself hunched over, fighting against the pain. He knew if they didn't stop the siren, that a sound like this could potentially kill. It didn't happen often, but it did happen.

Behind him, someone let out a shout that was lost in Jeremiah's shriek. He was knocked off balance, but it didn't silence his scream. Sophia yelled something and threw out her hand, but whatever spell she tried was just as ineffective.

Then Jeremiah's voice cut off with a choked sound, and Lucas glanced up in time to see the siren clawing at his throat like something was around it, though Lucas saw nothing. Still, he wasn't going to waste an opportunity, and flung magic at the man, relieved when he was thrown back and smacked his head on the stone wall. He went down hard, and Lucas hoped it had just stunned him rather than killing him. Better still would be knocking him out for the duration.

The others had held back while Jeremiah was using his siren abilities, because if they'd stepped in front of him, they would have been injured as well, but with him silent, they didn't hesitate to join the fight. Nicolas hung back, content to fling magic, but Lucas had expected that, given that Nick was a witch. Sophia's shield spell helped there, but Julian was able to block the magic more effectively and quickly became their main defense.

Aaron partially shifted, proving he was some kind of feline—panther maybe, judging by the black fur—and leapt forward. Farid quickly shifted to his leopard form and met him halfway. The sound of snarls filled the room, echoing back at them so the fight sounded worse than it already was. They were fierce and shed a lot of blood—and very quickly—but Lucas couldn't focus on them, not when there were so many others all too eager to end them.

Theo rushed toward Lucas faster than he could move, and he braced himself to absorb the impact of an enraged vampire. They both went down, the floor cracking with the impact and vibrating through him. Theo tried to sink his fangs into Lucas's neck, but they couldn't penetrate his tough skin. Lucas tried to pivot and reverse their positions, but Theo managed to keep him pinned. Drawing his dagger, he started to use it, then hesitated for just a second. The easiest way to get Theo off him would be to kill him, but he really hoped he could find an alternative to that.

Vazi gave him that alternative, picking Theo up with one hand and flinging him toward the others. He hit them like a bowling ball, knocking over half the group. They wouldn't stay down long, but it gave Lucas time to get to his feet, and he took a second to assess the situation.

Julian continued blocking magical attacks, not just from Nick, but also from Joshua. Farid and Aaron were still locked in combat, though it seemed to him that they were both starting to slow. Erasmus was chanting, with a hand extended and partially clenched, while staring at Alicia. Since she was clawing at her throat much like Jeremiah had, he assumed it was the same thing he'd done to Jeremiah. Smart, since Alicia was also a siren. Brigit appeared to be standing there doing nothing, but he realized she was staring at one of the women. From his best guess, she had somehow caught the woman's gaze, like a snake-charmer, but in reverse. It wasn't an ability he'd known snake shifters possessed, but he wasn't going to question it.

And Sophia was actually in the thick of it, fighting off one of the men he'd never seen. His first reaction was to jump in and help—though she honestly looked to be holding her own—but he didn't get the chance, since something caused his body to lock up. It felt like he was a true gargoyle, trapped in a stone form, immobile and vulnerable.

"I don't fucking think so," Seth snarled, and whatever was keeping him in place disappeared as the god stalked forward and punched one of the men in the face, hard enough to knock the man out and send him flying back a good six feet.

With his body his again, Lucas strode forward, throwing punches and magic in equal measure. Before he knew it, only Farid and Aaron were left, both covered in far too many deep gashes. He stomped to them and grabbed Farid by the scruff, pulling him away from Aaron. The leopard twisted and took a swipe at him, but his claws scraped across his stone skin rather than slashing it open. Following Seth's example, he threw Farid away from Aaron. The shifter acted like a true cat, landing on his feet—mostly—and turning to snarl at them.

"That's enough," Aelia said in a firm tone, before she pushed her palm toward Farid. The fur receded from his body, his eyes rolled back, and he collapsed, nude, bleeding, and now unconscious. That wasn't something Lucas had thought possible by anyone but a god. Shifting wasn't a learned magic, it was innate, as natural to shifters as breathing. Forcing someone to shift had to take a monumental amount of power. It made him respect Aelia just a little more.

Aaron returned to his fully human form, panting and bleeding. Aelia hurried over to him and made a displeased sound at all the injuries. "I can close the wounds, but it won't feel good," she offered.

"Sorcery?" Julian asked, also breathing heavily.

"Mmhmm," she confirmed with a nod.

"Let me do what I can first?" When she nodded again, he laid a hand on Aaron's arm. The wounds did close, though much more slowly than Lucas was used to seeing. Then again, he had been spoiled, since he'd most often seen healing done by the son of Apollo. It wasn't perfect, but the man was no longer bleeding.

"We should go before they wake up and we have to do it all over again," Sophia suggested, though she had a bruise forming around one eye, and her knuckles were red from her own fight.

"I agree," Erasmus said, nodding.

Lucas nodded and found Sophia's side as she entered the code to the next door and they resumed moving deeper into the Athenaeum.

They ran into two other groups, also a mix of Nasaru and outside victims, though they weren't as tough as that first group. Still, when they reached the Vault door, they were more banged up, but still mostly intact.

"Check to see if you can get into the Vault before we leave," Sophia suggested.

Erasmus grimaced, but moved to the keypad, laid his palm on it, and entered his code. It flashed red, proving that Peter had removed his access after his apparent death. It could have just been habit—it was procedure to remove deceased members from the security—or it could have been paranoia. Either way, the result was the same.

"Okay, let's see if it'll let me in, or if he took me out of the system, too." Sophia repeated the same process Erasmus had, and it seemed to take longer than normal before it flashed green and the locks opened. "I was really worried that wouldn't work."

"So was I," Lucas admitted. "If he'd been smart, he would have removed all of our access."

"But he didn't, so we can get to work," Julian said, taking several steps toward the door.

Lucas nearly smiled at the man's eagerness. "Remember, you're looking for something to stop the Miasma, not on a field trip," he said firmly.

Julian waved a hand dismissively. "Just remember that I helped you get all this back. Later, when I ask to come visit the Athenaeum."

"Doesn't mean you'll get into the Vault," Sophia warned as she started for the location Athena had told her the entrance to the Miasma chamber was hidden.

"Good luck," Brigit told Erasmus's group before following after Sophia.

Lucas watched the five disappear into the Vault, hoping they would find something, because he wasn't sure stopping Peter would stop the Miasma from spreading. Worse, if it was, in fact, sentient, then without Peter to control it, it might spread faster. They had no way of knowing.

Sophia found the entrance and got it open. Inside, it was a set of stairs not dissimilar from the rest of those in the Athenaeum. Unlike the other stairs, they were dark and even Lucas felt a foreboding as he stared down them. That would be because of the Miasma, he reasoned. Knowing there was a pool of the insidious stuff not that far from them was enough to make anyone nervous. What really concerned him was the idea that approaching it might be the same as when they'd gotten closer to the Oskila chamber. All they needed was to get aggressive toward each other before they even reached Peter. Then again, he could feel the mild pull of the Oskila, so that could help.

"Don't suppose anyone kept some of Julian's headlamps, did they?" Sophia asked.

"I don't have a headlamp, but I can do…" Brigit trailed off, whispered something, and flung her hand like she was tossing a ball toward the ceiling. A small ball of light appeared just beneath the ceiling. It wasn't extremely bright, but it was enough to allow them to safely navigate the stairs and see any impending threats. "That," she finished.

"That'll work," Seth said, nodding and starting down the stairs.

It quickly became apparent that this wasn't going to be a short trip. The stairs just went on and on, growing less defined as they went. They certainly weren't as smooth as the other stairs, but those had been walked on for thousands of years by thousands of people, and these had been ignored.

After a while, the stairs changed to a slope, steep enough that they had to step carefully or risk sliding the rest of the way down on their asses. Not the high ground he was hoping for when they found Peter. And that was if he was actually in the chamber.

"Am I seeing things, or is there a light down there?" Brigit asked.

As soon as she mentioned it, Lucas was able to make out a hint of light that didn't come from her glowing ball. "We must be getting close."

There was a faint echo from below, and it sounded like someone yelling. "We're definitely getting close," Sophia whispered. She sounded nervous, but he understood. He found her hand and gave it a squeeze, knowing she wouldn't want him doing more than that right now. Though he knew how strong she was, he also saw that she was constantly trying to prove it to others. Something assholes like Jericho hadn't helped with. Who cared if she was one of the youngest aspides they'd ever had? Or that she didn't have as much experience? She was still intelligent and brave, and no one could have stopped Peter before he'd killed, not without a prophet's vision or the ability to go back in time.

"Everyone ready?" he whispered. He meant it more for Sophia, but not singling her out would make her feel better.

Seth and Brigit nodded, but Sophia stared at the light for a moment before she did as well. "It's time to end it," she murmured.

They continued down the last bit of the sloping tunnel to the Miasma chamber. Though there was a sense of urgency, they didn't run, because falling would put them at a disadvantage and provide warning. Peter might know they were in the Athenaeum, but there was no way he could know they were aware of the Miasma.

The sound of yelling grew more distinct as they got closer. Peter was supremely pissed they were back, and he was calling someone incompetent for not being able to find three people. Himself, Sophia, and Olivia, he assumed. He didn't hear Erasmus's name mentioned, so it was likely he didn't know his uncle had survived. Good. They might need that ace in the hole later.

A few dozen feet from the opening into the Miasma chamber, they could see inside. Peter absolutely wasn't alone. Lucas could see Carla's face, but the rest were turned in a way that didn't allow him to make out who was who. There were at least three, plus Peter. Fairly even odds, especially since one of his group was a god. Carla was going to be tough to subdue without doing her serious injury, though.

"Hold up," Lucas whispered, drawing them back a few paces. "I can see Carla in there, and at least two others aside from Peter. She's tough. I think when we get in there, I should handle Carla. Can't tell you about anyone else because I couldn't make any of them out."

"She is tough," Sophia agreed. "I'll handle Peter."

"How?" Brigit asked. The single word didn't have any shock or doubt in it, but curiosity.

"I don't know," Sophia admitted with a shrug. "Talking to him, to begin with. I can mention Erasmus being alive if I have to. That should at least distract him for a minute if it does need to get physical."

"You wouldn't rather I take care of it?" Seth asked, frowning. With concern, he thought, but he wasn't a hundred percent on it. Skepticism was also possible, but Lucas had a feeling that Sophia had the best chance of talking Peter down. Secretly, he could admit he didn't think Peter could be swayed from his current path, but he had to let her try.

She smiled sadly and shook her head. "He doesn't really know you, and we both know it'd be easiest for you to kill him. I know it may sound naive, but I'd rather he end up in the Ekklesia's prison or something."

"If you're sure."

Sophia lifted her chin, squared her shoulders, and nodded. "I am."

"If you need backup, just say the word," Brigit said. "But from what I know, I think if anyone has a chance of talking him into sanity, it's you."

That was a weird way of saying it, but Lucas really was leaning that way, too. Some of it may have been a lie, but Sophia and Peter had spent a good bit of time bonding and hanging out. And as much as he hated how Peter had pushed her down the stairs and strangled her, he was also aware that he could have just killed her instead of warning her. The fact that he hadn't gave Lucas a tiny sliver of hope.

"Thank you," Sophia said, glancing back to the opening. "But let's do it now before I lose my nerve."

"Never gonna happen." Those were Lucas's last words before they went to face the Athenaeum's personal demon.

Chapter 23

Lucas took a quick glance around the chamber before he focused on those within. There was a small platform of stone, almost like a beach, set just before a pool of an oddly pretty swirling emerald liquid—though he used the term liquid very loosely. At times, it looked more like a gas, and occasionally it seemed nearly solid. Whatever it was, it looked dangerous. It wasn't a big pool, maybe only ten or twelve feet across, and maybe twenty wide. The ceiling was low, which meant they didn't have a lot of room to move in.

He'd also been wrong. There weren't three people in there with Peter, there were five, and it was worse than he'd expected. Along with Carla, Peter had gotten Ray—who was an older but very tough guard—Sophia's mom, Heather, Sergei—who was a son of Apollo—and Josie—a witch of no small power. She wasn't a guard, but she was talented. Heather was probably the least dangerous person there, but he had a feeling she was there as a deterrent or distraction for Sophia.

Rather than lose what little element of surprise they had, Lucas went right for Carla. He only got two steps before they were noticed.

"Kill them," Peter snarled, taking a step back toward the Miasma.

Carla shifted before Lucas could get to her, and he was suddenly facing a jaguar. He was honestly sick of felines at this point, but he didn't shy away. It wasn't the first time he'd fought a shifter in their animal form, and it wouldn't be the last. Especially since he had yet to go up against one whose claws could easily penetrate his gargoyle skin. Besides, while jaguars were formidable, he'd rather fight a jaguar than a bear.

Seth used his powers to cause rock to flow up and encase Heather's feet, effectively limiting what she could do. It was a smart move. As an elf, she didn't have any latent offensive talents, and she'd been away from the Athenaeum for too long to have learned much sorcery. With her out of the way, he went after Sergei. If it was a friendly sparring match, it would be interesting to watch—god against demigod—but in this case it could be very, very bad. But Seth had the best chance of subduing Sergei without killing him.

Brigit split her focus between Ray and Josie, and from what little Lucas could see as he fought off Carla, she was doing very well. Which left Sophia to deal with the one who had masterminded all this chaos.

"Peter, please," Sophia said, keeping her distance from her cousin. "You don't have to do this! You can stop now, before anyone else gets hurt."

"You could stop, too, dear cousin," Peter said in a low, dangerous purr of a voice. "Accept my rule, accept that I will control not just the Athenaeum, but the entire world, and I will let you and your friends live."

"No, Peter. We can't," she said sadly. "You've already done too much, hurt too many people. You nearly killed me."

"I should have strangled you when I had my hands around your throat," he said cruelly. "It's not a mistake I'll make again."

"Why? Why kill your own dad? Why kill Thomas and Agatha? Why try to kill me?"

Lucas was barely able to listen to Sophia pleading with Peter. Carla was formidable in any form, and he was having a hard time just avoiding being pinned by her. In an effort to gain control, he kicked at her belly as she leapt, which spun her around in the air. At that point, it was too late to stop what he saw coming next.

Her jaguar body stretched and twisted as she flew, aiming to land on her feet, but Josie got in the way. One of Carla's paws, claws fully extended, raked over Josie's throat, causing blood to spurt. From as deep as it looked, the vein likely wasn't the only thing destroyed by Carla's claws. There wasn't time to feel guilt or grief, though he knew in an instant that even Sergei likely wouldn't be able to save her, even if he'd been in his right mind.

Carla didn't seem to care, but Lucas tried to fend her off and get to Josie. Except after what was probably only thirty seconds, Brigit caught his eye and shook his head. It was already too late.

While Carla didn't care, Peter did. He released a roar of rage that echoed around the small chamber, hurting his eardrums almost as much as the siren's shriek had. Everyone, Carla included, glanced at him, just in time for him to disappear. He didn't go far, appearing directly in front of Sophia. Lucas didn't have time to move, didn't even have time to call out a warning before he grabbed Sophia by the throat and disappeared.

For a second, Lucas's heart felt as cold as the stone he was made of. Sophia was gone, he didn't know where she'd been taken, and she was accompanied only by a murderous madman. Which meant four people he considered friends were currently standing in the way of him finding her.

Turning back to Carla, he felt his wings release from their magical prison, and his claws and fangs lengthen. The small part of him that was still rational tried to remember he wasn't supposed to kill her. The core of him, the protector, wanted only to get her out of the way so he could find his mate.

"Stand down or I won't be responsible for what happens to you," he said, aware his voice was deeper, more gravelly than it was in his human form.

Carla either didn't care, or the infection made her ignore the warning. It was likely the latter, since not a single infected person had spoken since they'd entered the Athenaeum. Snarling, with Josie's blood on her claws, she leapt at Lucas. No longer going easy on her, he lifted one arm and simply smashed it into her face. There was a brief sound of pain before the fur disappeared and she turned back to human. An instant later, she collapsed on the floor, unconscious.

Heather was still incapacitated by the stone surrounding her feet, and Seth was battering Sergei beyond what any mortal could have handled. The demigod was weakening, and it was clear Seth would defeat him soon enough. A glance at Brigit and Ray showed they were evenly matched, and part of him wavered, debating if he should help her first, or go get Sophia.

She took the choice from him. "Go! Get her," Brigit said before she landed a kick to Ray's midsection, slamming him against the rock wall.

Without hesitation, he raced for the doorway. As soon as he was past the narrow opening, he took to the air, hoping he would get to her in time.

Sophia had frozen when Carla had accidentally killed Josie, so hadn't even moved when Peter had appeared before her and grabbed her. That act was enough to break her out of her momentary stupor, and as soon as they reformed in the computer room—his sanctuary—she jerked back. Peter didn't let her go easily, and she felt his nails scratch deep as she yanked out of his grip, then retreated several steps.

She watched him warily, unsure what she could say to calm him—if anything could. He hadn't been stable before Josie had been killed, and her death seemed to have snapped whatever sanity he'd clung to.

Her shield spell was muttered under her breath, strengthening it, since it had obviously weakened. Otherwise, Peter should never have been able to grab her. But it turned out not to be necessary. The frenzied light no longer shone in his eyes, and rather than trying to grab her again, he let his arm drop. Rather than the enraged, insane man she'd seen only a minute before, he now looked miserable and defeated.

"Peter?" she asked, certain this was some sort of trap. He had pretended to be a loving cousin for a month—and a loving son and nephew for decades before that—so he was clearly an exceptional actor.

"You can't save me, Sophia," he answered, his voice bleak, his expression somber.

"What?" That wasn't quite the last thing she'd expected to hear, but it was close.

"That's what you were trying to do, wasn't it? Talk me down so you could save me?" He attempted—and failed—a smile. It was more of a pained grimace than anything else. "You want to make everything right."

"Why can't I?" Sophia asked, wondering at this abrupt shift in personality. She wasn't sure she believed it, but refused to squash that last bit of hope. "Just let me cuff you now and stop all this."

He shook his head and leaned back against the wall, running a hand over his bright blue mohawk. "You can't save me," he repeated. "The Miasma has too great a hold on me. It's had me since I was a boy and I accidentally stumbled across it. Stumbled into it, actually. And I do mean literally."

The idea of a child falling into the Miasma horrified her, and she wanted to hug him and apologize for what had happened to him. There wasn't time for that, not now. Maybe not ever. "We can find a way to save you. We got the Miasma out of Lachlan."

Again, he shook his head. "You didn't, not entirely. I don't think there's a way to ever fully cure someone who's had the Miasma inside them, and it runs through my body like blood."

"There has to be a way," she protested, unwilling to give up on him. Or to entertain the thought that everyone he'd infected would forever be infected. That was no way to live, if the gods would even allow them to live.

He laughed, but it was dry and sounded pitiful. "Sophia, I killed my dad, my great-uncle. I tried to kill you." His gaze fell to the floor and his shoulders hunched. "I caused Josie's death."

Josie. So the affection she'd sensed growing between Josie and Peter hadn't been feigned. He'd really started to care for her. Maybe he'd even loved her. That made it all that much sadder.

"Even if there was some miraculous cure for what ails me, how could I possibly live with myself with all I've done?"

"But it wasn't you, it was the Miasma." If he was telling the truth, but she had a feeling he was being more honest now than he'd ever been with her.

"Maybe, but it was my hand that actually committed the acts." His expression went serious, which was almost as scary as when he looked like a madman. "You need to kill me, Sophia. If you don't, I'm going to kill you and do even worse to the world. If you think the Athenaeum under the Miasma's influence is bad, then imagine the world controlled by its whims. With all the relics and sorcery we have used to fulfill its needs. It won't take long before every living being is under its control."

Sophia was shaking her head before he finished talking, and she backed up several more steps, as though putting more space between them would prevent what he was asking. "No. I can't. Even with everything you've done, I can't. I've never killed anyone! I take spiders outside and set them free instead of squishing them, so how can you possibly think I could kill a person? Especially family?"

Peter pushed away from the wall and began walking slowly toward her. "Because if you don't, then you're damning all of us, Sophia, and especially me. You'll be forcing me to continue to kill and manipulate and conquer, all to achieve the Miasma's goal of overtaking the entire world. Maybe all the worlds." As he spoke, his voice began to grow in volume, and she sensed he was starting to lose whatever lucidity Josie's death had gifted him. "If you don't kill me, then I will kill you, and I will not be merciful about it!" he screamed, only feet from her, now, spittle flying from his mouth. "I will revel in it, and when you're close to your final breath, I'll find Lucas and make him watch as I end you. Then I'll string him up and take a chisel to him, carving pieces off his arrogant hide until he's nothing more than a pile of rubble."

"No," she breathed, as much for the image his words presented as for the fact that the Miasma was clearly regaining control over him. Though the thought of killing him wounded her in a way little else had, her hand eased toward the knife Lucas had given her. It was only on her hip, easy to grab. The knife may be the only thing that would allow her to survive this encounter, but the thought of using it put a deep crack in her heart. Killing him had always been a possibility, but somehow, it had been easier to imagine when she'd thought he'd been the one in control, not the one being controlled. She only had to hope that killing him would truly be saving him—and all those who were under the control of him and the Miasma.

"Oh yes," he crowed, the insane gleam back in his eyes. "It will be a joy to kill him and every other pompous asshole who thought they were better than me because they were stuck in the past and I was looking toward the future. And the ones I don't kill will bow to my every whim!" No longer was he the cousin who had given a damn about not just her, but the entire planet. The cousin who had nagged her into watching movies and taken her on a picnic to get some sunlight. The cousin who had worried about her. Now he was nothing more than the Miasma's tool.

Tears filled her eyes as she resigned herself to the fact that she would have to end his life, but she blinked them away, afraid they'd obscure her vision and throw off her aim. She might have to kill him, but she didn't want him to suffer one second more than was necessary.

"I'm so sorry, Peter," she whispered, before quickly casting the twin spell. As her duplicate appeared directly in front of him, close enough to touch, the real her darted forward, hoping he'd be distracted enough to miss her approach. Except he flung out a hand with a hissed word, throwing a ball of shimmering green magic through the intangible copy of her, and right into Sophia's chest. It hit with enough force to knock her back, and the twin disappeared.

She hit one of the desks hard enough to make her cry out as the edge slammed her lower back, but she couldn't afford to be distracted by the pain. A physical fight was out of the question, at least until her nerves stopped screaming, so she decided to literally fight fire with fire. She narrowed her eyes on him and spoke the new spell Olivia had taught her. His shirt caught on fire, distracting him more thoroughly than her first spell had. While he tried to beat out the flames, she pushed herself away from the desk and pulled the knife free of the sheath. Before she could get close to him, he kicked at her, but the training Lucas and Steven had given her rushed back, and she tried to dodge out of the way. She might have managed it, but trying to move like that made pain flare in her back where the desk had connected, slowing her movement just enough to have his foot connect with her hip.

Before Sophia could fully recover, he went with what seemed to be his favorite move—darting out a hand to grab her throat. This time she didn't fight it, but let him pull her closer, despite his shirt still flickering with flames in some places. Forcing her hand to lift, tears slipped down her cheeks when she shoved the knife into him as hard as she could, barely feeling the flames licking at her skin.

Peter's eyes widened with shock, but she wasn't sure she'd hit anything vital. Her training thus far hadn't included weapons—or the best places to hit with them—so she pulled the blade free and sank it into him again, then a third time. On that third blow his knees buckled and blood trickled out of the corner of his mouth.

She fell to the floor with him, her weapon still buried in his chest, her hand around the hilt. Not wanting to hurt him more than was necessary, she spoke in a shaky voice, extinguishing the fire. Her arm stung where the flames had licked at the skin, but it didn't hurt as badly as her heart. "I'm sorry, Peter," she said in a barely audible voice as his body weakened too much to support him and he fell to one side.

Sophia let go of the knife and caught him clumsily, lowering him as gently as she could as he stared up at her, mouth working, though no sound was coming out. Curling her legs beneath her, she held him close as blood flowed freely and the color leeched from his face. She couldn't stop crying, especially when it registered that he no longer looked crazy or sad; he looked relieved.

This wasn't how she'd wanted this to end. She'd been sincere when she said she wanted him to live, albeit in a cell. She had so little family left, it had hurt to even think of Peter dying, yet she'd been the one to wield the blade. Her mind might believe it was a saving action, but her heart wasn't so easily convinced.

"I'm so, so sorry," she whispered, running a hand over his disheveled hair. "I wish I'd known sooner. That there was something else I could have done."

"Don't," he said weakly, attempting to shake his head, but he barely moved a fraction of an inch. "Saved. Me."

Her throat tightened and she pressed her lips together to contain a sob as tears continued to stain her cheeks, just as his blood now stained her fingers. She couldn't say anything, so just held him during the last moments of his life. A life which had been tortured more than anyone could have guessed. Adults—even those several centuries old—had trouble dealing with a hint of the Miasma, so for him to have been exposed so young was unthinkable. He'd had no chance.

Peter tried to smile at her, though with the blood around his lips it looked more like a horror-movie grimace. Only a heartbeat later, he stilled. His eyes remained open, but she could see there was nothing in them. Not anymore.

Unable to contain herself any longer, she closed her eyes and let the sounds of grief come. She knew she should go see if his death had freed the others from the infection, but the little boy he'd been deserved at least a minute of grief. As did the last bit of innocence she'd lost when she'd given him the salvation he'd asked for.

When she could get herself under control, she eased him off her lap, sniffling and trying to ignore the blood covering her. It wasn't easy, since the smell of it permeated her clothes, the metallic smell making her a little nauseous. Standing, she looked down at him, wishing this wasn't how she'd remember him. So she focused on the traits he'd been known for. The blue mohawk. The eyebrow and snakebite piercings. The sleeve tattoos.

Frowning, her gaze landed on a gold cuff on his wrist. It wasn't something she'd ever seen him wear before, nor did it look at all his style. He was punk, not antiques, and that definitely looked old. But she'd have to wonder over that later. Right now, she had to find the others and figure out if the infection was gone—or if killing Peter had only been the first step to victory.

Chapter 24

Sophia would have been happy to never see Lucas's knife again, but there was no telling how many infected were between her and her allies, so she forced herself to pull it from Peter's still body. Grimacing at the blood staining it, she forced herself to ignore the crimson as she peeked outside the room. She didn't see anyone—friend or foe—and carefully stepped out, turning back toward the entrance hall. Right now, she really wished she'd learned Lucas's invisibility spell. The last thing she wanted right now was to fight someone else she knew and liked. Especially since she was alone and would have fewer options than the more experienced fighters.

She really, really didn't want to kill anyone else. Not today, not ever.

She was nearly back to the entrance room when she ran into a ghost. It took several precious seconds to realize she wasn't face to face with Josie. It was her twin, Angela. Grief and remorse hit her hard, but Angela didn't give her time to truly feel either before she slammed Sophia against the wall with magic. Sophia barely kept her head from smacking the stone, and tried the twin spell again. Infected, it seemed that aside from Peter, the Nasaru didn't have quite the same reasoning skills as they did normally, so Angela fell for it, turning her focus to the false figure. Her hand flew out, but the magic didn't affect the illusion the same way it had Sophia, causing the woman to frown and cock her head in confusion.

When her feet hit the floor again, Sophia thought a quick apology, then hit Angela with a quick telekinetic blast. Since the witch wasn't paying attention to her, it landed where Sophia intended, causing Angela to crumple where she stood.

She spared a moment's pity for the woman who didn't yet know she had lost her twin sister, then hurried on, hoping that would be the last person she ran into before finding friends.

Luck was finally on her side, because the next people she ran into were Olivia, Evane, Suni, and Rune. She bit her lip to avoid embarrassing herself. Sobbing with relief was hardly a good image for the head of a place like this. Even if everything had gone to hell on her watch.

She had no idea that her eyes were red and a little puffy from the tears she'd already shed.

"Sophia? Where are the others? Where's Lucas?" Olivia asked, hurrying across the distance to her.

Sophia backed up quickly, unwilling to touch or be touched while Peter's blood stained her clothes and skin. "I don't know. Back in the Miasma chamber, maybe? Peter..." She had to stop and breathe for a moment before she could continue. "Peter grabbed me and teleported us both to the computer room."

Olivia's brow knit with concern and she stopped, within touching distance, but she kept her hands at her sides. And her eyes dropped, taking in the blood covering Sophia's clothes and hands. "Is he..."

The grief tried to rise up once more as Sophia nodded, and rather than try to force the words out to explain, she just held up the bloody knife. It was enough. "But it didn't do anything. It didn't work," she admitted. "Angela...She attacked me after."

"Shit," Evane spat. "Wasn't that supposed to stop all this?"

"That was the hope, yes," Olivia answered without looking away from Sophia. "The Oskila Vazi blew in here should have calmed them down, and...without someone to control them, they should have stopped attacking."

"Except the Miasma is still inside them," Sophia murmured as she tried to figure out plan B. No, it was more like plan C. There had to be some way to force it out of these people. The tyet had seemed to work, but Peter had verified it had been a temporary fix; like putting a bandage on a broken bone. And this stuff was older than even the oldest god, so they couldn't help. But there had to be something. The Anunnaki might not have sealed this stuff away as well as she would have liked, but they couldn't have been so irresponsible as to create something this powerful and dangerous without putting in some sort of fail-safe.

Shit. A fail-safe. Like the one in the hidden room she'd been visiting. A room that had held a grimoire containing a spell to control Miasma. If that spell really worked, then maybe she could force all the Miasma to exit everyone it had infected and return to the chamber below. She might even be able to force it to remain dormant. But only *if* the spell really worked.

"I have an idea, but I need to go alone." Olivia she might be okay with knowing about this room—the woman had proven herself ultimately trustworthy—but the others weren't even Nasaru. And she remembered Erasmus saying he doubted the door would even open if someone other than the aspida was there. A way of protecting the texts within.

"No," Rune said, being as short-winded as ever.

"Look, it's not someplace—"

He shook his head as he cut her off. "No. You won't be alone."

She frowned as she studied his face. He appeared calm, but there was a stubborn set to his jaw. And while she didn't doubt he'd protect her, would he keep the room's existence to himself? Except...she wanted to trust him. She wasn't sure why, as she'd never been the sort to immediately trust strangers. Maybe it was Blanche's recommendation, or the way he and Brigit had dropped everything and come to help immediately after hearing she needed it, but she decided to trust him. "Okay." Looking back to the other three, she said, "Keep looking for others who are infected. If possible, move them all to the entrance hall where we left the others."

"Okay, but...be careful, Soph," Olivia instructed. "I'm not ready for a new aspida yet."

Sophia gave her a smile she was a long way from feeling. "Don't worry. I've got the viking with me," she said, nodding to Rune.

They parted ways, though Sophia started to move at a much quicker pace than they had with the rest of the group. It aggravated all of her injuries, but she wanted this done. She wanted everyone safe. "I think I know a way of getting the Miasma out of them," she told him. "Problem is, it's in a secret location only the heads of this place are supposed to know about. It's why I wanted to go alone. I'm also not sure I can get in with someone else with me."

"How?" he asked, his eyes moving constantly, searching for threats as they reached the stairs and started descending.

She needed a moment to figure out which how he was wondering about. "A spell. I have no guarantee it's one that'll work, but it claims to be able to control Miasma," she admitted. "I'm hoping I can use it to force the Miasma out of everyone—here or outside the Athenaeum—and back to the Miasma chamber."

"Good." It was all he said. No concerns, no further questions, just the single word. Normally Sophia liked people who spoke a little more than he did, but keeping it short and sweet was kind of refreshing in a way. On the other hand, if he'd kept up constant chatter, it might take her mind off things, at least for a minute.

The stairwell was clear as they passed the residential level, and she paused at the door to the aspida hallway. Every single former aspida, right back to the first, the one who'd rescued texts from the Library of Alexandria, was honored here. Each one had their urn on a pedestal, with a stele behind it, naming all of that aspida's achievements. Even Erasmus had one here, which was kind of creepy now that she knew he was alive. Especially since they'd burned 'his' body and placed the ashes in an urn. Which begged the question of who exactly was now in his urn. Or what, since the gods had been involved.

"Can you wait here?" she asked. "This is the only way in and out, so no one would be able to get to me with you standing guard." And it would let her mostly keep the room a secret. Its exact location, anyway. And hopefully, if he was at the entrance but not in the room itself, the door would open. If it didn't, she'd ask him to wait in the stairwell.

He scowled down at her and said nothing.

"Please?"

His eyes rolled toward the ceiling and he sighed, turning so his back was to the hallway and he could watch the stairs.

"Thank you," she told him, turning and hurrying down the hallway. The door thankfully slid open and she quickly stepped inside, letting it close behind her. She was probably safe now, even if she didn't have Rune. As far as she was aware, only she was able to open the door. Well, the patrons could probably manage it, but she wasn't afraid of them attacking her.

Not wanting to waste time, she moved straight to the desk and started flipping through the grimoire with her clean hand. It took her a minute to find the page she was looking for, and she blew out a breath as she began to read. After the warnings—which every spell in this book had—and after she'd muddled through the odd form of Greek, she glanced down at her hand and started to laugh. It was a good thing no one else was there, because she was certain it sounded as hysterical as she suddenly felt. The laughter quicker changed to tears, and it took her a few minutes to compose herself.

Some spells required only focus and a specific chant to work, like the shield spell, or even the teleportation spell she'd gotten out of this very book. Others, like the one to break Peter's ward, required physical components. This one? Oh, it required a true sacrifice. Specifically, something she literally had at hand.

> *Controlling such a primal essence is not, and should not, be easy. If you are foolish enough to dare such a task, then you must make a monumental sacrifice. Two things are required if you hope to force Miasma to accede to your demands; your own blood, drawn fresh from your body, and the life's blood of one you love. Nothing less than death to one you hold close to you will satisfy such dark*

magic. Nothing less would be powerful enough to bend the Miasma to your will.

I must warn you again—this is not something that should be undertaken lightly. The act of murder leaves a stain on the soul nothing can erase, and even if you dare that, the strain the magic places on your mind may be too much to bear.

Sophia dropped her head and wanted to cry again. Not because she didn't think she could do it, but because she was very much afraid the warning was right, and that she would always feel guilt for Peter. She already suspected that she'd feel the hot blood on her skin long after she'd washed it off.

Later. She would deal with that later, hopefully with Lucas's arms around her.

The blood was still wet, so hopefully it would work, because she wasn't going to have anyone else sacrificed for the fucking Miasma. Too many had died already. The chant needed was simple, at least, so she read through the words several times, committing them to memory. Yes, she could cast the spell here, in secret and safety, but she wouldn't know if it had worked without a victim in front of her. She would hate to end the spell prematurely and waste her unintentional sacrifice. Peter's death would mean something. By saving him, she *would* save the Athenaeum.

Leaving the room, she walked back to Rune. "I need to find Lucas, then we need to go back to the entrance."

"The spell?"

Sophia nodded, starting to understand his shorthand. "I found it, but we need to hurry."

He grunted and nodded, starting to head further down the stairs.

They'd only taken a few steps before she heard something she recognized as wings. "You hear that?"

"Wings. Large," he agreed, bracing for an attack.

Such preparations weren't needed, because the next person they saw coming up the stairs by air was Lucas, in full gargoyle form. Never in her life had she seen such a beautiful sight.

His eyes found her and he folded his wings, landing hard on the stairs then immediately running up the last few steps to her. He picked her up and crushed her to him, which she needed so much, but she had to be careful to keep her right hand away from him or risk losing the blood she needed for the spell. The other arm went around him and held him tightly as she buried her face in his shoulder.

"You ever do that to me again and I'll turn you over my knee and spank you until you can't sit for a week," he warned, though his face was pressed against her hair.

The rough stone of his skin was a little abrasive, but she didn't care. He was alive, and so was she. And now she had the person she trusted the most to watch for signs the Miasma infection was clearing.

"It wasn't my choice, believe me," she whispered. "And while I'd love to just hold you like this for the rest of the day, this isn't over and we need to hurry."

Lucas set her down but didn't fully release her. "Peter? He's still around here somewhere?"

She shook her head and fought to be able to tell him what had happened, but she wasn't ready to voice that horror, not yet.

"He is no longer a threat," Rune said. "We need to go."

Lucas frowned and glanced between them. "Go? Go where?"

She was grateful that was what he latched onto. "The entrance. I have a spell I'm hoping will force the Miasma out of everyone, but I need to be in the same room as the victims so I can tell when it works." So she could tell if it worked.

"One spell and this is all over?"

"I hope so."

"Then let's go." He released her and reached for her hand, but it was her right and she yanked it behind her back before he could touch it. That was when he noticed the blood covering her. "Fuck. Are you hurt? Who did that?"

Honestly, she was hurting. Adrenaline and grief had masked the worst of the physical pain, but she was feeling every injury she'd taken in the last hour. "It's not my blood, and I'll tell you, but please, later?"

His jaw clenched and he didn't look happy—he looked like he wanted to tear someone apart for hurting her—but he nodded. "Let's go get rid of the Miasma."

Chapter 25

Lucas's emotions were all over the place. Fear for Sophia's safety hadn't yet abated, and he was furious she'd been hurt. Her throat was bruising, as were a few other places, and she had blood all over her. It might not be hers, but the fact that it seemed to have coated her right hand and the knife meant it had likely been shed by her. Peter's? Rune had said he was dead, so it wasn't outside the realm of possibility, but it hurt something inside him to think of Sophia having to do something like that. She was strong enough, yes, but just because she could, didn't mean she should have to. Still, that bloodied knife said a lot. As did the fact that she didn't want to talk about it.

When they reached the top of the stairs, he saw the two recon groups had gathered back in the entrance, proving they'd cleared the top floor. Knowing Athena and Olivia, they'd probably gone over the residential floor, too.

Suni was busy checking on their temporary prisoners, probably ensuring their sleep spells were intact, as well as healing any wounds that had been missed. Or ones that just hadn't been tended to yet, as he saw faces that hadn't been here when they'd first arrived.

Olivia walked over to them, her face relieved. "Good. You're safe." Rune made an offended noise, and she flashed him a quick grin. "I know you were with her, but I'm allowed to worry, so don't get your panties in a twist."

Sophia nodded. "I am. Though we didn't run into anyone since I saw you."

"Good. Did you find the spell you were looking for?"

Sophia drew in a deep breath, like she was having to brace herself for the answer. "I did. And I need to do it now. And I mean right fucking now." There was a hint of desperation in her voice, which worried him a little. He was as eager for this to be over as she was, but he had a feeling it was more than that.

"Great!" Relief bloomed on Olivia's face, which Lucas understood. In a few minutes, this might actually be over. "Is this a focus and chant sort of spell, or something more complicated?"

It was doubtful anyone else noticed Sophia's right hand flexing around the knife, but he did. He noticed most everything about her, and that single action had his eyes narrowing as they waited for her answer.

"More complicated, but I have what I need. Or will in a moment."

"How's that?"

Instead of answering, Sophia looked over at Suni. "Can you wake one of them up?"

"I can," Suni said, straightening from checking on Jericho. "First, I want to take care of you, though."

"I'm fine," Sophia argued, but Suni shook her head.

"I'm a healer. I know you're not fine. You can do the spell, but I'm healing you before I wake anyone up."

Lucas was glad she pushed, and even happier when Sophia gave in. "Fine."

Suni laid a hand on Sophia's left arm, in one of the few patches not coated with blood. He watched as the budding bruises on her throat faded, and a stiffness he hadn't noticed eased.

"Thank you," Sophia said with a touch of a smile.

"You're welcome. Now, do you have a preference on who you want me to wake?"

"Catherine," Lucas answered. "She's a dryad, and since we're underground, she's not as much of a threat as some of them. Like him," he said, inclining his head to the ice elemental.

"Which one is she?"

Olivia pointed to the blonde woman, asleep off to the side. "That's her."

"Before you do that," Lucas said when Suni started in that direction, "Sophia, what does this spell entail, and is it dangerous?"

He could tell by the look on her face that she wanted to lie, but nodded after a second. "It is."

That didn't surprise him. A spell meant to do something like this would be legendary, and legendary spells were never without their risks. She'd already taken too many, and he was sincerely afraid her luck was going to run out eventually. "Then let me do it. You've already had to get the wards down, then whatever happened with Peter. Let me do it."

She shook her head. "You can't."

"Why not? I know more sorcery than you do. It can't be that complicated."

"Gimme a minute," she told Suni and Olivia, pulling him to the side.

"Sophia? Love, what is it? What's so bad about this spell?" he asked, cupping her cheek gently, careful not to scrape her with his skin. Everything inside him was on high alert, so he couldn't force his body to shift back. Not yet. He'd probably remain in his gargoyle form until the Miasma was well and truly gone.

"One of the ingredients...It can't be easily obtained."

"What's that supposed to mean? If you have it, then you can just give it to me."

"No, I can't," she whispered before holding up her bloody hand. "Not unless you want to kill me or someone else you love."

That was close to the last thing he'd expected her to say. "What?"

"It requires the caster to kill someone they love," she said, voice empty but for a slight tremor.

Oh gods. So she really had been the one to kill Peter. And it explained why she had yet to clean the away the blood. He was sure she wanted it off her more than anything, but was forcing herself to endure the extreme discomfort it gave her, both physically and emotionally. She was a remarkable woman, and he wished she wasn't right in this instance. He would give anything to have been the one to wield the knife, to take that guilt and this responsibility from her.

"No, I can't do that," he agreed softly, pulling her into a hug, though this time he was as mindful of her right hand as she was. "But I will be there beside you for every second, and then I'll take you straight to the bathroom so you can clean up. And anything else you need to do."

"Thank you," she breathed, sinking into him for the moment she allowed herself. "I love you."

"Love you, too." He kissed her lightly, then looked back to the others, who were politely not looking in their direction. "Let's get it over with?"

"Gods yes."

They walked to Suni, who was standing beside Catherine, along with Olivia and Rune.

"Anything we need to know about this spell?" Olivia asked, studying Sophia's face.

Sophia shrugged, avoiding Olivia's gaze. No doubt she didn't want anyone else to know the source of the blood or requirements of the spell. At least not yet. "Just that I have no guarantee it'll work. That's why I want Catherine awake, so we can see if there's a change in her personality, back to how she used to be. I've noticed none of the infected have spoken aside from Peter, so that'll be a good indicator."

Olivia nodded. "Fair enough. Then whenever you're ready, Sophia."

"Suni? Can you wake her up?"

The healer nodded and bent, brushing her fingers across Catherine's hand. It was all that was needed to remove whatever had been keeping the woman asleep. Catherine jerked into a sitting position, and Suni quickly stepped back. Evane moved in front of her, not taking any aggressive action, but clearly protecting his wife from a potentially dangerous woman.

Catherine looked around and her gaze landed on Sophia. Letting out an animalistic snarl, she tried to lunge forward. Samara stepped forward and, in a move too quick for Sophia follow, had Catherine turned around so her back was to Sam's front, her arms pinned, effectively immobilizing the woman. It wouldn't prevent her from speaking, but the only sounds she made now were angry growls.

"I've got her," Samara assured Sophia in a calm, confident tone, not even having to work to keep Catherine subdued. "Do what you need to do. She won't hurt anyone."

"Thank you." Sophia closed her eyes and shifted the knife to her left hand, poising the blade over her right palm. Suni cleared her throat and shook her head when Sophia looked at her. "Is something wrong?" she asked.

"No, but I assume your blood is a component of this spell?" Suni asked.

"It is," Sophia confirmed.

"I know a lot of sources—especially pop culture—go straight to cutting the palm in cases like that, but it hurts unnecessarily. And if you didn't have a healer here, it would also limit the mobility in your hand. Might I suggest you go for the back of your forearm instead? It won't hurt as badly."

Sophia considered that for a moment before she nodded. "All right. Thank you." The knife went back into her right hand, making Lucas frown in confusion, but after only a few seconds of hesitation, she sliced into her left forearm. She gasped and her eyes went wide at the sting of the blade, and he wanted to kill Peter all over again for causing her this pain.

"Lucas," she said, offering him the knife. He took it and watched as she slapped her bloody hand over the now bleeding wound, making him frown. She actually rubbed her hand over the wound, letting out a gasp and wincing as it irritated the already raw nerves. "Here we go," she whispered before she began chanting.

It felt wrong, rubbing Peter's blood into her arm, much less an open wound, but Sophia did her best not to think about it. Instead she focused on what she was doing, trying to force the Miasma out of everyone, whether they were inside the Athenaeum or not. To push it deep below the Athenaeum, where it couldn't hurt or infect anyone else. To free not just the Nasaru from its grip, but protecting the entire world from its twisted, innate ambition.

She kept that image in her head as she spoke the words she'd so recently memorized, but the spell was quickly draining her. It sapped her strength harder than the sundial relic she'd used not so long ago, and at the time, she'd thought that was nearly unbearable.

Her knees tried to buckle, but strong arms quickly wrapped around her and kept her upright. She didn't say a word, though she wanted to thank Lucas for the help. She couldn't let her focus waver, though, not if she wanted this to work. Not if she wanted to make sure all of this meant something. That Peter and Josie and all the others hadn't died just so the Miasma could continue to spread. Peter had asked her to save him, but she was going to save everyone. This was how she could truly be an aspida and make those who loved her proud. How she could make herself proud and turn this unbearable situation into something she could handle. She would protect the Athenaeum in the only way she could.

Sophia felt something begin to build in her chest, slick and strong, and she pushed away confusion that it wasn't spreading outward. The now familiar syllables continued to roll off her tongue, though everything inside her was starting to grow weak. Without Lucas keeping her upright, she'd be on her knees at best, and flat on her face at worst. Even speaking was starting to become difficult, the words trying to slur.

Minutes passed, and nothing seemed to be happening but for that silky pressure inside her chest continuing to grow, like layers added one by one onto a pearl. Catherine was still straining against Samara's hold, trying desperately to break free and get to Sophia.

A hand settled on her shoulder and warmth spread through her. It wasn't power, not exactly, but it was some sort of mystical energy. The limbs that had begun to feel leaden and useless were able to support themselves. She wanted to look and see who was helping her, but didn't dare take her eyes off Catherine.

As if the extra energy pushed her over some unknown threshold, that ball of power trickled outward and she saw something begin to happen. At first it was barely visible, just a faint wisp, like steam rolling off a fresh cup of coffee. Then it grew and coalesced into something impossible to miss. Yellow-green mist trickled out of Catherine's nose and mouth. As Catherine's struggles began to fade, the mist hovered in front of her, growing larger with each passing breath.

Hopeful, Sophia glanced over at Jericho and saw the same thing was happening to him. It was happening to everyone who had been infected—including Olivia and herself. That terrified her and her chant faltered, but the hand on her shoulder squeezed. It wasn't a gentle squeeze, though it obviously wasn't meant to hurt, just remind her to keep going.

The ephemeral substance that had pulled from each infected person flowed together into one large mass. It shimmered, much like the Miasma in the chamber below had, twisting in and around itself. Writhing, though Sophia didn't know if it was in protest or pain, or if she was just attributing qualities to it that existed only in her mind.

The mass began to fall toward the floor—no, it was descending, and not hitting the floor, but sinking *into* the stone beneath their feet. Moving toward the Miasma chamber? She could only hope, but that meant she needed to keep going, until she was certain it was safely hidden away again. She closed her eyes so as not to be distracted by Catherine asking what had happened and continued chanting.

Even with the extra energy from the person holding her shoulder, she felt herself growing weaker again, but she was determined. The Miasma *would* return to the chamber, and it *would* remain there, dormant and waiting, until the end of time if she could manage it. She never wanted to go through this again.

There was a conversation behind held behind her, one she ignored until the hand on her shoulder squeezed again. Rune—who was attached to that hand—spoke. "You can stop."

Sophia hesitantly opened her eyes and looked at him. "How do you know?" she asked, voice scratchy due to the constant chanting.

Rune didn't answer, just folded his arms over his chest and looked around at the others.

"I do agree with him. I don't feel any lingering trace of the Miasma here any longer," Athena said, looking at Rune curiously.

"Good. That's good," Sophia said, smiling tiredly. "We need to make sure it really is out of everyone, though. And let those on the lower levels know it should be safe."

Rune didn't say anything else, but inclined his head to indicate she should look behind her. She half turned—with Lucas's help—to see Seth and Brigit, along with her mom, Sergei, Ray, and Carla, coming out of the stairwell, confused looks on their faces. Confused and, in Heather's case, something else Sophia couldn't interpret, but she refused to meet her daughter's gaze. Great, another thing to hurt her heart.

"It's done," Seth told her with a triumphant grin. "I don't know what the hell you did, but this big ass ball of greenish mist just floated down through the ceiling and into the rest of the stuff. We waited a few minutes, but it didn't do anything after that."

Her eyes closed again, and she nodded, beyond happy that could stop. She was able to stay on her feet thanks to Rune pumping energy into her, but she was still exhausted. "Can one of you divine people get in touch with Vazi so his group can get back up here?"

"If they can drag Julian away," Lucas muttered, making her almost smile.

"Already done," Seth assured her. "They'll be here in a minute. Because yeah, they did have to drag Julian away. Athena, we might have to specifically ward this place against Julian so he won't sneak in."

"That won't be necessary," Athena assured him with a shake of her head. "As soon as we've put all our protections back to how they should be, the labyrinth magics will be intact. He will not be able to pass through without an escort."

"Sophia? I like the guy, but I do not want him to be a constant visitor," Olivia said, grimacing. "Especially not since you just had to make me head curator."

Sophia gave a hint of a smile. "Best woman for the job."

She desperately wanted to get out of there and take a hot shower, but couldn't, not until she'd seen for her own eyes that everyone—especially her grandfather—was all right. And it might be best to explain the blood on her hands before that. Get all the unpleasantness out of the way.

Erasmus and the rest of his group walked in. Other than Julian, the mortals seemed thrilled, proving Vazi had passed on the news. Julian looked like he wanted to cry, and she didn't even need to ask why. She knew how interesting the Vault was, and understood the desire to spend hours exploring it.

Vazi looked as serious as he ever did. She would be surprised if he even knew how to smile, much less laugh.

Her grandfather came straight to her and cupped her cheek, his expression going solemn as he searched her expression. "Tell us, quickly. Then let Lucas take you somewhere for a little while."

Lucas gave her a squeeze, and she nodded. Though her voice wanted to come out as a whisper, she pitched it to carry throughout the room, hating how hoarse she sounded right now. "Peter's dead. And before anyone here marks him as a villain," she shot a glance at Vazi, "you should know he was innocent. Like everyone else in the Athenaeum, he was infected. His infection just began decades ago, rather than weeks. I can't—I won't—blame a child for stumbling across something not even the gods can protect against. And yes, he did horrible things, but it was because of the infection, not because of his own desires." She took a breath and fought against the tears that wanted to come again, but she refused to let them fall while she had dozens of people watching her, listening intently to her every work.

"You should all know that just before...just before, he had a moment where he was himself. If you need further proof that he was not the one you should be blaming or hating, then know that he asked me to kill him. To save him. To prevent him from doing anything else to hurt someone else."

"That's enough," Lucas whispered against her ear. "If they need more details—if you decide they need those details—they can get them after you clean up."

"He's right," Erasmus said, and she saw he had no qualms about letting his tears show, his cheeks damp, his eyes shining. "If anyone has earned it, it's you. Olivia and I will take care of things until you're clean and have taken a few minutes for yourself."

"Thank you. Can you make sure everyone who was infected is brought here?" she asked as Lucas let go of her and took her hand instead, starting to lead her to the stairs. "I'll talk to them when I get back. Some probably need healing."

"We'll take care of everything until you're ready," he promised.

"Damn straight," Olivia agreed, a fierce look on her face, but like Sophia herself, it looked like she was fighting tears. "We've got this."

She was glad, because, just for a few minutes, she wanted to be responsible for absolutely nothing.

Chapter 26

WHILE THEY WERE IN sight of others, Lucas did little more than hold Sophia's hand and lead her toward the stairs. Once they were out of sight, out of the stairwell, he scooped her up in a bridal carry. She had her pride, and he was happy to help her keep it, but he also refused to suffer or allow her to suffer. The fact that she curled into him rather than resisting such a hold told him just how close she was to her breaking point. No, he was pretty fucking sure she'd already reached that point, she was just holding back the flood of emotions by sheer stubbornness. He admired that even as he hated everything about this.

Quickening his pace, he carried her through the common room and down the hallway to her bedroom, pausing only to swing through the kitchen to grab a bottle of water. He managed to open the door without setting her down, and was relieved when he saw it hadn't been trashed in her absence. It wouldn't have surprised him if Peter had ordered all of her things destroyed when she'd teleported them out of the Athenaeum and to safety. Then again, for all he knew, there was magic protecting the aspida's chamber, just like there was in other areas.

He ignored the bedroom and went straight to the bathroom. Setting her on her feet, he reached in and turned the shower on.

"Hot, please," she whispered in a tight voice.

Without hesitation, he adjusted the temperature as high as he could without reaching a point where it would physically harm her. "Whatever you need," he told her when he turned back to her. He was sure she didn't want to see the knife any longer, but he refused to leave her to put it out of her line of sight, so set it on the counter, as far from the shower as possible.

He cracked open the bottle of water and offered it to her. She took it with more reluctance than he would have expected, but once she sipped, she kept drinking until a full half of the bottle had been drained. "Better?" he asked when she handed it back to him.

She nodded, but said nothing, just pushed past him and stepped under the water fully clothed. It might be shocking under normal circumstances, but in this case, he got it. The blood wasn't just on her skin, but her clothes as well. He glanced at the knife and made a note to clean it before she had to deal with it again, then joined her in the shower. Wet clothes were a minor inconvenience, and he wasn't going to let it stop him from giving Sophia whatever comfort she needed. If it was for him to stand there looking like an idiot, he'd do it. If it was to hold her while she cried, he'd do that too. He might even join her.

Peter had become a hated figure, not just in his eyes, but to everyone who knew the situation. Then to find out he'd been trapped by the Miasma since he was a boy? Had regretted what it had made him do so much that he'd asked his cousin to kill him? It was heinous. As was the fact that she'd been forced to kill someone she loved. Yes, to save him—to save them all—but it was still an act more difficult than just about anything he could think of. Especially for someone so kind-hearted.

For a minute, then two, Sophia just stood beneath the water, letting it pour over her face, turn pink, and flow down the drain. Little by little the drying blood washed away, but he wasn't sure it was helping her as much as she had hoped it would. When her shoulders started to shake, he drew her back just enough to get her face out of the water and wrapped his arms around her.

Sophia turned in his arms and grabbed hold of him as she began to cry. Nothing delicate or ladylike, but deep, gut-wrenching sobs that tore at his heart and made him wish the Miasma was something he could fight. Something he could punish for what he'd done to Sophia and her family. And to the Nasaru.

She couldn't do anything but cry out all the grief, the guilt, the sheer exhaustion that had built in the last month. And she wasn't entirely convinced it was over. Yes, the Miasma was back where it belonged, but it didn't feel finished. Maybe that was just because of her mom's reaction, but she didn't think so. After all, they had to undo everything the Miasma had done through Peter, as well as make sure that whatever had been used to cause all the storms and other natural disasters was destroyed or safely stored in the Vault. Even if she was torn on that, she knew Vazi would insist on it. She couldn't even really blame him. Yes, her instinct was to preserve all ancient knowledge and relics, but she'd learned the hard way that not everything should be saved.

"I know, love," Lucas whispered against her hair, gently rubbing her back and gently rocking her as she waited for the heat of the water to penetrate her skin. The shower was full of steam, but she felt cold to the bone. "Take as much time as you need. I'm not going anywhere, and everything else can wait."

She loved that he knew what she needed right now. Something stable. Someone who wasn't going to turn on her or force her to do something else that would haunt her for the rest of her life. Her mom couldn't be that for her, not if she couldn't even look at her. Her grandfather loved her and wasn't going to turn on her, she knew that, but she wasn't sure he was stable, either. He'd already faked his death once without telling her, so she knew the fear that he'd disappear again would linger for a while. It might not ever truly fade. But Lucas? He'd been there for her since day one. They hadn't always been on the best of terms, but he'd protected her, taught her, even when he hadn't really seemed to like her. He'd even been thinking of her the night she'd jumped him after her grandfather's funeral. A lot of guys would have just accepted what she was offering, but he'd made sure it wasn't something she'd regret. And she hadn't. She'd never regret ending up in bed with him, not that time or any time that had come after.

Eventually the tears began to slow and the sobs to ease, leaving her weak, shivering, and only able to hold on to him, but still he didn't let go.

"Feel any better?" he asked in a soft voice that wrapped around her like a hug.

"Maybe a little?" She loosened her hold enough to lean back and look up into his face. "Is it always this bad?"

He didn't ask what she meant; there could only be one 'this' she was talking about. "The first time is always the worst, but I would say no. What you're going through? It's beyond what most people experience. He wasn't just family, someone you loved, he was someone you learned had been innocent. He was as much a victim as anyone else—yourself included. So no, it isn't always this bad, but I'm going to make sure you never have to go through anything like this again."

She loved him for every word, including his promise, but she smiled and leaned up to kiss him lightly. "Nice thought, but you can't promise that."

"Yes, I can," he said firmly. "Most aspides never have to use deadly force. The Athenaeum has never been invaded before, and aspides don't tend to go on the riskiest retrievals, so their exposure to true fighting is minimal."

"I hope you're right, because my stint as aspida has been nothing but trouble." She glanced down and grimaced at the clothes plastered to her body. "I should get out of these clothes, actually clean up, and get back out there."

"You should," he agreed, "but no one is going to blame you if you need to take a minute."

"I will. I can't say I'm the head of this place and then run away and cower while everyone else is busy working out there," she said, stepping back and peeling the shirt from her body. She tossed it to the far end of the shower, where it landed with a plop.

"Fine. But after you get things sorted, you're taking the rest of the day off. You have Nick, Olivia, and myself for a reason. Hell, you've got Heather and Erasmus, too."

She wished he hadn't mentioned her mom, but nodded. "Fine." The rest of her clothes went the same way as her shirt, and he undressed, too. They were quiet as they washed up. He got out before her as she had a great deal more to wash off, and she heard the sink running, but it wasn't until she stepped out to dry off that she saw what he'd been doing. The knife was clean, showing no signs of Peter's blood.

Tears stung her eyes again, and she closed them to get herself under control. "Thank you."

He trailed his fingers down her back and kissed her cheek. "It was the least I could do. I can't go back and undo it, but I can remove the evidence."

"You're going to want to send someone to the computer room, them," she muttered as she toweled off her hair. Though she was turned away from him, she could see in the mirror that he was watching her, brows furrowed.

"That's where he took you?"

She nodded. "I guess the part about him loving his computer wasn't a lie."

"I think a lot of what he did or said was actually truth," Lucas said thoughtfully. "If he had been controlled by the Miasma for so long, it was patient, in a way. Being patient, it probably didn't care about a lot of his actions, so long as he pushed forward with its plan. So his love of computers, how much he enjoyed spending time with you..."

"Him falling for Josie," she whispered.

"I don't think there's any question about that," he said, running a hand gently down her back. "Come on. Let's put some clothes on you before you get cold."

It was a good point. Somehow, in the last week, she'd forgotten that it was a few degrees colder in the Athenaeum than she was used to. Not surprising, given it was underground. It wasn't uncomfortable, and she'd get used to it again, but right now, standing naked in the bathroom, she was starting to get chilly.

She dressed in comfortable clothes, less concerned with looking like the aspida than acting like it. Besides, everything else she was about to do would be uncomfortable, so the least she could do for herself was not add to it with uncomfortable clothes.

By the time they got back to the entrance hall, everyone was gathered, including the strangers who had been brought in and infected. Before Sophia addressed the faces that turned toward her, she walked over to the gods, surprised to see the rest of the patrons had shown up. That made her a little nervous. She'd gotten used to Seth, and even started to adjust to being around Vazi, but having Athena, Isis, Hecate, Thoth, and Mimir there as well? She'd be terrified if she hadn't hit her emotional limit. At this point, she felt numb. Brittle, maybe, but numb. These were well-known and powerful gods. Okay, so Athena seemed kind of normal, and Hecate was kind of cool, but it didn't diminish what they were.

"I'm sorry to interrupt, but there are a lot of people here I don't know. I don't think they're part of the Athenaeum, so I'm concerned with just letting them go, since they know about the Athenaeum now, and where it is," she told them.

"We were just discussing that," Isis said, her voice the most beautiful Sophia had ever heard. It went beyond even what sirens could accomplish. The accent heightened the smooth, sweet voice that was just a touch deeper than she might have imagined for the petite goddess. "You are correct in that they are not Nasaru, but it will be a simple matter to muddy their memories. They will not be able to find the Athenaeum, nor will they understand what it is."

"Really?" Sophia asked, relief soothing her tight shoulders. "That's great. I didn't really want anyone else to die today."

Hecate shook her head. "It isn't necessary. We'll take care of it." She waved her hand, and the unknown people disappeared. "They're somewhere safe until we can deal with their memories. But I think there are some people wanting to know exactly what happened—and that includes us."

Oh, right. Only Seth, Vazi, and Athena had heard what she'd said before, and it had been pretty brief. Grimacing, she nodded. "Sure. And thank you."

"You're welcome."

Sophia turned, nearly running into Lucas. She had a feeling that would keep happening for a while, at least until he got over seeing her disappear with a madman. Stepping around him, she moved to stand between the sphinxes that guarded the stairway, where everyone could see her.

"Listen up!" Lucas boomed as he stood beside her, and a half step back.

The conversations that had filled the room died off rapidly, and she had dozens of sets of eyes fixed on her. Emotional limit or not, it made her a little sick to her stomach. To try to combat it, she found Olivia's face in the crowd and focused on her. Olivia was the safest person out there. She wasn't a god, had never let her down, and had become a good friend.

Lifting her chin and taking a deep breath, she began to speak. "I know a lot of you are very confused. I can't go into every detail now, but I will tell you the basics of what happened. Years ago, when he was a child, Peter was infected by something which forced him to do terrible things. I want it to be very, very clear that he *is* innocent, and as much a victim as anyone else," she said firmly, letting her gaze move over the crowd as she waited for that to sink in. "But yes, he is the one who killed Thomas and Agatha. He is also the one who poisoned Erasmus. Dion is and was innocent. And yes, you may see that Erasmus is alive. He knew something was wrong and was determined to find out what. Appearing to die was the best way he and the patrons could think of to find out." She glanced briefly at those patrons and, despite her numbness, felt a hint of irritation about having witnessed Erasmus's supposed death.

"A few weeks ago, Peter started to infect the Athenaeum. It was in the water, so every time we bathed with it or drank it, we were getting more and more infected, until the behavior of nearly everyone was violent and irrational." Sophia couldn't help but glance at her mom, but the bleak expression she found made her quickly look back at Olivia. "I want you to know that none of it was your fault. If you said things you regret, or attacked anyone, it wasn't you. I really want to stress that. It was not your fault," she said, enunciating each word. Despite her assurances, she saw several guilty expressions in the crowd. She got it, and knew it would take time for that to fade.

"Today, we were able to get in and get to Peter. He was briefly able to talk to me before he..." She closed her eyes and swallowed against her suddenly rolling stomach. "Before I was forced to kill him." Opening her eyes, which were strangely dry, as though she'd cried all she was able, she went on. "Afterward, I was able to clear the infection from everyone, but I do want to have each of you checked, just to make sure nothing lingers. But as far as I know, you should all be back to your usual selves." She really hoped that was true.

"I know you're all still confused, maybe feeling ashamed for things you remember doing, or just not feeling right, which is why we won't be resuming normal activities for a while. I want everyone to recover, both physically and mentally. If anyone needs to talk, I'm here. Or hell, I'll find a therapist. Whatever we need to get back to normal. This is our home, and I'll make sure it's fitting of the name again."

She stepped to one side, clearing the path to the stairs. "For now, you're free to go. I suggest going to the kitchen or common room, at least until you can be cleared by a healer or magic user who knows what they're looking for. And after today, if anyone needs to talk to me, my door is always."

People still wearing confusion on their faces began to file past her to the stairs, though the group who had entered the Athenaeum with her remained where they were. Even the patrons left, all except for Seth, Vazi, and Athena. When the Nasaru were downstairs, she looked at all the people who had stepped in to help her reclaim the Athenaeum.

"I want to thank all of you, too. You didn't have to help, and you sure as hell didn't have to swear to never speak of this place. I'm in your debt."

Wade shook his head. "No, you're not."

"He's right," Kara said, nodding. "Seeing what it did to your people? It's terrifying thinking of what it would have been like if it'd gotten out into the world. Helping you helped all of us."

"Besides, saving the world has sort of become what we do," Evane added with a smug smirk.

Samara jabbed her brother with her elbow. "You didn't save the world last time. Mom did."

"I helped," he protested, but she only rolled her eyes.

"Was anyone else seriously hurt aside from Josie and Peter?" Sophia asked, interrupting the twin's bickering.

"There were injuries, of course," Suni told her. "That was inevitable with that level of violence and how outnumbered we were, but there was only one other death."

"Who?" she asked, afraid that she'd just lost someone else.

"Kirk," Olivia answered.

A halfling, if she recalled correctly. Part mer, part witch. One of the guards. She glanced at Lucas and saw his brow furrow. "We'll see he's given the honors he deserves," she told him.

"We will," he agreed.

Turning back to the others, Sophia said, "You're welcome to hang around for a little while, and I'd appreciate your help in making sure everyone is clear of the Miasma, but you can go if you—"

A woman appeared in the middle of the room. She was in a white dress that resembled a Grecian gown. Standing a little taller than five feet, she had a soft, curvy body that said mother to Sophia. Not overweight, just soft in a way that made Sophia think of hugs and cookies. Her black hair was pinned up and curly, and though her overall demeanor was calm, her brown eyes were frantic.

"Grandmother?" Athena asked, sounding as shocked as Sophia felt. But Athena historically only had one grandmother, which made Sophia think this was Rhea—the mother of the gods. "What are you doing here?"

"I need your help," she said, focusing on Athena.

"Of course, Grandmother," Athena answered instantly, walking over to the other goddess and taking her hands. "But what's wrong?"

"I need help finding my daughter."

Athena cocked her head, her brows knitting together. "Your daughter? What do you mean? None of my aunts were missing last evening."

"Thousands of years ago, I had a child. Not your father or any of the aunts or uncles you know, but another goddess," she began, glancing at Vazi, who frowned at the attention.

"Don't look at me. Not only am I older than you are, Rhea, there's no possible way I could be the father of your child," he said, folding his arms over his chest.

"No, you're not," she agreed, shaking her head, "but you should be concerned with this child, too."

His eyes narrowed and his shoulders tensed. "Why?"

"Because she's half Lemurian."

In a flash, he was in front of her, towering over the smaller goddess, his face stony. "You'd better explain that. Now," he warned darkly.

Seth rested a hand on Vazi's shoulder, but he looked stunned. "Take a step back, Vazi."

"Not until she explains," Vazi argued, making no effort to move even a pace back.

Rhea simply looked up at him for a moment, unintimidated by his anger. "My daughter's father was a Lemurian god, so as I said, she is half Lemurian. Except I haven't seen her since Lemuria sank. And before you ask," she said before Vazi could say anything, "she was not affected by whatever affected the rest of your pantheon."

"Then why haven't you seen her?" Seth asked.

Rhea shifted her focus to him and the frenzy in her eyes went to cold anger. "Because as soon as Lemuria sank, my son abducted her. She has been under his control ever since, and every single time I have attempted to free her from his abuse, he nearly killed me."

Seth and Vazi exchanged a look, and Sophia was wondering what any of this had to do with the Athenaeum. Had Rhea just sensed the presence of two Lemurian gods and hoped they'd help, given the girl's lineage? If that was the case, why hadn't she gone to them sooner?

Seth turned his attention back to Rhea. "Zeus?" She nodded and his jaw clenched. "I swear, that man has more and more to pay for. One of these days, I'm going to rip him to pieces and the entire planet will rejoice."

"As his mother, I should chide you for that sort of talk, but I'm not ignorant to my son's character," Rhea said in the tone of someone already grieving. "I will do nothing if you move against him, but please, Dania has been his for far too long. I need to see my daughter freed from him."

"Why are you just now asking for help? And why here?" Vazi demanded.

"Because I have reason to believe he...lent her to someone here."

"What do you mean, lent her to someone here?" Sophia asked, forgetting her awe at standing in front of the mother of arguably the most famous gods in history. Though she wasn't going to forget about the tidbits about Zeus.

"Why would you believe that?" Erasmus asked at almost the same time.

"Dania's powers...she can do the things that have been happening across the planet in the last week," Rhea began hesitantly.

Lucas frowned. "What do you mean things? The storms and disasters?"

Rhea nodded. "And while most of the gods are concerned with the unusual weather, he has acted like it's nothing more than a light rainfall."

"This is true," Athena murmured. "I hadn't paid much attention, not with all that was going on here, but thinking on it, she's right. He cared more that his dinner was well cooked and on time than discovering the source of the weather."

"So your daughter—Dania—you think she's here in the Athenaeum?" Sophia asked, wondering how much more she was expected to endure before she would be allowed to rest and start trying to put all this behind her. It would never completely go away, she was aware of that, but it had to get better. Right?

"I do," Rhea said, nodding and walking toward Sophia. "Please, find my daughter," she begged.

It struck her just how much Rhea loved her daughter. It wasn't like a god to beg. Most didn't even ask, they demanded, but Rhea was willing to do anything to get back the daughter she'd been unable to rescue for thousands of years. Sophia couldn't even imagine how much that had to hurt.

Sophia looked from Rhea to the others. "Did you bring everyone you found to this room after the Miasma was gone?"

"Everyone," Wade agreed, while Suni said, "I didn't come across anyone else with the power level of a god."

"She has to be here," Rhea argued, shaking her head. "There is no single god other than Dania who could have done what we've seen in the last week."

If Rhea was right and Dania was here, had been controlled by Peter, then there weren't many options. But she did know of one place Peter had used that none of the others would have known to check. They didn't even know it existed. She glanced at Lucas and suspected he was thinking the same thing. "There is one place we haven't searched. Peter...he did some work there." She looked at Olivia and Erasmus. "Can you two get people settled and make sure everyone's okay and free of infection while we go look?"

"Of course," Erasmus said. "I know they'll have more questions, and despite your words, there will be concern."

"We've got it. You go find the goddess," Olivia told her without hesitation. "If this goddess has been Zeus's plaything for millennia, she deserves to be found and freed now."

"Agreed," Sophia murmured. "Try not to mention the Miasma. I don't want anyone knowing about it unless necessary." They consented and left to do as she asked, and she blew out a breath. "Come on. Let's see if your daughter is there," she told Rhea before starting for the stairs. It was expected when Lucas fell into step beside her and Rhea was a step behind him, but she was a little surprised when Athena, Seth, and Vazi followed after them. Then again, if this goddess really was half Lemurian, of course Seth and Vazi would want to meet her.

Athena? Well, Dania was an aunt she'd never met, so that made sense, too.

Divine families were extremely complicated. It was no wonder that ancient people had done their best to stay out of their squabbles.

Chapter 27

THEY WENT DOWN TO the hidden door Sophia and Lucas had discovered only a few days before fleeing the Athenaeum. Lucas remembered how to open it, and they went into the hallway, only for both of them to stop at the entrance to the room they'd nearly died in.

He pointed to the table, which held several relics. "Last time we walked across this room, several of those relics activated, filling the room with water and a sea serpent," he warned. "We nearly drowned." Since the sea serpent statue had broken and been repaired it might not come to life again, but he didn't want to risk it.

Vazi waved an impatient hand, and every relic disappeared. Lucas didn't know whether he'd sent them somewhere or destroyed them, but he wasn't about to ask. He wasn't an easily intimidated man, but he knew better than to poke at an already pissed off god, even one who was sort of a friend. Besides, if Sophia didn't quibble about losing those relics, neither would he.

"Go," Vazi directed.

Lucas went, though he ensured he was just ahead of Sophia, just in case the room had other traps they hadn't discovered before. When he opened the door to the next room—to what Peter had been using as a kind of workspace—he cursed and shoved the door open wider before stepping back, not wanting to get plowed over by angry deities.

In the middle of the room was a raised stone platform. Last time, he'd thought it looked like an altar. Today it held a woman, hopefully one who was sleeping, because she didn't move. She had hair as black as Rhea's and looked to be about the same height—just over five feet. She was dressed in a Grecian gown, similar to what her mother wore, but it was definitely more revealing. Unlike her mother, she wore only one piece of jewelry—a wide silver cuff on her left wrist. With the thin fabric of her gown clinging to her unconscious form, it was easy to see she was beyond slender. No, she looked gaunt, like she'd been starved for weeks. Despite that, her face was pretty, with delicate features. But even in sleep, she didn't look peaceful.

"Dania!" Rhea shoved past him and hurried across the room to the altar, taking Dania's hand in one of hers and laying the other on her daughter's cheek. "Dania," she sobbed, a tear sliding down her cheek. "She doesn't look hurt," she said, relief in her tone.

Vazi and Seth weren't far behind her, with the former frowning at the unconscious woman. "Why isn't she waking up?" the latter asked.

Rhea lifted Dania's hand and slightly turned her arm so the light glinted off the cuff. "Because of this, I believe." She lowered Dania's arm and focused on the younger goddesses's face, stroking her cheek.

Athena stepped forward, staring at the cuff in horror. "Is that...one of the Enkrateia?"

Rhea nodded.

"What the hell are the Enkrateia?" Seth asked before Lucas could.

"Horrible things I believed to have been destroyed centuries ago, when my father banned the creation and existence of powerful relics."

"Great, but what are they?" he asked again, studying the cuff, but making no move to get closer to it.

"A set of cuffs, one gold, one silver. Essentially, whoever wears the gold cuff can absolutely control the person wearing the silver cuff. And I do mean absolutely. This would have allowed my father or Peter to have forced her to use her powers as they willed. Or to sleep until they said to wake. It's said that the wearer of the gold cuff could even command the other to die and the cuff would make it truth." She shook her head, still staring at the metal on Dania's wrist. "And without the gold cuff, it will be impossible to remove the cuff from her wrist, even for a god."

"And Zeus isn't about to give us that cuff," Seth said with no small measure of disgust.

Sophia said nothing, not wanting to draw the attention of agitated gods to her, but she eased closer, frowning at the cuff. It looked familiar, but her head was still muddled from everything that had happened. That she'd done. She tuned out the arguing about how to help Dania and tried to search her memory for where she'd seen another cuff like that. It was definitely unique. An inch and a half wide with symbols—spells, she assumed—etched into the metal.

"What's wrong?" Lucas whispered in her ear.

She shook her head and answered just as quietly. "I've seen something like that before, but I can't remember where."

He frowned and glanced at the cuff. "The Vault, maybe? We've saved other relics from being destroyed, so we might have found a set of those cuffs."

"No, not the Vault." She thought it was in the Athenaeum, though. And not in the aspida room, either. There weren't any relics there.

Something like that definitely wouldn't have been stored on any other level of the Athenaeum, so where... "Oh shit."

"You remembered?"

"Yeah. One sec." She closed her eyes and, though she hated to remember what she'd left in the computer lab, she forced herself to picture it as clearly as possible. Specifically, the nearly identical cuff she'd noticed on Peter's wrist. She tried to bring every detail back, knowing she couldn't pull it to her without a clear image. Holding her hands out, cupped, she whispered the spell, relieved when she felt a cool weight land in her hands. Opening her eyes, she saw the gold cuff resting there. Blowing out a relieved breath, she gingerly picked it up with two fingers. It was bad enough that it had been used to subjugate a woman, but the fact that it had come off her dead cousin's wrist wasn't helping. "Zeus didn't have it," she said in a voice raised to carry over the arguing of the guards. "Peter did."

They turned, and she found it extremely disconcerting to have the attention of four gods on her, but it took only a moment for their focus to shift to the cuff. Rhea moved to take it, but Vazi beat her to it, snatching it out of Sophia's hand and slapping it on his own wrist.

Rhea started to protest, but he ignored her and moved back to Dania's side. With a gentler touch than she'd realized he was capable of, he removed the silver cuff from Dania's wrist. As soon as it was no longer in contact with her skin, both silver and gold cuff disappeared. She wasn't sure to where, but she hoped it was right into the middle of a volcano.

No one should have absolute control over another.

Once the cuff was off, Dania's eyes opened. There was no slow slide from unconscious to conscious. It was like flipping a switch. One moment she was asleep, the next she was wide awake. Her eyes—blue, Sophia saw—locked on Vazi, then the other faces around her, and she began to freak out. There was no sound, not even a gasp, but her eyes widened and her breathing turned rapid as she scrambled off the altar and across the room on all fours, putting distance between her and the unfamiliar gods. The room began to shudder, and it took a moment for Sophia to realize it was an earthquake—or at least the start of one.

Seth frowned and his shoulders tensed, then the rumbling lessened, but didn't completely subside.

"Dania. It's me. It's *Matera*," Rhea said soothingly in ancient Greek, tears tracking down her face. She moved around the altar, but didn't get any closer than that, having realized the same thing Sophia did—Dania was terrified. Then Sophia realized something else; she was staring at the men like they were about to attack her. If she had been kept by Zeus for thousands of years, it made sense. Even if all he'd done was withhold food and force her to use her powers, it still could have traumatized her. Hell, there was almost no way she wasn't traumatized.

"I think the guys need to leave," Sophia said, careful to keep her voice as calm and level as possible.

"I agree," Athena said, her voice sad. "Would you three wait for us outside?"

Lucas frowned at Sophia, but when she nodded, he started for the door. Seth was only a moment behind him. Vazi took a little longer, but when Athena said, "Vazi, please," he went, but his reluctance was obvious.

As soon as the men were gone, Dania relaxed, but barely. The slight trembling of the earth stopped, at least.

Sophia wasn't entirely sure she should be there, as she wasn't a goddess and had zero experience in calming down trauma victims. She couldn't bring herself to abandon the woman, though, not when she'd been used by one of Sophia's people, even if it hadn't been his choice.

"None of us are going to hurt you, Dania," she said in the same form of Greek Rhea had used. She stayed where she was, so the altar was between her and the frightened woman, hopefully making herself seem like less of a threat.

"We're here to help you," Athena added, also in Greek. "Look at your wrist. The cuff that was controlling you is gone."

Dania didn't seem keen on the idea of taking her eyes off them, so lifted her arm in front of her face, letting her see her now bare wrist without allowing them to be out of her line of sight. She gasped softly and brought her other hand up, rubbing at her wrist, assuring herself her eyes weren't deceiving her. "How?"

To Sophia's shock and extreme displeasure, Athena and Rhea both glanced at her. It made sense given that she had found the cuff, but it didn't mean she liked it. "The man who was controlling you, making you cause all the bad weather, is dead."

"Who...who killed him?" she asked in a voice that was a little hoarse, like she didn't have much practice in speaking. That made Sophia's heart break a little. As did the answer she had to give.

"I did," Sophia said softly. "And when we realized what the cuff you were wearing was, I got the cuff he had, and Vazi—the tall blond man who just left—used it to remove your cuff. We're here to help. That's all."

"We are," Rhea said desperately. "I'm your mother. I've been trying to find you, to free you, since the moment you were taken from me."

"My mother?" Dania asked skeptically. "I was told my mother gave me to...to *him*," she said, the last word holding more disgust, more rage than Sophia had ever heard infused into a single word.

"No!" Rhea said, shaking her head adamantly. "I would *never* have given you to anyone, my sweet girl. I adore you and always have. And I have never stopped trying to find you, to free you." She took a single step closer to her daughter, doing her best to appear maternal rather than threatening. "Please, try to remember. I would take you to Lemuria frequently, to see your father and play with him. When you were five, your father took you out into the ocean and you two played, causing little storms so you could watch the rain and lightning hit the sea, so you could learn to control your powers."

Dania frowned, but it seemed she was trying to remember rather than displeased, so Rhea went on.

"He had a doll made for you, one that looked like you. You carried it everywhere. You even slept with it. When you ate, you insisted she eat, too." Rhea gave a shaky smile. "You called her your little twin."

"Mikro Dania," she whispered.

Rhea nodded, the smile firming. "Yes, that's right. You lost her once and cried for an hour straight until your father found her."

"Papa," she whispered. "He...he had one blue eye, one gray?"

Rhea nodded again as more tears spilled down her face. "He did, yes. You were so upset that both your eyes were blue, until we told you they changed, much like the sky does depending on the weather. Sometimes they were blue, sometimes gray, sometimes green."

Dania slowly nodded. "I remember that," she said, her voice so quiet, like she was afraid admitting it would make those memories disappear like smoke. "I...I remember you fighting to get to me when he took me. Remember him hitting you so hard I wasn't sure if you'd ever get up again."

Rhea's breath caught, but she nodded. "I did. I always will. He may be my child, too, but it gave him no right to you, and no right to harm me. I have *always* tried to get to you. And I don't know why he gave the cuff to someone else, but I am so extraordinarily happy he did, because it meant I was able to ask them," she gestured to Athena and Sophia, "to help me find you."

Dania's eyes flicked to them. "You found me?"

Athena motioned to Sophia, so she smiled, though she didn't feel happy in the least. "I did. I'd actually found this room a little while ago, so I knew to look here. I'm just glad you were here."

"And I never have to go back to him?" Dania asked, looking back at her mother.

"I would die before I allowed that to happen," Rhea vowed.

"I'm scared," Dania admitted in a tone Sophia never thought to hear from a god.

Rhea began approaching Dania, though she kept her steps slow and careful, not wanting to startle her daughter. "I know, and you have every right to be." When Dania didn't freak out again, or cower away, Rhea moved closer, crouched, then opened her arms in the offer of a hug. But no matter what memories had come back to Dania, she didn't seem to understand what Rhea wanted, not until those arms came around her in a warm embrace. The single act of genuine affection, of true love broke both of them.

Dania let out a sob and her arms jerked up and clung to Rhea, while the mother of the gods simply closed her eyes and held the daughter she hadn't seen in so long. Both wept, Rhea silently, Dania with a release of emotion no one could blame her for. And while Sophia's day had been horrible by any estimation, she could only hope she would never have cause to grieve for so many years of torment and terror like Dania now was.

Wanting to give them some time, Athena and Sophia quietly left the room. Lucas was just outside the doorway, obviously waiting for them. Vazi was pacing like a caged animal, with Seth watching him, concerned.

"Where is she?" Vazi demanded the second he saw them.

Athena made a hushing motion and kept her voice soft, though she was clearly as moved by the reunion as Sophia was. "Dania finally remembered Rhea, at least a little. We're giving them a few minutes."

"She belongs in Lemuria. In Thelaria," he said in a tone that suggested no one argue with him.

Athena paid no attention to the warning. "She belongs with her mother," she told him firmly. "Her father is gone—at least for now—and at least one of her brothers has severely abused her. And as much as I love my family, I am no more ignorant as to their natures as my grandmother is. Hades and Hephaestus would no doubt treat her well, and I believe Hera would as well, but can you imagine Zeus finding her again? Or Poseidon? Ares?"

"Which is why she belongs with us," Vazi argued. "She isn't safe with the Greeks, which leaves the other half of her heritage. Zeus tried to destroy us. He tried to prevent Seth from finding Lemuria. He failed, just as he has failed every time he's tried to find and infiltrate our home. It is the single place she would be safe."

"I wish I didn't agree with you," Rhea said from behind Sophia. Dania stood beside her, holding her mother's hand. Her eyes were red from crying, and she watched all three men warily, but she didn't cower. She didn't seem confident, as there was no raised chin or set shoulders. More, it seemed like she was fighting to keep her feet where they were. "I would love nothing more than to keep her by my side for the next thousand years, but I am part of the pantheon he rules. If she stayed with me, he would eventually find me, and I will not allow that to happen," she said, voice and eyes fierce, a wave of power pouring off her.

"We can keep her safe," Seth promised Rhea. "We can keep you safe," he repeated, looking at Dania and offering her a warm smile.

"How?" was Dania's single question. It was in English this time, which startled Sophia, especially given there was no hint of an accent.

"Long ago, when our pantheon was whole, we made it so only Lemurians and those we've given permission to can even find our home, much less step foot on it. Zeus will *never* get so much as a glimpse of Lemuria," Vazi told her, gentling his tone when he spoke to her. Sophia noticed he'd kept doing that. He'd snap at one of them, then treat Dania like she was delicate. It made her think better of him. He might be a loud, callous asshole, but he wasn't completely insensitive.

"What would make me safe from you?"

Vazi's jaw tightened, but he remained patient. "I am not a man who would ever exploit or abuse those weaker than me, whether they are man or woman, adult or child, mortal or god. I attack in battle, in war, but I would never default to violence without just cause. Seth is an even better man than I am, and we are the last two Lemurian gods—aside from you."

Dania said nothing for several minutes as she and Vazi stared at each other. It was some kind of battle of wills, and Sophia wasn't quite sure what was going on, so she didn't interrupt. Besides, while Rhea and Dania had temporarily allowed her to forget what had happened, it hadn't lasted, and she wanted to be near Lucas. All she did was link her fingers through his, but it was enough.

"You want me to go live in the homeland of my papa?" Dania asked.

"I do," Vazi answered simply.

"Is it just the two of you?"

Vazi shook his head. "No. Seth's wife and father are also there, along with a few others we call friends. Some of them are upstairs, and helped with the issues in this place, which allowed us to find you. And there are good women there. Women who wouldn't stand for us abusing you even if we were so inclined."

Dania glanced at Rhea. "Can my mother live there, too?"

"Oh, I can't," Rhea said sadly, stroking a hand over Dania's hair. "I'm not Lemurian, I'm Greek. And Zeus would be able to track me there. It might not be enough to allow him to step foot on it, but he is crafty, and could probably make life very difficult for everyone there."

"But she can visit," Vazi allowed. "Others do. And we would never think to cut you off from your mother. And you won't be a prisoner, either."

Dania had one last question, this time for Sophia. "You trust these men? Their Lemurians?"

Sophia had no idea why Dania wanted her opinion. Maybe because she was the only woman here who wasn't a goddess? Whatever the reason, she couldn't not help where she could. Besides, she truly liked Seth, and Vazi was growing on her, so she didn't have anything bad to say. And beyond that, being open and honest was the best course of action here. "I quite literally have trusted Seth with my life. I haven't known Vazi as long, but I do trust that he won't hurt you. I actually think he'd kill anyone who tried." Out of the corner of her eye she saw Vazi tense, but she had a feeling it was because she'd hit a little too close to home, though she wasn't sure why, since it didn't really seem like something he was trying to hide. Dania made the number of Lemurian gods three, so she mattered to him. "As for the other Lemurians, I've known them for even less time than Vazi, but like he said, they helped us stop the man who was using you for your powers. Besides, Seth's wife is pregnant. He wouldn't allow anyone near her that would pose any kind of threat to either his wife or unborn child."

Her answer garnered a thoughtful nod from Dania as she looked back to the Lemurians. "I will go. For now," she qualified.

"Do you want to go there now?" Seth asked. "I'm sure you want to get away from this place."

"I do."

"I'll be back for the Lemurians once we get her settled," Seth told Sophia, before he, Vazi, Rhea, and Dania disappeared.

No one spoke for several moments. "Please, for the love of all the gods, tell me there aren't going to be anymore surprises," Sophia said.

"I really wish I could," Lucas said, kissing her cheek. "Let's go back upstairs. Get it finished, so you can rest."

"I'll come with you, to make sure all is well, then I need to meet with the other patrons and get started renewing the protections on the Athenaeum," Athena said.

As they walked up the stairs, Sophia had to know, "So...Did they choose the name of this place because of you?"

Athena laughed. "Well, I was the first patron. What else were they going to call it?" she asked, allowing them to make the rest of the climb with a little less weight on their shoulders.

Chapter 28

THEY FOUND EVERYONE IN the common room. Literally everyone. The Lemurians, Julian's friends, and every single member of the Nasaru that lived in the Athenaeum. That meant the large room was crowded and voices echoed off the stone in a way that threatened to give Sophia one hell of a headache. But the arrival of Sophia, Lucas, and Athena had them all growing quiet, the silence spreading across the room as they noticed the returning trio.

"So it's really over?" a woman's voice called from somewhere near the middle of the room. Sophia couldn't spot the woman or identify the voice. "Things can go back to normal?"

"It's really over," Sophia confirmed. "And yes, things are going to go back to normal, though I know it'll take us a little while to get there."

"That's for damn sure," a man muttered.

"Dion really didn't kill Agatha?" another voice called.

"Are you sure Peter was innocent?"

"What the hell did he infect us with?"

"What was so important that the gods were here?"

"Who are these other people and why are they in the Athenaeum?"

Sophia fought the urge to rub her temples as they began to throb. That or just run away. She'd hoped some of those questions would have been answered by Olivia and Erasmus, but either those two had been closed-lipped, or the Nasaru had waited for her before asking these questions. It occurred to her that maybe they wanted her to confirm those answers, but she dismissed it just as quickly. Erasmus had been aspida for decades. Of course they would have trusted any answer he'd have given them.

Unless they were also pissed that he'd faked his death.

"No, Dion didn't kill Agatha. I've confirmed that with a hundred percent certainty. Yes, I'm sure Peter was also innocent. He was infected by the same thing you all were, and no, I cannot tell you what it was." She made sure her voice was firm on that answer, as she did not want to spend hours deflecting, but there was no way she was going to tell more people about the Miasma. The fewer who knew of its existence, the fewer who would go hunting for it. "The nature of that substance is why the gods were here. As for the others, they're friends. Of Seth, of Erasmus, of ours. With all of you unable to help us, we had to look outside the Athenaeum. But you should recognize at least some of the names, such as Suni, who is a fantastic healer, or Julian, who is a scholar in his own right."

There were grumbles at her refusal to answer the infection question, but her short speech calmed them down. They went back to talking amongst themselves, but Heather separated herself from the crowd. Sophia tried not to tense as her mom approached, a look of abject apology on her face.

"Sophia...I..." Heather shook her head, tears filling her eyes. "I am so very, very sorry. For everything. I know you said it wasn't our fault, that we were being controlled by whatever was infecting us, but the way I acted...It was unforgivable."

"It wasn't your fault," Sophia repeated. "You didn't mean it. I know that." She did, but could admit to herself that it would take some time for her to forget. That might not be fair, and she was going to do her best to treat her mom like it had never happened, but it had happened. The pain she'd felt had been very real.

Still, she didn't object or evade when Heather stepped in for a hug, even returning it, savoring it. Heather continued to repeat how sorry she was, how much she loved Sophia and hadn't meant any of the nasty things she'd said, and Sophia just continued to murmur that it was okay, that it hadn't truly been Heather.

Several minutes later, Heather was able to draw back and give a watery smile as she stroked a hand over Sophia's hair. "I'm so proud of you. No other aspida has ever had to repel an invasion of the Athenaeum, and you did it against the Athenaeum itself."

Sophia shook her head. "I had help."

"Even so, it's still impressive. No one person can do everything. It's why the Athenaeum isn't a one-woman show, but has dozens of people doing various jobs."

That brought another thought to mind, and after her mom stepped back, Sophia found Olivia and Erasmus in the crowd and walked toward them, with Lucas stuck to her side. "So...I have an important question," she said when there was a break in their conversation.

"What question is that?" Erasmus asked.

"Since you didn't actually die...am I really still aspida? I mean, I know magically it passed to me, but isn't this a job you can't quit? And since you didn't actually die..."

Athena answered before Erasmus could even open his mouth. "Normally that is the way it works, but for the plan to work, the role of aspida had to truly pass from Erasmus onto his successor. And before you ask," she added, smiling warmly, "no, we did not deliberately choose you because of your relationship to Erasmus. The magic of the Athenaeum chose, as it always does."

Sophia had expected basically that answer and nodded, though she wasn't sure if she was relieved or disappointed. It might have been nice to be able to be a curator, but on the other hand, there was no way she'd ever run into anything as aspida that was as difficult as dealing with a Miasma infection. Right? She'd just gotten the really fucking hard stuff out of the way first. Shouldn't it be smooth sailing from here on out?

There was one more question she needed an answer to, and turned to Erasmus for this one. "You're staying, right? I mean, just because you're not aspida anymore doesn't mean you can't stay."

He beamed at her and drew her into a hug. "Of course I'm staying! Not only has this been my home for the entirety of my life, I want the time to actually get to know my granddaughter. I do think I want to do a bit more travel than I used to, but I will absolutely stay. I think I would make a fantastic curator."

"Good. Because you definitely owe me that getting to know you time."

He chuckled and drew back, giving her hands a quick squeeze before he released her. "You will have as much as you like," he promised.

"Dammit, Sophia. Aren't you done yet?" Lucas asked from behind her, his voice aggrieved.

Surprised, she turned and looked up at him. "What? Why?"

He huffed and grabbed her hand, tugging her into him with just enough force to have her body slamming lightly against his. She stared up at him, wide-eyed, her free hand ending up on his chest. Not to push him away—she couldn't imagine when that would ever happen—but to help brace herself.

"You were taking way too fucking long," he told her before he lifted her until only her toes remained against the floor, and kissed her. Despite the sizable crowd, it wasn't a chaste kiss. Despite her mom and grandfather standing there, watching them, he held nothing back. Normally she'd dodge or protest such a kiss in such company, but it was such a passionate, intense, loving kiss that she forgot all about their audience. The hand on his chest gripped, and she strained to get closer as she returned the kiss, completely losing herself in him. Even when a few people chuckled, and one or two let out catcalls, she just kissed him like it would never end, like it was their first kiss and last rolled into one.

When he broke the kiss it was abrupt, though she would have preferred to ease out of it, if only so she could regain her wits. Before she could, he gave her a cocky grin. "We're getting married," he told her, keeping her pressed against him.

"We are?"

"We are. And you're not saving the Athenaeum or the world anymore."

"I'm not?"

He shook his head. "You're not," he confirmed. "You're giving me gray hairs."

She had just enough presence of mind to shake her head. "You're just looking in the mirror in gargoyle form."

Lucas chuckled and gave her another kiss, though this one was both chaste and brief. "No, it's definitely you. But is that all you have to say?"

"What do you want me to say?" she wondered. "You didn't ask me, you told me."

"You could still say okay."

"Okay," she said, smiling, surprised she could be happy after everything that had happened in the last twenty-four hours.

The grin he gave her now was gorgeous and just as happy as she felt. "Good." Then he was kissing her again. This time, she dimly heard the cheers and calls of congratulations, but she didn't care. She might later. Right now, she wanted to bask in the fact that everyone was now safe, the Miasma was back in its chamber, and she was getting married to a wonderfully frustrating man.

She'd worry about everything else tomorrow.

It had been three days since Sophia and the others had invaded the Athenaeum and saved the Nasaru from the Miasma. Explanations had all been given, and they'd started putting things to rights again. Damage caused during the fight had been repaired, and they'd put books and relics back on their appropriate levels. And since Sophia had moved into the bedroom reserved for the aspida, Erasmus had moved into her old room. The room that had once been his son's. Unlike her mom, he had seemed pleased by the connection rather than dismayed.

The day before had been a hard one for everyone, as they'd held funerals for Kirk, Josie, and Peter. They had been just as horrible as all funerals, and Sophia genuinely hoped those would be the last ones she'd need to attend for many, many years. Their ashes now rested in the crypt alongside Dion's, now that he was no longer shunned even in death.

Penny had gotten a side promotion to tech, giving her the job she'd originally asked for. She'd been hesitant, given Peter's tenure in that job, but had eventually accepted. Her first task had been to find any holes or back doors that Peter had programmed into their security. Sadly, it had taken her only a few hours to discover that he'd had many.

Erasmus, Sophia, and Olivia had begun ensuring the Vault wasn't missing any materials, and were relieved to find it didn't seem to have been touched. Peter wouldn't have needed it to cause the damage he did, not when he had Dania, but none of them could figure out how he'd locked the gods out of the Athenaeum.

While they'd been working on the mundane repairs, Athena and the other patrons had worked on the protections. The labyrinth had been restored, and they could now safely come and go. They'd also reinstated the wards. Not just that, they'd improved upon them. While they all hoped they'd never have to deal with this sort of thing again, they'd taken what had happened and used it to give themselves options, just in case it did.

Sophia and Erasmus had taken their own precautions, making notes in several books in the aspida room about the Miasma chamber. It might be the wise decision not to spread it around what was beneath their feet, but they'd both decided—with input from both Olivia and Lucas—that future aspides needed to know about the potential danger. But they all knew the spell to control the Miasma wasn't one lightly taken. Not only was the cost high, they weren't exactly sure how she'd survived to complete the spell. Rune, they'd decided, must have been a much more powerful witch than they'd realized. So she'd called for Seth, who had called for the rest of the patrons, and they'd added more layers of protection.

Prior to this, after finding the hidden door that led down to the chamber, there had been nothing to prevent someone from reaching the Miasma. Now there was a wall of solid rock, helpfully created by Seth, to block the passage down. Hecate had added another layer of protection, creating a ward that would make anyone who tried to enter the passage feel extremely uneasy and want to leave. Isis's contribution had been an illusion that would turn people around, so they ended up right where they'd started. Thoth had etched spells on the inside of the door to make it harder to open, and would hopefully prevent anything from escaping. Mimir created another doorway just before the chamber, which somehow would require wisdom to pass. And Athena had devised a series of magical traps, just in case the other protections didn't work. Then they had ensured all traces of the Oskila were cleared from the Athenaeum, which relieved everyone who knew of its existence.

It might not be perfect, but it was damn close, especially since they intended to make sure no one else found out about the chamber.

Even with all that, there was still one more thing left to do—aside from getting married. After dinner that night, Lucas kissed her, then left the room so she could take care of the last thing that had been weighing on her mind.

Pulling out her new phone, which had been programmed with the numbers of all the Nasaru, outside contractors, the Lemurians and others who had helped her reclaim the Athenaeum, and the number she was calling now.

"Hello?"

"Hi Blanche," Sophia said, rubbing her free hand on her jeans. "You got a minute?"

"Sophia! Does this mean you got the Athenaeum back?" Blanche asked.

Sophia had sent her a text the night they'd gotten control of the Athenaeum back, but it had been extremely brief. Just enough to ensure Death didn't come in and wipe out all the Nasaru. "We did, and the Miasma is back where it belongs. We've even taken precautions to make sure no one can ever do that again."

"Good. That shit sounded scary."

"It was." Though that was an understatement. "And I've got to thank you. Brigit and Rune helped a lot. Especially Rune."

"I'm glad. I'm sorry I couldn't help, but..."

Sophia shook her head. "No, it's okay. I get it. And I'm sorry that even the three who died had to. Though that brings me to why I called."

"Oh?"

"At one point I...My cousin, he was innocent. He'd been infected, too, but worse than the others. Apparently, he had been since he was a kid," Sophia explained. "I had to kill him," she said softly.

"Oh Sophia. I'm so sorry," Blanche said with genuine sympathy. "It's bad enough to lose a loved one, but to have to be the one to do the deed is so much worse."

"It is. I was...I was hoping there was some way I'd be able to talk to him. You know, how Death let me talk to Dion? To make sure that death really did save him like he was hoping." It was a big ask, she knew that, but she had to try.

"I think I can do one better. Give me a minute and I'll call you back?"

Sophia wasn't sure what would be better, but she nodded. "Of course. And thank you, Blanche. I really appreciate it."

"Not a problem," she said before hanging up.

She turned her phone over in her hand while she waited for Blanche to call back, but after two minutes had passed, she felt a yank in her solar plexus and the room around her dissolved, only to reform as an entirely different room. It looked like a throne room, but the walls, floor, and ceiling were made of a gray stone with veins of blue, silver, and red. Pretty, but definitely not a place she'd ever seen before. Then she realized there was a woman sitting on the arm of a throne, beside a man who sat in it properly. A man she recognized and honestly feared. The king and queen of death; Blanche and Death.

Well, fuck.

Sophia slowly crossed the room toward them, her gaze continually flicking to the extremely intimidating man. "Um...Blanche?"

Death's wife was a pale beauty. Her black hair hung just past her shoulders, framing fair skin. Her eyes were blue-gray, and her lips were currently curved into a satisfied smirk. She wore all black—cargo pants and a form-fitting tee-shirt today, along with boots.

Her husband was tall, muscular, and more than a little scary, even without the ultimate powers of death. His hair was almost as dark as Blanche's and just long enough to be called shaggy, but in a handsome way. His eyes were nearly white they were so pale, and like his wife, he wore all black. Unlike her, his arms were covered in black and silver swirls and symbols.

"I told you I could probably do you one better, didn't I?" Blanche said, leaning lightly into Death's shoulder.

"You did…"

"She told me what you did, and what you've been through," Death said, his voice deep and a little on the grouchy side. Sophia figured if she dealt with death literally every second of her life, she'd be grumpy, too, so didn't hold that against him. "Normally I don't go around reuniting families when one is dead and one is alive, but I've decided to make an exception this time." He looked up at Blanche and rubbed her thigh. "Go ahead, *ara*."

Blanche grinned and rubbed her hands together. Lifting one of them, she snapped, and Peter appeared before her. He looked almost identical to the way she'd last seen him, except there was no sign of the stab wounds, and his mohawk was straight and perfect.

Peter's eyes widened with panic. "Sophia? No. No, no, no. You weren't supposed to be here. Not yet. You killed me. That should have made things better."

Sophia swallowed, though her mouth had suddenly gone dry. "I'm alive," she promised him. "It didn't make anything better, but it gave me the tools to do it."

He studied her closely for a moment. "You're really alive?"

"I am. I promise."

His brow furrowed as he nodded slowly. "Then what do you mean, gave you the tools? Is the Miasma is gone?"

She shook her head. "Not gone, no, but contained. I...There was a spell. I used your blood, and mine, and I was able to pull the Miasma out of everyone and put it back where it belonged. No one is infected anymore." She took a step toward him, then another, and hesitantly lifted her hand.

"He's solid here," Blanche said in a sober voice. "We'll give you two a few minutes, then send you home," she said before both she and Death disappeared.

"I'm so sorry, Sophia," Peter said, not seeming to have noticed they hadn't been alone. "I couldn't stop myself. And not in the way people say when they just don't have self-control. I literally couldn't stop myself."

"I know," she assured him. "And I told everyone that. I made sure they knew you were innocent. That you were as much a victim as everyone else."

"But am I? Was I?" he asked in a whisper. "I did horrible things. Killed people who didn't deserve it."

"But it wasn't you," she said, closing that last bit of distance and wrapping her arms around him in a hug. "The Miasma and its counterparts, they're literally irresistible. Even gods can't protect themselves from it, not for long."

Peter clung to her like she was his lifeline, and she was content to give him what comfort she could, for as long as she could. "How could you blame yourself when you were a child when you were exposed to it? If a god can't resist it, how could a kid?"

"I know, but...I remember doing those horrible things. It was like watching the most realistic movie ever, except I couldn't turn it off."

"I know," she whispered, rubbing his back soothingly. "But it wasn't you. Just think of it like a movie, and remember it was. Not. You." She leaned back enough so he could see her face and the sincerity on it. "I mean it. I don't blame you. I told that to the rest of the Athenaeum. They put the blame right on the Miasma." Maybe not entirely true, as she knew not everyone was convinced, but it wouldn't help him to hear that. Besides, it was mostly true. "Have you...have you seen your dad?"

Peter ducked his head and shook it. "No. I'm afraid to. All he knows is that I killed him," he muttered.

That was something she could help with, if Blanche was willing to do her one more favor. "Blanche? If you can hear me, can you do me one more teeny favor? I promise I'll owe you one."

Blanche appeared in front of the throne, alone this time. "You don't owe me. Consider this me repaying Erasmus for helping me out."

Sophia wasn't sure she liked taking Erasmus's favor, but didn't say anything. He wouldn't mind, in any case. "You remember the man Death summoned in my office a few weeks ago? Dion?"

"Sure."

"Do you think you could bring him here, too? He's Peter's father, and I want to make sure he knows Peter wasn't actually the one who killed him."

Blanche gave Peter a sympathetic look and nodded. "Of course." Another snap, and Dion appeared beside his son.

It wasn't unexpected when Dion recoiled, but Sophia reached out to stop him. "It's okay, Dion. It wasn't him."

"What do you mean, wasn't him?" Dion asked, glaring at Peter, who looked even more downtrodden than before.

"He was infected by something called Miasma, and had been since he was a child," Sophia said gently. "It caused him to do things that were out of his control. But when he had control, he did what he could to make things right. He...he told me to kill him, to stop him."

Dion studied Peter for a long moment. "Is this true?"

"It is, Papa," Peter whispered. "I never would have hurt you, or Uncle Erasmus, or any of the others. I didn't want to hurt anyone."

"And you're certain of this?" Dion asked Sophia.

"One hundred percent positive. I wouldn't lie about something like this. Peter is innocent. His body committed the acts, but his mind wasn't on board."

Since this wasn't Dion's first summoning as a ghost, he knew the deal. Or at least enough to look around until he spotted Blanche. "My lady, could I ask a boon?"

Blanche cocked her head. "You can ask."

"When you send me back, could you send my son with me? It sounds like we have many years to make up for, and many things to discuss."

Blanche smiled. "Of course." Her gaze flicked to Sophia. "Say your goodbyes, so I can send them home."

Sophia gave Dion a hug—the first she'd actually ever given him—and whispered against his ear, "I promise. He is innocent, and he regrets what he was forced to do. Just treat him like your son."

"I will," he promised.

She turned to Peter, giving him a hug as well. "Be patient with him," she murmured. "It's hard to change what you thought you knew."

"I'll give him centuries if I need to."

She nodded and stepped back, not caring that her eyes were damp. "I'm so sorry the Miasma brought both of you here before your time. You're missed, I promise. And loved."

"Thank you, Sophia," Dion said, while Peter tried to give her a smile.

Smiling at them, she looked behind them at Blanche and nodded. One more snap, and both men disappeared. Only then did she allow her breath to catch or her eyes to close, so tears tracked down her cheeks.

Blanche touched her arm. "That was a good thing you did. Not everyone would give a thought to the dead, not like that."

"It was the least I could do," she said, opening her eyes. "They were both innocent. Both victims of the Miasma. They weren't the only ones, but I think those two suffered more than just about anyone." Except maybe Josie and her twin. "I don't know how much you interfere, but there's a woman named Josie. She died just before Peter did. I'm pretty sure he was in love with her. Her death is actually what caused him to ask me to kill him to save us all."

"I'll see what I can do. But you need to go back to your home now. Just don't forget to give me a call now and again, when there isn't a world-ending catastrophe happening."

Sophia smiled and brushed the tears from her cheeks. "Count on it. Maybe you, me, and Olivia can have a girl's night sometime."

Blanche grinned. "I think I'd like that. Until then, take care of yourself."

Another tug and she was back in her bedroom. Lucas had apparently just returned, so looked startled at her sudden reappearance. "I take it you got in touch with Blanche?"

Sophia crossed the room and wrapped her arms around his waist, pressing her cheek against his chest. "Peter's with Dion. And I have a feeling Josie will be there soon."

He kissed the top of her head. "I have no doubt. But you need to think of happy now."

"That is happy," she corrected. "But I could go for some more happy. What'd you have in mind?"

He chuckled. "How do you feel about going for a bit of flying?"

She looked up at him and smiled. "Sounds wonderful." And maybe the freedom of being in her owl form high in the sky, dancing with her gargoyle fiancée, would set the rest of the world to rights.

Epilogue

LUCAS WAS NOT A patient man. He hadn't been able to wait until they'd left the others before telling her they were getting married, and he hadn't wanted to wait for them to actually tie the knot. Which was why, a month after they'd wrested control of the Athenaeum back from the Miasma, they were having a wedding.

Sophia was over the moon, even if the month hadn't given her much time to plan.

They'd decided on the Athenaeum for the venue, partly because Sophia wanted to replace bad memories with good. The guest list had been a little trickier. The Nasaru, of course, and Lucas's family. They couldn't leave out the patrons, because doing anything else would be an insult, and she really didn't want to insult the gods who protected the Athenaeum. The people who had helped them retake the Athenaeum rounded out the list, and since that included Vazi, Blanche, and Death, she was a little terrified. Seven gods and the lord of death? What could go wrong?

The mind boggled.

The Nasaru had been happy to help with all the details, which took a lot off her mind. Farid was a surprisingly good baker, especially for a guard, and had made the cake. Multiple people had taken on the task of decorating the entrance hall and making the food for the reception. And Hecate had gifted her with the most gorgeous wedding dress Sophia had ever seen. It was deceptively simple, with narrow straps, a sweetheart neckline, and a full skirt. And unlike modern wedding dresses, this one wasn't white, as white hadn't been the color of choice for weddings in ancient Greece. Instead, this one reminded Sophia of the night sky. It was a pale blue that went darker and finally to black around the bottom hem. Silver stitching around the neckline and bottom hem made her think of stars, as did the rhinestones—she hoped they were rhinestones—that decorated the bodice, the bottom three inches of the dress, and the train. It was also as light as a whisper and as soft as a caress.

She loved it.

Sophia had asked Olivia to be her maid of honor, with Lucas asking Steven to be his best man. She'd debated asking Erasmus to walk her down the aisle, but before she could, he'd asked to officiate. They'd accepted, but she couldn't decide if she was upset or not. Yes, the whole faking his death thing still stung, but she did love him, and had been able to spend time with him over the past month, which had been wonderful. But it was okay, really. She didn't need to be walked down the aisle. And it wasn't a huge wedding in any case.

The best part of such a short time between the engagement and wedding was that Sophia didn't have the time to get nervous, especially not with the aftermath of the Miasma she had been dealing with. Of course, now that she was in her dress, with Olivia putting the last touches on her hair, those nerves tried to rise. Not as strongly as she'd expected, she realized. Maybe because she had absolutely no reservations about marrying Lucas. He was perfect for her, and she was going to be surrounded by everyone she cared about. It was a day for smiles, not jitters.

"You look beautiful," Heather said from where she sat on the edge of Sophia's bed, sniffling and dabbing at her eyes with a tissue. Their relationship had settled over the last few weeks, and though Sophia might never really forget about the way her mom had acted when she'd been infected, she'd truly forgiven her. "I wish your father could see you like this. He would be as proud as I am."

Sophia did, too, as this whole process had made her miss him more than she ever had. It had always been difficult for her to really hold a lot of emotion toward him, since she'd never met him, but fathers were meant to walk their daughters to their grooms, and she didn't even really know what he looked like. Okay, she knew he'd had hair like hers, and green eyes like she and Erasmus did, but she'd never seen a photo of him. Heather hadn't been able to bear having such things around.

"Don't you cry," Olivia warned as she adjusted a curl. "Neither of you. I hate crying."

"I'm going to cry," Sophia said with a grin. "Isn't it a requirement when you get married?"

"Oh shut up and hold still. You're almost done, which is good because it's almost time."

"Actually, it is time." The still unfamiliar voice from behind her had Sophia glancing in the mirror to see Athena, standing there with a smile, decked out in what Sophia thought of as the stereotypical Greek goddess garb. A Grecian gown of pure blue, it flowed over her exactly how those things were supposed to. She looked beautiful and definitely like a goddess.

"Pfft," Olivia said dismissively. "There is no wedding without the bride. She just needs one...more...second." She fussed with the curls, and on the last word, leaned back and nodded. "You were right to nix the veil," she decided. "It would hide my fantastic work."

"She's right," Heather said, getting to her feet and offering the bouquet she held. Like the dress, it was deceptively simple. It was just a small bunch of flowers, all alien to Sophia, but beautiful, with the petals mirroring her dress, in that they faded from the palest of colors to a blue so dark it was nearly black. That, she was told, had been a gift from Seth, which made her think they were from Lemuria, since she couldn't think of any flowers with that kind of coloring elsewhere.

"You really do look beautiful," Heather said, carefully embracing Sophia. "I'm going to go so I can see Lucas's face when he sees you."

"All right. Thanks, Mom."

Heather only smiled before she left. Athena whispered something to Olivia, also smiled, then she disappeared to take her seat in the entrance hall.

"You ready?" Olivia asked, checking her own dress in the mirror. She'd been happy when Sophia had said Olivia could pick out her own dress and had gone with a deep red sheath that looked amazing on her.

Sophia lifted her bouquet to her face, inhaled the subtle, exotic scent. "I really am."

Olivia linked her arm with Sophia's and led her out of the room. "Then it's time for me to tell you there's been one little last-minute change to the wedding."

Nerves truly hit now and she stopped for a second. "What's wrong?"

"Not a thing." But her voice held mischief, which really worried Sophia.

"Uh huh. Then what's the change?" she insisted as they made their way down the hallway, then to the stairs to where Lucas and their guests waited.

"You'll see. Just a second."

"Olivia..."

"It's not bad, I promise. But I also had to promise not to say anything. I just want you to be prepared that something is coming," Olivia said, relenting that much. "So no fainting, all right? This is a good thing."

Sophia was skeptical, but said nothing as she gathered her skirt so she didn't trip, then made her way up. Halfway there, she stopped, because a man in a very nice suit stood there, waiting for them. Except she didn't know him. She'd met Lucas's brother the day before, so it wasn't him, but why was there a stranger in the Athenaeum?

She turned to Olivia, who only smiled, patted Sophia's arm, then strode around the man and continued upstairs.

"Sophia," he said in a voice choked with emotion. He smiled, but his eyes were watery.

"Do I know you?" she asked hesitantly as she studied his face. No, she didn't know him, but there was something...familiar. She couldn't place it, but she realized she didn't fear him. That could be partly because of Olivia's reaction, but that wasn't entirely it.

He shook his head and came down one step. "Unfortunately, you don't. You never got the chance, and I will forever regret that."

"I don't understand." She really didn't, but she was starting to feel the urge the cry.

It looked like he wasn't sure what to say, and he even started to speak a couple of times before he had to pause to clear his throat. Finally, after taking a deep breath, he moved down one more stair. "I'm Gregory Regas. I'm your father, Sophia."

"I don't understand," she said again, though the words were breathless this time. "My father died before I was born." It didn't stop her from really studying him, though. He didn't look like a dead guy. No, he looked very much alive, with brown, shoulder-length hair, a light tan, and bright green eyes. His eyes? They did look like hers. Hers and Erasmus's. Even Dion's eyes had been that same shade.

Another step was taken, and he nodded. "I did, yes. But maybe I should give you a message that will clarify a few things?"

"Clarity is good," she whispered.

"Your friend Blanche, she said to tell you this was your wedding present from her." He cocked his head and smiled proudly. "Are you really friends with the wife of Death?"

That did it. "Dad?"

"Yes, baby," he said in the same quiet tone, the pride melting into love with a hint of sadness.

She had just been thinking about him, how she'd never really thought about him and how her wedding had made her realize just how much she had missed growing up without a dad. And here he was. She doubted very much that he would be allowed to stay, which meant she needed to make the most of the time they had.

Barely remembering to keep hold of the flowers, she hurried up the last few stairs separating them and threw herself into his arms. He caught her and wound his arms around her, hugging her tight as she pressed her face against his shoulder and put the waterproof mascara to the test. There might be people waiting on her, including the man she loved, but she thought they'd all understand once they knew what was delaying her. Olivia certainly wouldn't allow Lucas to worry, not when she'd clearly known who he was.

The bachelorette party they'd thrown her had obviously allowed Blanche and Olivia to bond, at least a little, and she was glad for it. Because right now she just wanted to hug her dad until she stopped crying. No, that wasn't all she wanted.

Leaning back enough to look up at him, enough to see that his cheeks were as damp as hers, she gave him a trembling smile. "Will you walk me down the aisle?"

"I was really hoping you'd let me."

"Good. That's good." Her eyes widened and she glanced past him. "Does Mom know?"

He smiled and nodded. "Apparently Blanche and another of your friends thought it would be best if she didn't see me for the first time when I was walking you down the aisle. They didn't want to spoil your wedding, so Blanche brought me early this morning."

Heather had known and hadn't let on? Okay, so the mother of the bride being emotional on the day of her daughter's wedding was expected, but still, Sophia would have expected to see some sign.

"I had no idea everyone here was that good at keeping secrets," Sophia said with a laugh.

"It is kind of what they do. And your mother tells me you're aspida?"

She nodded and smiled. "I am, though Grandpa helps, since he's not actually, you know, dead."

"I'll bet he does. And I want to hear everything, but we should go get you married first. And I need to meet the man who thinks he's good enough for you."

It was such a dad thing to say that she laughed and gave him a hard hug. "He's a very good man," she assured him before he took her arm and led her up the rest of the stairs.

She could hear the murmur of voices just feet away, and she took in a deep breath, looking up at her dad. "I'm so happy you're here. I'm going to owe Blanche big."

"Not for a present, and she assured me that's what this was," Gregory told her, patting the hand on his arm. "But I'm happy, too. And I just want you to know that I love you. I've loved you since the moment I knew your mom was pregnant. Since I first felt you move. Being gone doesn't change that."

"I love you, too, Dad," she said without hesitation, surprised to find that she meant it. Before now, she'd just loved the idea of him, but having him here? There was no question.

At some signal she didn't realize they'd given, the murmuring outside quieted and the first strains of the wedding march began.

"Ready?" he asked.

"Absolutely."

They stepped out, and she saw the crowd of people—including the terrifying Death, because of course he'd come to her wedding. But then her gaze landed on Lucas and everyone else disappeared for her. He stood at the far end of the room next to Erasmus, Olivia, and Steven, wearing a tux that made him look even sexier than he normally was. And he stared at her like she was his world, his eyes already gray from the emotion in them.

She really, really loved that man.

As Gregory walked her toward him, she noticed that he wasn't the only one Blanche had brought back for her wedding. Standing next to her mom—who both beamed at them and cried—were Dion and Peter. She really was going to owe Blanche, but decided it was absolutely worth it.

They stopped in front of Lucas and she just stared at the man who was about to be her husband. "Be good to her or I'll be back," her dad warned Lucas before he kissed Sophia's cheek and passed her hand to Lucas.

"Always," Lucas answered without looking away from Sophia. He took the bouquet from her and passed it blindly to Olivia, who chuckled quietly.

They barely heard as Erasmus spoke, thanking everyone for joining them and speaking of love and marriage. He actually had to clear his throat when it was time for Sophia to say I do, and poke Lucas when it was time for him to place the ring on her finger, because they were so absorbed in each other. But Lucas definitely heard him pronounce them husband and wife, because he didn't wait for permission, just drew her into his arms and kissed her dumb.

Around them people cheered, and a few laughed when the kiss went on longer than might be polite, but she didn't care. They'd not just survived the Miasma, they'd beaten it, and even rescued a goddess and rediscovered the Hall of Records. She had absolutely earned her happily ever after, and that was going to begin today.

About the Author

Meg M. Robinson is a fantasy author who lives in north Georgia with her husband and a small menagerie of animals. She's goofy and a little dorky, which greatly amuses her family.

She's obsessed with crows, sea turtles, and houseplants. And, of course, books. When she's not focused on either reading or writing a book, she enjoys playing video games, archery, and baking.

www.megmrobinson.com

Please consider leaving a review for this book. Reviews are extremely important for authors, but especially indie authors like me! Believe me, we appreciate it!

* 9 7 8 1 9 6 0 2 1 8 0 7 0 *